Other Books by K. Adrian Zonneville

American Stories

Carrie Come To Me Smiling

Z

Great Things, A Novel

To Dance Among The Stars

To Sail The Barren Seas

Lost Dog Found

The Sperling Chronicles

Sequel; An Ian Sperling Saga, The Tour Continues

A Life in The Wings; My Sixty Year Love Affair With Rock and Roll David Spero Memoir

Tales of The High Seas and Lowlands

By

K. Adrian Zonneville

This book is dedicated to those who seek. Whether they seek knowledge, truth, family, love, respect, compassion, the right chord and word, God, the Devil or the deep blue sea. Seek your passion, chase your dreams, love with every fiber of your being and give with a full heart.

Acknowledgements

No project is ever completed without the assistance of others. No album, no construction, no business, no book, painting, or poem. You need inspiration and guidance, someone or something you love, friends, pets, something outside yourself. I am the luckiest person on the planet as I have all those things. So, to my wife who allows an old man his passion and the time to pursue his love of writing, to my dogs, Harper and Greta who make me get off my ass and move about the town when I can't think, to my children who inspire me every day. Thank you.

To Janet Sipl for her brilliant artwork over the years.

To Linda Wike Calkins who keeps me on the straight and narrow when I get lost in my flights of fancy, she pulls me back in and makes these stories so much better. She also tries to rein in my misspellings, grammar, and where to put commas.

And to Tom Misuraca for playing golf and cheering me on.

Dublin 1843

He coughed.

The smoldering peat smoke wafted into the loft where he lay, irritating his nose and throat. He coughed again as he inhaled another lung full of smoke. He was glad, the coughing would cover the whimpers and sobs left over from another battle with Pa. He used every calming exercise he had learned while attending first year seminary school. He wished the noise of his hacking would cover his Pa's disappointed rant rising with the smoke.

"I just don't understand why the boy has to be so contrary. He's the eldest and as such he should follow his father's bidding. The priesthood would offer him a lifetime without want," his voice rose with his indignation. "He would never be more than a half day from Dublin. It's not like he has to go into the wilds and try to convert the savages fighting over the scraps left in the potato fields. He'd have a future with Mother church."

Listening from above he could hear his ma defending him. Well, defending him as much as she dared. She knew far better than to rouse her husband when he was in this distemper. She would like to blame it on the drink but she knew, the drink only brought out his true self. She had known that when she married him but thought he would outgrow the deep-seated anger and frustration that was his heritage.

She attempted to reinforce the boy's argument against Mother church. Explaining to her husband what she and her son had discussed, his overpowering desire to see the world. The church would provide succor of soul and body but not of his mind. He wished to experience life not hide from it in some monastery wallowing in poverty. The booming indignation mother's response had awaken threatened to shake the very rafters of the cottage.

"Not every priest takes an oath of poverty. Those are monks. They live in those monasteries and avoid contact with the rest of humanity while they ponder the complexities of God. Priests have more important work, packing the Lord's wisdom and laws into the heads of malcontent boys!" His voice had quieted until his admonition, in a strained whisper, barely carried to the boy he knew listened from above.

"I'm not going back!" The voice attempted bravado but fell well short of the mark. The crack and squeak hadn't quite aged its way out of his timbre and he sounded more like the petulant child he was attempting to outgrow rather than the man he felt his fourteen-year-old self to be. The sound of the creak of weight on the first step of the ancient wooden ladder stayed his tongue from trespassing further.

His mother's voice, though anxious, endeavored calm to quiet the anger about to ascend the heavens. A final creak ended the discussion when pa's foot left the rung.

"He'll do as told!" The pounding of the last nail and the beginning of the final act.

Thomas McDermitt would not be studying the proper techniques to push God's words into hard heads come the second term of seminary. He'd make a run for it and this time he would succeed. Not like when he was just a child of eight attempting the same run for freedom. He had been stupid, thinking no one would notice a child traveling by hisself. He'd hardly made towns edge afore some meddling midwife had caught him by the ear and found where he lived. Brought him back like a captured prisoner. Though when it all come down to it, wasn't that exactly what he was? A prisoner of his own ma and pa.

Hostage to their every whim, like he had not a say in his own life. His own damn life! It weren't his life! It were theirs to do with what they wanted; his wishes be damned. He knew he shouldn't swear, not even in the privacy of his own head, God was everywhere, but he didn't care. He was a growed man and he'd make his own way in this world.

He'd plan it better this time, that was all. For one thing he was bigger now, almost full grown. Just a couple thumbs shy of six foot with growing yet to do. He'd need some filling out and muscle added but that'd come with time and work.

Question was, what kind of work? He weren't trained for much but reading, writing and praying. He hadn't a clue, he just knew he needed to move, to travel, to see other lands, meet folks other than those of the town and seminary. One thing he'd learned in the seminary was there was a whole world out there just for the discovering and he wanted to see all of it, especially America.

He'd heard the seafarers as they 'd spin tale after tale while sucking down whiskey in pubs near the wharves. They spoke of faraway lands filled with exotic and strange people. Women who bounded about their villages with little or nothing on. And the men of those villages hardly taking note of the bare breasted nubile bodies as if it were as natural as sunrise. He heard men talk of the darkies in Africa and how some of them ate man flesh. Of the tigers, lions, reptiles of the rivers that were twelve-foot long maneaters, and giant beasts with trunks as long as the yardarm on a ship.

Thomas wanted to see these wonders and to travel to the new world. That new land over the ocean that had thrown off the yoke of his majesty the king. A new land with new ideas of freedom and equality. They had founded a government based on the people not a monarchy nor a pope. It excited his imagination no end. A priest would never in his life have the opportunity to experience such marvels.

He'd even struck up a kind of friendship with one of the darker members of a crew. His skin the color of midnight, his eyes bright orbs that seemed to shine of their own light. He spoke a kind of English, an odd inflection to his words, though Thomas could understand him. Well, most of what he said.

According to the priests of the seminary, this man had no soul. He was not loved by God because he worshipped savage gods and knew not the love of the Christian God. He was bound for hell, yet Thomas saw something in the man, some spark of a soul in his eyes and the way he treated others; giving where others needed, helping out those with less than he had. He was a good man, with a rich life, having sailed the seven seas a hundred times and survived. How could God not love such a man?

And he'd been to America! He'd seen what lay beyond the ocean. Though he warned Thomas of the terrors and horrors of the new land. They bought and sold people what looked like him like they were livestock, not better than cows or sheep. In fact, he said cows and sheep were treated better than black folk over there.

Thomas had reiterated that he thought black folks was treated fairly poor right here in Dublin.

"Yeah, but they ain't selling me to nobody!" The dark sailor had laughed hard.

Still, the new world called to Thomas. He yearned to see, to live, to roam this virgin land. They said any man with the want to and willing could become a rich man over there. Well, he was brimming with both qualities. Question was how to get there?

He'd have to hop a ship, that was his only escape, a stowaway they called it. He knew they might throw him overboard for the audacity of sneaking onto their ship but they might let him work. He was big enough; he just wasn't certain he was bold enough.

He would have to have patience, not be brusque with pa, be kind to ma and make them believe he had changed for their desires. It wouldn't be easy. They wouldn't believe at first that his heart had been turned so quickly or easily. Aye, he would still have to put up some kind of battle, though not as vehement as he had. A little conciliatory behavior could go a long way. He knew he could do it. His life depended on it.

The month had passed, if not peacefully, at least without any grand eruptions from pa, though Thomas had been very careful not to light any fuses. Now, here he was nestled between several large crates in the belly of a fine ship he just knew had to be headed west to the new land.

It had been far easier than he had hoped. There were no guards keeping an eye on the gangplank, no lookouts looking out for wayward young men with escape on every breath. Just sleepy sailors getting one more good night before setting sail. The gentle rock of a ship at dock lulling all aboard to dream of calm seas and new worlds.

Chicago 2025

Tom jerked awake. The scent of the sea and Ireland still fresh in his nostrils, though how he knew what the sea smelled like or what the Ireland of hundreds of years ago would look like, he couldn't discern, as he'd never been within five hundred miles of the ocean let alone crossed such an expanse. He was a born and bred Midwesterner living in the wilds of Northside Chicago. He had no love of the sea, no want to leave dry land. He was not one for great expanses of water. He had no desire to go out on Lake Michigan, even when associates invited him out on their yachts and power boats.

His eyes focused on his light tan hands, still holding the pen he'd been using to calculate figures and code before entering it into the computer. A light skinned 'Black' man who fit in no round, square, or octagonal hole that he'd ever found. Too light for black folk, too dark for the white. Just a cat without a real home.

He wasn't 'tanned' he was tan; it was his color by birth. He chuckled at the irony when he considered that coloring made him 'Black' by definition of ethnicity. This was America and everyone had to be categorized by their color. More than height, intelligence, economic status, sexuality, or personality, it all came down to color. And if you weren't pure white and Christian then you were another. Another color, another race, another suspect religion. And he didn't fit neatly into any of the categories America wanted to cram him in.

Black men didn't write code, especially financial code. Code to run the white corporation's billing, payroll, incomes and outgoes, deep intense code. And black men especially didn't do it by writing it out in ink and paper. But Tom wasn't just anybody, he was the best. They called him a genius, a once in a century intellect, All wrapped in a large, tan, slightly overweight body. And he was tired. Tired to the bone as his 'tiger nap', as his momma used to call them, proved beyond a doubt.

It had been a hard couple months but he hoped the check coming his way would make it all worthwhile. He was mid-forties and in good shape but his family history told another story. Men didn't live much past fifty and he wanted to enjoy some of what he had left. He wanted to retire early, earlier than anyone he worked with would hope, but he was done. Maybe that was why he dreamt of the ocean. Maybe he would go to an ocean, any ocean, and stick his toes in the waters while he wondered where he came from.

Like most African Americans he hadn't a clue past a couple generations. There were sparse records of some granddaddy's and Grammy's, great aunts and uncles, some blood, some not, but the knowledge of these antecedents piddled out before the turn of the last century. He thirsted to know more. Who was he? Where did his people come from? They obviously were slaves a couple hundred years ago, most black folk knew that, but from where? He had white in him, his features and light coloring told him that, but from whom and where?

Well, he wouldn't find out today. He rubbed tired eyes and focused on the chore at hand. They wanted these codes deployed before the end of the week and he hadn't completed the expense coding for their year ends and that was where his retirement was coming from, not from dreams and fantasies of Ireland and the high seas. Fantasy did not pay his bills, reality did.

He thought he should've married and had a family by now and yet work, worry, and low self-esteem kept the women at bay. Children! He almost laughed out loud. Why would he want to pass along defective genes to another generation? Sickle cell would probably kill him as it had his father and grandfather, either through the disease or through self-medication for pain that would eventually cause his self-destruction. Best keep that one contained to him, a last generation.

Right now, he had to keep his mind from wandering all over hell's half-acre. Pen to paper, mind to work, concentrate on the project at hand, worry could wait. It always did, until right around bedtime. If he worked out the last few bugs in the coding, he could enter them before sleep began eluding him while he tossed and turned in bed. Then popping awake and chasing what he might have missed sometime around 4 a.m.

He rubbed his eyes again, this would have to wait until the morning, however that was defined. His mind floated, drifted, a lace leaf riding a gentle summer breeze on a lazy afternoon. It searched a place to rest. He fought the urge but only just, even the finest pencil required a rest and sharpening, he would close his eyes for a few minutes to refresh then begin again. Just a few minutes to recharge.

Between The Devil
and The Deep Blue Sea

1843

The hard pitch of the ship banged his head against the wooden hull bringing him immediately to a dazed conscious state of confusion. Where was he? Oh, the ship, the sea, America. He was wedged between several crates and the hull of the ship while it bounced along choppy waves. He hadn't considered the voyage might be rough, he had never seen the sea beyond the protected bay on the east side of town. Now he was being tossed about like a loose barrel on the lips of a rickety cart, lurching, rolling, down a cobblestone road, while being banged over and over against the rough surface of the inner bilge. This was awful! He was quite certain that whatever might still remain in his stomach from supper last night—it was last night, wasn't it?—was about to spill forth onto into the bilge water collecting at his feet. He had to get out of the belly of the beast, discovery be damned.

He stumbled onto the deck and hung his head over the side emptying what little contents remained.

A strong, coarse hand grabbed him by the back of the neck and pulled him hard, back, away from the railing. "If was up to me, I'd just push ya over the side with the rest of the flotsam, but Cap'n says to bring ya to him. You might wish for the sea when he's done wit ya."

That grubby, coarse hand steered him along the rolling deck to a short ladder leading up to, what he was soon to discover, was the Captain's quarters. The cabin had a bunk, a desk, a chair, and a captain. His steps had found it difficult to find purchase on the rolling deck and the abrupt jerking and bobbing of the ship, though the mate who maintained his grip on Thomas' shoulder seemed not to be bothered. The mate had banged once on the captain's door and opened it just a second before the voice hollered, "Come!"

The captain was a gruff appearing man, not in a pirate or brigand sort to Thomas' way of thinking, more of a man who had circumnavigated the globe many times and survived a life on the sea. He'd seen men like this as he ran errands about town. You couldn't live in a port town without running across their kind. They weren't mean or harsh, just hard from the sea, from life.

Most of those who made their life on solid ground thought they understood the seafarers. After all, didn't they do the same as the merchants? Plying their trade on known routes, though those routes might be across the mighty oceans. And instead of traveling between towns they rode between continents separated by hundreds, if not thousands, of miles of water.

The major difference betwixt those land locked and those who rode the waves was sailors had no rules except what the sea demanded. The land locked thought sailors were reprobates who were forever running away from whatever they had done on one piece of land toward what they would do on another. The only difference between merchant mariners and pirates was who had the bounty at any particular time. Each one hoped to have possession when it truly counted, as they sailed into port. This man had held onto his fortunes by skill, might, and wile. He was not a man to be trifled with.

If Thomas had any hope of remaining on the solidity of the deck and not attempting to swim toward shore—a shore he had no inkling where it might lay—then he had best either be very honest or the best liar on the high seas.

Now here was the boy of fourteen face to face with a man who had faced down storms, pirates, and wars and survived them all. Thomas swallowed hard, his legs trembled, threatening to give way leaving the boy sprawled across the floor. He prayed to his god his legs would not betray him.

"So, another rat stowed aboard my ship." The Captain glanced at the mate standing behind Thomas, hand never letting up on the pressure on Thomas' shoulder. "Did he steal anything? Or eat from the lockers?"

"Not that I've been able to determine, Cap'n," quoth the hand.

"So, what are ye doin' on my ship?" The captain locked eyes with Thomas.

His knees began to buckle, he took a deep breath and lied. He lied like the Lord himself put the words in his mouth.

"I'm recent an orphan and had nowhere to go," he wanted to sound strong, filled with bravado, the arrow fell short. "I thought maybe to make my way to America and place a claim. I thought, I hoped, I prayed once found you would let me stay and work my way. Maybe you could use an extra hand, someone willing to learn, to work hard, to, to, to..."

"No plan, eh?" The captain spit into the brass spittoon at his feet. "What makes ye think you could be a sailor?" He looked the big kid—and yes, he could tell he was a kid—up and down. He was big, the question was, was he worth the trouble of training. Big didn't mean smart, and no matter what landlubbers thought, you had to be smart to sail the open seas. You had to read the wind, feel the currents, guide the ship by stars and experience, you didn't just hop a ship and become a fucking sailor!

"No." There it was. Honest. Truth spilled like fish guts on the deck. Thomas was done for, he couldn't lie, well, he couldn't lie any more than he had already. He might not be an actual orphan, though in his mind he had forsaken his family or they had forsaken him! Wasn't that some kind of orphan?

"Well, I'm guessing since you was hiding in the hold you got some rest. I'll let you stand watch through the night. If you don't fall asleep, fall overboard, fall down and skin yer pretty little knees we'll feed ya in the morning and see where we go from there. Irish," he pointed at the deck hand holding Thomas prisoner, "find him an oilskin so he doesn't die from the spray and chill and secure him to something so we don't lose the oilskin if he falls over."

Thomas had no more taken up his position at the bow of the ship when her nose dipped as she rode the downside of a wave and then caught the upside on her nose. The wave broke over the bow and thousands of gallons of sea water grabbed him by the scruff of the neck and threw him to the deck. He skidded along the hard wooden surface and would have washed over the side and out to sea had not the lines they tied him to between foremast and rail held.

He lay for several seconds to see if anyone would come to check on his well-being. A chasm opened where rescue should have appeared. There would be no one. He wanted nothing more than to lay where he was, curled up in a fetal position and weep for his mother. But she was a memory now by his own choosing. He spit up a few yards of sea water before grabbing hold of the deck rail and pulling himself up onto his very unsteady feet. There would be no help from his mother, the crew, the captain, or God. Which, on this vessel, the two were the same. Holding tight to the rail with both hands he stood, tall, thin, wiry, and weak, facing the onslaught of wind and wave determined to last until morning.

And so began Thomas McDermitt's trial at sea.

Is Reality Any Kind of Escape?

Present Day

Tom started awake.

He was in bed though did not remember climbing into the comfort. It was his one major luxury, a king-sized bed for a large man shouldn't be a luxury though the cost made it so. He hadn't cared at the time as he had the cash and he needed room to lay out and sleep, especially with a ninety-pound dog, a Beardie, who loved him so much she had to sleep on top of him. He loved feeling the weight of her love, the in and out of her breath and knowing there would never be another being on this planet that would love him as unconditionally. Well, not since his mother passed.

He could taste the sea water, the saltiness, and fish, or what he thought sea water and raw fish tasted like. He was drenched in sweat though it could've been the wave that almost took his life while he slept. Though why he dreamt what he dreamt was baffling. He could understand it if he dreamt the dreams of his slave forebearers. The sweat and death in the belly of the slave ships coming from Africa. He'd seen programs and documentaries on the conditions and horrors of that crossing. It had brought nightmares for weeks when he was younger. These dreams were far distant from anything he had read, viewed, or experienced.

His pillow was wet as if he had spilled the contents of the ocean on it yet knew he hadn't. It was drool and spit. He slid out of bed so as not to wake Sherry Louis, his Beardie, to shower off the dream and the sweat. He still had a few bugs to work out before he deployed the code but he felt confident he would have it done by the time his eggs were ready.

He whistled—well, he blew breath through puckered lips, a light wind in the silence—as he ran the debugging software, he, himself, had designed. Others had offered much if he would share his programs but he knew if he did, they would find a way to boot him off the programming 'team'. They would take his work and claim it as their own. He didn't have the wherewithal to fight the biggies in court, so he kept his work to himself. They could try and bust his encryption but they never would, at least not until someone came up with a quantum computer.

He had a meeting via zoom just after he wolfed down breakfast. These would be across several time zones and with every major player involved. He should be nervous but after more than twenty years of design, implementation, and success he just couldn't bring himself to worry.

He shoved a forkful of piping hot western egg bowl in his mouth. He immediately regretted his haste. It was only seconds out of the microwave and still scalding, as two minutes of forcing molecules to vibrate until they created intense heat will do. He took hard, deep, fast breaths in and out, in and out, hoping to cool the egg mixture before it melded his mouth shut. He could've spit it out, but who has ever done that?

Not off to a stellar start on the day. His confidence was not shaken, but stirred just slightly, as he slowed his consuming down so he could chew without fear of self-immolation. He knew the movers and shakers, the high muckity mucks of this conglomerate on the Zoom with the largest tech concern in the nation plus more than a dozen of its offspring, wanted his secrets. Yes, they wanted the coding, the software he had designed but they also wanted his encryption and his methods. The question was, how much would they be willing to part with to obtain such sorcery.

And that was how he thought of his software, sorcery. It was a combination of math, algorithms, and 'spells,' spells he had created to make everything work together to create the desired effect. Eye of newt, bat spit, some bailing wire, and hope. You could rule the world. Well, the world you created, but a world nonetheless.

He thought he might just let it slip that he was thinking of optioning his trade secrets, if the numbers worked. Not a hard sell, not even an offer just an aside, like he'd slipped by letting it be known. Bait the hook and see if anything would nibble at it.

The Zoom meeting began as it always did with several levels of identity verification and encryption, something Tom heartily approved. One could never be too secure when online, especially when discussing sensitive material and software. The last he, or the reps of the conglomerate he was to meet with, wanted was for any leaks in their conversation. A slip of the encrypted lip could make it possible for any eavesdropper to take said code or programing and use it for their own nefarious ends. All involved wanted it only used for the nefarious ends they paid for.

As the dozen heads began to appear on Tom's screen, he recognized the usual suspects. The CEO. CFO, COO, CTO, head of research and development, as well as those who would hear his words and understand the software and then translate it to the brilliant minds at the top of the pecking order. The lords of industry would then nod knowingly, while the nerds spoke to each other in their own special language. The Poohbahs of tech would not understand a word, but that was why they paid the nerds so much money. If the nerds ever revolted every business on the planet would fail, while those ostensibly in charge ran around with their hair on fire and no one with a pail of water.

While Tom pointedly directed his conversation to the heads of the divisions and companies, he essentially spoke to those who knew what the fuck he was saying. He hadn't noticed while the unnecessary intros were being made but there was a new head in the Hollywood Square down in the right-hand corner and, oh, what a head it was.

She was stunning in a minimalist way. A scant amount of rouge, eyeliner to accent not distract, no lipstick or whatever women slapped on their lips to make them shine, black hair pulled back in a simple ponytail. He found himself doing something he hated when he saw people doing it to him, he tried to guess her ethnic heritage. Impossible. She seemed to have the best qualities of every ethnicity on the planet. He guessed her to be a bit younger than himself, late thirties-early forties. Her skin was smooth, though she had a few crow's feet about the eyes and around her mouth, which only intensified her beauty. She looked him right in the eyes, something not easily accomplished when there was so much technology and protocols in between, but it was like she was sitting across a small table from him in a seductively lit café and reading his soul. Saying he was distracted was like saying he noticed the sunrise over the mountains.

The meeting began and he spoke by rote. He had explained most of the ins and outs of the technology to the tech guys many times before. This was just a reiteration and update on the new protocols and changes to the software. Later he would remember kind of hinting at his desire to possibly, maybe, he might be thinking about licensing his creations. Subtle like a slip of the tongue, but they took notice. She stared hard into his eyes as if reading what he wasn't saying while, obviously, letting this tidbit slip.

He was having difficulty concentrating, thinking, finding words. He was, in a word, sidetracked. He couldn't take his eyes from this woman and she couldn't seem to take hers off him. Tom knew he wasn't a handsome man, not classic in any way. Oh, children would not run from him screaming in horror but he was never going to turn a pretty woman's head. And yet, this stunning example of humanity seemed like she saw and heard only him. Interesting.

It hit him like an obvious pitfall ten foot wide and thirty foot deep. That was why she was here, to distract. They were playing him! And he didn't care for that one bit. He tore his eyes from the woman, it felt like pulling a band aid off an old and thoroughly scabbed over gash. This was going to bleed for a while.

He thought he might be sweating from the effort of avoiding this woman's gaze. Shit, he hadn't even noticed her name or title in the chyron below that perfect face. She hadn't uttered a word. The other Techies and R&D folks were asking rapid fire queries about the sustainability of the new code and how often it would have to be updated. If that was included in the package. All questions he had fielded a dozen or more times over the years with each of these meetings. There was no need to stop and consider each answer.

He answered each query with assurances all could be taught, modified, or amended as need be. Either he could send along debugging patches, if needed, or would teach those in position to understand and write their own fixes. His eyes betrayed him. They could not avoid the overwhelming longing to just take a glimpse of that face.

She smiled. It was not a predatory grin as if she had won a contest of wills, more filled with a joyous knowledge that he could no more avoid looking at her than she could looking at him. Though her gaze was far deeper than his superficial glance at beauty and the unattainable. She seemed immersed in his intelligence, his thoughtful replies, never talking down to anyone and going over every aspect until those with the need understood what he had created almost as well as he did himself. She weighed his elemental worth and found him to be pure.

"Are you really thinking of licensing this work to the corporation and only this corporation in perpetuity? You would give up your secrets to this one conglomerate?" She was saying something, asking something, he couldn't quite grasp. She wasn't asking him if he was selling his secrets, she was asking him far more, like, what was he going to do with the rest of his lonely, barren life. A life that had been defined by his work, his creations. Who would he become? She wanted to know his plan. She was interested in him as a human being not as a content creator. And why had she referred to them as 'the corporation', rather than us?

Who the hell was this woman and why did he want to open up his every thought, fear, insecurity, and desire to her? Fuck! It was as if every other face on both screens blurred, then disappeared and only hers remained. It was then he noted her square had no identification. No name. No title.

Had this woman, somehow, hacked into this seemingly impregnable Zoom call? If so, how had she? Tom knew if he'd wanted to, he could've found a backdoor to slip in. Though he would've preferred to remain unnoticed. Her whole bearing was of someone who wanted to be noticed, wanted his attention. Though no one else, not one other person on the screen, seemed to note her presence.

He had to focus; questions were coming from all quarters as the higher ups realized what he was talking about. They could own everything if they could come up with a number between what he obviously wanted and what they obviously didn't want to pay. And Tom no longer cared. Whatever they offered, and he knew they would try and short him, it would be more than he would ever need or could spend if he lived another hundred years. And that, he knew that would never happen.

The questions ceased, everyone satisfied with the outcome and the promise of the meeting. Tom was just happy it was over and he had given just enough away without naming a price. Let them stew. He had maintained his composure throughout, thanks to years of mindless meetings and explanations, but he was spent. He wanted nothing more than to close his eyes and sleep for a few days while they contemplated what he had intimated and came up with a number. He found he cared so little for the number it shocked him. This had been about an astronomical cash out, now he just wanted peace. He told them they could talk more later when they'd had a chance to discuss among themselves.

Maybe he should go to the beach, any beach, he knew there were plenty of them on both ends of the continent. He could just go to the airport and buy a ticket for someplace near one, the airline people would know. Or he could get on the computer and find a beach. Though he didn't want to look at the screen, not yet, not until it went dark. Until he did.

She was still there. Looking right at him. Her face now filled an entire forty-inch monitor, you could see every blemish, every flaw, every single mark on her face. If she'd had any. Yet, there were none. She was just as perfect as she had been when just a couple inches in size.

She smiled. He blushed. God, had he ever blushed in his entire forty-four years? Not that he could remember.

"Nicely done." It was a compliment to his mental acuity, his wit, his sense of humor and humanity. She approved of him. He hadn't thought about anybody's approval since ma had passed. He liked it.

The words asking for her contact information were just forming on his lips when she faded away. It was possible he had manufactured this perfect woman in his tired mind. But if he hadn't, then he should be able to squeeze out her information when they sealed the deal.

Who was he kidding? A woman like that would have no interest in a mid-forties man of average appeal. He needed to sleep for a few days. They'd contact him with their offer but until they did, he didn't want to think, to plan, to do anything. Except maybe go put his feet in an ocean.

His head flopped back on the pillow, his eyes closed and he slipped beneath the waves. The scent of the ocean called him, strong, pungent. The sound of waves crashing on a beach far, far away soothed and comforted him as sleep overtook any further thoughts.

Lessons of The Sea

1843 Fall/1851

The ship rocked.

The heavy sea tossing it like a cork in a wine barrel on a wagon racing down a dirt and stone lane. Thomas was secured by tethers to the mainmast and crow's nest to forestall a headward plunge onto the deck. A few weeks ago, he would have been spilling meals from the past few days onto that deck but he had time at sea now, he could now stand at the apex of life and act as lookout while they passed the Horn of Africa.

The few weeks at sea had taught him how to swab a deck properly, and yes, there is a proper and improper way to do such things. How to climb the rigging, and hoist sail until his hands were bloody and his back was burning with pain. How to run from fore to aft in a tossing sea, and what fore and aft meant, as well as port and starboard. He hadn't become a sailor, not yet, but he was in the right current. He learned he hated the drudgery, the repetitious chores that wreaked havoc on the muscle and bone yet learned to love the sea.

He had, also, learned over those past few weeks they were not heading for America. They were, in fact, heading in the opposite direction and had no plans of ever docking in America. Though devasted by the news, Thomas adjusted quickly to his new reality. He'd had a long talk with himself on a clear moonlit night filled with a hundred thousand stars that maybe this wasn't such a horrible way to live, for a while.

He was just past his fourteenth birthing day by a few months, he had time to reach the new world. That is if he lived through their journey traveling the seas of the old world. Right this moment, with the seas tossing him like a die and the wind whipping about him while singing a siren's call from her depths, he didn't like the odds.

The Cap'n had made a gambler's choice and run closer to the Horn than most did. He had seen the storms further out to their south, and wishing to make haste, had chosen an inner passage. It might have been an astounding choice and brilliant had they not come close to wrecking upon some well-hidden rock formations further out from land than they should have been. Now it was Thomas' job to keep them off any other clever rock piles that might have plans for a ship lunch.

Of course, the great weakness in that line of thought was Thomas had to steady himself a hundred and twenty feet off the tossing deck with howling wind and spray in his face and keep his eyes searching for any disturbance on the surface of a very disturbed ocean. He had the Cap'n's looking glass but that didn't help much when you were being thrown around like a leaf on the wind. He braced hisself against the mainmast and did his best to plot them a course that would not lead to death.

Hours passed like days, the day dragged into a month twenty-four hours long, but finally they made it through the worst of it. His muscles shook and trembled from the effort of remaining upright. At long last one of the other crewmen stuck his head over the side of the nest and smiled; relief had arrived. Thomas could come down and get something to eat and then rest. Relief it was. Now, all he had to do was climb down the rigging with every limb quivering and shuddering and not lose his grip or miss a hand hold with hands that could barely form a fist, tumbling him to his death.

The look of respect the others gave him as his foot touched the hard surface of the deck was the most satisfying reward he had ever received. That was until the Cap'n hisself came out and shook his hand and pronounced him a full and true seaman. He would eat hearty, have a cup of rum, and sleep 'til eventide.

Days became weeks, which turned into months and grew into years. Thomas had hit a growth spurt during his time at sea and was now, by a head, taller than any man on the ship. His body had filled out with the backbreaking chores of sea life, loading and unloading cargo, and survival. He was now first mate and noticing the Cap'n was getting long in the tooth, long in the beard and short in his temper, he would soon need to make the choice of retiring somewhere with what booty he had squirreled away or find himself being replaced by force. Thomas had decisions to make.

The crew respected him, he was a good seaman and a fair first mate. He had learned the ropes quickly and thoroughly. He knew not every cargo was legit, sometimes you had to traffic in contraband when no other cargo was available. And he had learned the hard way that you weren't always the merchant ship, sometimes you flew the skull and crossbones. Survival is survival and a man has to make his living with what the Lord provides.

Though truth be told, piracy had its limits. He had always cautioned the men not to take any lives unless absolutely necessary. Take their weapons, incapacitate the ship, though not to the point of stranding the crew. Unless they wanted Navies out for their blood, they would just take what they wanted and leave the other ship with the ability to make it to the nearest port. By then 'Avenging Mother of The Sea' would be in another of the seven seas.

It wasn't a bad life; they would make port, satisfy urges and drink themselves broke, then head back out to sea. If one was smart, he would squirrel away a few doubloons or whatever the coin of the realm might be and not let that knowledge pass your lips. Thomas found hisself wishing for more. You cannot grow up the son of a well-to-do merchant and not long for the stability of home. He had left that stability to discover the world, his worth, and make his fortune in the new world. He had discovered the world. He itched for the rest.

His new plan—God, how many years had it been since he'd set off on the old plan—was to stick with the ship, not drink up his share of the bounty, and find a place to hide what coins he collected. And with the crew being the crew, changing some in each port, none would be the wiser of his change in habit. He could stow away a large portion of his share, especially shares from ill-gotten cargoes. Then all he had to do was find a way to force the Cap'n's hand and finally make his way to America. Or maybe Canada, if that's all that was offered.

These were his thoughts as the ship gently rocked at anchor. Several hundred yards away palm trees waved in strong breezes coming up from the south and promised adventure. If only the Cap'n would get off whatever island girl he was humping so they could catch some of that beautiful breeze.

Thomas sighed. As much as he dreamed of finally setting foot on America, he had to admit this was a fine life. He was still young, somewhere near to or over twenty, if years counted. But he was far older by experience. He had no concrete idea of how long he had been at sea. They had circumnavigated the globe more than once and were now halfway around her again. He had a nice stash hidden away to start his new life; as long as the ship didn't sink, that is. That was the one possible death nell to his dream, though truth be told, it would probably be the death of him as well.

He sighed again. If that was to be his fate then so be it. He guessed he was dead already to his family and wasn't that where you found your life, your roots, your first breath. If they thought you dead, then dead you were. They had ported in Dublin not four months ago and he considered trying to find his family but then thought better of it. They probably had forgotten about him by now. There were five other children to worry about. He had given them the gift of not having to contend with a malcontent, unruly, and rebellious child. There was no need to find them and have a very contentious home coming. Let him lie beneath the waves in their minds, let them forget and be happy with what they had.

Those were the daydreams of a ship lolling at anchor in the leeward side of a tropical island in the South Pacific. Most of the crew was ashore taking their leave of young island girls, island drink, and rest. He had the ship almost to hisself. Well, he and a half dozen others, but they left him to his thoughts and he left them to laze in the hot summer sun. He looked up. Not a cloud in the sky, typical of the South Pacific. He had discovered, after spending months crossing this massive ocean almost five years ago and now being back for the past two, utopia was deathly boring. He wanted action, to be moving, to feel the waves tossing and threatening them every second. It was only skill and luck that had kept them alive. Now, he was just bored.

As if Tangaroa, the Māori god of the sea, heard Thomas' thoughts and was kind enough to provide a distraction, the cry from aft roused him from his stupor. Thomas mentally chastised hisself. He had been so distracted by the absence of activity he had not kept watch on the mouth of the bay. They were about to come under attack!

There was a ship rounding the craggy western side of the mouth of the bay. He pulled the spyglass from his belt and looked to see if it was freebooter or just another merchant taking advantage of a prize sitting unprotected and with only a skeleton crew aboard.

No flag. A ship, not proclaiming pirate or commissioned. He had to assume they were probably mutineers trying to make one big hit before they went and hid their shame in a pub. They would drink up whatever they had stolen and then find themselves in need of another chancy encounter. Thomas was not amused.

If they were mutineers, they would be unruly, disorganized with each man out only for himself. Thomas might only have a skeleton crew but they were trained and had sailed together through some very intense, near disastrous voyages. They knew each other and how to fight as a machine.

Thomas was unarmed as the first man made it over the rail. He grabbed a belaying pin and lay the lowlife out on the deck. He turned to see another coming from the same direction. One of his mates hollered his name and Thomas turned expecting an attack from behind. Instead, he caught the cutlass tossed his way. Pulling it out of its' scabbard he turned to face the, now, two men coming at him. He smiled. Well, he wasn't bored now.

It didn't take long before they were outnumbered two to one. Thomas knew that each one of his men was worth at least three of the others. It wasn't arrogance, it was simply truth. His men were seasoned sailors and fighters, they knew how to work as a unit. They were well fed, strong, and trusted each other. They were also fighting for their ship and the crew on leave. It was up to them to protect all that each man held dear. The dozen who had rowed up silently in their launch were scrawny, half-starved, weak, and completely out classed as fighters. They were thieves coming to rob the larder while the owners were ashore. They thought they could subdue the skeleton crew with their numbers. They had severely underestimated the condition and will of the crew.

Now, six of them lay dead and the others were disabled and would be no further threat. Thomas had the crew gather them up and toss them over the side to their waiting launch. They could try and paddle their way back to the ship now hoisting sail at the mouth of the bay. If they made it, they made it, if they didn't it was only a couple thousand miles to one of the continents. He wasn't being cruel or he would've thrown them overboard and into the sea.

He turned his attention to the island; peace had settled on the ship; he'd keep a keen eye out so they would know when the Cap'n and crew were returning. He hoped it would be soon, he was ready for open water.

His wait was short as he saw the activity on land increase as Captain and crew hastily made their way, half-dressed and stumbling, to their own launch resting on the pure white sands.

"Gentlemen, the Cap'n returns! Let's swab the deck so he doesn't have to see how we spilled all that blood over his pretty ship." He grinned and the crew laughed as they pulled up sea water in buckets to clean up the remains of battle.

"I doan unnerstand," spoke the Cap'n in his manner, "Why ye dinna send someun for us t come hep yez."

"Well, as I explained we were somewhat busy at the time and, to be honest, I couldn't spare a man to come find you. Besides, it was obvious from the first man they would not be much of a threat." Thomas stood; legs splayed far apart so his head would not keep bumping into the low hanging beam of the ceiling.

"Deh ya see which course they was bearing? Maybe we should gae and fine them an return tha favor," Cap'n wanted his ounce for the audacity of them attacking his floating domain.

"Sorry, I saw no need to care. They were malnourished, completely disorganized, and the ship was riding high. I assumed they had nothing worth chasing them for. It would take us to god knows where with little chance for reward." Thomas shrugged. He thought the whole affair well-and-truly done and chasing them a waste of time. They should find more lucrative pursuits.

"Aye, I sees yer point. Yeev become a good mate with clear thinking and a levelhead, someday ye'll make a greet cap'n of yer en!" Thomas knew he had been dismissed and was happy to be above decks where he could breathe fresh air instead of whatever his Cap'n reeked of.

As they hoisted anchor and made ready to raise sail. Thomas stood at the rail for one last look at the tropical paradise. He had seen the look in the Cap'n's eye when he pretended admiration. Thomas knew the man felt threatened by how efficiently the crew had reacted and how much all now respected his first mate. Thomas had no doubt the lord of this ship was already planning on ways to rid himself of this upstart.

At one time Thomas had thought the man felt his years and wanted to find an island like the one they were departing. To spend what little time he had left in the arms of a young girl and feasting. Now he knew, the Cap'n would hang on to his power with every last ounce of life.

Thomas thought his greatest desire was to sail to America, get off the ship, and start a new life. Now, he knew his life depended upon that outcome.

All he had to do was stay alive until he could make that outcome come about.

That's What Friends Are For

Current Day

Tom sat gazing out the window at the great lake shimmering in moonlight. He sipped his Barnett Cabernet Sauvignon enjoying the silky-smooth, full-bodied wine. He did not have expensive taste in most things but he was of the belief that life was too short to drink cheap wine. The Barnett was not expensive, as wines go, but at almost two hundred dollars a bottle it wasn't cheap. Especially not at a joint like this. It was a nice restaurant sitting atop a lovely hotel with a magnificent view of this truly great lake. You could see for miles on clear evenings, which this was, though not quite far enough to see the state across from where he sat. He always thought of it as his great lake. From here you could imagine you rested on a tropical island somewhere in the Caribbean or South Pacific, except when winter blew hard across its open waters.

His friend, Chester, was coming to meet him for dinner. It'd been a minute since the two had found a convenient evening to get together and pass time in old stories, mutual acquaintances, catching up on the minutia of the day, and whatever else might waste some time and distract from the mundanity of life.

Tom needed distraction. He couldn't stop thinking of the woman on the computer. He also couldn't find out who she was. No one from the zoom meeting remembered seeing the woman on their screen, which would have been impossible if they had seen her. Nor did they have anyone who matched his description of her in their employ. He had spoken to each under the pretext of passing along another fix or assuring himself they had all they required.

Tom feared that he'd been hacked, though he could find no evidence of such, and he believed it to be unfeasible. No one had mentioned his slow dance around selling or leasing his secrets, though that call would come from someone much higher on the mountain than the nerds. Still, too much hung in the air for his liking. He considered rescinding his veiled offer. The thought that these bean counting technological imbeciles were trying to toy with his head and emotions was insulting. But still...

Chester grinned from ear to ear as he pulled out the chair opposite Tom. This cat had apparently caught a very large and tasty mouse, just the amusement Tom required. He had known Chester since high school They had bonded out of necessity. The greasers, wannabe gangster goombah types, who were neither gangsta nor Italian just greasy, always had to show their lack of intelligence and over developed musculature by intimidating and beating on those smarter and smaller than they. Enter Tom and Chester.

Neither of them had the physical stature to match intellectual dimensions. Small, weak, nerds didn't stand a chance against large, Cro-Magnons. Those who invented the wheel were being rolled over by those who used those wheels and loud mufflers to unnerve the studious.

Those same intimidators spent most of their time as adults standing in and out of the unemployment line. Their hope was the government they hated would bail them out with a check each month as their places of employment closed due to economic realities. They may have hated the concept of unemployment insurance, but they still cashed the checks while waiting for another repetitious, mundane job to open up. They never seemed to grasp the concept of acquiring new skills, learning new trades to survive.

Tom and Chester had thrived as the economy morphed from manual labor to more technology intensive professions and remained friends, though not close enough to get together regularly due to their natural inclination for introvertedness. It was funny to both men that that was the quality that seemed to keep them together, the need for isolation and both grokking exactly what, why, and comforting in it.

In most things they were quite the odd couple. Chester came from an upper middle-class neighborhood on the outskirts of the city. Tom from the inner city. They probably never would have met if not for the bussing craze of the 1970s. There they found their commonality, intelligence, — both easy targets for the musclebound – and loneliness. Neither man had ever been a chick magnet. They had bonded.

Now they would meet when the stars aligned and neither was neck deep in intellectual pursuits. Time didn't matter, whether months, weeks, or years passed since they had shared a meal and a couple hours, they both loved getting lost in egghead stuff—though Tom was a computer nerd and Chester's interests were more literary. Forgiving someone lost in their own thoughts for weeks at a time was easy when you had wandered down the same path so many times, you'd worn a groove.

"You look extremely filled with joy," Tom smiled at his friend's obvious mood.

"Football season starts Tomorrow!" Chester's excitement could not be contained in his small, frail body. He loved the sport of football, though due to physical limitations had never had the pleasure of being thrown unceremoniously to the hard ground after running for a loss.

Tom thought it odd that the man cared about a sport where those who participated had been some of their worst antagonists, but it seemed Chester couldn't fight his upbringing. His father was a big man who had played in high school, college, and then spent most of his time in and out of the operating room. Seems his body could not hold up under the duress of getting knocked around week after week. Now the man had dementia brought on by chronic traumatic encephalopathy (getting whacked in the head too often).

Still, Chester had been brought up a fan of the local NFL franchise and would die a fan of the game, there was no accounting for reason or rhyme. Tom on the other hand cared for only one 'sport,' chess. He would sit mesmerized by a tournament on the FIDE YouTube channel. To each their own.

"And how do you think your glorious Bears will fare this season." Tom tried to keep the mocking tone out of his words but succeeded only in emphasizing.

Chester gave it a pass. "Superbowl baby!" Ah, fandom, how blind is the love of the game. "What's new with you?"

"Thinking about walking away from the game." There, he'd said it out loud. Kind of off the cuff. He'd put the words out there into the endless cosmos which in turn would put into action the final act.

"What? You can't walk away from what you love!" Chester was aghast. His friend had talked of nothing his entire life, not sports, girls, cars, travel, nothing, except his love of code and program creation. It was his passion.

"Loved, past tense," corrected Tom. "Passions come and passions go. I've created, written and produced for almost thirty years, I want something else." He said the words but they had lost some of their conviction between tongue and ear. He pumped up the enthusiasm, "Life is about change. I need to alter the trajectory of my course."

"Bullshit!" Blurted the shocked Chester as the waitress came over to take their order. "I'm sorry," he apologized.

"Tame compared to some I've heard," she smiled. This woman was a pro.

"Two of what he's having," he said pointing to Tom's glass, "and whatever he wants. Please." He remembered his manners, "Then we'll eat, thank you." He turned to face Tom as the waitress left to get the wine. "Why?" It was a simple question yet contained all the wonder of the universe in one word. Chester was having great difficulty processing this new information.

Tom told him of his offer to sell or lease his secrets to this massive conglomerate with stipulations attached that could not be voided and what he thought they might offer him in financial remuneration. He then explained his inner need to find his roots and maybe travel to where his people originated. It wasn't until he explained the nuts and bolts that he told Chester about the woman. The woman who, apparently, only existed in his mind or in his computer or in his dreams. He didn't know, but he wanted to find that out as well. He completed the story just as the last sip of wine from his first glass flowed down his throat.

"I think you're having a breakdown." Chester's tone was dismissive, though it could not hide his concern. He had watched his father slowly slip beneath the waves of dementia, he feared he was observing the same in his friend.

"I'm fine, just tired of the same old same old." Tom was frustrated at his friend's response. He should be happy Tom wanted to live a life rather than spend his life running in the same circle. Yes, he could continue coding, programing, and living in his head, but he found he wanted more. Maybe it was the press of years on his back. Forty-four to most was hardly old but forty-four to Tom was closing fast on the end. If his family genes held, he might have a decade, not much when you wished eternity.

"I can reasonably assume you have given this great thought and considered all aspects and downsides of this move," now Chester was back to his old analytical self. "What are the percentages you will find what you are looking for?" He was referring to Tom's antecedents, to the possibility of finding some connection to people he'd never heard mention of, nor, apparently, had anyone in his family. Chester was an upper middle class white man who could trace his heritage back two hundred years without consulting a book or genealogical website. He had no idea what it was to feel as if you had no anchor or line tethered to the past.

Add the addition of this woman 'on his screen', and Tom's reversal of life course was extremely concerning. Especially as Tom readily admitted, no one in the meeting remembered seeing this apparition. Tom was chasing ghosts and even if he found this particular spirit what would he do? Chester knew of Tom's fear of premature death and wondered if this wasn't some distraction from facing the inevitable. And if it was, who was he to scotch that distraction.

Tom was his friend, his only friend, and if he loved the man as such, he should rejoice in his decision to take what was offered and run with it. He had no scions nor other family that he cared to bequeath his fortune to why not blow it on chasing phantoms in the night. Besides, the numbers Tom tossed about would last him several well wasted lifetimes. He was being arrogant and selfish; he should be basking in his friend's joy.

He caught the waitress's eye, held up two fingers, in the international signal for another round, mouthing 'please' and motioned they were ready to order when she was ready to take it.

The Gods of The Sea Given, and Taketh

Late 1851

Thomas was in ill humor when he spied where their course was to take them. Cap'n had decided another lesson was required for the young sailor, deeming the last few since they had set out from their tropical paradise insufficient. Cap'n was pissed that the crew had taken to the first mate. A first mate still green and not yet a real sailor in his book, certainly not well-seasoned. He required some hardening to refine the 'niceness' out of the man.

Heading east out of Tahiti toward the South Americas they spied the ship that had set upon them as they lay drifting. Their sails ripped, hanging limp in the slight breeze they hardly were making a knot. She listed to port side as if tired and near death. Cap'n decided to put them out of their misery.

In the privacy of the captain's cabin Thomas had pled the case that maybe they should be saved, it wasn't their fault that their captain had sent some to raid the 'Avenging Mother of The Sea', they had done what any sailor would do, followed Captains orders. But Cap'n's mood had darkened even more than normal by the crew's reaction to their First Mate saving his ship. His ship! Shit! They prized him above their own Cap'n! He would have none of Thomas' pleading and begging for these scallywags' lives. He would send them below where they could tell their murderous tale to the fishes and whales.

They set upon the ship with calm precision and merciless finality. They had discovered a small chest of jewels and coin, but that was the extent of her treasures. The men had put up a weak and pitiable defense but all had come to the same end. Cap'n had them burn the ship as she wasn't worth towing for scavenge.

Thomas had been sick to his stomach. It was so unnecessary. It was cruel and barbaric. Oh, Thomas had killed his fair share of men but that had been in a true battle, he had been attacked and had only protected himself and his crew. These men could barely hold their weapons. Swords with points down, boat hooks hanging from fingertips, empty eyes, empty souls seeming to almost welcome death.

The Cap'n had unleashed his tirade at Thomas' reaction calling him weak like a woman. The men had laughed though without levity. It was fearful, tinged with a strain of anger. They, too, had not enjoyed the butchering. The mood on the ship had darkened with his tongue lashing of the first mate they respected. If he had hoped to bring his crew back to their loyalty to him the Cap'n had misjudged the situation horribly.

The Cap'n had stayed clear of his men for a fortnight, interacting only when necessary, until the lookout spied another vessel moving slow and low in the water. A prize worth investigating. And an action which would raise the men out of their doldrums.

They had failed to contract any cargo on the island and the Cap'n was desperate for something to pay off the crew and win them back to his side. This pig in the water seemed just ripe for the slaughter. Merchants become pirates when circumstances demand.

They would sail close, nice and friendly like, maybe hove to, say hello. And when the guard was down, they would strike and take whatever booty wouldn't slow the 'Avenging Mother' down. And whatever the other ship was hauling looked to be enormously heavy and heavy usually meant expensive.

Cap'n was flying the flag of Britain, he had several country's flags stowed, using whichever was convenient to the situation. The British flag usually guaranteed any ship would welcome them unless they were Portuguese or Spanish. Some bad blood would not wash out. This time it worked perfectly. They were welcomed as friends, the bosuns whistle singing them aboard.

While Captain entertained Captain with the help of the surgeon, enjoying a fine meal and glasses of wine, first mates, bosuns, boatswain, and carpenters shared a cup or two of rum. The crew settled back in the calm of the evening to enjoy a night of peace. They were awarded one hour before all hell broke loose.

When Cap'n pulled his pistol and shoved it under the chin of the portly merchant Captain the struggle soon was over. Very little loss of life, loss of blood, though great quantities of loss of trust and pride.

If Thomas thought he wanted out before this event what happened next cemented the idea forever. They made ready to hove to, the lines loosened and made ready, waiting on the Cap'n. As Thomas watched as the Cap'n had his arm around the neck of the Merchant Captain, whispering something in his ear, as if imparting a great truth or secret. The man jolted, turning hard and stared Cap'n right in the eyes. The retort of the pistol at his temple was the last thing he heard. Cap'n pushed him overboard, laughing he scolded the merchant's crew, "Don't be trying to folla us where were headed, as were headed ta hell. If'n anybody asks ye, tell em Jolly Red took ya fer it all!" Grabbing a swing rope and jumping he cleared the fifteen feet between ships like a young crewman, laughing all the way.

Thomas stared at the sea where the other man had slipped beneath the waves. Horrified he turned as the Cap'n came strutting up behind him. He thought for a moment about decking the older man but knew that Cap'n kept another pistol in his belt behind his back.

The Cap'n read Thomas' thoughts and grinned, "Good choice, boyo, good choice."

As they sailed away from the theft and murder, several of the crewmen made their way aft where they could remove the sheet of sail covering the name of their ship. The other crew would never know who had murdered their captain, only Jolly Red. Something Cap'n had made up on the spur of the moment.

Yes, tests, Cap'n loved tests and he was testing Thomas now. He either had to prove himself worthy of this ship and crew or he would die in the trying. Thomas knew, the one thing Cap'n desired most was Thomas' failure. He also knew he would not give the despicable man the pleasure.

It was now an unsettled crew with anger and distrust simmering just below the surface. They did their best to hide their feelings from the Cap'n though Thomas could feel the resentment like the heat from an open kiln. This powder keg was getting ready to blow. He had to keep a lid on it until they could reach civilization and turn this murderous sonofabitch in to the proper authorities. Thomas may have done some things that had left black marks on his soul, but a murderer he was not.

Days passed, the ship making good time, as they made way for the tip of South America. Soon they would come 'round and head north, that was where Thomas would make his move and end this sin.

He pulled out the eye glass, telescoped it to the full extent and took one last look at the virginal passage he would navigate around the Horn, The Drake Passage. Though this would be his first time navigating the passage, he knew what he had to do and where his course lay. The men trusted his instincts and he believed in himself. The question was, did

God? That was who he would need most of all to make his initial crossing. One last test of the first mate by his Cap'n.

Thomas took the helm as they made the turn eastward and into Drake's Passage. He knew instinctively where he wanted to go, he would trust those instincts to get them through. He steered towards a trough that looked as if it would hold just long enough for them to use it to enter the passage. As the bow of the ship entered the promised trough the crest collapsed and pulled the bow under. A forty-foot wave washed over the forecastle, back across the deck and the bridge knocking all except Thomas to their knees.

He kept upright by virtue of his grip on the helm. He saw all the crew remained safely on deck courtesy of the belaying lines. They had been knocked around like lawn pins but were soon upright again. He called his apology but did so with a great laugh so they would know he was in control and they had nothing to worry about. Cap'n scowled as he saw their trust in the man increase. The young sonofabitch was enjoying this. He might sink the ship, but he'd go down with all hands laughing and cursing every god of the sea.

Thomas was attempting to read, to feel the currents and the wind, an impossible task considering the wind whipped and swirled to and fro from every direction. The currents danced and pirouetted to the commands of the insane wind and the angry sea lords. Thomas would make the ship dance with whatever tune that played. He had hoped to find a rhythm in the sea but found only chaos. He would use the chaos as his guide.

This was where thousands of men had fought and died attempting to tame the savage conditions and bend them to their will. Thomas would take what was given and try to steal a little good fortune. He knew it would be two full days to make the passage in these conditions and he would be at the helm the entire time. The crew would rotate allowing men to rest tired, beaten bodies. Thomas would not be afforded that luxury.

It took every ounce of strength he had to hold the helm, make minor or major adjustments as needed and remain standing. This would be his final test. If he passed, the Cap'n would have no choice but to honor him and the crew would be his for the taking. The thing was, he had no desire to take them. He wanted to sail north once through the Drake and find a place to finally land in North America and disembark this life. But first he had to survive this crossing.

The spray from another towering wave as it broke over the port side soaked his already drenched body tossing the ship like a child's toy in a tub. His arms ached, his legs trembled, his lungs burned from sea water and bellowing into the howling wind. And they were only a few hours into the trek. There was no way of reading the waves, the wind seemed to have a mind of its own, its only purpose, to destroy the ship and crew. Thomas wished he was anywhere but here, but here was where he was and he would have to make do. Somewhere there had to be reason, nature had reason, he knew that because God did not create chaos, He created order. That was what he had learned in seminary school and he would take that knowledge to the grave, though a watery grave it would be.

They came up from a deep trough and crested the monster, the spray and a million gallons of seawater washing over the length of the ship. Anything not secured more than sufficiently washed overboard and out to sea. The men had secured lifelines along the length and breadth of the ship, if they lost anything of import it would not be human. All hatches had been battened down and doubly secured, it was all they could do.

The seawater was cold, cold to the bone. -He and crew were soddened, waterlogged. They forced trembling hands and stiff fingers to achieve the impossible task of sailing this tiny vessel through a very angry sea. They might have given up, hidden below deck, and prayed for a quick death but for the visage of the tall, muscular first mate with a death grip on the helm, grinning from ear to ear and shouting his defiance at the gods of the seas and any others who might be in the neighborhood.

It was a visage to bring either terror into the mind of the sane or glee into the hearts of those deranged enough to ride the death wish with him. Thomas heard one of the crew scream into the wind, "if'n there be any who can get us through, it's that crazy sonofabitch at the helm!"

Thomas was fairly certain the words were not meant for his ears but it made him more determined, more dead set on, and hell bent to conquer the wind and sea and deliver ship and crew to safety. It was then he heard the terrified scream. It was either a warning or a pleading prayer to God.

He turned his head slightly to starboard where he thought the scream may have been birthed and was greeted by the sight of the monster rising from the depths of hell at the bottom of the ocean. Thomas had never believed the ocean was a living breathing entity. It was just the way that sailors had always referred to her. He believed it now.

The wave continued to grow by the second until it towered over their seemingly insignificant vessel. He had no time to bring his poor ship about and face this thing head on, it had surprised them and would roll them into the miasma. He called to the men and they grabbed whatever might act as life rafts and provide them with a chance at survival. Thomas did his best to wrestle the helm to try to get the prow of the ship turned away from this horror and let the stern take the brunt, but he was too late. They would be another victim of the Drake Passage.

It crashed with an earsplitting thunder with enough force to drag the ship under with every man-jack of them now about to become part of the ocean food chain. The ship rolled under the turbulent sea, up above the seas raged and crashed, down here life moved in slow motion. Each man knowing their only chance to live was to hang onto the only true-life raft that presented itself, the ship. If they could maintain their hold on anything solid there was a slight chance the ship could right itself and the air trapped inside would pull it to the surface.

The first casualty was the mainmast which snapped with the power and weight of the wave. It should have boded disaster except it now no longer acted as a drag on the rolling ship allowing the carcass to spin more freely. The foremast was the second as it snapped at the deck level and caught in the rigging acting as a drag on the bow and spinning the ship. Two crewmen who were secured to the prow, breath held deep in their lungs about to give way, found the strength and determination to cut the mast free just as the ship righted itself and began the assent to the surface.

She broke the surface just as the men were losing consciousness for lack of air. She tossed and turned in the violent waters but they were still alive. Thomas had somehow clung to the helm and was now attempting the impossible to steer her in any direction that the wind blew. They did not have the rigging to fight this storm and had to try and ride it out. Like ragdolls the crew was hurled and hove to around the deck, the only thing saving their lives were the safety lines. It wouldn't have mattered either way, as not one had the strength to do more than pray in their head and take their last few breaths before the sea pulled them back under.

Thomas held steady believing there had to be an exit, a route, a trough to take them away, to save what was left. He never saw it but felt the tug, like the great hand of God pulling them to some semblance of safety. The current had caught them, pulling them away from the brutal confluence of Atlantic and Pacific.

She settled into a rhythm as the current towed her east. Thomas pried his fingers loose of the helm and slowly sank to the deck. Exhausted, he closed his eyes to thank God, just for a moment. A weak grip on his shoulder, softly shaking him brought him back to reality. He tilted his head to where he could see the grinning face of one of the crew. He was laughing and yelling at the skies, bout the craziest, luckiest sonofabitch'n first mate on the sea.

Thomas' mind was muddled, disoriented, missing, he had been where? Where had he been? Lost in a dream of young men strolling in the sunshine discussing the finer points of what God meant by this passage or some other parable. Those had been happy times. Times without death hanging over your head every day and nature testing skill, strength, and will to live. Well, he had lived for another day. The question was would the ship? He had to get hold of himself and survey the damage. And find the Cap'n.

He should be, by all rights, standing and bellowing his displeasure at first mate and crew. Demanding they rise from their stupor and set things right, yet it was quiet except the sea. She never slept, never lay still, never lay quiet.

He roused himself to go check the Cap'n's cabin.

He knocked once before pushing on the door to enter. It did not budge. He knocked again harder and put his ear to the door listening for any sign the Cap'n might be in trouble. Nothing. He pushed harder attempting to crack the door open. Nothing. Now he rapped hard on the door with a closed fist loud enough to wake the dead, if any might be in there. Nothing.

Putting his shoulder to the door and bracing his feet against the bulkhead, he strained with every muscle and sinew until the door cracked. It did not open, the wood shattered and splintered. With a fist tightly clenched he began to pound on the splintered wood until a hole appeared and he could get his hand inside to try and pry away whatever might be against the inside. He could feel something wedged against the handle, a chair, maybe, or some other wooden object. He pulled until he was certain the muscles in his arm might tear but could feel it ever so slightly give way. He renewed the effort until the wooden chair gave way completely and the door swung open.

The interior of the cabin was destroyed. The legs of the central table bolted to the floor were the only sign of any furniture still remaining. Pages of books scattered amongst the bedclothes that hadn't been washed out the smashed quarter gallery lights. Any sign of life had been completely washed away. Along with the Cap'n, apparently. There was no sign of the man and no place where his body could hide.

Thomas thought it must have been when they were forced under the raging sea and rolled. The million stone of frigid seawater was too much even for the leaded glass of the lights. Cap'n had thought himself safe from the weather, the waves, and the wind. The sea had found and claimed him. Thomas was now master of the Mother.

He turned and saw several of the crew taking in what he already had seen. They worked out the meaning same as he.

"What do we do now, Cap'n?" One of them ventured.

"First off, don't call me that. If I am to be anything I will be Captain, I want no connection to the man who bore the other moniker." He began throwing whatever was left of the previous occupant's belongings through the smashed glass. "Secondly, let's get her as shipshape as we might. See what can be repaired, what jibs still are usable and if any of the masts are still attached anywhere to the ship and if they can be rigged and sail hoisted. We need to have some maneuverability if we are to have any hope of staying alive long enough to find a port." He nodded to himself assuring he had set in motion their best chance. "And if luck should hold, and we can gain control of our wounded dear heart, then we sail north, to America and any that wish, may find dry land with me. The rest may go wherever their freedom takes them." He smiled. The Cap'n had always avoided America like a plague infested cesspool, Thomas would at long last find that land and opportunity he had yearned for.

The forested cove showed her pretty face two days after the final crumb of food, that hadn't been tossed overboard or spoiled by being exposed to sea water, had been consumed. Almost to a man they had come to the conclusion their luck had run out. Thomas had been a good man, a good first mate, and their good luck charm, but even the big man couldn't hold off the specter of death forever. They would die on the ship crippled at sea. All hope was lost.

Until the cry of 'Land-Ho' rang out from the prow. Then silence as the exhausted, foundering mate rubbed his eyes before shakily holding up the spy glass and repeated the call while pointing towards the west.

"Heading and distance, Mr. Hanson," cried Thomas surprised by the energy and clarity of his own ragged voice.

They limped into the protected cover of calm and deep green. The men grumbled slightly when Thomas order them to drop anchor but he wasn't taking any chances the ship might drift away while they foraged for food and fresh water. And a new mainmast and fore.

They had jerry rigged the broken headsail which had conveniently gotten itself tangled in the securing lines and clung to the ship as its own life raft. It had not been steady or sturdy but, by the gods of the sea, it had held long enough for them to have a chance at life. Hell, the ship had held together with no more than a few leaks and listing to the port side but she'd been a tough old broad holding them in her arms until she could find safe harbor. They would lovingly now patch her, use pitch to seal what they could and fill their own bellies. A spot like this had to have game, and at this point they didn't care what it was, boar, deer, rat, or snake, anything to sate.

They spread out to survey their new surroundings hoping to discover some kind of game that wouldn't require extraordinary strength or energy to bring down.

Though they could hear the rustling of brush as life traversed through the forest and birds filling the trees, they saw nothing. That was until one of the more senior seamen noticed the cocoanuts and bananas hanging from the trees.

He knew of these delicious fruits from his many years at sea. He also remembered you could eat the roots of many plants that could take the place of meat. Yes, they could survive here while they replenished supplies and repaired their Mother.

The men settled into a comfortable routine of foraging edible vegetation while others cut down a sizeable tree for the new mast, not quite of the size and height they would have preferred but it would do. The spare canvas stored below decks had survived the underwater adventure so sails could be fashioned and hoisted. Within two months, near as anyone could tell, they were once again seaworthy, or as seaworthy as they ever would be until they could dry dock.

Several of the men had made noise about remaining in this jungle paradise until they realized they would be their only company. No natives had shown themselves, and they knew from experience that if there were any native folk about, they would have come a-calling. Curiosity was an impossible enticer to resist. There had not been any sign, footprint, broken artifact, sound, or sighting. They would all board and go where Thomas headed.

As they sailed out of the cove and pointed the prow north it was a wan but contented crew that manned the ship. They had lost weight before finding salvation and lost a bit more with their vegetarian diet, supplanted by whatever fish they could catch in the cove, but now they believed they would live, they believed in Thomas and they believed in the 'Avenging Mother of the Sea'.

My How Sushi Can change Your Life

Present Day

Tom slowly ascended to the surface of consciousness from the depths of R.E.M sleep. He was rested. That, in and of itself, was quite extraordinary and welcome. Glancing at the digital clock on the nightstand he was taken aback by the number glaring at him, judging him, and finding his slothful self wanting. He had slept for fourteen hours. He knew he was tired but, shit, that was bordering on coma.

He pulled back the heavy curtain and blinked in the brilliant sunlight. Jesus, it was four o'clock in the afternoon. He stretched. He wanted to chastise himself for wasting a day, though was rest and recuperation really wasting a day? He had worked his ass off getting all the coding right, the programing set and worrying about whether his veiled offer would be noted and contemplated.

He realized he had dangled the possibility but not an exact price. He should have tossed an exceedingly high estimate, a starting point, figuring they would require a ballpark to play in. He had left it entirely to their own imaginations. Either way he didn't care. He really did want out. He wanted complete freedom; the complete freedom only a huge basket of cash could provide. If these people wanted to fuck around, they would find out he had others just as interested, just not as stingy.

He'd get a nice hot cuppa and a cinnamon roll, one of his few vices, and then check messages. No need to hurry, the day would begin when he was more aware of it. He flipped on the laptop and set his coffee and roll down next to it.

Then, before he could tap in his password, the video tile opened down in the right-hand corner of the screen.

It was her. He caught his coffee before it spilled over the keyboard. WTF?

"Y-y-you," he stuttered. It was a stupid, monosyllabic response and he was pretty sure his voice had cracked like a third grader.

She smiled. "Sleep well?" There were depths to the question he thought he would drown in if he chanced to chase down their meaning.

"Yes," keep it simple stupid. A woman of this beauty and intelligence would detect every single weakness in his crumbling façade. Shit, Tommy would detect every one of his weaknesses while playing pinball and discussing quadratic equations. Why was he sweating? "Fourteen hours' worth." His response was sheepish as if admitting such shiftlessness would highlight a major flaw in his character. "I've been working hard and not sleeping much lately." The defense rests.

"Working on the retirement plan?" How would she? Oh, she had hacked into the call the other day and it wouldn't take a genius to figure out why he was asking what he was asking of those who had the wherewithal to grant what he asked. "How's it coming together?"

It was none of her business and she had no right to pry! "Don't know yet. I think they are trying to make me sweat for a few before coming back with an offer." He could no more refuse this woman anything she wanted to know than he could sail the seven seas with his dreams.

"What if we would double what you think fair plus give you residuals in perpetuity?" She was like a siren out of a Greek tragedy. She sang so sweetly and enticingly he couldn't refuse.

The laughter began at his toes, racing through his body until it erupted from him like Vesuvius in 79 AD! And then it would not be staunched. He shook with uncontrollable laughter, tears cascading down his face. He was insane with the ridiculousness of this entire intercourse. And that's exactly what it was, she was fucking with him, seeing how far she could lead him along, tempting him, bringing him close to orgasm only to pull back with frivolity.

Finally getting hold of himself physically and mentally he wheezed to a stop. "In perpetuity, that's rich," he had regained his control. "If you know so much about me and my intentions then you would know 'in perpetuity' is around another decade." He wanted to laugh again but the audacity of stating his death sentence out loud to another person, even one inside a computer, made it all too starkly real. Tom had never told anyone—except Chester—his fear and reality. He had now.

She smiled that all knowing, conceited grin. "What if I told you your fear is misguided and you could live a much longer life than you give yourself credit for." She waited while that sank to the bottom of his soul. "You may have been misled," she teased. "First off," she continued, "you have never been tested to see if you have the gene for what you fear, and number two, even if you did there are infinite possibilities of ways to cure what you don't have." She nodded to herself and him as if the point had been cemented into the foundation.

Tom studied her every movement the way her mouth made words, her lips, did her words synch up with what her mouth formed. Each blink of an eye, breathing, did her hair move naturally? He searched every known way of detecting AI but he could see none of them. The way the crinkles formed around her mouth when she pronounced certain vowels, the way her pupils changed with the intensity of her words. NO, there was no way she was AI generated, she was real. The question again was why? Why was she coming to him? Why was she making this offer? How did she know his most secret fear? And, why was she so certain he was wrong to fear it?

"Who do you work for?" Why hadn't he asked that in the first place. It should not have surprised him that his desire to retire might leak and once it did there would be a number of mega syndicates wanting his encryption methods, his advanced security, and engineering methods. All would be willing to bid for what he had in his head.

But he didn't want those secrets to wind up in the wrong hands. They could prove to be very dangerous if someone with illicit intent were to integrate them into their system. Though they would never know he had installed a very small back door, undetectable, hidden under a hundred layers of minutia. That was his personal security measure against abuse of his brilliance.

"I don't work 'for' anyone. If I did, I would work for all of humanity. I, like you, would prefer to keep your inventions out of the hands of those who would use them to rule over their competitors." She appeared to search for a better answer to his question but couldn't seem to formulate or contrive anything satisfactory without giving away completely whatever it was she proposed. Smart. "Look you want to know your history, yes?" He nodded though he hadn't wanted to. She already seemed to know too much about him, he didn't wish to confirm any more than he had. "How about as a sign of good faith I do some research and pass it all along to you?"

It was tempting but Tom's cautious nature finally kicked in. "I don't want it here," he said pointing at the computer, "You've already proven to me that nothing is secure. You do your foraging and ferreting and when you have something we'll meet, in person, face to face. Then we'll talk." He reached over to turn off the machine just as she said in a curiously playful tone,

"I will look forward to that with great anticipation."

His stomach growled its displeasure. How long had he been sitting here talking to 'Her'? It was getting dark outside and his impatient gastrointestinal tract had waited long enough, he required sustenance. He glanced at the now hard cinnamon roll he'd completely forgotten about during their conversation and sighed. Well, he might need to eat but had no desire to prepare said necessity. Time to throw on a light jacket and head out into the earthly pleasures that awaited.

The beauty of living in an upscale, citified neighborhood was the plethora of offerings that didn't include fast food or chain restaurants. Most of the folks who dwelt in this area liked upscale or, at the very least, decent quick dining. That was where Tom would head. He didn't want a sit-down meal, he wanted something to grab and go. Something tasty that he could subsume without thought so his mind could work out the fourteen million questions rolling around the inside his cranium.

Sushi. Perfect. Without anyone to share it he could walk and eat with his fingers with no one the wiser. Sometimes man had to revert to Neanderthal and shove the sushi into the gullet with fingers rather than chopsticks. Tonight, he was going Paleolithic. Maybe sashimi to go with!

The light rain began about four blocks from his apartment. It wasn't a heavy downpour nor did it show any predilection to go there. He might get washed but not drenched as he made his way home. He pulled the hood up on his jacket to try and keep the rain off the plastic tray of sushi he was now furiously shoving into his mouth before the fish could get wet. He chuckled. He should be more concerned with his own deteriorating condition. Ah well, as his mother used to tell him, he might be sweet but he wasn't likely to melt in a little bit of rain.

The flashing red and blue lights startled him, he almost lost the grip on his dinner, saving it just before it slipped from his, now, wet fingers.

"Hold where you are!" commanded an authoritative voice.

Tom turned to see who was yelling at him. They didn't have problems in this neighborhood. It was quiet, peaceful, wealthy. Everyone felt safe and secure behind their knowledge that the lower classes never ventured here. You could walk with impunity, never bothered by the homeless, the beggars, the street. So, to have an officer of the law speak to him in such a manner was disquieting. Maybe he had misjudged and eating sushi and soon sashimi with the bare hands was an infraction of the law.

"Are you speaking to me?" Tom kept his tone even, respectful, but not timid.

"What are you doing wandering around this neighborhood?" It was a question and a command. This guy wanted answers and would have them.

"I think you might wish to speak with a little more respect to a citizen," Tom's intention was jovial, not threatening, just a light poke at the servant of the people.

"I'll show you some respect!" The anger rose to the surface like a serpent out of myth.

Tom had done nothing to arouse such passion in this man and now he felt his own anger coming to the fore. He turned to find rage and a pistol aim at him.

"Drop what's in your hand!" Screamed the now, apparently, out of control policeman.

"It's sushi," Tom's words were steel. He shocked himself as he had never been ill tempered. He had led a life without interaction with hate, bigotry, racism, or being talked down to by authority figures. He had always considered himself on a par with anyone. Now he was being treated as a common criminal in his own neighborhood and he found it infuriating.

"I said drop it or I'll shoot!" This man was losing his shit and Tom was losing patience.

"You're going to shoot a man over sushi? Are you insane? Look for yourself," and Tom shoved the half empty tray of sushi towards the cop.

The gun was steady as death as the cop—were those sergeant stripes on his shirt?—tightened his finger on the trigger. Life has a way of slowing down at points like this, as if to give you time to comprehend the last moments of your life. Tom shouted defiance.

He could not remember if he heard the shot but he felt the shock of pain as the bullet entered his shoulder. He knew in his heart his mother would be so disappointed but he knew, with the shock of pain, he had howled, "What the fuck!" as he lost consciousness.

The Smallest Islands Hide the Most Precious Treasures

Spring 1852

The sea had her dander up as they made their way north hugging the coast of Brazil. They would stay within sight of the coast as the seas were far less vicious in this close and if they did have to abandon ship, they could most likely swim their way to shore. Once around the Nordeste of Brazil they would plot a more northerly course into and through the Caribbean. There Thomas hoped to find a friendly island where they could hunker down, complete more repairs to their leaky, listing vessel and regain some of their own strength and stamina. It had been an agonizing few months, but they had survived. On the sea, sometimes that was enough.

The wind came around from the east-northeast to west-southwest and became a gentle, comforting breeze as they entered the Caribbean, as if welcoming them. Thomas felt himself relax slightly, his neck and shoulder muscles loosened, his back lost some of the intense pain that had burrowed in and found a home, with the promise of good weather, warm breezes, and the possibility of friendly shores. He also knew that America was now within reach.

He considered Cuba as he stared at the torn and tattered remnants of the map but decided to keep to the lesser outposts of mankind. News, even on the oceans, can travel faster than winds can blow limping ships and he had no idea if their exploits under the Cap'n had won the race to this part of the world. One of the first things he planned to do once they found any kind of safe harbor was to rename the Mother and remove all references to their previous master.

If they could escape their past, they could have a future.

There were options galore for a merchant ship in need of refitting, almost three dozen on the leeward of the Lesser Antilles but most were occupied by nations Thomas wanted nothing to do with; at least until he found out which way the wind blew and if it had carried ill will their way. He settled on St. Maartin. Unlike many of the islands throughout the Caribbean this island had been split in two with two separate nations laying claim to it. Thomas felt safety lay in the disfunction and distrust of two.

She was a pretty young woman, not more than a stone's throw from being a girl, and she smiled at him as he walked the plank from ship to shore. Thomas had been at sea for months. He had survived storms, battles, and actions he was shamed by, yet all he could do was smile back. Oh, he'd lay with an island girl if she caught his eye but not as a customary practice, he didn't come looking for sexual release, and he always felt the guilt instilled by the seminary for months after. This stop was not about satiating his carnal needs, it was about refitting and satiating the needs of Mother. So, he walked on by.

He wanted to find the master of the harbor and see to repairs. After a quick search and a few questions, he found the man, though master might have been more honorific than earned. He was half drunk, reeking of bad personal hygiene, and a worse diet. The need to spend a few less minutes in bars and a few more in water emanated from him like an ill wind. Thomas had met worse. He knew he reeked to high heaven himself but he had been at sea for most of the past year and endured more than most. He also knew he would cleanse his journey from him as soon as business was taken care of.

"Any chance of refitting my ship?" Straight to the point and assuring the harbor master he was speaking to the ship's captain. "We had a rough go of it coming 'round the horn." The man didn't need details, they had lived, and every man-jack knew of the Drake, that was all that was pertinent.

"Ya," well, that was good. He spoke enough of the mother tongue to understand Thomas' needs. "Whatchu got need of?"

He could've asked for gold or silver first but he hadn't. Usually that's all these blighters wanted, maybe this was one of the more decent sort. It would certainly make up for the stench.

"Mainmast, rigging, mainsails and fore. Oh, and some pitch for sealing a few leaks while we bail the bilge," if they could acquire these it would assure they could make it north to America or Canada. Thomas knew he didn't want to settle in the south as he, being Irish and knowing the degradation of serfs and slaves, had no desire to be near such again. If he could make it to New York or up into Canada he could start anew.

"Gonna cost," Heavily accented extortion was still extortion, the question was the price heavier than the accent.

"How much?" That would give him a beginning point to haggle.

"Thirty for labor, a hundred for the cloth and I'll throw in the rigging for another fifty. You cut down the trees for the masts and haul them to yer vessel." Thomas was shocked by how reasonable the price was. He assumed the guy would try to squeeze every coin out of his pouch he could get. After all, Thomas was at the disadvantage here, his was the ship in need.

"Why so reasonable?" His suspicion was screaming at him.

"You take me with." So, that was it. This slug of a human had probably made enemies from here to Europe and back and was not well-loved on this spit of land. Probably hated if his appearance meant anything.

"You will bathe before stepping one foot on my ship," Thomas could live with much but this malodorous pig was not going to stink up his ship. The crew would mutiny.

"Two weeks, den we go. Money first." He held out his hand as if Thomas would come in here with a full purse.

Thomas reached deep inside his torn trousers and pulled up a leather pouch. He weighed it in his hand before opening it and pouring out what he needed before handing the rest to the master.

He folded the rest in his palm. He nodded his agreement with the oaf before heading out to buy some refreshments and distractions for the crew. Work would begin soon enough, they'd known misery, hunger, thirst, pain and suffering long enough. It was time for pleasure.

But not for him. He wanted to cleanse himself and sleep for a week, though that would not be possible. A night in a soft bed would certainly be welcome, he grinned.

He found the large, thatched building that served as tavern and inn and handed the proprietor, a heavy-set brown man with a friendly bearing, half of what he'd held back from the harbor master.

"My men will be here soon, make sure they are well taken care of with food, drink, and whatever they need. Do not fuck me or I will return in a foul mood." They grinned at each other sealing the deal. Thomas would head back to the 'Avenging Mother'—soon to be Daughter of The Sea—to let his crew know as soon as they belayed and finished painting the new name, they could enjoy themselves, but not so much as to get themselves killed! He loved the sound of their laughter.

The young woman remained by the end of the dock and smiled once again as he passed. She was more than pretty, he decided. A rich brown, like fine leather, with brilliant white eyes and teeth that lit up the dock. Yet, the teachings of the church weighed heavy. It was one thing to bed a woman on the other side of the world but here he was close to civilization and Mother Church. Here Christianity could be felt in the air. His soul would suffer no debasement in the sight of God.

He walked by the girl and onto the ship to grab his one remaining shirt and trousers with the least number of holes. If he was going to bathe, he would want the freshest clothes he had, though fresh was in the nose of the beholder.

He checked around the small village and found no actual bathing establishments, it would seem cleanliness might be next to godliness but that god hadn't yet visited this island. He must be on the Dutch side of the island for certainly the French would be bathed in perfumes and flower petals. He would find himself a nice, secluded cove fed by fresh water if the gods be kind, to wash off the last few months.

Finding said cover, he sat in the tepid water staring out at the sea enjoying the last light of day. He had scrubbed himself with sand and pumice, found along the small beach, to alleviate some of the scum from salt, sweat, and the refuse of the ocean.

As he stood in all his glory for one last peek at the setting sun, he heard a giggle from behind. Without thinking he turned to see who might be spying on him. He saw her cover her face at the sight of full-frontal nudity. He should have quickly covered himself but was too tired and had been too long away from civilization to care.

He shooed her away as he made his way back to the beach and his clothing. He wanted nothing to do with her or anyone, just a soft bed. He held the thought; would this place even have that comfort? He would need to ask the innkeeper at the establishment where the men would be three-quarters drunk and working on finishing the job.

Yes, the fellow told him, he had just the thing but it would be another silver, a gold if he wanted to use it the whole time they were there. Thomas cared not a whit for the cost, it was ill-gotten in the first place and it was supposed to be used to begin a new life. Well, hello new life.

It was a full-size bed, with sheets and a pillow. Thomas was dreaming. He pulled off his clothes, slipped between the sheets and dreamt before the pillow wrapped his head in heaven. Dreams came and went; most he would never remember but one stood out. He was in a land he did not recognize, a bizarre land that was like no other he had ever visited. They had carts but nothing pulled them, they moved of their own volition. The streets were smooth and the people wore clothes that were almost lewd, showing skin that only a wife or husband should ever see. And yet, he felt at home here until someone yelled at him. He couldn't understand what was being said. A different language though familiar inflection, shouted in anger and hate. Thomas wanted to know what had brought out such hate but felt a sharp pain and he died.

Well, in the dream, in reality he awoke with a start to find he was not alone in his bed. Who the hell? When had she come in here and why was she unclothed? She didn't wake with his abrupt movement just curled in closer to him, hugging him like a child.

He wanted to shake her awake and toss her out of his bed, but he couldn't. There was something so innocent in the way she clung to him, as a cub would cling to its mother for safety and succor. He lay back down and tried not to think of her naked body touching his own.

He awoke at the breaking dawn with her still beside him and him in a state of arousal. He had to slip out of the bed and rid himself of this spear. The last thing he needed right now was to despoil some islander's daughter even if she had initiated the comingling. He tiptoed over to the chamber pot in the corner and as quietly as he could relieved the pressure. She did not stir.

Guilt set anchor in his heart, though he didn't know why. He had done nothing. He couldn't be responsible for his body reacting in a natural way to the situation, yet he couldn't shake the deep seeded feeling he was at fault here. Maybe it was her pure innocence. Maybe it was because he found himself attracted so strongly to a dark woman. Though he'd bedded brown island women before, this was different. Maybe he thought the devil had a hand in this; forcing black on white, savage on Christian, it was against God's will. The races should never interbreed. They told him as much in the seminary and his father had beaten the same into his soul. Yet, she was. . .Too young, screamed his mind! Too naïve! Too different. Too perfect.

And a sound sleeper, thought Thomas, or an excellent actress. He grinned in the burgeoning light and donned his 'clean' clothes. He would see what presented itself to break his night's fast and bring her back some as well. He felt responsible for the girl though he could not fathom why. He hadn't used her nor had he encouraged her actions. He had not invited her to his bed and had only comforted her there. Yet, she was stunning in her beauty and innocence. He thought someone should watch over her, if only while their ship was being refitted.

He brought her some fruit and a bowl of water which she ate while he attempted to ascertain her status and where her parents might be. She spoke only island talk. He guessed it was her native tongue. She had never been taught French or Dutch or, certainly, the King's tongue. This was going nowhere. He thought it best to take her to the innkeeper, who was also one of the dark people, and see if he could obtain any information.

As soon as Thomas showed up with the girl the innkeeper took a step back with fear in his eyes.

"What you doing wid THAT girl," there was terror, accusation, and confusion in the question.

"She seems to have attached herself to me. She doesn't speak any civilized tongue that I can tell, only her own. I thought, maybe, you could interpret what she wants, or who she is, or where I might find her parents so she can go home." It was a rational list, as far as Thomas could tell. He only wished to help this child before she got into real trouble with someone less scrupulous than he.

"As far as I know, no parents. She might be child of the jungle. She might be witch to beguile. She might be Voodoo woman, unclean, cursed and bringing curse to anyone who touch her," Thomas would have laughed had he not run into superstitions and believers many times over the last few years. He knew from experience that belief was sometimes stronger than what you could see with your own eyes. This man feared this child.

"She's an orphan?" Thomas searched for an ounce of compassion.

"Don't know, don't care. She come out of jungle a while back, naked as birth, talking her gibberish. Old woman in town say she touched, by god, by devil, by spirits of forest, but she touched. Some give her food hoping she will bring dem luck, some mock her and taunt her to see if she really witch. Some want to burn or drown her to find out, most try to stay away, keep trouble from dere door." He crossed himself, though Thomas did not believe the man was Christian, just covering his bet.

"She will be under my protection until we leave. I want it known no one is to hurt her in any way. Do not bother her or taunt her or retribution shall be mine!" Thomas had been away from Seminary school for the better part of a decade but the teachings driven into him, though hidden deep, could be excavated easily and would rise to the surface with passion. He was a Christian man; it had been beaten into him since he was a child. And though he may not always have followed scripture he still knew the importance of treating each other as one wanted to be treated and how Jesus wanted us to treat the powerless and weak. He would take care of this lost child of God. Maybe he could teach her some of the King's Tongue and the words of the savior.

He had found his purpose in life, for now.

She was his constant companion, his shadow. At first it drove him to distraction that every time he turned around, she was underfoot. He had to sleep with something on, no longer au natural, so she would do the same. He could not in good conscience sleep with a naked young woman at his side, and she would sleep nowhere else.

He had made arrangements with the innkeeper for her to have separate quarters yet every morning he would find her snuggled next to him. He would once again chastise her and send her away but she would only return the next night. He had fed and cared for the stray; the stray was stray no longer.

The work progressed on the ship just as the Harbor Master had promised. Thomas was amazed by how well the natives of the island followed the instructions of his crew, creating a new mizzenmast, Topgallant, rigging, and stripping small trees for yards. It would not be up to standard but it would be a far cry from what they had limped in on. She would be more than seaworthy soon.

So, what to do with the girl. He had taught her some of the King's tongue and she was keen to learn everything he was willing to teach; but she couldn't come with them. What would he do with this child when they got to the new world? He had his treasure but no idea how far that would get him in this new land. He couldn't claim her as his child as one look would put the lie to that. She would have to stay here where she was born.

He found it interesting that this orphan wandered untouched through this outpost of civilization. She was more than comely, with fine, strong features, a womanly figure, yet walked through a seaport without fear. He wondered why no man had made a play for her. He'd asked the innkeeper what he knew and the only answer he would get was to stay away from the girl. She was poison. There was something evil about her, that was it, no further explanation.

He finally set the girl down and decided to mime what he was trying ask her. Showing her how men and women interact, kissing his hand, and caressing himself in a sexual way. Better to mime on himself, he thought, than to use her. At long last she seemed to get what he was asking.

Her face went cold, her features froze. Her eyes locked on his as she mimed back, pointing at where one, two, three, four, maybe five men stood surrounding her. She mimed trying to get away from them as they crowded in on her. The terror on her face and her movements was all he needed to see what she saw. She mimed fighting each, one at a time, then two, three, until she threw herself down on the ground, kicking and screaming as she continued to fight. Until she could fight no more. She closed her eyes, went completely still and the tears pushed their way past her sealed lids.

She got up from the ground and ran to him. He held her in his arms, gently, stroking her hair, and promising her that would never happen to her again.

That evening he questioned the innkeeper once again, this time with knowledge and fact. The man hung his head, not able to look Thomas in the eyes. Nodding, as he confirmed everything that Thomas had discerned from the silent story he had just witnessed.

"Yes, they raped, viciously," he whispered. Shame covered his features, his body slumped.

Thomas could feel his fury rising. He would have answers. Who had done this? Where were they now? If they be sailors, what ship? The man remained silent until Thomas grabbed him by both shoulders and shook him until he gazed directly into Thomas' eyes. "What happened to them? Where are they?" He demanded an answer.

"Dead." The word final.

Thomas stood, still holding the man's shoulders, waiting like the harbinger of doom. "How?"

"Accidents, they say, every one of dem. One fell from crow's nest on calm day. One off a cliff on 'ta other side of the island. One found dead in his bed without a mark on him, though his face was a mask of terror. The fourth got drunk and drown and the fifth hung himself rather than wait. Nobody know nothing about how they all could die, the only thing in this world connecting them was dat girl. They had never met before that night. Dey get drunk together." He spit, and crossed himself, "Take what you will from that, but stay clear of that girl if you value your life."

Thomas pushed the man away. He, like any sailor or man of the time, had his superstitions but he could never believe the girl was the cause of five men dying, no matter what they had done to her. She might wish them dead but wishing ain't killing and killing ain't by accident. He now knew he could not leave her here or someone would get up enough courage to kill her and cleanse the island of her evil.

She would have to come with him.

And The Lord Said, Heal!

Present Day

Tom could feel the cool rushing through his veins. That was a good thing, his mind reassured. The drugs were riding roughshod through his blood stream on their way to the source of the pain and if blood wasn't flowing, carrying that pain suppressant, it would mean he was more than likely dead. He remembered the cop pointing the gun right at his heart and the hate and fear in his eyes, maybe that was what made him miss his target by inches. Tom had raised the container of sushi to reassure but apparently this cop found the Dragon Roll and Sashimi terrifying. Maybe he'd had bad sushi, gas station sushi, and the memory of his illness plagued him. Who knew what evil lurked in the hearts and minds of men?

Tom was paying the price now. They must be infusing ice into his veins and arteries because he shivered with the piercing frigidity coursing through his body. Maybe they were using ice chips to staunch the blood. The chips would lodge themselves in the arteries, slowing the flow of blood to the wound, but before they could do harm the ice would begin to melt allowing blood to flow at a lesser rate. And maybe the drugs they were infusing caused this kind of thinking. Either way, he lived, and that would be a very good first step.

He floated outside his body and observed all the activity buzzing around his prone, naked form. He should lose a few pounds, thought the almost expired. If he lived, he would take better physical care of himself, he promised. He had always kept his mind well oiled, tuned up, and running at peak capacity but all that time in front of a computer monitor and scratching on legal pads had taken its toll on his midsection and what little muscle tone he'd ever acquired in life. Yeah, maybe a gym membership or he could try walking and see how that went.

Oh, that's right, that's what got him here in the first place. He had decided to walk to grab a bite and then walk in the rain home. The Hoodie! Like a brilliantly lit marque inside his head announcing the opening of smash Broadway hit came his answer. The Hoodie was what done him in. The cop had seen a rather large black man, though he was far more tan, tromping through a posh neighborhood in the rain and rather than reason out why this might be occurring allowed his racism to kick-in and take over. 'Must be one of them from the inner city come out to bother some good, decent wealthy white folk or break into their well-appointed homes and rob them, rape them, or some other horror. Yeah, well best thing to do is when the colored fella attacks you with raw fish is shoot the sonofabitch!'

If Tom would have been conscious, he thought he might've laughed at the absurdity of the whole fucking scene. But he wasn't and it wasn't really that funny, more sad, but he was alive. Maybe he could still meet that stunning woman, if she wasn't AI or something weird like that. Yeah, the drugs definitely had kicked in. He'd loved to have introduced her to his mother, she'd be so proud of him. The chubby egghead standing there with a hologram of a stunning woman pretending to be his date. Maybe death wasn't such a horrible option.

Voices intruded on his aimless mental wandering. They were in a language he could not comprehend and Tom was pretty good with languages. He wasn't necessarily prolific or fluent on more than a few but he could grasp words here and there which would give away any language, except the one being spoken.

He wasn't shocked, per se, just confused, though upon further reflection, as he had the time and no other distractions, he shouldn't have been. People in the medical profession here in the states, came from all over the world. They would learn all their universities had to offer, add in medical schools being subsidized by US interests, come here, add a few years working the front lines at hospitals and one-off emergency rooms and you had built a medical establishment where those practicing were just happy to be making a few hundred thousand a year, less than the expectation of the home grown.

Still, the words niggling at his brain tantalized. He wanted nothing more than to swim to the surface and see who spoke. There was power in the words, they contained fear more than syllables, consonants, and vowels, there was a power, maybe, or a magic he could feel. Though to be honest with himself, he had never believed in magic or unseen power, sleight of hand, yes, real magic was not possible to the reasoned mind.

He heard his name spoken over and over and over until he had no choice but to crack an eye and see who the fuck wanted him. He saw black hair atop a youthful male head with Asian eyes and a white lab coat. The woman's voice calling him, speaking to him did not match the motion of the lips on the man, nor did the gender. He heard the words, 'lucky. . . a couple inches to the right or lower. . . somehow missing the third ribs, dancing through without touching, exiting. . . impossible,' and he closed his eyes. It was like trying to watch classic sci-fi movies from the 50's where they didn't use subtitles but overdubbed a voice that fit the person like a cheap suit bought from a secondhand store in the wrong neighborhood.

He wanted whoever was in charge of masking his pain to stop, if only for the nonce, until he could clear his mind, his hearing, his understanding of what the hell was going on around him. Then, maybe, just maybe, he could grasp what was being discussed in such intricate detail, as he was quite certain it applied to him.

A young woman filled his head. A woman he had never met, never known, had never seen in passing, yet there was a connection, though tangential. She was dark of complexion though still not black as he understood the color, more a deep brown, a brown of such depth and richness it pulled the eye and all thought into it. He was drowning in another human being and there was no shallow end to save him. She was pretty, though not stunning like the woman in his computer representing his deepest desire. As his thoughts touched on the woman of his dreams and computer display, her face took over the monitor screen inside his head.

His perfect woman smiled at him. It was lovely, friendly, well-meaning though he could feel the tug of sexuality behind the innocence of that face. He wanted to yell at himself to stop this childish yearning for someone and something that was as far from ever becoming reality as him walking on the moon, yet he couldn't. He wanted her.

The young girl he had seen or imagined earlier came back into focus. She was saying something to him, though he couldn't hear a sound, just observe the earnestness of her features. She did everything in her power to convey a warning or alert him to some coming danger. He wanted to laugh long and hard, it was out of a bad movie and juvenile.

Well, shit, the danger had already come and shot him in the shoulder. If this was his guardian angel or somesuch shit, her timing stunk. He was clinging to life, he thought, though it could just be a flesh wound. The man who had not felt the slings and arrows of pain and suffering since tenth grade, wouldn't know the difference. He should sleep and see how the world fared once he'd chased these demons from his mind.

The sound of open waves greeted him as he slipped beneath the conscious world. The scent of salt air, the breaching whale off the port bow combined with the sounds of an old Irish sea shanty—he thought it might be *'Leave Her Johny Leave Her'*, as reimagined by a 1920's jazz band—yanked him back out to a sea he had never seen, never experienced yet called to him and pulled him to her. Lively, spirited, flights of fancy about coming home riding a lilting, light melody became the soundtrack of his dream.

The Sea Teaches What You Are Willing to Learn

Late 1852

Thomas cried his joy to the clouds scudding across the sky, laughing and rejoicing at the sight. His exhilaration at catching sight of the breaching giant sent chills up and down his body like an electrical shock. He was not a whaler; this was not a whaling ship and Thomas was thankful. It was one thing to go against a ship filled with bloodthirsty pirates or British navy regulars who thought you were, but this enormous creature put fear and awe to the very core of his soul. He could not imagine wanting to do battle or, god forbid, killing such a glorious animal. It was beautiful, magnificent, powerful in its presence. He would miss the glory and majesty of the wide-open sea, but it was time.

He had acquired a young woman who was his responsibility. The crew would land on their feet, he was gifting them the ship fully provisioned with the profits from the Caribbean cargo. They should be happy for the chance to secure their own future, if only they didn't drink it away.

He hadn't noticed Roisin—the name he had bequeathed the girl, apparently never having been christened, Roisin Dubh, the Black Rose—as she stood watching him from the bow. He thought the name was fitting and she had to have a name. It boggled his mind that no one had ever given this woman a name. Yes, she was an orphan, maybe orphaned before her mother could find her name, but certainly over the ensuing years someone would have noticed she was nameless. But, then again, here in the Caribbean where these people were nothing more than chattel, bought and sold, used then thrown away, why did you need a name?

He had seen the first year of the potato famine and knew that families unraveled, blew apart due to starvation, poverty, and violence. Hunger killed more people than war, more than piracy, more than sin and yet no one ever focused on solving the crisis of deprivation. There was glory in dying of war, of the battle for the high seas and treasure, but what was there to a death by dereliction. Shame, that was the epitaph. Never mind the fault was not yours. It mattered not that the state allowed your death in the hope someone stronger would take your place. You were peasants and peasants could be bought by the barrel load. Shipped in and out, as need be. They were there for the privileged, livestock, one died to be replaced by another. Yet, what peasants lived was still several steps up from what slaves lived.

The meek may inherit the earth someday, but only after the rich had plundered and stripped it of anything worth a farthing. The promise of the bible would never come for the poor, the starved and neglected. The dumb bastards died. It was like a sick joke. The church supported the moneyed class, who in turn supported the church and they all told the same lie; you'll get your reward in heaven. And if that turned out to not be true who would know? The dead told no tales.

Thomas shook his head to dispel the wicked thoughts that had begun to take root and blossom. He caught a glimpse of her from the corner of his eye and Roisin smiled at him, as if reading his thoughts and pleased he stepped away from the darkness of them. He swore there was something otherworldly about the girl. Not too long in the past they would have drowned her or burned her at the stake—hell, weeks ago—but he found her enticing, though forbidden.

She broke the momentary eye contact, turning her attention to the whale breaching once again. She stared at the mighty beast as if beckoning it to where she stood at the prow of the ship. The behemoth made one more leaping, dancing motion with two calves following in her wake before turning and swimming directly towards the ship.

Thomas stood frozen at the sight of this monster from the deep barreling towards his ship on a direct course to ram it and take it to the bottom of the ocean. He swore Roisin smiled, her eyes locked with the great beast, pleading with the magnificent creature to come to her. At long last Thomas found his voice and called to his crew to brace for impact. Each man quickly grabbed rope to tie themselves off or wove themselves into the rigging hoping to stay with the greater portion of wreckage.

Thomas watched in horror was the three whales slid through the waves sleek and silent as death toward his vessel.

They were going to die, and with only a few weeks away from docking at the town of New York. To be so close only to have it taken away was more than his rage could bear. He hollered to the helmsman to come about to the port side hard. He ran to the bow. Bracing himself he grabbed Roisin around the waist to assure she would not be tossed overboard by the sudden change in direction. He buttressed himself between the points of the bow.

The ship plowed head on toward the three whales. Ten meters out they veered off, one to port, one to starboard and one diving deep. A plume of sea mist geysered from the blowhole of the giant to the starboard showering the deck with stank water. Relief flooded the Mother, but relief would not sink her, only raise her crew her in jubilation.

The crew cheered their captain and his quick thinking, assuming with little or no actual facts, that he had avoided the collision by coming about and heading directly into the threat. Thomas thanked providence, for he and Roisin were the only ones in position to witness as the three whales clearly choose to veer off rather than sink the ship. He didn't know if it was God, fate, or the brown woman standing next to him and he didn't care. They would bring the ship about heading to the NNW and the New world.

His thought had been to bring her into the port of New York where they could offload their cargo, find a buyer, and go their own ways. He looked down on the small woman at his side and it hit him, he had not thought of her as a woman, only as a girl until this moment. There was something different in her, she had aged, not a few years, more like she had matured until complete, as if she had lived a lifetime in the last few hours. She didn't appear old, just whole and filled with life.

She smiled before turning and quickly walking down the length of the ship to follow where the whales had continued swimming after avoiding the ship. Had she influenced? No, she was just an island girl, unlearned, unschooled, brought up in the jungle, apparently alone, but a survivor. That was the undeniable fact that niggled at the back of his head. How does a child, and by all accounts a very small child, barely out of the arms of her mother, survive alone in a jungle? Even one born to a people of the jungle would surely perish within days; yet she had not. She had grown into puberty from what the harbor master said and had wandered into the town full grown, though without the ability to speak in anything other than garbled sounds and gestures. How?

She turned back to him and smiled a big toothy grin as if she could read what he'd been thinking, showing her pride at accomplishing something he thought impossible. She closed the distance between them, hugged him close, like a child to her parent, her protector, before bowing her head slightly and heading to the cabin they shared.

Damn! Had she? No, she couldn't have somehow asked the whales to avoid them. She was not a witch, nor did she have some kind of voodoo, supernatural powers. No one did, except the Lord. And she was not the Lord! He thought he had seen every possible coincidence in his travels but the world was grand and held many secrets, this interaction with the monsters of the deep was just another example of how the Lord works in mysterious ways. Then, again, maybe he was tired and the glare of the sun off the waves made it appear they had avoided ramming the ship at the last moment; that they had never been on course for the ship in the first place.

He turned to go to their cabin and, as he did, he caught the former harbor master of the island leaning against the starboard rail grinning at him. He had seen. Or thought he had seen what he wanted. He had warned Thomas about the witchy woman, Thomas had chosen not to listen, the man's eyes seemed to say, now he would suffer the consequences.

As stupid as it would make him sound, he had to ask. He made his way to the cabin where Roisin waited. She waited because she had come to know the tall, handsome barbaric captain and she knew his mind. He was a seeker; he could leave no stone unturned when he wanted to know something. He would come to satiate his curiosity. Yes, he would most certainly come.

Thomas called to the helmsman that he had the ship while Thomas went below. "Keep her on course for freedom," he waved as he slid down the rails of the ladder.

This wouldn't take long, he would ask her if she had enticed the whales to change course, she would deny, as any reasonable human would, and Thomas could get back to dreaming of the New World. He almost ran into her as he entered the cabin. She stood, patient as the sea, apparently waiting for him. Well, this should only take seconds.

"Roisin," he began, though his thoughts jumbled gazing into her innocent stare. How could he possibly think this sweet, guileless child could have forced the monstrous beasts to alter their course. It was ridiculous and absurd.

"Yes," she said into the ensuing silence.

"Nothing." He shook himself from his temporary stupor and made to leave.

"The answer you are seeking," she said softly and without any evasiveness, "is yes."

"How do you know what I came to ask?" Now he was getting spooked. What if she could read minds? Could she know exactly what he was thinking while he stood there silent?

"What you were thinking was plain as the light of the full moon. I can read your thoughts in your face," she said as if that weren't an earthshaking proclamation.

"You can read my mind?" He asked pointing to his head.

"No, I read your face. It is very, um, very..." she stumbled searching for a word in his language so he would understand what she wanted to say. With her hands she gestured to her own face and moved it in expressive ways.

"Expressive?" He took a shot, trying to read her miming.

"Yes. I think that is right. I read your face and it tells me what is happening in the head," she grinned as if that explained everything. And maybe it did.

Thomas realized she wasn't using some supernatural, demonic power to know what he thought, she was just observing his expressions and interpreting them. He relaxed now more convinced he had come here on a fool's errand. He turned to go back on deck.

"You no want to know if Roisin ask whales to not sink boat?" She seemed surprised at the change in direction he made.

"I realized how silly it was to even suspect, to think..." he blushed with his embarrassment.

"I ask them. They thought it silly I would think they would sink boat with me on it. They love me, as I do them, they would not harm me or those I am with." She spoke as if this were the most natural thing anyone had ever discussed. Of course, she asked them not to ram the ship, and they had agreed without a second thought.

Thomas sat on the only chair still remaining in the captain's quarters. He sat silent making every attempt to get his thoughts, his mind, his reality around what the girl was actually saying. He couldn't.

"You are saying that you somehow silently asked those monsters of the sea, beautiful though they may be, they are mammoth in size, to not sink the ship and they just did as you told them to?" It was as succinct as he could say without sounding even more daft than he felt. He had seen many wonders throughout the world, had witnessed miracles of nature only God could have created and saw magic practiced by wizards who turned out to be charlatans who only wished your last copper. But she was asking him to believe something impossible, she could talk to animals and they would do her bidding.

"I tell them not, I ask them to be kind and they say yes," she said it again as if this was the most natural thing in the world. She spoke the words bewildered that he would find this unusual.

"Have you always been able to tell the natural world what to do and they obey?" He knew he was saying something different than what she meant but it was easier to understand if he believed she could order them to do her bidding, like a trained dog might, than to believe she merely asks and they, out of the kindness of their savage hearts, accede to her wishes.

"They do not obey, as you think of it. They do so out of the kindness of nature." She spoke to his blank expression and knew she had to try and explain better. "When I was alone in the jungle of my island—those who birth me threw me into the wild because they think I was bad medicine. I guess, even as baby, they could see I was not like them, not like anyone in village. I think they hope I become more like the people as I grow, but I didn't. I never talk, not like them.

I am happy alone and without people. I talk to the jungle and call out in my small voice to the animals who live there. I knew, in my heart, they would take me and I was not something to fear. And, one day my parents go into the jungle with me and leave without me. I was found by a small tribe of monkeys. They make me one of their own until I became too big. They find I not fit in with them either. A few pull me out of the bush and with the help of sloths lead me to where my people should be.

"But they were not my people, they were new white mans, like you, but cruel. If they sense any weakness they will come in for kill, not for survival like animals do, just out of cruelty. Some came and held me down, while others did horrible things to me. I could not shout. I had no words to describe the horror as animals would never do that to each other and I do not believe my people would either. They laughed and poured their evil drink in me then left me in my jungle to die. I did not. I lived. My jungle came for me and healed me. I could not tell them what happened. I did not have any way to tell them that they would understand. But they knew I had been bad hurted. And they could see in my head who had done this." She broke down weeping at the memory. She valiantly tried to settle her pain and speak but there were no words.

"What happened to the men who did this to you?" He knew what the Inn proprietor had told him but he wanted the truth from her.

"They die. Some by accident, it is said, some beaten to death by unknown others. Maybe my jungle take them. Maybe my jungle had had enough of these evil men, who took from her, her children, kill her babies and her trees. They had come from far away to harm her and kill all life. For what? Their shiny pieces of metal?" She spit on the deck. "I do not morn for those who were taken, I morn for my home that they tore by the roots from the mother." Silence wrapped the cabin.

Thomas could think of nothing to say, no words of comfort, nothing to take the pain away from her. He stood and hugged her close. He wanted to weep for her, to go back and tear apart everything sick and demented about that island hole, but he was years too late. All he could do now was comfort and protect her to the best of his ability.

The thought came slowly yet rose to the surface like that breaking whale. "Did the harbor master know of all this as it happened?" Now he wanted the full picture. When the man had told him of her past, Thomas had the sense he was keeping something from him. He wanted to know what, and long before they made dock.

"He knew. They his friends. When they start to die, he say I do this thing. I laugh at him. How can a little girl kill big, strong men? What power do I have? This is when he calls me witch. I do not know what this means but all others do and they rip off my clothes and prepare to burn me, I think. Big fire, angry people, frightened people who don't understand the ways." She shivered at the memory. "This is when my jungle come alive and the big water too!" Her voice rose in pitch and timbre. "One of the big fishes, the whales you call, come into where boats come to stay and water spring to life out of her head, then another, and another until the big fire is dead. Now my jungle friends make big noise, screeching, howling, making bush move with their motion. The people they become very afraid now, they throw my clothes at me and tell me to leave, go back to my jungle. But I shake my head. I stare each in their sad little white eyes, I point to Mother, this my ground and I will stay. If any harm come to me, I will destroy everything. I make myself known and what I will do. Fear rules their lives, this I have seen, and they now fear me. They leave me food and water to leave them alone. It is lonely but I know the pain of lonely and while it hurts, you get used to it." She sighed and his heart broke.

How could people be so cruel? A child, and because she was different than them, they would have nothing to do with her. Superstitious fools, afraid of their own shadows. This is what religion has brought. He knew it in his bones. Well, his religion, the religion of Thomas was not such. He would protect her with his life. She would know love. Something she had apparently never known.

Though his heart was pure in this thought and plan he didn't realize the large barrel of unknowns he was about to open. In his mind she had never known love. Not from her parents, not from the village, not from the whites. He hadn't considered the love she had felt from the creatures of the jungle, those who had instinctively taken her in and raised her as their own. He hadn't considered the love she felt for the jungle itself, as if it were a nurturing mother that protected her and cared for her. The comfort and safety she felt in the arms of those entities, the animals, the plants, trees, insects, and reptiles that held her. How she felt that same safety with him.

What he completely failed to consider was she had never known love from her own. She had never been in love, had someone love her as lover, or cared for her as a close friend, a confidant and that she had no way of knowing there might be a difference.

Sometimes It's the Drugs That Clarify the Mind

Present Day

Tom was groggy as he came out of the drug induced stupor. The nurse entered his room with a smile and a syringe. Her rubber soled shoes squeaking their way to the side of his bed. He wanted to tell her not to inject what was in that syringe into his intravenous tube but his mouth wouldn't form the words. His mouth was disconnected from his brain and no messages were coming through. He flopped his left arm over to where he thought his right arm might be. An excellent idea though his aim was woefully off.

It did distract her attention from the errand at hand to his action. She stopped. His eyes moved slowly back and forth in an effort to convey a 'no, please'. She got it immediately. One cannot be a nurse or care giver without empathy and a sixth sense of what needed doing and what needed left alone.

"Had enough time off?" She chided lightly. "Let's give it a few and see how you feel when I get back." She smiled warmth and understanding as she patted him gently on the shoulder.

Tom felt his entire body relax, he would sleep but he startled back awake. He didn't want to sleep right now. He fought the effects of the drugs with every bit of willpower in his possession before he realized it wasn't the drugs that brought the relaxation, it was the lack of same. He was at peace with his decision to forego more narcotics. His mind demanded functionality and would not be denied. Yet the stress of the past week, or several days or a month—he realized he had no concept of how long he'd been here. And where, exactly was here?—was pulling him under, just like the ship he was on earlier.

What ship? He'd never been on a ship in his life. It was the dream. He'd been on a ship in his dream. So real, he could feel the pressure of the water pulling him down, his lungs burned with the demand for oxygen. He remembered it as if it were real, not a nightmare from weeks ago. He fought with every bit of strength he had to remain conscious, but the pull was too strong and he succumbed.

The dream came immediately. A young woman, a brown so deep as to be almost black, and a white man in the throes of passion. Not in the present day but in a century past, when it was forbidden. Whites and blacks did not couple back then except as master and slave. The wrongness of this filled his soul, he tried to wake himself but he was too deep into the dream.

And yet this didn't feel wrong. The girl wasn't being forced, he wasn't taking her against her will, she had given herself freely to him. She was the one who had initiated the love making. The feeling of wrong faded from his heart replaced by love? Right? Something deeper? He couldn't tell, he only knew he required sleep, bizarre dreams or no and so settled into sleep.

Though peacefully sleeping Tom couldn't help but wonder as he wandered through his dreamscape why for the first time in his memory he was dreaming in such clear detail, crisp and sharp, like real life. Intellectually he knew he was dreaming and though submersed within those dreams, he still knew it wasn't real. And yet, it was. It was as real as his everyday life. The puzzling thing was not that he never dreamt, it was that the subjects and context of those dreams tended to be more mundane. He dreamt of coding, the equations and concepts that wouldn't fit together. The problems that occupied his mind during the day would force their way into his subconscious seeking answers to riddles he couldn't grasp consciously. Those were productive dreams, problem solving on a basic level. He'd never had need of escapism, it held nothing for him. Apparently, that had changed.

When had that occurred? His mind wandered a barren desert devoid of information. This was beyond his capacity as a logical, well-reasoned, balanced individual. Something had triggered these wanton treks into the fantastical. When had they begun? That is where you should seek answers.

With the woman at the Zoom meeting! She had been a distraction to concentration and purpose. Her very presence promised something he knew to be outside the pale and, yet, he couldn't help but desire the most desirable woman he had ever beheld. Was that it? His well-ordered life had been turned inside out because of a woman who, apparently, so far, didn't exist. The others involved in the meeting paid her no attention. When she spoke, they did not respond. Only he seemed aware of the stunning creature in the corner of his monitor. Her appearance was followed quickly by his desire to go to a beach, any beach as if that was where he would find his roots.

His people, obviously, had been brought to this country from across the great Atlantic hundreds of years ago. So, shouldn't it be natural he would wish to go to the sea to find the answers to where he had come from. No. Thousands of African men and women had been forced into the bellies of the slave ships and brought to America where there was an overwhelming hunger for human chattel. To try and narrow down which ship from which coast carried which of his ancestors to their nightmare, especially when records of the slave trade were scant at best, was an impossible task.

The Dream Road beckoned and he dutifully followed. Now, it became his own personal Christmas Carole without the Christmas. He found himself as a very young man being taunted and punched by one of the big kids at school. There was nothing racial about the abuse, the school had been integrated years before and though there remained a certain degree of animosity it was not something most of the students were aware. Mostly that purview belonged to parents and grandparents. Kids didn't notice color unless they were programmed that way by ignorance and hate. This was not that.

He was being abused simply for the sin of having an outstanding mind. It wasn't anything he bragged about or taunted other students with, just what was true. He was smarter than any of his peers, hell, he was brighter than most of his teachers, if the truth be known, though, again, he never flaunted it. The problem is you can only dumb yourself down so much. At some level, the brain refuses to cooperate and commands the body to respond accordingly. His had during class where he answered 87.5% of the teacher's questions leaving the other 12.5% to his classmates. It wasn't that he desired to show off, he just couldn't abide the pace of class with each student being asked questions to which that child had not a clue of the answer. Boredom was the motivator; beatings were the reward.

He took it in stride. He was a chunky kid and the blows could not inflict a deep enough pain that he cared. Oh, the psychological bruising would last for an extended period but it too would scab over and heal.

He jumped ahead to his passing of the driver's test. The written test had been simplicity itself, the driving and maneuverability sections proved slightly more problematic. It wasn't that he didn't know how or couldn't pass the mechanics of it with flying colors on a closed course. It was submersing oneself in the vast steaming pot of humanity that behind the wheel boiled several levels of terror. After three tries he passed and was awarded a license to drive. It would be one of the last times he would get behind the wheel.

The first level of terror was taking into account every other driver on the road that raged at his driving style, slow and steady wins the race. The second level of terror was the 'talk'. This was when all the kids whose skin was shaded slightly darker than white got sat down by the parental units and told about the popo; the police. 'If you are ever stopped,' said as if there was a possibility that it wouldn't happen, the guarantee was implied, 'sit up, turn the dome light on in the car, and stay perfectly still until instructed otherwise!'

"But what if I haven't done anything wrong?" was his naïve reply.

The admonition was repeated in a much more stern tone to reinforce they would greatly appreciate him coming home to their loving embrace. They did not wish to make a journey to the morgue to identify someone who could not follow directions. He decided there was no need for a car of his own or for them to forgo an evening out so he could have the custody of the family vehicle. He would walk or take the bus or stay in and read. They would have no worries about bringing him into adulthood as opposed to burying him in the local cemetery.

The dream road brought him forth to his life in the current epoch. Corporate life had provided him with the much-needed medical coverage and comfortable retirement, the safety net. He had lived a contended existence, if not filled with great joy, neither was it cursed with great hardship. All he had to do was keep his head down, don't rock the boat, and pray no one noticed him. He'd left one day in a fit of independence and recognition that life was not eternal and happiness was not a corporate benefit.

He found he could make a very good living working at home, only interacting with the rest of the species as need and financial reward dictated. Zoom calls now sufficed where in the not-too-distant past physical presence would have been a requirement. Technology had been a great improvement in his quality of life.

There had been, once again, no overt racism in the corporate world, if you did your job well, they saw past any other mitigating attributes and a certain level of freedom was accorded. Though he found once he walked away from corporate life and into private design there was a different kind of freedom and it was refreshing and far more satisfying. But, then again, that probably had more to do with corporate culture. He knew of people, associates, who had remained in the corporate world, black, white, brown, yellow, men and women, gay and straight, who had suffered under the yoke of dysfunction that is woven into the structure of mainstream America. They had never been exposed to nor had the chance to taste the joy of their occupation. They had been threatened, cajoled, and beaten into submission by loss of the benefits of corporate life by those who feared losing their own tiny slice of power.

Just like the cop. Fear ruled in modern day America and it asserted its power over all it subjugated. People were cowed into believing they required a certain kind of employment or they had failed at life. They would fail their spouses, their kids, their parents. Without the buttress of the mega Corp, you could not survive. Tom smiled in his dream state, that was an assumption he had proven wrong. He had dared to live outside that belief, he had charted his own course, lived his own life, that was until some cop carrying the fear, hate, guilt of his forefathers took umbrage at extremely good Sashimi and a Dragon Roll.

Still, he was alive, he should be grateful, that's what his mother would have wanted him to feel. And yet, he couldn't quite bring himself to that hallowed point. As a matter of fact, he felt something akin to anger, not gratitude. Now that he seemed to be shaking off the chains, the bonds of narcotic pain relief, he found a new emotion had been born; anger, wrath, the indignation he'd never had just cause to feel previously.

He knew intellectually that his 'people', the multi-hued spectrum of humanity, had suffered at the hands and will of the pure. He had been saved by his usefulness either in assisting those physically superior in his youth to succeed academically or creating programs and coding for the giant corporations in adulthood. His worth had buffered him from the worst of ingrained bias. Not anymore!

He wanted retribution! Though he knew he didn't have that fight within him, not yet. First he would have to make the connection with the savage warriors he instinctively knew to be his forebearers. The necessity to dig into his past, as far in time as possible, to find his true self was now not just a curiosity but a driving, raging force within him. Once he knew of his proud beginnings, of his tribe and where they ruled back on the Dark Continent, he would find a way to connect, to plumb the depths of their courage and strength and become what they had been.

No longer when he saw his reflection would he see the white that had been forced into him by the enslavers and rapists of the past. He had seen, truly seen, the difference between the black man in America and the black man in his purist form from the Motherland. He couldn't strip the Caucasian DNA from his genetics but he could purge it from his soul.

He would have his day in court. He would hold the system responsible for disrupting his life at this crucial point. He was supposed to be consummating the greatest deal of his life, instead here he lay, recovering from stupidity. Righteous indignation filled his soul just as the squeak of rubber soles on linoleum announced the entrance of his very punctual nurse.

Not All Dangers Wait Below the Waves

Late 1852

The ship bobbed on the calm sea; no wind filled her sails. They barely moved under the hot, intense sun. They had been becalmed for two days now. It was frustrating on a dozen different levels, none of which could be alleviated without wind. It was the sailor's lot to find oneself stranded in the midst of thousands of miles of ocean and, though there were always some kind of currents, find yourself sitting, waiting, hoping for the gods to provide either wind or proper current. The gods were not always in the mood.

Thomas was fluctuating between demanding the crew find something, anything, to do rather than lollygag about the deck and understanding they had already done every chore conceivable to alleviate their own boredom. To add to his frustration was the knowledge of how close they were to their ultimate goal. The New World was just over the horizon to the west. He swore if he reached his hand out, he could touch it, yet it tantalized from a distance.

Roisin had taken to their shared cabin not wishing to be where the crew could allow their unoccupied minds to entertain lascivious methods to entertain themselves while bobbing into nowhere or to blame the 'witch' for the lack of wind. What little breeze there was forced its way through the repaired aft windows. She had been born and bred of Caribbean jungle, she knew heat and how best to keep it at bay.

She thought if she asked in a respectful way that the wind would come, yet she didn't want this voyage to end, not now, not too soon. She smiled as she looked at the future and, though it would not bring the life she most desired, it would bring more pleasure than she could've dreamt in her jungle. The sun would set soon, that would bring him and that made her rejoice.

He was a good man for all his faults. He was gruff, demanding in his way, but always respectful of her. It was not something she had been accustomed to. He would protect her from the wants and desires of his crew or any who might entertain thoughts. And she knew as long as she was under his protection, they would stay clear, though she cared not one bit for the way the former harbor master leered at her when they would chance to meet on the deck. He frightened her. She knew him to be cruel, though not personally, no, he would have his men visit what horrors he devised. She knew he didn't like the idea of her on this ship. She knew he blamed her for the deaths of those who had viciously attacked her. It had not been her; it had been those who loved her, those of the jungle, they had visited jungle law upon the evil. Now she would catch him in deep conversation with crew members, whispering his venom in their welcoming ears.

Thomas would hold her when they slept, keeping her fears and the visions away from her sleep. She would reward him and he would, in turn, reward her with a future for her people.

Boredom, the lack of purpose, the paucity of burning off any energy made Thomas realize he would probably not sleep tonight. One had to have reason to sleep, have exerted a modicum of labor, toil, to warrant sleep. He had done nothing but seek wind where none existed. Thomas was not a man disposed to inaction. He knew from his time at sea there were always times when the sea forced you to be still, to take time to consider life and your place in it, but she would reward you with a ride such as they'd had coming around the horn of Patagonia. For all the terror that little jaunt had brought it was preferable to sitting, becalmed, for days.

He watched as the sun slowly slid beneath the waves and dusk fell across the vast ocean. He would go study the charts for the umpteenth time, wishing his ship closer to shore. Wishing never made the wind rise or a ship move, just increased the level of frustration. He should go below, pretend to read, or chart their course until forced to make an attempt at sleep. Roisin would be there. Her presence comforted him though her future brought fear.

He had heard how the whites in the new world treated the blacks. He tried to convince himself it couldn't be as bad as he'd heard sailors describe in harbor dives across the globe. No one could think so little of another human being to treat it so. Though the men he'd met, those who told the tales, swore whites in America didn't consider blacks to be human. They were chattel to be whipped, driven, fed just enough to keep them alive, and worked until the feeding became unnecessary. Thomas swore he would never let such a fate befall Roisin.

She sat on the hard wood deck of their shared berth, eschewing the lone chair in the cabin, staring out the back windows of the Captain's quarters as if attempting to use her will to bring the wind. Looks could be deceiving. She didn't turn at his entrance, she didn't have to, she knew exactly what he looked like, tired, worried, wishing only to be moving and it would only sadden her to see him like that.

"Are you hungry?" Her voice soft like a lover's touch, "should I see what cook might put together for you?"

"I hunger, but cook will have nothing in his larder to satiate my craving." He slumped down in the lone piece of furniture remaining after the washing out of debris months ago, including the former captain. "I can taste it in the air. Even without any wind to bring me the news I know she lays just to the west of us, though I would prefer to find dockage further to the north. I do not like the tales and horror I hear of the south. Some think they would try to take you from me and I will die first." His irritation born of inaction and the possibility that some of these barbarians would attempt to take someone who belonged, no, not belonged, meant something to him rose his ire to the point of violence.

She got up from her seated position without using aid. She was so natural in everything she did, she seemed to fit wherever she was. She didn't stumble or stagger with the motion of the sea, it was as if she were born to it. She stepped behind him and lay her hands on his shoulders. His muscles were tight as the rigging in a heavy blow. She began to work the knots out of his shoulders. Her hands felt warm, almost hot, through his thin shirt. He could feel his body relax; his mind soothed by her ministrations. Soon he felt his eyelids become heavy, too heavy to hold up. He wanted nothing more than to sleep, but the bunk was over there and he didn't think he had the energy to walk that far. His eyes closed and he slipped into dream.

She lay next to him in a large feather bed. Both of them in the natural state as God had intended. She stroked his arms and chest before softly, passionately kissing his lips. His mind screamed! He had to stop this before it went too far! Hell it had already gone too far. She was just a child. Well, maybe not a child but a young woman, too young for him to take her like this. He chastised himself for thinking, dreaming such debauchery.

She kissed his chest murmuring this was what she craved. He was doing nothing wrong. He was not forcing her into a coupling, she was coaxing him. Still, he fought the carnal urge, the overwhelming desire. She climbed on top of him to reassure him this was her doing. He struggled against this slip of a woman but her strength, her need, was greater than he. He felt himself slip into her and she rocked.

She rocked with the rhythm of the waves, moaning her pleasure, her breath coming hard and fast, he could feel the explosion building in his loins. His arms enveloped her and he pulled her to him. Her small, firm breasts resting on his chest were all that was required to ignite and he gushed into her. Spent they lay there in his dream murmuring, whispering, cuddling until he fell into a deep dream sleep.

Somewhere in the back of his mind his conscience awoke and shame threatened to overcome any feeling of satisfaction or joy he'd felt. He knew he shouldn't have done this! It was just a dream, his mind reassured. If he could hide his desires in dreams, it would alleviate the possibility of it ever happening in the waking world. From far away, somewhere down around the equator a breeze was born and would soon go in search of a ship.

Thomas felt rested and at peace as the sun climbed back to her position high above them. He knew he shouldn't after a dream such as that, yet it seemed far away, not real at all, after all, it had only been a dream. After all, didn't they both remain clothed without any indication anything untoward had taken place? The day passed as all had since the wind had deserted them, hot sun, little to occupy the body or mind, and waiting. Roisin seemed no different. She acted towards him as she always had. And why shouldn't she? Because he had a tawdry dream? If he didn't let on, she would never know and he had no intention of allowing that tidbit of information to ever leave his tortured soul.

If he thought the dream had been torrid the night before, the dream lovemaking the second night would have shamed a harbor whore. Yet there was that feeling of right about it, a feeling he wished would not have been present. It was one thing to have these nocturnal forays into sexual fantasy but the proper response would have been shame and guilt, there was neither present when he awoke.

She smiled that innocent, sweet smile. Dear God in Heaven, how was he to live with himself, taking care of her during the day yet ravaging her in his dreams at night. He had to separate himself from her before he acted on these despicable thoughts.

He would allow her the cabin and he would sleep under the stars on deck. When he was a stowaway being tolerated by day there was nowhere else to sleep on the ship each night but in a hammock on deck. Most nights it was wonderful. The gentle swaying of the ship, the night air, warm and comforting, he missed the freedom of being a small halyard on a large ship. The only time he was noticed is when he messed up. All he had to do was perform his duties and chores properly and no one of any station took note of his presence. Yes, the hammock was just the salve to soothe his perverted soul.

The gentle rock of the ship quieted his nerves, the creak and groan of weathered wood on weathered wood and halyards at rest was comforting in its familiarity. He stared up at a million stars filling the night sky. Thomas thought that this was his favorite time at sea. Night, becalmed, hundreds of nautical miles from mankind, with nothing but the sea and God to guide him. He thought they would bring a clarity of thought, of soul. His mind could rest, the nightmare/dream would fear to tread in such a pure, unspoiled atmosphere. He slept.

The dream came slow as if inviting him to dance one more time. It was soft, seductive, playful. She came to him in innocence, cuddling in his arms just as she did when they slept. He could feel her breath caress his chest. It was sweet with the fragrance of the jungle, wild, enticing, beckoning him to taste the perfect unsullied fruit. Tempting him with promises of love, fulfillment, ecstasy. He shook his head, though whether just in dream or while he rocked in the hammock he couldn't know, only that this could not be consummated again.

He heard a moan, somewhere in the distance, as if from across the calm sea. It was her moan from the bunk in their shared cabin. Nothing could happen, he knew in his heart, physically while they were separated. Still, he tried to find a way to wake from where he knew the dream was pulling him.

He knew in his heart where this could only progress and though he knew it to be dream, not reality, he wanted nothing to do with spoiling her again.

It mattered not how or where in reality it happened, he would remain just as guilty as if he held her down and forced her. Something that was anathema to him. Not that he was adverse when island girls would willingly lay with him, but he would never rape another. And he felt it mattered not that she gave herself willingly in these erotic dreams. It was that she was young, naïve in the ways of man. Though she had seen some of the worst of mankind, she still remained untouched by the brutality they had unleashed. To her in his dream state she might be giving herself to him out of love or gratitude, he could not accept such a gift from someone he thought of as a younger sister under his protection.

He found he could not resist her need. And that was exactly what he felt, she had a need for him to enter her, to make love to her, to complete her. He didn't know why and wished he could run away, but she grasped his manhood and held him in place. Her grip was strong and he was not about to fight her with it in her grasp. Better to allow the dream to continue to completion. The problem was she seemed unable to be satisfied. So, over and over, they completed the act until he was worn and could not continue. She cuddled in his arm and they slept. And once again he was filled with a sense of wonder, completion, rightness, and a surprising lack of guilt.

He woke in the morning quite alone as the sun winked at him over the eastern horizon. He stretched and smiled at the day. Any remorse he might have felt now washed away by reality. And there was a nice breeze coming out of the South-southwest which he could tack along toward the city of New York.

Roisin came out on deck for the first time in three days. She glowed in the morning light nodding good morning to each sailor as she passed them on her way to the forecastle where Thomas stood with spyglass to eye searching the horizon for what; only he knew. She could see very far without the use of such by asking any bird flying overhead what they saw and they would show her, though she kept that information to herself. This crew was already leery of her and superstitious about her being on board, though she had caused no disruption. She'd heard a few accusing her of being the reason for them being stranded in the calm. It had made her laugh under her breath. Why would she wish them to be stuck in the middle of the ocean? What could that possibly accomplish? They would not know of the dreams! Though, superstitions are not usually the property of the intelligent.

She found her own unease increasing as she thought about what life would be like in the white man's city. She had known her share of white people, but they had come to her jungle and had been forced to adapt to her island as it would not allow them to conquer. Now it would be her who would have to adapt to a foreign culture. She barely spoke the language, though Thomas had been pleased with her progress she knew she still made many mistakes while trying to express herself and ideas. This would be worse.

Then there was the matter of slavery. She had been lucky to be born in and of the jungle. No one had ever had the skill to catch her in the wild. When she had been drawn into the village on her island by what she knew would be her future arriving, she had frightened enough of the local whites to keep them from trying to force her into slavery, not everyone on the island had been so fortunate. She had no idea how far slavery had spread throughout this new world. Would she be taken from Thomas and sold into some horror? He would die to keep that from happening; she knew that he would fight a hundred to protect her, but he would lose and she would lose him and hope.

On the third morning after the hammock had proven insufficient to rock away the carnalval of his dreams, with a light fog and mist on the sea came the vision of New York City, it was disappointing. They had heard stories of this place as the center of banking and commerce for the New World instead they were greeted by buildings that had the feeling of temporary, almost ephemeral, slipshod, and filthy, something to hold a place until a real city could be constructed. Thomas thought it would outshine his home of Dublin yet it paled by comparison. It was a babe compared to the grown, ancient parent back home. It gave off the appearance of a country town only larger, but just so. He expected to be greeted by the sight of farms and pens filled with cows and pigs when they disembarked. If he was seeking grandeur, great beauty, to be inspired by this new land of opportunity, equality, intellectual freedom, and joy he was sorely mistaken.

The city sat like a forgotten idea on the banks of the Hudson. It was now a place where you swept those idealistic concepts under the rug and pretended no one would notice. It was poor by European standards. He was not greeted by great works of art, sculptures, buildings that celebrated mans' need to express his own magnificence before God. No, this was a harbor pub that catered to the basest impulses of any sailor trying to drown his loneliness before setting sail one more time, hoping for a romp with a cheap floozie and praying he didn't get syphilis. Still a quarter mile out and with the wind tacking out of the west, the stench of man greeted the hopes of the naïve.

Thomas' first thought was to turn about and keep heading north until they could breathe but he had cargo to offload and sell. He'd promised his men once they got to this new, pristine—he laughed maniacally in his head—land, they would get what they could for their troubles and then he would leave. Maybe Canada had maintained some semblance of civilization, they were, after all, still under British rule.

The docks were busy with loading and offloading. Thomas' first course of action was to find the harbor master and see if he could find a buyer for the bananas, coconuts, and sundry Native made baubles and artwork he had brought with him along with Roisin. And no, she was not for sale!

The Harbor Master was not a hard man to find especially since he was headed towards the dock where Thomas was walking the gangplank with his first mate on his heels. There is something about city officials that makes them easy to find. Maybe it was that look in their eyes where you could see them counting how much they could skim off the top of any cargo coming in. Or maybe it was the swagger that seemed inbred in men endowed with a modicum of power. Cocky came with the feeling that one was superior to the next class of human down from them, whether that was true or not, someone had bequeathed this rodent with a tarnished scepter and a title. He reminded Thomas of the harbor master currently waiting impatiently aboard his ship, whose name he had never bothered to give and Thomas had never bothered to seek.

"What's yer cargo? How long ye plannin' on remaining in our great city? Do you already have a buyer or would ye like I should recommend?" Here, his eyes lit up with the reflection of gold and possibility of his own plunder.

"We carry fresh fruits and art from the Caribbean. Looking for a buyer, a fair man with silver, and a place to rest for a day or two. Someplace clean that don't much care about the condition of sailing men months at sea. Matter of fact, if ye know of a place that might have a tub with clean water to scrape a man clean that would suit us just fine." Thomas smiled as he had seen captains back home do, and the one he had adopted as they traversed the sea lanes, to relax the master. They would not be staying in this cesspool. The Master seemed pleased he could sheer these fresh sheep and send them on their way none the wiser.

"With whores or would ye prefer something monkish?" When he grinned, Thomas thought the man should just allow the last few teeth their freedom as they appeared like lonely vessels sailing a dark and barren sea.

"Up to each man how they wish to rest and relax." He shook his head at the implication that all sailors were the same. "I'll guarantee they have enough coin to assure they will eat, drink, and enjoy their stay in your fine city." He almost spit the last word as he took in the filth, stench, and lay abouts that defined the docks.

"And what would you be seeking Captain?"

"Peace, quiet, and a soft bed," Thomas spoke quietly as if contemplating the deeper meanings of the question.

"No one to share the bed?" This man had a mind that could only focus on the lascivious.

"Don't need one," came a familiar voice from behind him. Thomas turned to find the former harbor master of Roisin's island glaring at him with a wicked, disgusting grin.

"Got himself a darkie witch," his tone a challenge, daring Thomas to deny, "Picked her up on an island I was stranded on. Allowed me to come this far wit him but this seems to be the end of his decency. I've been asked to leave without so much as a copper in my pocket."

"I believe you have plenty to sustain you from robbing the ships that made port and the natives you forced into labor." Thomas' tone was far more menacing. He'd had enough of this lewd, disgusting excuse for a human being. He knew the man had skimmed a large percentage off the dockage and off the payment for labor, he could now leave of his own accord or Thomas would joyfully assist.

"You got colored aboard?" Now the New York harbor master scrutinized the young captain.

"I have a friend of mine, and she will stay on board unless I can guarantee her safety." Thomas' words were steel. He would not back down. Yes, he would like to allow her the freedom of moving about the city, seeing someplace foreign to her, expanding her knowledge of the white man and his civilization but not at the cost of her actual freedom. He had no idea what these men in New York thought of slavery, pro or con, and he was not about to risk her life on his ignorance.

The former master's laugh was dismissive yet depraved. Thomas wanted nothing more than to shove it back down into his bowels where it had originated. He kept his calm. Seminary school remained deeply embedded in his psyche, they had taught him control and peace, he gripped both in an iron fist. "Oh, you couldn't pry them two apart wit a crow iron. She a witch and got him in her power, is what she is. Shoulda drown the bitch while we was out t sea." Now the man's hate and fear for Roisin came through each syllable. There was more here than Roisin had told Thomas, he would question her once he was back aboard ship. For now, he just wanted to find a buyer and be gone from here.

"We got nothin' agin coloreds, not we think they be equal to a white man, but we don't much care for enslavin' none. You be Irish unless I lost my ear for me home," now the Master of New York harbor became a friend from home. "My people might not ha' been slaves, but we was treated poorly." The understatement was typical of those who had suffered. Never people to complain outside the home, they always would downplay their own pain while understanding and empathizing with others.

"Dublin," Thomas replied, "though a few years to the south of where I stand now. Preferred the sea to the cloth."

The Harbor Master nodded in understanding. "Liam," he offered his hand, "and as long as yer here in my harbor you are under my word. No one will trouble you nor anyone wit ye." They shook and Thomas relaxed ever so. "My folks kept after me to make the same devil's bargain with them priests but I got no need o' them nor their caterwaulin' about the rewards of dyin'. I prefer my rewards while livin' while I can still taste the rum and feel a full belly while lyin' with a purty girl." From the other 'master' that might have come off as rude or lascivious but with this man it was just good-natured jibing.

"Find me a buyer and I'll find you a cup of whatever you want and fill yer belly as well," Thomas took the man's hand once again, two boys from the Emerald Island now standing on a dock on another island thousands of miles away.

Liam gripped Thomas' hand with both of his and nodded, he would help his fellow countryman out. He then turned to glower at the man standing just behind Thomas. He didn't like contemptuous, lewd people. Oh, an off-color jibe about fucking was allowable but you didn't denigrate another man's woman, no matter her color, her looks, her former profession, or her temperament, you didn't have to live with the woman the fella did. And if he could put up with her failings and specialties t'was none of yer concern. The sooner this Dutch piece of dry rot took flight the sooner the air would clear.

"Whatever ye be needin' you let me or one of my crew know and it's yours. Also I'll tell ye where some of the quarters of our fine city to avoid if'n you and the lady wish to stretch the legs and grab something to eat that ain't been in a barrel for several months," he grinned as he steered Thomas away from the former harbor master of a tiny island.

Business completed and new life just waiting for him around the corner, Thomas whistled an old tune form his childhood as he made his way back to 'The Daughter of The Sea'. He knew Roisin would be pleased to find she could explore this new land—well, as long as she was by his side— and eat something with more substance than the gruel they had aboard the ship. Yes, it was going to be a fine day.

As they readied themselves for their foray into the new world both Thomas and Roisin felt light of heart and soul. Here was a place that would accept whatever their relationship was without judging or looking askance. They were not a couple, per se, just very good friends hoping to keep it that way. Dreams be damned, thought Thomas.

Cleaned up and dressed in the closet thing they had to finery, he in waistcoat and white bell bottoms, hair pulled back and woven in a tail, she in a hand-woven island dress, simple but elegant. He would show her the greatness of his people, their buildings, their culture, as much of that as he might find in this small city, and their food. He was excited about exposing her to the best of the white man's ways.

As they came on board to the good-natured hoots and whistles from the crew, they could not help but smile. Most of the crew had come to accept whatever the relationship their captain had with this pretty, yes, they had to admit the black woman was pretty, woman. They manned the rails to show their respect for captain and friend. He was good man, far superior to the man he had taken over from. They cheered their joy though the cheer was cut short.

The sound of angry protests and drunken revelry turned their heads in the direction of the dock. Thirty men came strutting down the dock making for the Daughter. Some were armed with batons, broken rods of steel, some were armed with knives and a few had swords. Thomas felt his temper rise to a dangerous level.

The riffraff came to a halt at the end of their gangplank.

"Want I should pull her up?" Thomas heard a sailor standing to his right whisper. He shook his head. He would meet this threat as he had all in his life.

"What is the meaning of this?" He demand of the rabble.

They took in his six-foot-six frame, the muscles bulging beneath the waistcoat like snakes fighting to be freed and took a step back. One filthy stench of a wasted life stepped forward emboldened by a belly full of rum.

"Word is ye got yerself a witch on board, and we don't much care for witches," and the men surrounding him cheered him on, "this is a godly city and we won't let no blasphemers, no children of Satan, step foot and despoil our fair town." And again, the drunken followers of god cheered and took sips to cleanse the soul.

"I'll give ye to the count of ten to clear the way or you'll be meeting yer maker quite sooner than ye thought this morning. For all who live by the sword shall perish by the sword, saith the lord Jesus." Thomas stood unmoving at the top of the gangplank and began to count.

"Don't let him frighten you, he's got nothing and the Lord ain't going to save him and his witch. You've got to defend your town or it will soon be run over by black devils and their worship of demons. They've come to take your souls, to take your women, and everything you've worked for. If you let one in, then they all come in. Don't you keep all yer blacks in the south where they know how to handle them savages?" It was the former master, the Dutchman, from St. Maartin. He grinned his revenge at Thomas.

Obviously, the man had kept himself busy over the last hour or so buying drinks and stoking anger. You could never go wrong filling the ignorant with booze and hate if you were looking for someone to work up the stupidity and violent tendencies necessary without dirtying your own hands. And he had found the bottom of the barrel.

"Would you care to put your accusations to the test?" Thomas took a deliberate step down the gangplank toward his intended target. The Dutchman took several steps back until he was once again in the center of the mob.

"If you think you can fight your way through to me." His words half-heartedly laughed and challenged, though his eyes betrayed him.

Thomas unbuttoned and removed his waistcoat. He handed it to Roisin who made to beg him to not do this but changed her mind at the anger in his eyes. There would be no turning back until one man was dead.

"There's only the one of him you got to get through to get to her," the vindictive harbor lackey screamed at the drunken horde. "He means nothing, it's the witch we needs find and drown along with her evil ways!"

Grumbling joined fear to a crescendo of ignorant hate. They knew nothing of Roisin and cared not. She was a black woman from far away and their nascent leader was a white man who spoke their language, though with a distinct accent. Still, he spoke to them in a way they understood. They may not know much but they knew an influx of foreigners was pushing them out of work, the masters of their profession had told them so. That was why their wages had been dropped so low a man could hardly buy a mug of rum. Never considering most immigrants landed in New York for a short stay before venturing out into the vast unknown of the wilderness to the west. It was time for some payback on their unfortunate circumstances. Besides the rum was running low. As one, with courage from a bottle and bolstered by numbers, they made their way to the end of the gangplank..

"First man that steps foot on that plank is dead," Thomas' tone was cold truth. He was not here to negotiate, he was here to protect his ship, his crew, and her. He might die, the possibilities were extremely high, but he would take his share with him. If a man wasn't willing to die to protect what he loved, he wasn't willing to live with himself.

A large dockworker with sword in hand charged up the gangplank, screaming his defiance and courage as he closed with Thomas. He swung widely, no surprise considering the level of alcohol in his blood, Thomas ducked under the blade, came up with a powerful fist to the chin and watched as the man fell into the bay. Still, there were more than enough to take him down if they could overcome their growing fear and indecision.

His crew lined up behind him, they had seen enough and their captain needed them, they would stand with him until the end. Grabbing boat hooks and belaying pins his men lined the rail, these drunken riffraff would not step foot on the deck of The Daughter. His crew were men that had fought off and been pirates. They had sailed and survived some of the most dangerous, life-threatening seas. Drunken rabble were nothing compared to the Drake Passage.

Seeing the determination and ferocious gleam in the eyes of well-seasoned seamen gave pause even to the drunkest of the refuse gathered at the dock side of the gangplank. The former harbor 'master' attempted to cajole and embolden the mob but the steam had escaped and they began mumbling about not believing in witches or spells and such and maybe a cask of rum would go well with a bite right about now.

As the discussion continued Thomas noted another group of dockworkers making their way towards the melee with a single-minded stride. They carried batons, clubs, and wooden bullets as well as an attitude of glee at the imminent brawl. They were going to enjoy whacking a few heads and tossing more refuse into the bay.

The combinations of angry sailors and fresh reinforcements took the rest of the wind out of the sails of the aforementioned rowdies, they turned to return to the nearest pub.

"Come back ye scurvy cowards!" Demanded the man too weak to fight his own battles.

"You let us know when you've worn him and his friends down enough and we'll come and finish the job," yelled an anonymous source to gales of laughter.

Healing Can Be Such Sweet Pain

Present Day

Tom drifted in and out of foggy consciousness, every time it felt as though he would breach the surface his dreams would pull him into the depths. It was the scent of bacon powering through his dormant olfactory senses like a bulldozer through a shotgun shack that brought him ravenous into life.

They had stopped or, at least, lessened the doses of pain numbing chemicals so the trip returning to the land of the woke was smoothed over, not the harsh ripping from the womb it had been. He smiled. Bacon. Was there a more glorious smell in the universe. He knew intellectually what bacon was doing to his cholesterol and therefore his health but moreso knew the pleasure he would experience before it would kill him. The squeak of rubber soles on linoleum rang out like the hallelujah chorus of breakfast.

Her smile pleasant as she reacted to his reaction to breakfast, hunger was always a good sign in a hospital. They wanted you to eat so they were not forced to insert another tube to do the job. His eyes fluttered, blinking away the last vestiges of sleep. Real sleep, not drug induced, fell away with the realization they were bringing him real food to go with his real sleep. Not soft porridge or Jell-o, or some other slop, but bacon and, unless he was still dreaming, scrambled eggs. Soft food yes, but with flavor. Look, his now not piqued mind cooed, those little packets have salt and pepper! It would be a good day.

Her eyes were soft as she placed the tray on the moveable table found in every hospital room in the world. Her hair tight in a neat bun to keep it out of her way while she worked, streaks of grey showed age and hard work, though kindness showed pretty. She had been with him throughout this ordeal, he knew that instinctively by the way she cared for him. And that was it, wasn't it? She did care for him, not just as a patient but as a person, it was inherent in her gentle soul and bearing.

She pushed the table over to where it hovered over his prone form before grasping the remote control for his bed and powering him up into an almost seated position. The better to comfortably eat.

"Did you sleep well?" A simple question, just something to say.

"Deeply, I think, though I am tuckered out. I never usually dream. Oh, I work things out while I sleep, mathematics, code, glitches, and bugs. My mind has a way of sorting through problems while I leave it alone, but I don't dream...stories, I guess. And I have been living a series of stories that confound and confuse me. It's like I am living another life in my sleep to the point I wake up more tired than when I went to sleep," he shook his head as if he could waggle and jiggle his thoughts into their proper places.

"It's not unusual for the drugs to intensify your subconscious. We often hear of patients who, when they come out of surgery, feel as though they have regained consciousness in a foreign world. For some it is just a momentary feeling of disconnection, for others it can be days until they settle back into reality. But this too shall pass," she patted his shoulder in a reassuring manner as she made to leave. "Though some have felt their journey into the nocturnal fantasy was more real than what they came back to, just as you have. That they lived another life simultaneously with this." She waved her hands to include all of creation. "It's a curious condition."

"Well, I don't know where I would come up with the life I'm living while deep in sleep. It has no bearing on anything I have ever know, read about, thought about, or dreamt of previously." He tried to sound nonchalant though the look she gave him showed he had not been entirely successful.

"Maybe it's from a past you don't know much about but is trying to impress itself upon you," she grinned as she warmed to the subject making her way back to his bedside.

"I don't think I've ever been a white sailor," he laughed, "I think I would remember that. And if it's from stories of my past, well, no one ever mentioned white sailors in any branch of my roots." He grinned his disinclination to go along for the ride.

"Maybe, but from what I've learned most black folks don't know much past three or four generations in the past," she looked away from him as if she knew she had crossed a racial line and was apprehensive of his reaction. "I watch a lot of PBS and Henry Louis Gates Jr. Sorry if I stepped out of line. It just seems anything is possible when there are no facts pro or con for a theory. Have you ever thought of delving into your family's past?"

Now Tom had to laugh, "I was about to embark on just such a journey when I discovered sushi and bullets do not pair well."

"We'll get you out of here in another day or two and then you may resume your journey. Is there anyone we should contact about your 'misfortune'?"

"No, there is no one, but I sure could use a laptop and access. I know you can't get mine, but I can log on if someone has something decent I can use," now hope came to the fore as he realized he could maybe complete his proposed deal while laying abed.

It was early that same afternoon when she returned carrying a small HP laptop and a beaming smile. "I had my wife bring mine in from home. It's just sitting there waiting for me to start writing again." She handed him the machine.

It was not a high-powered business, professional computer like he had but he could make it work. He had no need to write code or solve inconsistencies, just to communicate. It would do very nicely.

"Thank you..." Tom blushed with his realization of rudeness for never asking her name.

"Ruthie." And there was that beatific smile that lit her eyes and made you feel as welcome as a lost boy returning to the embrace of his mother.

"And you're a writer?" He didn't know why that should surprise him but it did. This woman in her middle years whom he assumed to be pleasantly ensconced in the niche life had placed her.

His reaction to the gift of the use of her computer, her mention of her wife, and that she was a writer evoked the almost identical reaction in her. She thought it was peculiar that he wasn't taken aback more by any of the revelations. Ruthie, in her own way, found it refreshing that he was as impressed by the writer credit as her marital status and kindness. He accepted her as she was, it was not a response she was accustomed to.

"I have been writing a book for the past decade, so I am not certain I qualify for the title but I try. It's silly, I know, especially since I hardly sit down and write more than a few words a week, but I haven't given up." The words were wistful and wishful. The kind used by someone of little self-confidence when saying something slightly embarrassing in its presumption without substance. She found it necessary to add the qualifier.

"But it is a pursuit you enjoy, yes?" She nodded her affirmation. "Then you should take pride in the doing. Oh, I know it is far from done," he added to stave off her unnecessary defense, "You haven't quit. Not on the story, not on yourself. A few words a week, right now, and I'm guessing between work and family it doesn't allow hours and hours of time to wander in the literary forests," again, she acknowledged the truth with a nod, "any progress is considered progress. If you love to write then write, it will get done when the story is told." He opened the computer and pushed the power button.

"And what is it you do?" she had borne her poetic soul, she expected like recompense.

"I work for myself, though am about to retire and go off on my journey of self-discovery as you pointed out so succinctly before. I find I crave an anchor to my past." He hesitated on the phrasing. Why had he chosen the word 'anchor'? It was not one he usually would bandy about. He normally would have said connection or link. His dreams were insinuating themselves into his normal life. "I am a computer scientist, I create code, cyber security, software applications, suites, and script."

"You're a nerd!" Ruthie clapped her hands in a display of childish joy. "You create, like any other artist or writer, just nerdier!"

Tom could not help but grin in self-consciousness and grateful admission to the truth. He had never thought himself an artist or writer. Yet did he create stories any less convoluted or interesting—well, to him and other nerds— than the great writers of fiction? What he created he created from the same ether as novelists, their own minds. Now, he laughed at the presumptuousness of it all. This woman was delightful in so many ways.

That was the thing with those not of the master race— the straight, white, male, those who felt so terrified they were losing their power to those less deserving—they didn't want to be raised up above the former rulers of the world, just equal. The brown, black, gay, lesbian, bi, trans, queers, different people, the oddities of society who only wanted what the white males had, nothing more just the same rights and opportunities. Here was common cause. A black, well tan, man and a lesbian writer. He thought the sun shone brighter in his room than he had ever seen. He really had to get out into the world more and meet these weirdos.

"Don't tell me, your wife is an artist, isn't she?" He asked as if it were the most natural question in the world before he realized it was.

"She does paint," admitted Ruthie through her smile, "but actually she is a financial advisor. She handles much of the investing for our group of oddities."

"I may wish to join your elite eccentrics once I am freed of the pain and suffering wrought by an unjust corporate representative of society. For now, I have work to do before I have the investment to make," he began punching in passwords and secret codes to access his personal cloud.

Instantly his emails began flowing down the screen, There were the usual hundred or so bullshit sales pitches, promises of riches if he'd only click on the link, or politicians who had bought his personal information for a dollar so they could hound him for every nickel they could squeeze out of his pockets, and just general annoyances. He clicked on 'select all' and flushed.

He clicked on his secured personal email, of which only a half dozen people were privy to, and there was only one lonely email, from Chester. Shit! Nothing important just an invitation for lunch and conversation but it had come several days previous. Chester would be wondering. Tom composed a quick synopsis of the events of the past few days, careful to explain he was healing, doing well, nothing to worry about, he would be home on the morrow or soon after. Though would not be up for dining out for a few. Although, if Chester wanted to show up with some sushi—he still had a taste for it and it hadn't been the sushi's fault—Tom would not be averse to a roll or two. Now, onto the business account.

No sooner did the emails begin popping up than did her window open in the bottom right-hand corner. It would appear she had pinned her presence to a permanent spot on his screen.

"Interesting," came a joyful exclamation.

Ruthie's continued presence caught him off guard, he'd thought she had exited the room but had, instead, remained in case he should require any assistance cranking up her machine. It was so in character he couldn't be upset with her.

"I'm sorry, I have some personal business to attend right now but I would enjoy continuing our discussion later today, if that would be agreeable."

Ruthie patted him on the shoulder to seal the deal, pointedly without glancing or peeking at his screen. She was truly a trustworthy human, he grinned. He would enjoy working with her and her wife.

"I didn't mean to interrupt," the perfect face on the screen was concerned she had finally overstepped. "A friend?" She couldn't contain her curiosity.

"My nurse," he replied without thinking and immediately regretted the flippant tone.

"Your what?" For someone who seemed to know every single thing about him and his health she was abruptly surprised and troubled.

He spent the next ten minutes explaining his circumstance and how it had come to be, while answering a multitude of rapid-fire questions about the exact timeline and actions involved. Finally satisfied he was in no danger of expiring any time soon she summed up her feelings with, "You shouldn't have pointed the sashimi!"

Tension evaporated like rubbing alcohol on a hot surface. The conversation took a welcome turn as she reported she had done some initial digging into his family. Skipping over the past two generations, of which he was well versed, she jumped back a hundred years to where she believed his grandparents had been born and generally to whom. Tom was impressed with the thoroughness of her research and how quickly she had moved. She had said she would provide him a voucher of good faith and here she was, though they were supposed to meet face to face. Yeah, well shit had changed and it wasn't her fault.

She had followed possible lineage to western New York, near Buffalo, or somewhere in Canada, though that was the white side and it was blurred in supposes, maybes, guesses and leaps of faith. She could prove none of the truth of that ancestry, just a supposition. The darker side of the family proved a bit more elusive. She had followed the possibilities to Michigan but could go no further as the line then disappeared.

Tom should not have been astonished at the revelation of white ancestors and yet he was. It was one thing to think or acknowledge intellectually the mixing of races it was quite another to have it confirmed. That could only mean one thing and that was that at some time in the past one of his white forefathers had most likely raped one of his great, great grandmums.

The stunning woman waited patiently as realization, anger, shame —for which he had no cause, as neither he nor his great grandparent had had a choice in the act. She was probably terrified, and physically and psychologically damaged for life—and finally acceptance as there was no changing the past. She felt for him or so her countenance expressed. But she could no more change the past than he. These were the sins of the country and all had to bear them; or should.

"You've held up your end of our very loosely woven bargain," said Tom evidently pleased with the outcome. If he was to be honest with himself, and shouldn't everyone attempt the same, he preferred doing business with this woman rather than the soulless representatives of the grand corporate world. His gut told him he could trust her, her word would be sacrosanct and if not, she would be no different than the corporate whores waiting on word from him, though far more pleasant to gaze upon. "though how can I be assured you have the resources to accommodate my needs?" Still a pig was a pig no matter how you dressed it and it had to be faced if you were to own it.

"The remuneration has already been deposited into your secure account at the Pacific National Bank of Nantucket," a small private concern serving the well healed of the nearby Martha's vineyard. They prided themselves on their confidentiality when it came to who their customers were, the level of their wealth, and their transactions. A private, non-government insured nor overseen equity management firm. Her deposit would not be detected nor scrutinized by any SEC or IRS busybodies. He would not be taxed nor penalized.

Tom rested his hand on the keyboard, indecisive as to whether to open another tab and check the voracity of her claim before deciding if trust was to be the coin, then both had to use the same currency. She watched his eyes and read his thoughts. Most people never knew how much information passed through their eyes; it was like the news ticker on Times Square. He wanted to check whether she was telling him truthfully, something he could've done and probably would do once the video call ended, but he refused to check her honesty while she watched. He was trusting her. Apparently not a gesture he was used to employing.

She couldn't blame him. He had spent the better part of his adult life dealing with the shysters and bullshit artists that are employed by mega-corps for just this situation. They could lie with perfection, their eyes empty as their souls, their smile like a dagger to the heart daring you to gaze into their faux genuineness and honor and dare call them out on their lies. She had lived the life, which was why she was here now.

Her lips pulled at the corners as they fought the crooked smile aborning. The last thing she wished was for him to believe she mocked him or give the impression she had won this bout. She wanted his trust more than she wanted his secrets. It was time to lay her cards on the table and play her most outrageous gambit. Truth.

"When do they think you will be released?" Information first.

"Tomorrow, day after they think at the latest," he sighed. He was tired, tired of healing, tired of laying abed, tired of playing games when he hadn't a clue what the rules were or who he was playing against. He wanted his freedom, he wanted out.

"And when do they think you are up to having company and conducting business?" Tread softly, stealthily so as not to spook the prey. Though prey was not the word she wished, at one time it would have fit like a well-tailored jacket, but now, it wasn't how she thought of him. She wanted a partner, someone trustworthy and decent. Well, in for a penny.

"Who knows, but soon or I'll go insane with nothing to occupy my mind. I require action of the cerebellum." He lay back on the raised head of the hospital bed wishing he could say what he wanted but knowing if he did, she would never feel comfortable in his presence.

"I'll contact you the day after tomorrow and see how you are feeling, and if you are feeling up to it, I'll bring lunch and we can spend some time together discussing many things. Then you will take a few days to consider everything I impart to you and we will see if we can form a relationship which allows you to begin your new life, your journey, comfortably. I don't mean just financially, but in your heart, soul, and mind." She gave the impression she was seeking something not in her immediate field of view. Whatever she sought was far from where she sat.

His heart skipped, stopped, started then leapt like a principal danseur. He was going to meet this stunning, brilliant woman, eye to eye, in the same room, together alone. He could feel the sweat forming under his arms and down his back, nervous as a thirteen-year-old virgin preparing for prom with the prettiest girl in his class.

"Yes, that would be fine," he said staring at the ceiling and thinking of code and mathematical equations to slow his breathing and pulse. Could he wait another few days for that to happen? He wanted the conversational intercourse to happen now. He wanted to think of another way to phrase that as well. "I would prefer something other than sushi, I'm certain you can understand the reasons. Also, please understand that I tire easily so I don't mean to be rude so if I let go a yawn or seem distanced, it is all part of the healing. My discomfort level will also be of concern as I am spurning any opiates or other mind-altering pain medication." She should know his full mental and medical condition.

Her expression was kind, forgiving, and accepting of his limitations. "Not to worry, I'll be gentle and patient." And she was gone.

Now, what the hell did that mean?

The thought ran through his mind before his eyes slammed shut, as tired caught up with healing. His body and mind were fatigued to exhaustion and dragged him down.

The Sea Giveth New Life, The Land Promises Naught

Late Summer, Early Fall 1852

Thomas thought to keep Roisin sequestered in the captain's cabin for fear the sight of her walking freely on board would ignite the ignorant masses again. She, of course, refused to hide from hate. Wearing her finest island wrap she paraded about the deck like she owned the ship. Stopping to talk convivially with each sailor until she came to stand as his equal by his side.

As they both gazed down the dock, they could see staggering spies creep down from the public house where the rabble had retreated. They watched them watching the ship. Thomas knew from experience it would only take a few more rounds and an increase in membership of the Idiots Brigade before they would once again unearth their scrap of courage. It wouldn't be long before they would mass in a mound of wretched excrement and try to force their way through a mutual sphincter. Liam might be inclined to send some reinforcements; Thomas would prefer to avoid involving the Harbor Master in a war not his own.

He deliberated options as the deck hands and dock hands continued skillfully to swing block and tackle discharging his cargo. As he watched and considered their options, he realized the best course of action would be to collect his coin from the Master and push off on the evening tide.

His desire to see, feel, and possibly settle in this new world did not supersede his desire to keep Roisin safe. As well as his crew, he reflected. If push came to kill, he knew his men would stand behind him, and her, and he had no desire to put them in harm's way. They would make for Canada, which he understood to be just as beautiful and free as this America, though with less of a burden of hate.

He noticed the Master strolling down the dock as if he hadn't a care in the world, a purse heavy with coin swinging in his right hand. The man had pluck, Thomas chuckled, and balls the size of a three masted schooner at full sail.

"Ya fear naught," grinned the ship's captain as he welcomed the Master onboard.

"T'ain't naught to fear. If these scum want work or any chance to sign on, they best respect the office, if not the man. They won't belay a Harbor Master unless they enjoy being black balled all up and down the coast." He held out the purse for Thomas to inspect.

Taking a cursory peek, he noticed gold and silver coins sharing the soft, warm luxury of the supple leather pouch. Even with each man receiving an equal measure it would still provide him all he would require to begin his new life. Well, alongside his somewhat ill-gotten gains during several voyages between Singapore and the end of the world. Merchant or pirate, sometimes it was hard to discern betwixt and between.

Thomas was not a greedy man; he would share with the men who had remained loyal to him and the ship. If they wished to stay here that would be their decision. If they wished to find what the north held for them, he would welcome them with open arms. He also knew that by making such an open show of bringing a large purse filled with currency recognized by every country on the map, the Master was telling Thomas it would be in his best interest to move on. He wasn't implying he wouldn't stand with the ship and crew, just that he would prefer not to be forced into a decision. Thomas shook the man's hand and gripped his shoulder in camaraderie. The minute the last bale of goods left the ship they would make ready to leave on the even tide.

As the sun began to descend below the western horizon, they cast off, just as the, now, very swollen, gang of dock scum began to make their way down the dock once again. At their fore was the former dock master from St. Maartin, torch in hand, spittle spewing and spraying from his almost toothless mouth as he egged the mob on. Promising them riches and bitches.

He reared back lighting the bottle of rum in his hand and made ready to toss it onto the ship. The belaying hook that took root and sprouted from his chest forced him tumbling backwards where he dropped the lit bottle, spraying its fire on several nearby louts. The rest scattered saving themselves rather than attempt to douse the flames on their former comrades.

Thomas turned to see one of the crew grinning ear to ear appreciating his handy work, never noticing the gleam in the eyes of the woman standing directly behind him. If he'd have been a more superstitious man, a man of belief rather than of learning, he might've believed she had something to do with the act, but Thomas prided himself on his common sense and life learning. There was no such thing as magic or witches, just human interactions and free will. He had seen too much of the world not to believe that.

Sails hoisted in the burgeoning western breeze they moved smoothly, tacking out of New York harbor and down to the Atlantic. Near as he could discern from a few quick and pointed questions during the very short time in New York, his best shot at avoiding any more of America was to stay well out to sea until he could hug the coast up around Nove Scotia and New Brunswick coming around to Quebec. He could then sell or transfer his ship to his crew or another and then continue down the St. Lawrence either by a smaller vessel or wagon to the interior. It would take some time but could be accomplished before weather set in. He hoped neither crew nor friend minded cold and snow.

The weather stayed fare and the wind steady, as if they knew this would be Thomas' final voyage, even if he, himself was unaware in his bones and his heart, though he knew he had sailed the great oceans for the last time. It had been more'n a decade since he had stowed away and been discovered on this very ship. He had seen, experienced, lived a life he could never in all of eternity have dreamed, but it was time to settle. The thought of putting down roots on dry land sent a shiver up his spine. Could he live without the rhythm of the sea? Could he breathe air not touched and seasoned by all the life in the ocean? Would the itch, the need, the desire to be somewhere, anywhere, drive him batty? Only one way to discover the truth of his destiny, to live it.

Thomas would meet with his crew as they closed in on Quebec. Some deciding required attention. It would be a simple meet, they all knew the circumstances, what Thomas planned for his life and now they had to decide what they would do with theirs. They furled the sails and allowed the ship to ride the night current. There was no fear of running aground this far out in the bay, all the men could sit together on the deck and discuss.

Thomas called the meeting to order by thanking his crew for all they had survived together. He recounted some of their adventures to gales of laughter, cheers, and somber remembrances. He then reiterated what his plan was, to leave the ship in Quebec and venture inland. The question at hand was what did the crew want?

He laid out what he thought were the best available options; they could take their share of what the sale of the ship would bring plus what they were owed and settle in Canada as he was intending; they could buy the ship from him and those who wished to remain here in the north, elect a new captain—a completely novel idea as captains usually captained a ship from strength and fear—hire on another crew and continue their ways; or they could follow Thomas inland and begin new lives as dry landers.

Most laughed at the idea of dry lander living as an impossibility, though there were one or two who did not dismiss it out of hand, including, Thomas noted, the crewman who had taken down the former harbor master of St. Maartin. The vast majority decided they would like to keep the Daughter of The Sea and live between pirating and merchant men, which ever paid the best at the time. None wished to remain in Quebec as they had heard it was far more French than English or Irish.

Thomas grinned; it was what he believed was the best option for these men. It was what they knew, what they excelled at, and what they loved. He was ready with his proposal for the price of ship and everything else on board, he would only take what was rightfully his. And the only two things he wished to take with him were Roisin and his hidden chest. He proposed they cede their share of earnings from the cargo sold in New York and the deal would be done.

It would give him enough of a stake to secure his new life and not concern himself with income for several years. It would be a bargain for the crew as they could never have afforded this grace any other way, and he would feel in his heart that he had paid them back for their loyalty, courage, and hard work. You cannot put a price on a man's life, but you can help him achieve his dream.

Once safely docked and settled in Quebec it took several days for Thomas to settle all with the crew and prepare to head upstream towards the east end of Lake Ontario. He had attempted to explain to Roisin what was happening and the why, though she was having trouble comprehending the why. She had met and come to know Thomas because of this ship. It had provided her freedom from the superstitions and intimidation of the island people. Not her people, they were happily ensconced deep in the dense jungle, but the Spanish, French and Dutch half breeds and mulattos of her island.

People without a sense of belonging anywhere because they were racially and ethnically of supposed different tribes. They didn't fit with any and none would claim them. They would have benefited from clinging to each other and forming a new tribe, but, instead, they searched for and found an 'other' to dismiss as less than human and of sorcerous git. Someone they could all scorn.

The ship had carried her far from scattered fear and revulsion into the outright and deep-seated hatred of white people towards all black people, who they feared and believed were coming for their livelihoods and women. The ship had protected her from coming to harm and now she was to leave this safe place. For what?

Thomas had been her savior, her friend, her protector as well. Now she had to choose between the two. She knew the ship, her crew, and what life was onboard. What Thomas offered now was completely unknown. The days in Quebec were warm enough this end of the summer but the nights promised a change that would not be welcome. There was a chill on the breeze, a scent she was not familiar with, water yet different. People spoke of the coming snow and she couldn't grasp what the word meant. They had no corresponding word in her language or culture. Frozen water that came from the sky and buried whole cities, froze rivers, streams, and people. In the end she knew what she had to do. Swallow her fear and hope it didn't consume her from the inside while the frigid winds destroyed her from the outside. She would follow Thomas.

It would take them just over a month to make the trek bouncing between river boats and portaging, with a few days rest in Montreal. Thomas accepted this fact and was satisfied they would arrive before the winter snows. To Roisin this sounded like death by torture, trial by something she could not imagine before she would finally either come to terms with this new life or die in the attempt.

She would have to learn who the trees were if she were to friend them and who the animals were if she were to take them into her confidence and trust their counsel. Maybe that was what the spirits of nature were attempting to tell her. Yes, the trip would be arduous and long but it would give her time to adjust to this new land and her children, both plant and animal.

She had heard the tales of the wild red men who inhabited these lands. They were savage and bloodthirsty. It chilled her blood more than the wind until she realized that was what the whites said about her people and any that were not just like them. Actually, they said that about anyone who was not of their immediate tribe or family. Roisin decided she would like to meet some of these savages to find if they were more like her or more like the cruel Europeans.

Several of the ship's crew decided they would also accompany Roisin and Thomas to the great lake they sought. These men had sailed the seven seas, they could not imagine any lake that could compare with the vastness, grandeur and spirit of the sea. Curiosity can be a great motivator. Men like the sailors of The Daughter of The Seas sought adventure and exploration. The want to see what lay over the horizon, what great riches were held where the sun set. The pull was too much for many a man to ignore or fight.

The First Line in a Book, The First Note of a Symphony

Present day

The doorbell chime startled Tom awake. He hadn't realized he'd dozed off in the middle of the paragraph he'd been rereading. He was having some difficulty concentrating since being released from the hospital to his own recognizance. Ruthie had called a couple times a day since his release from confinement three days ago. She was a good egg. She didn't have to check in on him, as she had enough to occupy her in her own life. Wife, kids, job, a hefty portion of society that wished she and her kind would just disappear; that wasn't ever going to happen. She told him on one of their phone conversations that she wondered if the Straight White Male loving slice of society realized just how much their disapproval and hate motivated those they sought to relegate to the back alleys, ghettoes, and hidden clubs. If only they would accept the LGBTQ+ folks as equal, normal, and historically necessary. If they could only accept and appreciate the contributions to society. If they could only realize the possibility that those contributions created by LGBTQ+ people benefited all throughout history. All told, these accomplishments, combined with the insecurities inherent in all those who believed themselves superior, might be the cause of their derision. Such is the self-inflicting nature of man.

Why all this ran through his head while the door chimed again, he couldn't say, but he assumed whoever was leaning on the button was not going to evaporate. He rubbed the sleep and sand from his eyes, how long had he slept? It seemed his only activity since liberation was tossing and turning while he slept. He'd wanted to begin exercising, slowly, incrementally to regain some strength in his arms and legs but he was so worn out from sleeping it was all he could do to turn pages and read. The chime ran out once again.

Tom was finding irritation was as good a motivator as hunger. He wanted to throw open the door and share a piece of his ragged mind with whoever couldn't pull their fucking finger off the button. Tom was not one for cussing, not even in the privacy of his own head, but this sonofabitch was pissing off the healing patient. His shoulder throbbed with the movement while he lumbered to the door. Some pissant was about to get a large load of Tom's thoughts on patience and the definition of rude.

If he'd meant to make a statement with his mentally rehearsed storming of the front portal, he flubbed the dismount horribly, whacking himself in the head with the door when it caught on his outstretched foot. Stars, just like in the cartoons of his youth, danced, and whirled in front of his eyes. Maroon! He acidly chastised himself, though he was going to take it out on the intruder not the guilty party. Until she smiled.

"Uh, huh, well, uh, wha, uh?" The sounds slipped from his tongue like silver, the exhortation of a brilliant mind. Shit!

She held up a bag of take-out in offer of apology for her abrupt appearance. "Sorry, I should've called to tell you I was bringing lunch but I was afraid you'd try to dissuade me. I really didn't mean to surprise you, though, come to think of it, what did I expect. Grand error on my reasoning and conclusion." Again, that smile though this time filled with remorse.

"Please, please come in," he completed the opening of the door without further harm and waved her into his spacious apartment. Well, spacious for one person, more than enough for a genius, his computers, yes, he had several, and sparse furniture. Not that it was a mess, but it clearly reflected the condition of the man living here convalescing. There were a few empty to-go boxes on the kitchen counter, dirty dishes in the sink, a blanket scrunched up on the couch where he had fallen asleep while reading.

Tom quickly stepped around this vision to try and straighten up some of the area and at least give her a place to sit. He awkwardly apologized for the condition, saying it isn't usually like this, embarrassment evident in his every move.

She shushed him and told him to return to where he had obviously been before her intrusion. She would find what they required for a lovely lunch of rare hamburgers—she had called the hospital before making the choice to be certain it would fit his recovery. Lovely person that Ruthie—a salad, and milkshakes, strawberry and chocolate, his choice. The meat would require plating and warmed for a half minute in the microwave. It had been a bit of trek over here and she was certain the burgers could use a warm-up. They settled into the living room to share a meal as they belatedly met face to face.

Tom chewed as silently as he could manage—it was a very good burger—so as not to disrupt his thoughts. He couldn't believe this stunning and, from what he could discern, brilliant woman was actually sitting in his living room. He had believed her to be no more than a magnificent creation of AI. But flesh and blood was evident, there was no way a hologram could've carried the bag full deliciousness over here. AI shit wasn't THAT good yet and probably never would be. He knew.

She watched him out of the corner of her eye, trying not to be obvious that she studied him. He was exactly what he appeared on screen and what she had hoped. A large, soft, comfy man with a brain that knew no limits because he would never confine himself that way. He was not arrogant of his talents but wasn't ashamed or intimidated by his possession of them either. He could shed a couple pounds and get into shape but it was not a priority for him and, she realized, it wouldn't be for her. His mind was a beautiful wonderland of possibilities and she wanted to explore.

"Any idea why you are so gifted and brilliant when it comes to what you do? Special training, a fall on your head as child that kick-started parts of your brain none of the rest of us possess? Loneliness? Shy? Not good at making friends?" The questions were serious ones though she presented them playfully, not wishing him to read more into her inquiry than she meant. She had been around geniuses throughout her life. They were skittish, timid, retiring, almost as if suffering from a form of PTSD after a lifetime of abuse by those without the same mental acuity. Average people thought geniuses had some kind of magic or secret ability they refused to share with those of less mental capacities. Geniuses were also not known for their physical attributes and so were quite easy to intimidate with a few punches and shoves. Jealousy is not an attractive attribute.

Tom blushed as no one had ever been so straight forward about his abilities. They wanted to study him or use him or hold him up to his peers as what they could be if they only would apply themselves. No wonder the other kids thought so ill of him. But it wasn't his idea or want to be treated differently. It was just what adults did to show they had control over those they thought better than themselves.

"It's just something that was always there, like being left-handed or being good at baseball, some kids had something others didn't. They were born with it. The grand difference was no one beat you up because you could throw, hit, catch, run, or put a ball through a hoop from mid-court. They worshipped you. Brain loses to brawn almost every time, well, until someone has a problem no one else can solve then we become necessary. My gran used to call it a knack, like a little bit of magic I had in my head, where things just fell into the right holes and slots." He shrugged. He had tried to explain this to people, psychologists, counselors, employers, and government reps since he was a child. There was just no way they could grok what he could do because they would never be in his head to see how it happened.

"If you try to think about the how, the process goes hinky, is that how it is?" She waited while he weighed her words.

Was she trying to get inside his head or was she saying she did get it and wanted him to know? "Actually, that is probably the best description I've heard, not exactly but it captures the feel. I'm not sure the how or why, but it makes sense when I allow it to happen organically." He grinned inwardly; this woman might actually get it.

She took another bite of the warm hamburger and chewed thoughtfully, mulling over what she already knew with what his explanation added to the data. What she had discovered thus far was Tom, for all his brilliance and innovation, was as normal a human being as she had ever run across. He had no quirks, was not reticent to try and explain his 'gift' and didn't seem to feel the need to hide that he had such a gift. There was no need to act the genius, a squirrely, odd, offbeat, fringe human being. He wanted to fit in and if no one would let him, he was fine with that as well.

"What is it you really want out of life, right now?" Might as well get to the marrow of this bone.

"I want the world to stop and let me off. I want to go sit on a beach and count the waves, listen to the surf, maybe drink some tall thing with umbrellas in it. I don't know. I've been somebody's trained monkey since I can remember, even my own. I don't want to think for a while, to solve anything, to dance to tunes someone, not of my choosing, is pumping out like vacuous pop candy and expecting me to turn it into a symphonic masterpiece. I want to know who I am and why I can do what no one else can, even the best in the field. There has to be something in the family line, some gene that originated hundreds of years ago. Though I have to admit one would think it would have shown up in a generation before me. And again, this is where I get stumped as my knowledge only goes back two generations." His mood deflated as he considered the maze before him. A Rubiks would seem child's play compared to what he wished to discover. And that was the crux. "I want to stop thinking and start doing. I want to discover, to travel, to learn through osmosis by immersing myself into humanity. Humans are supposed to be adaptable. I want to find out if I am human!" The plea in his words almost broke her heart. His need to be a 'real boy', as Pinocchio had so succinctly put it, was as pure a want as any she had ever encountered. The question was, could she make it a reality. She could try.

"Let's start off easy, how are you?" It was a simple question, one to pry off the top of the can of pent-up questions and worries about life.

"Good, I think." He seemed to reconsider his answer, he wanted to say more, but would he? Silence filled the room like the scent of his mother, Este Lauder Azuree, if he remembered. Of course, he did, it was his mother's favorite. She always asked him the same question and he always responded the same. Though the realization slammed the inside of his head like a plank of wood made from understanding. They both asked it and they both sought more than he had given, they wanted honesty. He hadn't given that to his mother; he should try to gift it here. "I think I lay awake nights thinking and wondering if the cop had been more relaxed, less impassioned, would his aim have been more on target? Would he have put the bullet through my heart?" Silence, it was a load to expose.

"Ruthie told me that they had no explanation for why I was still alive. She said, the surgeon told her it was as if the bullet had a mind of its own and had charted a course through major organs, without causing any more necessary damage than it could, before exiting out the back. Again, between ribs rather than through," He shook his head in wonder as he had when she explained it the first time.

She began to say something but he raised his hand to still her. She leaned back into the soft cushions of the sofa to wait for what she was fairly certain was coming.

"See, I have lived with accepting death for so long, due to my family history, that I thought it could not hold any fear for me and yet, I find myself terrified that it was only chance that saved me that night. It would have been quick, instant. Pain one second eternity the next. I can't help but feel it might have been the best outcome instead of the pain and suffering that waits my actual demise. Sickle cell once it kicks in, early in life or at my end, is a horribly painful disease that never lets up. It destroys your lungs, kidneys, and brain and you are constantly aware of that destruction. You watch as you are slowly, painfully being taken apart piece by piece. Your hips, shoulders, knees, and ankles feel as though someone is constantly ramming a sharp ice pick into them and twisting it. Years will pass with no relief, ever. It is being tortured slowly, horribly every single day until you finally cease to exist, either from the disease or by your own hand." He wiped a stray tear from his cheek. He hadn't realized he was weeping as he described what his end would be. He hadn't thought about it in such vivid detail since that first attack and his death sentence. "Here was the solution and the damn cop failed me."

"Do you think you shoved the food container his way to force his hand? Do you think you wanted suicide by cop?" She had almost whispered the words, as if afraid of what his reaction would be.

Well, there was a conundrum he hadn't considered. Had he? A deep breath in through the nose and slowly released through his mouth bought time and relaxed him physically. If he had initially wanted to strike out at the temerity of the question, he forced that response to the end of the line.

"I don't know." There it was. He had to face the possibility that his mind had taken an offramp he never saw, or so he thought. What if subconsciously he wanted to die right there, to end the future he saw for himself. Had he moved just enough to forestall that end? Had his desire for knowledge of his family's past overridden the want to die? Was his nebulous journey more important than pain and suffering? He would require a great amount of time in solitude and contemplation to dig to the core of his mental and spiritual self to discover the truth of that line of inquiry.

"What you should know, and please do not ask how I got my information, I may tell one day but not today, you'll just have to take my word on this, but you have been ill informed medically. The pain and suffering you have experienced is not what you think. The chances of you having sickle cell anemia are close to nil. What you suffer from is a severe deficiency of vitamin D." The slight lift of the corners of her mouth transferred to a glint of mirth in her eyes. She allowed the information to force its way past his substantial fortress of belief and settle into hope.

"But I was told..." he began and she pulled a manilla folder from her shoulder valise. "Here are your medical records from the time you were a child to your current condition." She handed them over to where he sat. The words poised on the tip of his tongue awaiting the cry for freedom. Her hand stayed the release.

"You were told what they thought at the time. They took into consideration your symptoms, family history, racial medical histories, the technology of the time, and a mountain of assumptions and bang, you have sickle cell, even though it didn't show up in the tests." She allowed the information to disseminate and register.

"I still don't understand, even if they misdiagnosed when I was younger why was it never diagnosed properly at any time later in life?" His confusion and burgeoning anger apparent in his, now, wide open eyes.

"Missed opportunities. Maybe they thought the likelihood of you contracting sickle cell was such that there was no need to build your hopes when it more than likely would rear its ugly head at some time in the future. Maybe they never delved deep enough into the problem. Maybe they allowed a little inadvertent, innate racism to figure into their conclusions. All I can tell you is there is nothing wrong with you that a little vitamin D won't relieve. Take it in pill form or stand in the sun from time to time." Now she did smile, "You are awfully pale for an African American." Now she laughed and the angels sang in his heart.

Tom wanted to be pissed, to rip out his ounce or two of flesh for retribution for all the nightmares and worries he had suffered over the ensuing decades, but all the medical personnel who had initially misdiagnosed were all either ancient or gone; dead, buried, turned to dust years ago. Relief washed over him. He should be pissed. Instead he was giddy. But could he take her at her word? How could he not? She had given him all his medical records for the past four decades, all he had to do was read them, translate them from medical to English, and learn. Well, he was laid up for another week or two.

He paged through the reports pretending to read some, leafing through others, and actually understanding a few. From all appearances she was correct. They had misdiagnosed during his early teen years and never felt the need to correct the diagnosis. Assumptions combined with a societal bias against folks of color, doctors who were— especially in his youth--majority white and used a different scale to gage pain for whites and blacks, had led to a lifetime of misinformation and fear of a shortened existence.

If she was correct in her reading, and hope springs, he had been given a new lease on his new life. Whereas he thought he would never have the time to track down his ancestry, it would seem he would have both time and resources. Speaking of which...

"How does this information affect our agreement?" Might as well beard the lion.

"Only slightly," she was now all business, "what I propose is a subtle though significant change. As it would seem you are going to be wandering the planet for far longer than previously thought, I hoped I could give you an initial sum with a yearly stipend to more than sustain you for the rest of your natural life." Her body language said she was suggesting something he might not like but she was confident she could talk him into it.

"I guess that would depend on the initial stipend," he laughed. He found this face-to-face bartering much more fun than a conference call with six vice presidents and lawyers while the CFO, CEO, COO, and BFD listened in. This was personal and she was stunning.

She dug into her valise, which seemed to hold the contents of a small library, finding a small pad of paper and a pen. She rested the pad on her knee while removing the tip from the pen. Hmm, a fountain pen. Well, you had to give her points for style. She stared at the ceiling for several seconds before making a show of writing something on the pad. Placing the tip back on the pen she tore off the sheet of paper, folded it in half and handed it to him.

"I thought you told me you had deposited my remuneration into my bank account." He accused, though realization was dawning and she confirmed.

"It was a childish test to see if you would take my word; to see if you could trust me. I require your complete trust if we are to complete our negotiations." She waited. She'd known this confrontation was coming. What she hadn't been so cocky about was his response. This would be the tell.

"I guess I understand. It's just, I don't like people fucking with me. But I'll give you a pass on this one," now he grinned. He had to appreciate the way she played him, it was not a malicious act but a need to know.

"You really never checked? Even after we concluded our conversation?" She was taken aback at his lack of curiosity.

"I guess the money doesn't mean as much to me as it does to others, I have never worshipped the dollar. It is just a means to an end." It was his turn to take some pleasure at having astonished her. "And I have a comfortable financial cushion to sustain."

"Well then, let's see what you think about what I have offered."

"Wouldn't it have been easier and less dramatic if you just tell me the number?" Tom smiled. He couldn't help himself it was so ludicrous.

"Yes, but what fun is that? Don't you think negotiations should be fun! People get all testy because they think the person on the other side is always trying to screw them and so they try to screw that person first. It turns into a fucking contest. I don't want that and don't think you do either. This is how they do it in the motion pictures, I thought it would add a touch of frivolousness to our very delicate and extremely important interlocutions." She sat back on the loveseat and relaxed. Ball in your court, Mr. Webb.

Tom carefully opened the small piece of paper to reveal the amount she was offering. His grin widened as he took in what she had written. Nothing. It was blank. She was having a jape with him. The question was, what was her game?

"So, we start from zero?" His tone playful yet curious.

"I guess the question is, how much do you really want for your secrets?" Now she leaned forward and locked eyes with him. "I know what the big guys can offer. It is an enormous amount of money though with no back end. And no true guarantee they won't use every genius at their disposal to break your code and lock the back door we are all certain you have built in." Her eyes danced with the banter. "I am asking you what you need to make your dreams come true with an immutable guarantee that your secrets will remain the property of you and me. They will never be used for nefarious purposes nor for hostility against any person, country, or state. And you will receive a very generous stipend each year for the rest of your life. That leaves me the possibility for profit, control, and we both live happily ever after. You don't have to do another code or create another program or worry that your genius will be used for unsavory purposes." She sat back, took a bite of her now cold hamburger and waited. "Though you can, if you so desire."

Tom had to admit it was a beautiful offer. How much did he actually need? Yes, the mega corp would offer him the moon and stars but they also were greedy bastards with no morals or decency. They would not give a second thought to how his brilliance would be used. She may not be offering as much in the way of hard currency, she offered far more in integrity, morality, and virtue. Plus, she was so easy on the eye.

"You wish me to come up with a number of what I think is reasonable to seal the deal and begin my new life, yes?" Now the wheels were turning at an incredible rate. What did he want? Enough to travel to find his roots, enjoy some time just absorbing the world and maybe a nice Shepherd's Pie. He wanted to live in relative comfort, protected from further intrusions into his inner organs, safely respected enough that the next time he was confronted by authority they would treat him with a modicum of respect before opening fire. In reality, he had that now.

Fat Chance! His rational mind screamed. As long as your complexion was not pearly white and your features not northern European not all the money in the world could hold back the hordes of racism. Think of Sterling Brown or Bianca Williams, they had money, prestige as top tier athletes and still got fucked over by the police. Yeah, money don't buy everything unless you got the complexion to go with it.

His thoughts surprised Tom. He had always thought himself outside the victim mentality. Hadn't he been successful in business? Hadn't he been able to afford a lovely fourteen hundred square foot condo right on the lake? Yeah, he'd had to jump through a plethora of hoops to get the place, but didn't everybody? Or did they? He had never discussed what it took for him to be given the privilege of purchasing an overpriced piece of the American dream. Had everyone had the same hassle? It bore some investigation.

"What kind of music do you like?" The question came from far-left field, especially considering where his thoughts had taken him.

"Never thought much about it, I guess. Just noise in the background while I was trying to concentrate on solving issues," he stumbled the explanation as he returned to the present and his guest.

"You don't like music?" She couldn't hide her surprise, she almost laughed at the absurdity. How was it possible someone didn't like music? Not rock or jazz, or classical, folk or rap, but music, in general.

"It's not a matter of like or dislike it's more an issue of whether I notice music as anything but background noise." He now felt affronted by her attitude. Not everyone liked what everyone else liked, it was personal taste. Though how would he know about music, any kind, considering how single minded he had always been when it came to his job, his career, something he truly enjoyed, the doing, the solving, the creating. It wasn't work it was joy. Who needed music or distraction? Same reason he didn't own a television set, nothing for him.

"You have no outside interests? No hobbies? No pursuit of the finer things in life?" She was now shocked and a little saddened. How could someone this intelligent, this creative, not want some form of external stimuli?

Tom's innate insecurity was beginning to rear its ugly head. He had never been good at sports so they held nothing for him but humiliation. He had no artistic skills to speak of;

he couldn't draw, paint, sculpt, carve, and when he tried it only added to the ridicule brought on by the jocks. He could not play any instrument though he tried several and so thought music to be an annoyance rather than something to be embraced. He was devoid of the culture of his civilization, his society, his people, black, white, brown, or orange. He was a computer nerd who could make magic happen when sat before a keyboard. Once he had found his niche, his place in life, he blossomed and grew as a weed in sunlight and cow manure. What others could not comprehend was second nature to him, he hardly had to think about the simple codes he was writing. Hell, they almost wrote themselves. Now he was comprehending walking away from the one thing in life he had found where he excelled. What the hell was he going to do?

He had the quest for his ancestry, but would that satisfy his creative desire? It certainly was too late to try to learn to paint, play music, dance, draw, or pick up a sport. If you couldn't participate in those activities what good was watching them. He put the question to her. And then stopped her before she could answer.

"Oh my God, I just realized I don't even know your name!" The declaration caught them both by surprise.

"You may be the least curious person on this planet," she laughed and his heart sang. Maybe he could appreciate a little music. "Maybe in the history of this world. You never thought to ask before now?" She was truly aghast and tickled by the naivete, the innocence of the man. He was a treasure worth preserving. "Aoife." Which she pronounce, 'EE-fa'.

"Lovely." He whispered as his breath had been reclaimed.

"Do you speak Gaelic?" Again, he stopped her in her tracks. The man continued to astound.

"No why?"

"It's an old Gaelic name meaning 'beauty'," a self-conscious laugh escaped her perfect lips.

"Well, you are appropriately named, then," he blushed.

"Thank you," she tipped her head in acceptance of the compliment, "and as to your question I will just say, all art, music, performance of any kind is lost, it's invisible," she searched for the proper words, "it's meaningless without someone to appreciate it. Someone whose soul, for want of a better term, is touched by the work. Oh, the artist knows what they have created, yet will always seek someone's approval that their work has merit. It doesn't have to be millions; it can be a loved one who is honest about how the work affected them. For without honesty, acclaim means naught. You can learn to appreciate art as you can learn the difference between a six-dollar steak and a seventy-dollar steak cooked by a master. It's all in the taste." She grinned at her slight pun.

"You think I can learn to understand beauty?" He had never considered it possible outside of ones and zeros.

"You have already begun."

Tom was confused. Had he begun by understanding he had no understanding of art and music, literature, architecture, or style. He had no style, maybe that was it. Or, had he begun by appreciating the beauty of the woman across the coffee table from him? Didn't all appreciation of beauty begin at home when a child saw their mother as a vision of beauty? He was confused, but in for a penny...

"What I propose is that while you are convalescing for the next few weeks, I will expose you to certain styles of music and literature. You don't have to work, so we will use the time to ingrain some culture and possibly ingrain some healthy hobbies in your day to day to supplant your need to stare at a monitor." She rubbed her hands together in the universal sign of an evil villain about to embark on creating a creature. Though what kind of creature she meant to remake him into was yet to be seen. "I like the men I associate with to be well-rounded."

Tom patted his rotund stomach, "That I can do!" He smirked.

"You are about to embark on several journeys of discovery all at once that I hope will lead to a greater understanding of your primary quest. I hope you see that because you are an amalgamation of all your predecessors. your culture, your humanity is tied up in all those disparate paths. You are not black or white, protestant, Baptist, Jew, European, American, African, or Canadian you are a human being, and an exemplary example of the species."

Well, you had to give her this, she had mighty aspirations for him. The trepidation crept up his spine when he considered all she was going to try and stuff in his empty shell. It threatened to overwhelm. Though when he saw her, so earnest, so positive, so anxious to fill him with glory, he could not help but be excited at the prospect. He had lived an empty spiritual existence, not religiously, as he had no need for such, but culturally. Let the journey begin.

The More Things Change. . .

1852 Before The First Snowfall-Spring 1859

Thomas had been convinced by rumor and uneducated gossip that Canada would be more accepting of he and his friend. He had been sorely misled or mistaken. What passed for toleration in Quebec was thinly veiled racism. A kind of soft slavery where the 'darkies' were allowed certain access to public houses and public places due to the necessity of being close to an amenable master or mistress. They behaved themselves and therefore were allowed to be close to civilized society. Decency was displayed by beatings, rapings, and molestations that were less savage and for a briefer interval. Kindness by increment.

In the wilderness of Kingston things were less forgiving. It surprised him as Kingston was a fairly metropolitan city. It had been the capital of Canada for a few short years, was a primary military and naval town, sitting as it did on the banks of Lake Ontario where it could protect the empire from the marauding and barbaric Americans.

Thomas could not tell an inch of difference between the two peoples, even to the point of holding each other in the same low esteem. Both thinking the other was coming to steal their women, drink their beer, and conquer their vast magnificent lands. Yet neither seemed inclined to do so. They both preferred drinking to excess while extolling on the horrors of the other country and fighting amongst themselves. Not perplexing, as they both sprouted from the identical root.

Thomas found lodgings hard to come by in Kingston unless he was willing to house his negro in separate and far less equal quarters. His kindness toward her was considered unseemly and rather scandalous. It was one thing to fuck a negress, quite another to actually consider them part of the family.

The thing was, he wasn't sleeping with her, not in that way, more as a protector than a lover. She was in a very strange, cold, cold country with no one like herself in any way other than color. And the colored up here were as different from her as she was from a lizard. She was frightened and lonely, he only took care of her as he would any child. Dreams notwithstanding.

At long last he found a man who owned a small but well-kept cottage on the fringe of the city that was willing, for a steep price, to rent out to this odd couple. They settled into a routine that would not draw the ire of the local townsfolk and readied themselves for the onslaught of winter.

They had been warned that winter on the tail of the lake could be brutal. Thomas had sailed some of the most brutal and unforgiving waters of the world, he felt himself well steeled for what was to come. If his assumptions of the modernity of the people of Canada had been vastly unsound then his assumptions of his preparedness for the Canadian winter, the feet of snow produced by open waters and frigid winds, was egregiously erroneous.

The chill of September was quickly followed by the numbing winds of October, which morphed into the glacial and mind numbing cold of November, followed by months of stinging, freezing, biting, bitter darkness and misery that promised to never end. Death would be welcome and less miserable. Roisin began to fade into the white abyss of a Great Lake twilight.

Thomas worried the days and nights away, as he continued to brave the biting cold long enough to chop wood and toss it into the large fireplace that dominated the lower floor of the cottage. Roisin refused to climb into the rafters where he had set up a bed denying his entreaties that it was far warmer in the upper reaches than it was even in front of the blazing inferno. She feared being that much closer to where the sky god lived would only bring her to his attention and tempt him to come for her in the night while she slept.

It was near spring when her child was born. Thomas hadn't noticed the pregnancy, as he was distracted by her illness and failing strength. She hadn't gained much weight due to her incapacity to keep food down. Soup and thin gruel were all she could consume without immediately returning the meal to the cottage floor. She died that same night, with Thomas coddling the newborn boy while attempting to hold her and provide comfort. His grief threatened to end all three lives on the same eve.

The babe looked white, pale, which Thomas could only attribute to its tiny size and apparent sickliness. After attempting to keep the child alive with inept and ignorant clumsiness, he finally sought a milk mother in town. No white woman would come, telling him to let the bastard die and be done with an ill tiding, but it was all he had left of her and he would not allow that spark to die. He found a negress for sale who had recently birthed a stillborn child. As much as he hated the idea of purchasing a human being, the idea of allowing the sickly boy to perish was beyond comprehension. The deal was made, the woman moved into a shack behind the cottage, refusing his entreaty to move inside. She and the mulatto would live out back and the 'master' would live as he should.

The child and his 'mother' lived well, out behind Thomas' cottage. He would stop by often to check on the child and assure himself that the woman was eating and taking care of both. She seemed content with her lot in life and he consoled himself with his caretaker position, it was the best he could do in a world he could not change.

He chafed at his own ignorance and naivete. How could he believe that two countries separated by a river and a lake, no matter how big that lake might be, would be any different from each other. They had sprung from the same stock; the only differences were a slight disparity in how they worshipped the same god and a president as opposed to a king. Weren't they in essence sides of the same coin?

Here Frenchmen had learned to tolerate the Englishmen and across their southern border the Englishman had learned the necessity of tolerating any other white man willing to endure the harsh and foreboding wilderness. It was an immense land, from what he had heard, filled with savage red men, untamed massive animals and dangers that required heathens to tame and open it up for the civilized. Bring on the immigrants. If you filled the land with enough of them, they would tame it, and if many died in the trying, so much the better.

That was the way of man; find those with brute force and want of riches, toss them and their savagery at those who may have wished to live in peace and grateful for what bounty they had. Allow the barbarians 'open up the land' for those who would follow to settle it into civility. It was mankind at his best or worst depending on which side of the line you stood.

Now all Thomas wanted was a little retribution for the price Roisin had paid for the white man's craving to be first among all those whom they considered lesser. Success would hopefully provide the salve. But success at what? That was the question.

It was a mid-spring day when he sauntered down to the docks, a place where he found solace, as it had been his home and salvation for most of his life, until now. From the moment he had hidden away on the 'Avenging Mother of The Sea' the open waters of sea and ocean became his home, now he wanted to feel the waves beneath his feet once again. Waves, on an ocean or a lake, the impetuous nature of water and wind, took one's mind away from anything that might ail.

Thomas saw the old man slouched against the bulkhead of a tall ship at dock. He looked done in by time, weather, and fortune, his worn stained linen shirt had patches, rips, and frayed tails, trousers of sailcloth that looked incapable of catching a breeze. He was a lifer of the water whose time was running low. Thomas felt a companionship immediately.

"Just in?" He prodded softly.

"About out," the words rode a soft lake breeze filled with a chill that could only be death taking up residence.

"The years eat away at the kindness the waves bestow, eh?" Thomas could not help but love the man. He was every true sailor's future.

"True enough, but they could allow me one last sally," he coughed and a spot of blood stained the front of his linen.

"No one willing to take a chance on a skilled mariner such as yerself?" Thomas meant it as a comfort but he could see the man took it as offense.

"Don't be mocking the ancient, boy, if yer blessed you'll find yerself in the same skiff," this time he spit the bloody phlegm with intent.

"Don't take offense, where none was tossed. I meant you respect not mocking." Thomas saw the ire die a slow smoldering death.

"Who's the captain here?" Change the line and keep the bait fresh.

"I be," he coughed a laugh, "Captain and owner." He coughed a few more chuckles, "A captain and owner without crew or cargo, so be off, sonny, and leave me be."

"This be your vessel?" Thomas found his mood lightening and his interest piqued.

"Ay, why ye care?"

"Might be interested in buying the derelict if you be interested in selling. That is, if she is still seaworthy," now Thomas smiled, the dickering could begin.

A gleam was born deep in the old man's eyes. Life was making a comeback. "Well, I got five more just like her, if yer carin' to be doin' some honest trading," Yeah, he was enjoying himself until a few of the roughnecks hanging about approached.

"Cap'n Meg, you aren't trying to hornswoggle this poor dumb Irishman into buying these floating caskets are ye?" They threw their mockery in his face.

Thomas felt his anger rise. He was a big man, big at the shoulder and towering over these miscreants and craving a row. "I think they would suit my needs just fine, what are ye asking?" He ignored the ignorant.

"You can't buy these ships!" The larger of the three stepped forward.

"And why not?" Thomas held his ground.

"We were waiting on the old codger to breathe his last and then we could pick them up for a pittance," he smiled a challenge.

"It would appear you have lost the waiting game as this man and I were just closing our deal for this ship and the rest." Thomas turned to face the captain, "Do we have a deal?" He knew they hadn't set a price and from the look on the captains face he didn't care anymore than Thomas did; the ships were his.

"One condition," serious as a hard wind out of the west.

"Name it."

"I come with ye and ye bury me on the lake as the only fitting place for a lake rider to die," he spit in his hand. Thomas countered in kind and the deal was done.

"I have coin," Thomas whispered, as the three realizing they'd lost this round skulked away, not wishing a confrontation with the large sailor.

"What good is coin to such as I?" Meg coughed again.

Thomas nodded. "Guess I need to collect a crew or six."

Thomas threw himself into learning the lakes all spring. Captain Meg lasted longer than either man thought he would, giving them time to get to know a fellow good man. Meg had sailed the Great Lakes since he was a boy of nine, signing on as a cabin boy. He had never sailed the great oceans, had never seen them and could not believe they were as magnificent as he had been told. 'Tall Tales,' he said. Thomas assured him they were not.

Thomas had to learn a whole new kind of sailing and knowledge of the great bodies of water. He had seen the lake freeze over his first winter here and found it amazing any body of water that large could freeze solid. Now he had to learn to read the weather with a quicker eye and mind. Where you had some days to read an ocean, you had hours to read the lakes. They could be glass one minute and turn into raging monsters within an hour. He had witnessed and fought forty- and fifty-foot waves on the ocean but the fifteen- or thirty-footers on the lake would be more likely to kill you.

He found men who were trustworthy, at least as long as there was good coin, food and drink. If you treated men well, they responded in a more positive and beneficial way than they would if they thought you didn't respect, care, or were trying to fuck them. He gave them respect, they answered in kind. His vessels soon became the desired fleet on the lakes.

The more his reputation grew the more the growing city wanted to honor him with awards and hopes of reciprocation. He refused all entreaties. They would never have his affection, his loyalty, his camaraderie. He never went out of his way to explain why, they knew. He held them completely, as a society and community, responsible for Roisin's death, for their treatment of the child—who would never be accepted by their racist society. Thomas may have begun his life with a racist bent but that was because his father and father's father were racist. They had been brought up and taught the same as he had, the difference was they had never had any need to change their minds. They had never had any interactions with people of different cultures, races, ideas. He had. And his mind had been malleable enough at his young age to observe and see the similarities rather than the need for someone to look down on and denigrate, just to make oneself feel one rung up on another.

He succeeded where others only existed. Sailors came to him seeking employ as they knew how Thomas lived his heart and values. It was the middle of August, they were easing into the end of the season—something else he had never encountered on the oceans, shipping seasons, but when the ice came you left—when Captain Meg called him to come to his cabin. He was wheezing and coughing so hard he could hardly get his words out.

"Well, the sonofabitch finally found me." He coughed out a stream of blood, "I run as hard as I could and was lucky enough to meet you, young Thomas. You've been a good man to me and treated me with a respect I never got before. I need one more favor from you and I'll move on." Wheezing and coughing wracked his body.

"You know anything you ask with be granted. You gave me this life, these lakes, and much knowledge. Ask, my friend," Thomas took a deep breath to force his emotions back down. He had come to love and esteem the old man.

"I'll be gone soon, don't take me back to the land. I'm a sailor, give me a proper sailor's death and burial at sea," He had never been to sea but he had heard there were formalities of burial at sea, it sounded like a perfect way for a man to leave this life.

"I would be proud and honored to give you this gift." And the deal was done.

A brief thunderstorm pushed through as they made their way from Georgian Bay south toward Detroit City. Storms on the lake could be devastating or beautiful, capturing nature at her best. A small chop rocked the ship, laden with lumber, making its way through the Great Lakes to the shipyards on the upper Ontario by Kingston. They would sail down to where Lake Erie could take them east and the Welland Canal which would take them into Lake Ontario. The thunder clouds were dark black on their crests but illuminated brilliant yellows and reds by the setting sun. The beauty and majesty of these lakes never ceased to amaze the young Irishman. They weren't the ocean; but they had their own magnificence.

Meg took his last breath as the sun sank below the horizon. It was as if they both were extinguished simultaneously. The lake settled into a gentle rock as if giving comfort to the saddened crew. They wrapped Meg in sailcloth, the finest they had on board—Thomas would replace it when they returned home, a small price for such a good man—and hoisted him on their shoulders while singing 'The Sea Captain'. At the rail they held him high so the gods of the lake could see who they would hold in their hearts.

Thomas read from Revelations.

- "And the sea gave up the dead who were in it, and Death and Hades gave up the dead who were in them, and they were judged, each one of them, according to what they had done" And here we commit to the sea a good man who will be judged accordingly and found decent and beyond reproach.

And with that they slid Meg into Lake Huron to his final resting place. They each took a swallow from a rum bottle before pouring the rest into the lake for their Captain and friend. They would ride where the lake and breeze took them for the night. It was a pleasant evening with the wind coming out of the northwest but without chill or threat. Let the men have a night to see how respectful sailors honored the dead.

The rest of the journey back to the loneliness of Kingston only reinforced how isolated Thomas was from the rest of mankind. He was at home on the waves but could never be brothers with those who had taken his Roisin from him. The grief had taken up residence in his heart and soul and would not be moved. Even though those who crewed with him weren't personally accountable, they were born and raised by those he held guilty. They were good men and crew but carried the sins of their fathers.

Thomas was one of the very few, if not the only captain and shipper who employed both white men and dark. He had seen what hate did to men's souls and what hope did to men's spirits. He thought if he could force the two together it might equal out to humanity. The mountain was steep and appeared impossible to climb, but he had witnessed men forced together by circumstance come together in fellowship on the high seas, why not on the Great Lakes.

Cracks formed in the fortress of hate as men brought up to consider those of darker skin to be less than human, began to see how freemen of any color could rise to heights when allowed. The negroes Thomas brought on ship were escaped slaves from the southern United States seeking freedom and a chance. Once given that chance they would prove themselves worthy over and over while earning the respect, though sometimes begrudgingly, of their fellow sailors. Unfortunately, that did not translate to the townsfolk once on shore.

He could not change the world and he was tiring of being alone. He sat on the front porch of his stately Victorian home.

He had upgraded his living quarters not so much for himself but so Sofie, the boys milk mother and caretaker, would move out the shack she insisted on living in and into the main home. He wanted the boy to be taken care of like a white man, not like how they were forced to raise mulattos. They lived a solitary existence, the child, his caretaker, and Thomas. His obvious animosity towards the citizens of Kingston assuring the distance would never close. He cared not.

She showed up as he was lost in his thoughts. He hadn't noticed her coming up the front steps and standing directly in front of him. The day filled with the bright sunshine and cool temperatures of early spring, the receding scent of winter catching a slight breeze, and a flowered scent riding that breeze from the woman. He snapped out of his reverie to take in the stunning, young woman who silently regarded him.

Her hair was dark, her eyes green, her figure slim and well suited to the loose, well-tailored blouse and skirt, sans cage crinoline so it hung loose rather than taking up as much space as three human beings. Out of fashion it may have been, Thomas thought, the simple skirt was far more practical and less cumbersome, and therefore his opinion of this lovely young girl was of an intelligent, rational person.

"I am collecting to help build a Magdalene Asylum and orphanage, widows and mothers left bereft with children once a husband leaves her either by choice or death. I thought you might be interested in contributing." She stood; hands clasped at her waist as if expecting him to attack her for asking.

Thomas studied the girl, no, young woman, he corrected. He would've loved to lash out and would have had it been one of the busybodies who spent their days judging and condemning others they considered lesser than themselves. Then would go out to prove their piousness by doing deeds that their neighbors could only perceive as godly.

"And why would you assume that?" He asked pleasantly enough.

"Because you have suffered at the injustice and vitriol of others, and yet stood strong, spit in their faces. I thought you might wish to help those deemed lesser than," she stood her ground.

"Who are you, girl? I haven't seen you about the town and by your tongue you are not long here. Where be ye from?" His own brough slipped in and out as he traded with her.

"Mary Haggerty, from County Galway." She answered simply.

"Well, Mary Haggerty, from County Galway, how is it you know so much about me?" His interest was piqued in several areas of inquiry.

"I asked why a man such as yerself would be living all alone when he obviously has so much to attract a mate." She blushed, but only slightly.

"So, Mary Haggerty from County Galway is it a donation ye seek or is it a mate?" Now he smiled openly to take any offense from the words.

"For now, a donation will do just fine." And she grinned back at him.

He liked this girl, she carried not a whiff of sin upon her perfect self. They were married a month later, Yes, she was young for him, eight years his junior but at twenty-two years of age she was close to spinsterhood. She and her pa had emigrated from Galway in the fall which would explain how he'd never seen nor run into her before. He never would've known her with her bundled as completely as one needed in the Canadian winter.

There was a purity about her, unspoiled by the generations of seeking someone to dominate to make one feel better about oneself. She had no need to feel superior, only needed. Those green eyes would hold him as surely as the sea had. He knew he could lose himself forever just being in her presence.

He didn't know much about the westerners, as those from Dublin considered their kin on the cliffs of the Atlantic. They might as well have been from another country. They were considered country bumpkins to the sophisticated in the grand city of Dublin. She wasn't unsophisticated, she was honest and open, caring and giving, she had given him hope for a future.

She never questioned his loyalty or obvious love of the boy. A child in whom she could see Thomas even though he could not or would not see for himself. When she tried to bring up his evident paternal lineage to him, he would explain the impossibility of such a theory as he had never had sex with Roisin. He was her protector not someone who might ravage her. Though he could not erase the memory of his dreams about her, but dreams were dreams, not actions.

She patiently and lovingly explained she meant nothing by pointing out the striking resemblance. She did not accuse him of taking advantage of, nor attacking, his protégé, only what the evidence proved. She was as taken by the child as Thomas, it mattered not the parentage, only the child. She would love the child as her own.

As Mary and he sat in the formal dining room enjoying a glass of after dinner wine, a kind he had acquired a taste for called Ice wine, discussing the day's pursuits, the sound of a crash and breaking glass broke the serenity. Thomas jumped up from his chair and ran to the back of the house where the boy and his adopted mother ate their dinner. He had tried and tried to get her to eat at the table with them but she refused explaining if the town folk found out they would make her life a living hell.

She held the small child in her lap, covering him with her arms and protecting him in case another attack might come. Thomas ran to the window to see the mob milling out back.

They passed bottles to reinforce their courage. That would explain the broken bottle the lay at his feet and was the apparent cause of the crash and broken glass.

Thomas was not a man of violence until forced. He grabbed his rifle from above the door and stepped out on the back porch. They stood in a cluster about twenty yards from his home. Thomas knew they would have weapons of their own and he was in all likelihood going to die, though he would die protecting his home and those he loved.

He leveled the rifle at the heart of the group. He was a big man, easily as tall as Thomas himself, though not quite as broad at the shoulder, still he looked as though he outweighed Thomas by a good two stone. Thomas cared not, he had fought bigger men for far less.

"One step and one will die," he pointed the weapon menacingly at the big man.

"You'd kill a white man to protect them nig…," the word never found its other half as Thomas took the man in the shoulder.

He quickly reloaded the rifle while the mob stood stunned by his action. "Anyone else have an opinion on how I run my house?"

"It ain't right," came a voice that wanted so badly to be brave yet hid that bravado behind a tremor and the bodies of others. "ain't supposed to treat them like one of us." He completed his ignorance.

"You're right," Thomas shouted, "they are far better than any man jack of ya. And if you think to enter my home and bring violence upon them, Ye might want to pray to god afore you do, as you will be in his presence before you take one step into my home."

He felt a presence at his back though didn't wish to turn around to see who it might be. He felt the hard steel of his cutlass being placed in his hand. He held up both sword and rifle in challenge. "Any man who threatens me or mine will find himself waking up in hell. Now, leave my property before I run a few of you through just for the practice." They stood and stared; he took a step towards them with his cutlass waving ominously. "Git now or die!" another step and the mob lost what little fortitude the drink had bought.

As they meandered toward the center of town one man found a kernel of boldness as he turned and glared at Thomas, "ye can't be there every minute of every day." A malicious grin split his face as he turned and joined the others.

Back inside he found that Mary had taken the child and his 'mother' into the cellar and locked the door, bolting it from the inside and placing what she could against it. Thomas banged hard and hollered his name. He heard the tentative steps on the stairs as the three made their way to him.

"We have to leave!" Mary wept into this shoulder.

"I'll not be chased from my own home!" Thomas' rage continued to seethe.

"As long as we stay their lives are in danger." Mary was making it clear she feared not for her and Thomas but the child and his protector.

"Aye, let's clean up the mess and then allow me to give thought of what we should do," he nodded ending any further discussion.

Thomas did not sleep that night. He tossed and turned in the large bed he and Mary shared, until he gave up and went downstairs to pace and think. The bruises under his eyes lay testament to his lack of sleep.

After breaking the night's fast he strapped on his cutlass and without a word stepped into the morning sun. He required movement, to walk, to stimulate the brain, to work out a course of action. Several of his biggest and most trusted crew had apparently heard rumor and stood guard on his front porch. He guessed there were several more posted around the house. Wordlessly he nodded his thanks and stepped out for a morning constitutional.

He knew he couldn't continue living the way they had, that had been made abundantly clear. He should pack his family and leave this godforsaken town. And yet, this was his last connection, his last memory, his final moment with Roisin, he would not be chased from what they had done to her by their refusal to help.

It was down by the docks that he ran into an old crewman lounging, wasting time. He was an older man, no one would bring him on to crew, yet he showed up every morning in hope. He greeted Thomas as the two passed like ships coming into and sailing out of port.

"Ye look perplexed," tossed the old man in Thomas' direction.

Thomas raised his gaze from the wood planks he'd been counting and smiled at the elderly sailor. He stopped and stared hard out across the lake. Without thinking he unloaded his burden to a confessor he believed would take his words to the grave.

"Tis a tricky knot ye wish to solve." Said the ancient mariner. "Ye know, there are places where ye could send the boy and the woman where they might have a new beginning amongst their own."

"I love the child; I have no desire to disinherit him or the woman. Yet I cannot in good conscience keep them here where threat hangs over their heads like the sword of Damocles. There are no good solutions. I cannot leave my memories; I cannot endanger their lives." Thomas hung his head shamed he could not find a solution that would pacify his conscience.

"What if ye could send the boy and woman away where they'd be safe and ye could support them. They'd be protected from the hate. You could send them a stipend to assure their well-being. Would that do yer heart some good?" The old man grinned hope.

"Is there such a place?"

"I know of one west o' here over by Detroit. If'n you want to trust a man, I believe I could sail my skiff with them aboard and find that place."

Thomas was not in a trusting mood, but he had sailed with this crewman once or twice and though not close to the man knew him to be a good sailor, and that was a good a recommendation as he could ask. It would break his heart to send the child away, but not as much as it would break his soul if harm came.

It was Thomas who would never forgive himself if harm came to Roisin's child. He had promised her on her death bed to watch over the boy. This may not be the best solution, but it was the only one. He would never forget the mother. After several weeks of dancing, he came to the conclusion it would serve all best if he sent the milk mother and child away. He would support them in a comfortable lifestyle but would have no contact with either. They would be sent to Amherstburg, Ontario, four hundred miles to the west and a 'Black Town'. They would not face hostility or hate among their own. She might even find a mate and find some joy in life..

Mary Haggerty was a strong-willed woman and did not agree with her husband though she loved him dearly and knew he suffered greatly at his own decision. She agreed to the arrangement as she had no other choice but she would secretly communicate with the 'mother' and child for years.

Once the child and his caretaker were sent away the rest of Kingston attempted to warm relations again with Thomas and his new wife, thinking the child had been the wedge. They could not have been more wrong in their assessment. Sending the child away to possibly have a better life where it would face less hate and resistance only solidified Thomas' resentment of the town and her people. The fact they made overt attempts to win him over only deepened his animosity. He found he missed the child, but what was done was done.

Mary satisfied herself with her small circle of friends from before their marriage and her family. She had never made friends easily, as she had been as rigid in her views and values as Thomas. They did not suffer fools or bigots. Both had come from generations of those who found it necessary to belittle, look down on and hate on others in order to make themselves feel superior. Both had rebelled, both were quite comfortable with a bohemian life.

Katherine Ann McDermitt was born in the spring of the following year. She was the light of their lives. Both parents doted on her as the bringer of joy in their household. Thomas found he loathed going off to voyage with his two girls at home. They tugged at his heart every second of each day on the lakes. Where once he had found consolation on the deck of a ship, he now wandered, lost and alone. It was time to find his land legs permanently.

He had arrived back home on the evening of Katherine's first birthday just in time for a small gathering of close friends and family. They would celebrate the occasion as befitted the child of a prominent, wealthy, successful businessman in a growing town on the conquered frontier of Canada. Cakes, cookies, and presents, and a letter from overseas.

It would appear his success had not been confined to the lakes of America, people in his homeland had heard, even his father. The letter was from an associate of his father's letting him know his parents had both passed on. His mother several years previous and his father a few months back. This man wanted Thomas to know his father spoke highly of him and his dream. He may not have appreciated the course Thomas had taken to fulfill that dream but he had to be impressed by the results. There was no inheritance though there was a question.

Would he be willing to take on a partnership or consider selling his ships to an old countryman?

He showed the letter to Mary who only sighed. She wondered if his great love was taken away or sold, what would he do? She feared without his time on the water his anger at the town would manifest in other more destructive ways. She loved the man, she knew he was kind, loving, and tender but she also knew he could hold onto a grudge like a spar used as a life raft in the middle of the ocean.

"I am tired," he said to her silence, "I have been sailing more than half my life. These waters, all the oceans and lakes, take the life out of a man. Every muscle and joint aches, my back is bowed and my mind is weary. Maybe a change would do us good. Katherine could have a full-time father to teach her what you can't. We could be together instead of always sailing past. We don't have to decide right this minute but I think it deserves our consideration." He kissed her forehead before going out the front door to sit on their expansive front porch and smoke his pipe.

It took a year to complete the details of the sale. He wanted one more excursion with his crew to Georgian Bay and back. They would take Katherine's Wave, leaving the other five ships in dock for inspection and completion of the sale.

He would only be gone a few weeks and it would allow him to say farewell to his crew, his ships, and his life on the waves. There was sadness in his heart as they set sail, yet also a sense of excitement. It was the beginning of a new life, new discoveries, more children, and a house filled with love. He would not be his father. He would never demand his children do his bidding. He had made a fortune and they would be privileged to live the lives they chose. They would not be forced to work hard at physical labor or wonder where their next meal would come from. They could live lives dedicated to learning, music, the arts, whatever they wished. Yes, it was with hope, joy, and excitement for the future that they sailed out of Kingston heading west across the Great Lake Ontario.

A Stroll Through The Past with Stumbles Present Day

She had begun with old soul music from the sixties, something she thought he might have been exposed to by his parents or older friends. It was planting a flag in a barren land. The most important aspect of old soul, Motown, was that it appealed, literally, to just about everyone. You didn't have to be black to groove to Marvin Gaye. You didn't have to be a woman to sing R-E-S-P-E-C-T. You didn't have to be a musician or singer to appreciate Smokey Robinson, or The Temptations, Four Tops, Tammy Terrel, Gladys Knight, or Stevie Wonder. It hit you in the feels, it made you swoon with the tune, it made you want to dance even if you didn't know a step. It touched the soul, hence the name.

Tom had never really paid attention to dance music as he had never gone to dances. He was clumsy, nerdy, a bit paunchy, even as a child, and there was no reason to go somewhere where all those lacks would shine like a blinding light. He and Chester would hang out together playing mind games or reading deep Sci-fi. He stopped his thoughts; when was the last time he had really enjoyed a book? Not a science and technology tome, but one just for the fun of the story. Maybe when he was still in elementary school. Those few years before his genius changed everyone's perception of him and what he 'should' be doing with all that grey matter.

He listened intently to the Marvin Gaye album, 'What's Going On', and was impressed that conflicts, dealing with hate and inequality, the harsh realities of black life, the lack of opportunities, war, and death could inspire such magnificent music. Suffering and pain brought beauty and want. Need inspired true majesty and brilliance, not bubble-gum teen angst or love, but truth and exposing these inequities to the light of day by putting the words to music that drew the listener in. Music truly had charm to soothe or inspire the savage beast. He wanted more.

She brought him symphonies by Beethoven, Mozart, Shostakovich, Brahms, Mussorgsky, that without one word spoken or sung filled his head with stories and tales from centuries before. She brought opera and tried to force it down his parched throat, but this was his line in the sand. It was screeching and wailing and in languages he no longer had any desire to master. Taste, it came down to taste and this was not his.

Miles, Trane, Monk, Holiday, Bird, Mingus, Simone, Max Roach and Sonny Rollins, Chic Corea, and Herbie Hancock, oh my, how they filled his head and lifted his soul to heights never before experienced. He wanted to hear this live, not just on vinyl. So, she took him to concerts and jazz clubs- tiny, dark, nightclubs where the music filled every nook and cranny and the people listened with intent. It was marvelous.

The weeks passed in museums; modern art and the masters called to him. How had he missed all of this? He wanted it never to end. Aoife told him of the masterpieces hanging in Paris, Amsterdam, Vienna, and Florence. And explained that he now had the wherewithal to see them all. And the time. He wanted to share them with Aoife, though deep in the back of his reasoning, exceptional brain he knew he was nurturing childish fantasies. A preteen that never knew what it was like to have a girlfriend, a rotund teenager spurned by any girl he talked to as unacceptable, now attending concerts and museums with the most stunning, yes, that word again, impressive woman he had ever come across, and in the back of this logical, analytical mind he hoped she liked him. Dumb sap.

Though she appeared interested in his thoughts, his growth as a cultured individual, his complete assimilation into music, art, and philosophy, she certainly didn't seem interested in any romance or relationship. Why would she groom him like this if not because she saw something far deeper in him than he did himself?

Insecurity check! Because she didn't want to be associated with a shallow, ignorant, slob who just happened to be brilliant in one area. He was an idiot savant! But was that true? It's not that he couldn't understand or feel, have his soul touched by these great works, he had never been exposed in a way that opened his mind and heart to them. She was prying open a very tightly sealed can. Maybe she really did just want him to be 'well-rounded' mentally, spiritually, and artistically; not just physically.

And that was another thing, while they had been traipsing around to all of these finer things, walking miles a day sometimes, he had been losing weight and inches. Not so any stranger might notice the difference, but he did. He felt more buoyant, energetic, and healthy. His shoulder hardly bothered him and much of his previous pain was dissipating with the addition of vitamin D and walks in the sunlight. He had been almost a hermit most of his life, confined to artificial light and four walls filled with computer screens and not much else. His kingdom had grown by leaps and bounds.

Still, he had to check his new-found confidence at the door when it came to Aoife. She filled him so she wouldn't be partnered with a buffoon, that was all. While she was building her business with what he had created, she didn't want to always have to explain to him what life was. She was kind, she was patient, but in the end, she was also concerned with her own well-being and mental state. He should put fantasies on hold and just enjoy her companionship.

Besides, the first order of his own business was to discover his past. He craved the knowing of where he had come from. Who he was. Everyone needed to know their origin. He would concentrate on that.

He brought it up to her on their next outing.

"When do you think I can begin to spend some time in familial archeology?" He broached the subject over a particularly marvelous rendition of Augusta Savage's, 'Lift Every Voice and Sing', recreated by a local artist for an exhibition of African American Artists at the Art Institute of Chicago. It was a marvelous piece and it caught him off guard by how it moved him. This is what Aoife had spoken of so many times, when a piece of music, a painting, or, in this case, a sculpture dove deeply into the soul. He had been staring at it when she touched his shoulder and asked if he was alright.

"Why?" it was a whisper.

"You're crying," not accusation or attempt at shaming, more a pride that was palpable.

"I'm sorry," he began to push the words through his lips then stopped. He wasn't sorry in the least and he would not apologize for his honest reaction to this magnificent piece of humanity.

Aoife nodded as she stood silently by his side. She would say nothing more as she had no desire to shatter this moment.

They stood there for an hour or a few minutes or a week, time lost meaning, he was lost on a sea of beauty and import.

"I want to see the actual Augusta Savage piece, is it still on exhibit somewhere?" He closed his eyes in supplication.

"I believe it is. We'll look it up and go there." She spoke the promise.

"I think I need to get back to my original journey and find myself," it was an oath to himself. He loved what she did for him but it was time for him to get back to doing for himself. "Where do I begin?"

"Where you ended up," she grinned, "at the keyboard. Let's find a place for a cup of coffee or tea and open up our laptops. As you know, that is where most of the knowledge of the world resides!" That tinkle of laughter that lifted his heart and hopes rang out in the cavernous, marble space.

Alone, once again, in his condo, Tom was taken aback at the resources available to those with African heritages. Aoife had jump started his curiosity and shown him where to begin before leaving him to his personal search. He spent the first hours alone digging through centuries old records of slave owners and their 'property'. He guessed he had never had much reason to think about, or the curiosity if he was honest, to dig into the country's past. The fact that many of these former 'owners' would catalogue human beings with their cattle, goats, acres of land and other possessions tore at his soul in a way counter to how music and art had lifted it. It made him sick to his stomach. It was so cold, so emotionless, there was no feeling of care, love, or difference in a goat or man. To be honest it seemed these monsters were more concerned with the loss of a cow or bull than the loss of a human being. He wanted to strike out at someone, anyone, but who? He was a century and a half too late.

How had these enslaved people survived? The conditions were horrid. Their children bought, sold, and raped. Their wives bought, sold, and raped. The men beaten, whipped, and mutilated, worked, literally, to death. Tom wanted nothing more than to close the site, turn off the computer, and go on a rampage. That was not why he had opened this pandora's box, he had come to learn. To learn of his people, of their history, of their survival so he could be sitting in an expensive condominium drinking a glass of very expensive Napa wine and be exposed to that horror.

The strength of the slaves, these people ripped from their homeland and shipped in atrocious, unspeakable conditions, many dying as they crossed the ocean in the belly of the beast, only to be treated as less than chattel, amazed and inspired him. Yet survive they did, fighting to keep as many of their traditions and memories alive as they could through stories and songs across the decades of a 'master race's' attempt to breed, beat, and whip those precious pieces of their past out of them.

They continued to have their children knowing they would suffer as the parents, grandparents, great grandparents for generations had in the slim hope this would all end some day and they would find freedom and better lives.

They had, for one brief moment in history found some glimmer of that hope realized only to have the hatred, fear, and viciousness of the white man come down on them in the form of Jim Crow laws; the laws that again showed the savagery and cruelty of limiting rights and enforcing segregation. They had never met this 'Jim Crow', but they knew they hated the man.

Tom had to find a way to focus on his narrow search or he would lose his mind. It was one thing to 'know' these things had happened. It was quite another to be submerged in the vile, putrid, scum of immersion, knowing it was your forebearers who had lived it. He wanted to find these people in his past and thank them. He wanted to kneel on their graves and weep for their sacrifice; to let them know it had all not been in vain. He was too late to the table to serve his feast of gratitude. Still, if he could find his ancestors and learn of them, he could keep them alive in his life, let them know they had succeeded though it had taken more than a hundred years to do so.

And then it hit him. Had they really? Hadn't he, a successful, free, paragon of his race been shot for the sin of his skin? If he had been of the 'master race' wouldn't the cop have given him a ride home in the rain and stayed outside until Tom was inside to assure that he got home safe? Not shot him through the shoulder for the crime of Sashimi. Yes, they had made progress, but racism had not been bred out of white culture. Maybe it was too ingrained to ever be.

Tom shut those ideas from his mind. He couldn't change the present by living in the past. He had to find that nub of beginning and follow it through the decades to find what his part in this ancient play would be.

He clicked open the Federal Slaves Census Schedules to begin where he thought his people would be, 1850-1860. It was nearing the end of slave ships and human bondage. There may have been a story or a folk tale from when he was a very young boy that his gran had spoken of their coming to the new world around that time. Though he couldn't say for sure and there was no one he could ask, just a spark of memory sitting in an aroma filled kitchen and old people drinking wine, laughing, and believing things could change. Something bubbled on the stove, greens, he thought, while biscuits baked in the oven next to a pan of ham hocks and beans, grits would almost be done, that's what was boiling, he thought.

He fastidiously searched through the records trying to find any mention of the family name but came up empty handed. Maybe he was doing this wrong. What process did Henry Louis Gates, Jr. use on Finding Your Roots? He began at the end of the line, the person seeking information, and worked his way back. Well, if that was the way the professor went about it, Tom, the novice, should incorporate the same process.

He closed out the slave pages and shut down the computer. If he was going in search of, he wanted to do it with a clear mind. He wished Aoife were here. He wanted to bounce ideas off her. She had an analytical mind, much like his own, and he felt between the two of them they could plan a clear course of action.

He missed her. They hadn't spoken in more than a week and though he had led a monkish existence before her arrival he found he now missed the companionship. He missed the conversation, the learning, the laughter they shared. He discovered he no longer wished to be estranged from humanity. Well, to be honest, he could do without most, but he found there was much to be gained by exposure to the rest. One in particular. Sigh.

Focus, son, focus. Maybe a nap would be the best course of inaction at the moment, then start fresh this evening.

He woke slowly, groggily, something had roused him and he wanted nothing more than to return to the dream he'd been walking through. He couldn't remember exactly what it was. He knew he had been speaking to his parents about something important. He thought he might have been catching them up on his life since they had passed. The sadness threatened to overwhelm him. They had been gone almost two decades and yet when he thought of them, remembered them, it was as fresh as this evening though filled with remorse and loneliness. Every time this happened it only reinforced how lonely he was. Just him and his code written across blank screens.

Mingus played in the background. He didn't remember having music on when he fell asleep though his thoughts were fuzzy. And then the music stopped. He thought it was 'Reincarnation of a Lovebird' though he couldn't be certain, she had only exposed him to Mingus just a few short weeks ago. He'd learn the more he listened.

No, it was the buzzer announcing an unwelcome guest at the front door. Someone's timing sucked. He tried to ignore the buzz, buzz, buzz but the insistence wouldn't allow him to block it out. Sigh. He pulled on a pair of sweats and an old well-worn sweatshirt from his college days. How the hell it still fit he would never understand though he was a big man in college and still carried some of the weight.

He opened the door to her smiling face.

"Woke you again?" It was an apology without saying so. "My timing sucks, sorry." There it was.

"I'm so very glad to see you." He attempted to make it a light greeting but his need stuck its clingy, insecure face around the corner. Ah, well.

"I thought I should check in and see how goes the search and if I could be of any help," she stepped inside the condo without the aid of an invitation.

"Sorry, I should have asked you in," he blushed at his faux paus. "Would you like a glass of wine? Water? A sandwich?" He rummaged through his memory of what might be available in the kitchen and hoped he wasn't offering things he had no access to.

"White wine would be nice if you have a bottle open," she made her way into the kitchen to help herself. In her family once you have been to someone's home you were no longer a guest but a part of the family and did not expect others to wait on you!

"How's it going?" She asked from the kitchen as she poured them both a glass.

"Frustrating and infuriating." He answered, nodding his thanks as she handed him his glass. "How could I have lived forty-four years and not known how my people had been treated for centuries?" He gave himself a quick slap to the temple for his own ignorance. "I mean, I knew that slavery had happened, Jim Crow laws, but had never cared enough to delve into the horror, the dehumanizing aspect of all the wrongs done. Redling, Tulsa, Rosewood, Colfax, and dozens of other atrocities. I had to stop searching from the beginning, as all I found was hate. And, I began to obsess." He sighed his remorse for awakening an emotion he hadn't known he possessed. "So, I thought I should do what Henry Louis Gates Jr. does and start from the other end of the line and work my way back."

"Good plan," She grinned.

"The problem is, I can only go back two generations as that is all I know about. That was when I decided it was time to turn off the machine and try to rest and begin again fresh," he tipped his glass to signify the end of his synopsis.

"And here I am disturbing the flow of energy. Maybe I should leave you alone. Unless you would like a little assist." She tiled her head slightly in a way that magnified her beauty tenfold.

Damn, he wanted nothing more than for them to work together. Her strengthening his weak points and exponentially increasing his own abilities. Hell, he wanted to spend the rest of his life with this woman. It was then he realized that might be possible, as long as he never told her, showed her, exposed how he felt about her. If they remained friends, and only friends, well, and associates, he felt they could share that life and he would have to take what joy was offered.

"I'd like that." He tossed a sheepish grin her way before taking a sip of wine.

"Good, because I have some ideas on where to go from your dead end." She pulled out her own laptop and opened it after setting it on the coffee table between them.

Tom got up to retrieve his laptop from the dining room table where he did most of his work. As a bachelor with no social life, he had no need to have a dedicated work room or office. He enjoyed the large windows of his French doors leading out to a small patio. He could watch the world go by, kids playing, lovers walking arm in arm, the yelling of conversations between residents of his condominium community and passersby on the streets, he almost felt part of society.

He came back to the loveseat across from the couch where she sat and told her the sites he'd been using and where he thought they should begin again. She suggested they try the Afro-American Historical and Genealogical Society as a starting point which disseminated information and had tools for research that would be helpful.

Tom was impressed she knew about the site and, it would seem, many others. She had done her research about research. Why would a white woman know so much about researching black genealogy? The question was, was she even of all European heritage. She had an Irish name, but she had the eyes of an Asian, which many Black folk did as well, and though she had the green eyes and dark hair of the Emerald Isle, she had darker skin than one would expect from someone from that region of the world. She was an enigma he would probably never truly understand but was happy to have the chance and, hopefully, the time to try.

The Lakes Giveth, Take Away, and Giveth More

1865

It was early spring though the weather continued chilly as they sailed across Lake Ontario towards the Welland Canal and Lake Erie. Though a brisk wind came at them from the North-Northwest they were able to make decent time tacking across the Great Lake. By the time they reached Erie the weather had begun to turn warmer buoying the spirits of crew and captain. It would be a good final voyage. They'd had to wait for the war with the south to find a solution. Thomas wanted to sail right away thinking the atrocities would remain far south of them but Mary had begged him to wait not wishing him to find himself embroiled in others struggles. Thomas and the buyer agreed on the sale and allowing Thomas his final fare-thee-well.

Erie was accommodating, not smooth as glass but not rolling as she had a tendency to do when the winds played with her shallow depths. That was and had always been the threat of the shallowest of the Great Lakes, she could be calm and welcoming one hour and kick up like an angered woman the next. It didn't take much to anger this lake, it was almost as if she was waiting for someone or some ship to cross her just wrong and she'd make them pay a very substantial price. Today she smiled with warm spring sunshine on her back.

They kept to the north of the line denoting the United States from Canada as the great war between the states had wound down only months before and Thomas wished to keep himself and his crew out of the midst of any renewed flare up. He was glad the northerners had stood up to the slave owners in the south and had defeated them handily though at the cost of tens of thousands of lives lost and many, many more maimed for life. But Lincoln had Emancipated the slaves and they were to be free men and women from this point on. Thomas had his doubts, you couldn't force people to forego the hatred and attitudes of centuries in such a short time. He felt a pang of guilt and shame when he thought of how he'd sent the boy and his milk mother away, though he'd done more than any he knew would have done. Still, it rankled him and haunted his sleep. He had no desire to fight the Americans or to treat much more than he was forced to do.

These were the thoughts that occupied his mind as they closed in on Detroit where they would tack north into mighty Lake Huron and make their way towards the Georgian Bay. One more cargo of lumber and minerals. It would be a good payday when they returned to Kingston, the men didn't know it but they would all receive a very healthy bonus. Thomas smiled, it would be a proper sendoff for a crew that had been loyal, hardworking, and close to his heart. There was that pang again; it would subside with time.

The crew was in a jovial mood as they docked in the Collingwood shipyard. It would take several days to secure and load their cargo. So, time in a frontier town with frontier women and drink would be very welcome after crossing three of the five Great Lakes. Even with the weather in their favor they had spent almost two weeks on the water. Even the finest of sailing men required solid land from time to time.

Thomas found the discrepancies between saltwater sailors and fresh water to be laughable. He loved this crew, they were good, solid, hardworking men, but they had no idea what real sailors had to endure. When he was a saltwater man, he would be months on the oceans with little time on an island or port. They circumnavigated the earth a dozen times, each with its own terrors, dangers, and beauty. Hurricanes, typhoons, enormous waves thirty meters high with no land in sight and their only hope tacking directly into the leviathan praying to every god that might be available and some they may have invented on the spot.

Then there were the times they were stuck in the doldrums with little food or water for weeks or months at a time; death just over the rail. Hallucinations would come with dehydration and hunger. Many a good man succumbed to the hopelessness and mental degradation of the doldrums.

Add that there were the thousands of islands placed helter skelter across the globe where no white man had ever set foot, some friendly beyond measure, some measured you for the cookpot, some were uncertain what the best course of action might be.

Thomas felt the pull of regret on his heart, he loved sailing. He had since he'd fallen into it as a stowaway so many years before. He also knew it was time to move on. Life was about change not stasis. He had survived horrors unimaginable and known the camaraderie of true brothers. He would now know family and friend, the joy of everyman. He might feel the tug at times in his life and if he did, he could borrow or buy a good skiff and spend some days on the rolling waves of Ontario. He'd soothe the savage with a romp across the choppy, white caps of home.

And that brought another question to the fore, 'where would home be?'. He had spent years in Kingston but had never forgiven them their racist hatred of his beloved ward. He blamed himself, he should have left her on her island, at least that was a hate and ignominy she had known how to deal with. He had brought her here thinking he could improve her life and only brought her to a cold, lonely death. He would do better by his own get.

There was a feel around the house before he set sail, an anticipation he felt that might mean another child on the way. He hoped it would be a son. Every father wanted a son to carry his name. That was immortality. To carry your forebearers into the future. He became anxious to complete the buying and loading so as to begin the homeward journey into a new life.

He found himself being short with the men as the stevedores took their time moving, tying down and hoisting the lumber into the hold. He knew his men could only work as fast as the dockworkers brought the cargo to ship's side but he found himself pushing to get underway. The men could feel his anxiety, though none could understand. Sailors were not known as good family men. Most, if they had wife and get, were not around enough to make much of an impression and were usually running full sail even while the ship was docked. They did not, for the most part, take well to home life. They felt landlocked and adrift at the same time, wanting to be good mates but needing to be free on the waves. Thomas wanted to be home.

At long last they lowered the dinghies over the port side to bring 'Katherine's Wave' about and headed toward home. They would row the big ship well away from the dock before letting go lines and rowing back to the Katherine. The morning sun shone bright and promised an uneventful passage home. She sat low in the water with a cargo of lumber and minerals but not low enough to be trouble. Though she would be pig with light wind. The hope was for a steady westerly to northwesterly to push them south towards Erie.

On the third day they finally crept their way down the St. Clair River to Lake St. Clair which had taken them longer than they wished to reach the Detroit River and into Lake Erie. Thomas considered mooring in the channel until daybreak but he wished to get home and they'd made this journey a hundred times. They would sail through the night. The night showed no sign of storm or change and they were downwind. He would trim the sails and keep an eye to the west.

His first mate, a Lieutenant Merritt took first watch hoping Thomas would sleep until three bells. He needed the rest and Merritt enjoyed the time alone. He was a solitary man which was why he had taken to sailing back as a boy. He loved nights alone on the lakes and would have his way as most of the crew would be below catching what sleep they could and it would be just him, the helmsman, and a few crew ghosting about the ship's deck. Fog had moved in and set up as the air temperature dropped below the temperature of the lake. It wasn't thick enough to be a concern but the haze impeded his view of the western night sky, though he could make out the brightest of the stars and the weather remained pleasant.

Thomas relieved him at six bells. The crew had decided he required rest and though he would've loved to ream them from top to bottom he could not argue he felt rested and ready for the new day. Or so he thought. The light fog had remained throughout the night and was only beginning to dissipate with the coming morning. Thomas noted that to the east the sky was red, deep red. He stepped over to where the barometer was floating on its gimbles and noted the drop in pressure from the last reading two hours previous. It was not a slight drop but a precipitous one, storms were closing in. As if to highlight that fact several flashes of lightning exploded in the sky very quickly followed by cracks and peals of thunder right on their heels.

Storms were not coming; they were here and from the sound of it they were near on top of them. Thomas screamed the order to batten down everything not already tied. He had to scream to be heard over the resounding thunder. Men scurried about the ship tying down or tossing below anything that might become a weapon in a howling wind, which was increasing by the moment. The lake, apparently angered by the sudden awakening roared to life as waves began to crash hard against the port side of the Katherine.

Thomas yelled for all on deck to tie themselves to lifelines and brace for the raging thunderstorm. Normally there would be no worry when a storm kicked up on the lake but some, and this appeared to be one of them, could be monsters that would sink a ship and take her crew within minutes. Thomas was not about to let that happen. He took the helm and fought the swirling white caps attempting to find the flow and use it rather than fight what could not be won.

If he could just get the ship to listen to him. He watched in horror as men scampered aloft to reef in the sails. They had to reduce their profile to have any chance of controlling the ship. A sailor swung dangerously from a yardarm where he had slipped and now dangled more than thirty feet above the deck. Thomas tried to call to others to help, but his voice was lost in the tempest. The man continued to swing in the wind until the line broke throwing him into the turbulent sea. There would be no way to save the man, Thomas knew, he had to concentrate on saving the rest of the crew and his ship.

Who would believe that the shallowest of the lakes could kick up such great waves, but she was very angry and wanted her due. The grave danger was there was no rhythm to the storm, it felt as though it was coming at them from every direction. The wind swirled crazily, the waves fighting each other for dominance, the rain turning to sleet, threatening to freeze on the lines and yards. The decks would soon become impossible to traverse and then she would begin to breakup. If he didn't do something, find some miracle, they were going down.

He heard the mainmast creak loudly before there was an ear shattering crack and the weight of ice and water, with the muscle of sixty mile an hour winds snapped it like a twig. It crashed hard on the deck before rolling over the side. They had to cut her loose or there would be no way to control the ship and the mast would soon or late break through the Katherine's hull.

He saw men slipping and sliding as they attempted to make their way to the lines holding the mast fast to the starboard side of the ship. The ship listed to starboard with the wind pushing her and the weight of the mast pulling her down. Waves saw their opportunity and began to swell over the side taking men and loose barrels with them.

Thomas heard the bang as the mast swung out ten feet then like a battering ram split the wood of Katherine's hull. He screamed for all to abandon ship. Trying to be heard over the top of the squall he ordered them to try and find whatever flotsam they could hold onto and pray to whatever god they might hold dear. He saw men fighting for barrels or broken hatches. Pieces of his dear Katherine began to litter the waves, men clinging to whatever might give them a glimmer of hope. When he was as certain as he could be he said a quiet goodbye to Mary, to his child, his unborn, and his ship, then dove into his final resting place. The waves creating havoc overhead, as he sank into the swirling depths and closed his eyes.

The sun pried open eyes sealed by water and time. He floated on a raft of broken hull bobbing on gentle waves. Had it all been a dream? No, the raft proved that. The thirst parching his throat confirmed it. The sun was high in the sky, he figured around noon maybe a bit earlier. With what little strength remained in his body he rolled onto his right side to avoid the brilliant shards of light and possibly get a sip of water.

His foot kicked up against something, something soft that rolled with the waves, not hard like wood. He lifted his head. A body. One of the crew was all he could think. Then laughed a hoarse, coughing, bitter bark. Of course, it was one of the crew, did he think he picked up someone just passing by in the middle of the lake in the middle of a storm?

He raised his head slightly to see if he could see any others clinging to makeshift life rafts bobbing on the waves nearby. There was plenty of debris but he saw no others. Maybe they had caught a current and were making their way towards shore and maybe, yeah, maybe. He didn't want to think of what might've happened to the rest. Right now, he required water and to find out if he shared the deck with the living or the dead.

Thirst slacked he crawled, carefully so as not to tip the raft, to where the other man lay. Lieutenant Merritt, interesting. Had Merritt found him and saved his life? Or had he found Merritt? And did it make any difference? The man was breathing. They were shallow sips of air but he had a pulse, it was now up to Thomas to persist on that course.

He cupped his hand and brought sips of water to Merritt. He coughed hard as the water found a different course than the one charted by Thomas. Thomas waited a three count then slowly dribbled another stream into Merritt's mouth. This time he swallowed without coughing. It took time and patience, but soon he was sitting up and grateful for life. Though how long that gratitude would last was dependent on their resourcefulness.

The sound of lapping waves kept the silence at bay. The few birds overhead called to each other, conversing about the strangers floating on their feeding grounds. Thomas couldn't make out what kind of birds through eyes blurred from overexposure to water. Looking up caused sharp, stabbing pain; the brilliant noonday sun forcing him to look away. He rubbed them and immediately regretted the action, they were irritated and probably infected by the time in and on the lake. He closed them and listened, hoping the birds were gulls, as that would mean they were probably within a couple nautical miles from shore. He prayed to a god he hadn't believed in, in a very long time.

The question was, which way was the Canadian shore? He wanted to avoid the formerly United States as he had no idea whether they had truly settled their differences. And there was the fact he wanted to be home. He thought of his Mary, of Katherine, he had believed he would never see them again but now there was renewed hope. He just had to stay alive.

Merritt coughed and lifted his head, "Thank you, you saved my life." It was more a scratchy whisper but Thomas heard it over the slap of wave on wood.

He had no idea who had saved who and if Merritt just meant by giving him water Thomas had saved him, it mattered not. What mattered was survival and home. Well, they had fresh water, that was a gift. If this had happened on the open ocean there would be little chance they could survive, salt water would kill them quicker than hunger. They had to find a way to catch fish unless the storm had pushed them closer to shore than he could hope. He believed in luck, he believed in the miracles of the sea—he thought back on his last passage through the Drake Passage and shivered—he could use another now.

The sun made its own good time across the sky but now he knew which way was north and which way the slight wind current was taking them. The storm had come in from the northeast but the winds seemed to have settled into a more west-southwest flow which should, he thought, push them where they wanted to go. How far that would be and how long it would take were the factors he couldn't assess.

Thomas tried to remember where they had been when the storm overtook them, though, he chuckled to himself, it didn't much matter as he was quite certain the storm had blown them well off course. He recalculated, where had they been from which direction had the storm come, and how long had it lasted?. If this was still the same day and he had come to in late morning that meant the storm had blown through fairly quickly. The ship had been destroyed, he had gone overboard, and then found himself floating on the wrecked hull. He couldn't have been under the water for too long or he would be dead. He or Merritt had found this life raft and they had been allowed by fate to remain alive. So, it must have been after the storm had completely moved on. If the east-northeast wind had pushed them with any kind of consistency and the storm had thrown them to the west-southwest, maybe they evened out some. They should be within a dozen miles of shore. Theoretically, he smiled. It was an idea.

They would live. That was the conclusion he forced himself to came to. If they had to jump in the lake and swim they would live. Joy filled his heart, followed quickly by the realization that at least most of the crew had not.

As if in answer to his unspoken, unthought prayer a paddle from one of the Dinghies floated near enough he could almost reach it. He would have to slip off the raft, retrieve it and then return. Nothing to it, or there wouldn't have been, if he were not exhausted.

He gazed to the east, to where his loved ones waited for his return and slipped into the water. He swam the few stokes to the paddle, grabbed it and then turned for the return trip. The raft had floated in another direction. It was now thirty feet away and adding to its lead. He lay on his back holding the paddle with both hands and kicked furiously toward where he hoped the raft was headed.

Thomas was a strong man and a strong swimmer, every sailor had to be if he wanted to live on the waves. He chanced a quick turn of the head to where he hoped the raft would be. The heavens smiled as it was headed on an intercepting course to him. His head bumped the raft stirring Merritt. Thomas tossed the paddle on the raft before carefully, slowly pulling himself up next to it. He lay there gasping for breath and waiting for his heart to cease furiously attempting to escape his chest before sitting up, swallowing a large breath and beginning to paddle in the direction he hoped land lay.

The broadsheets were filled with stories of the wreck and the assignation of the American president. News of the wreck arrived as the few survivors washed up on the shores of the Great Lake Erie and made their way to towns and villages along the shore. They told of their captain's courage, how he had done everything humanly possible to save those he could and how he had at the very last gone into the tumultuous sea.

It was weeks before the news reached Kingston and the home of Thomas' assumed widow and child. Mary, or course, refused to believe any force under God would be mighty enough to bring her husband down. He was a large man, six foot six in his stockinged feet, broad at the shoulder and built like a Greek god. He had survived years on the ocean, through typhoons, hostile natives, and pirates, some mere lake would not have the power nor the audacity to take him from her. Her love would burn brilliant enough for him to find his way home.

Though as the days passed without word her hope began to weaken. Her hold on belief began to dissipate. She found herself slowly submitting to the possibility, and then she would straighten her back and refuse to consider any alternative other than the deep, heartfelt knowledge that he lived. If he had died, she would've felt it in her soul and she hadn't. He lived. There was no other choice.

Weeks passed, friends came to commiserate, to offer condolences, to give comfort and support. She sent them away from her door. There was no reason to commiserate, no need for comfort, and they could keep their condolences until facts proved otherwise. She began to think they came to reassure themselves that the man who had rejected them, the man who had harbored a black woman in his home as if she were completely human, or of the same race as good, Christian white folk, equal to them, was dead. The man who still blamed them, them, who were god fearing, fine, upstanding, civilized people, for the death the mother of that man's child. And chased the child and his wet-nurse mammy out of their good town. Though their words never said it, their actions and behavior did, good riddance.

Mary found herself despising them as her husband had and when he got back, they would leave. That, she promised herself. And come back he would. And if he didn't? She would not allow herself to consider the possibility.

It was early summer and hot for the time of year when there was a commotion on the street leading up to Mary McDermott's house. Gasps were heard, shouts of disbelief, mumblings of 'it can't be, a haunting at midday!' She stepped out on her porch and swooned at the sight. Her head swam and her legs lost their strength as she tumbled towards the hard wood floor of the porch. Her husband was marching up the street festooned in a swallow-tailed coat, Grey stiped pants, white collared shirt with diamond links in the cuffs and patent leather shoes as was his want, with a large gold medallion around his neck. As she slid down onto the flooring, he ran to catch her before she hit the hard surface. His strong arms cradled her as he told her how much he loved her and it was his love that kept him alive for these past few months. She clung to him for life as hard as he had clung to the raft that saved both his life and that of Lt. Merritt.

She looked past his presence to note that though some were seen smiling in joy at his return, others did not seem so pleased. She cared not; she had her husband returned. Her life was complete. His joy at having her in his arms was amplified tenfold when he noticed the great bulging of her belly and knew there was another life within. If he thought his joy could not possibly be greater, he found the little arms that now enclosed his neck and the joyful tears shed exceeded all expectations. Now he enfolded Mary, Katherine and their soon to be child in his arms and knew rapture.

That evening Mary's parents and some very close friends came to dine and to learn of his adventure and journey home.

After a fine dinner of quail, beef, potatoes, green beans, and apple pie they settled into the parlor with glasses of whiskey for the telling of the tale. Thomas kept the tale to the barest of facts as he didn't want to burden Mary with the horrors, the degradation, and harsh circumstances they'd had to overcome. She has suffered enough herself.

They had floated/paddled the several miles to the north shore, landing at an unpopulated spot somewhere between nowhere and death. A French trapper had found them laying exhausted and unconscious and brought them to his cabin. He and his Indian wife, though both claimed she was Irish, as Natives were being chased and slaughtered out of civilized Canada at the time, nourished the two castaways back to life. It took several weeks of convalescence before both Lt. Merritt and Thomas were well enough to travel.

They set out east hoping to find a white settlement, though the trapper and his wife knew of none, not traveling or exposing themselves to the animus of civilized society. They would need travel by foot as the trapper only possessed his one canoe. They set out through the wilderness following the banks of Erie and the sun and moon. Most of the large wild game had been decimated by the pioneers moving west but they would find enough edible roots and berries to keep them alive. They might even catch small game if they were clever and fast enough. They survived long enough to find a large settlement, Port Dover, on the west bank of the River Lynn.

It was there that Thomas could prove his bona fides, as he was a well-known commodity on the Great Lakes. They rested another week and would've stayed longer except Thomas' love and need for his wife and child, after being gone for more than a month, tugged at his heart. He was able to find passage to Toronto on a lumber barge from a friendly captain that Thomas had apparently done a good turn a few years back. It was fortunate the man was fully loaded and sailing out in the morning. They would follow the northern coast of Lake Erie to the Welland Canal on back onto Lake Ontario.

It was Toronto where Thomas was waylaid once again, this time by the Mayor of the city who presented him with the Gold Medal and chain for saving the life of fellow Canadian Lt. Merritt. A celebration of heroism followed, and a couple days wait for a ship headed to Kingston. And that was why it had taken him so long to rejoin his family. The story was cheered by several rounds of Huzzahs for his safe return and more than enough toasts to his health, his wife's sanity, his family, and his good fortune.

Thomas slept well that night not being roused from bed until ten bells. Mary informed him that the gentleman who had promised to purchase the six ships had honored his word on the five remaining as he had promised. He may have lost much by the loss of his ship and cargo but insurance would cover almost the entire cost, enough he could reimburse what crew still remained and had found their way back to Kingston. The profit from the sale of the five lake vessels would allow them comfort and leisure in their new life in America.

Yes, he told her, he had never given up on his dream of settling in America, especially when she had related to him how the townsfolk had reacted to his death. It was the final cut to the line that held them here. They would start anew in Buffalo. He could stay close to the lakes he had come to love and she could continue her clandestine added support of the child in Amherstburg. They could raise their growing family in the peace and prosperity of America. And she would keep up her secret communications with 'Mary' and 'Tom'. Unbeknownst to Thomas, she had been sending extra funds beyond the small allowance he had and missives to the both of them since she and Thomas had been first married.

Her family was torn by the news and begged them to remain close by. They could build a home outside of Kingston and only come to town on rare occasions, but Thomas would not hear of it. He wanted his children to have all the advantages and privileges his wealth could afford. They would attend good schools, hear the greatest orchestras, have museums at their disposal. They would become refined leaders of society, not ostracized backwoods bumpkins living far out of town.

He suggested that if they were that heartbroken by the decision to move why didn't they pack up and come with the family. Thomas had more than enough coin on hand to build two homes, side by side, and they would never have to be apart. Mary's father balked at the idea, but her mother jumped on board with both feet for the opportunity to be next door to her grandchildren and attending the finest cultural events. Mary's father had lost the debate, though he didn't mind.

Starts and Stops, Spits and Hiccups

Present Day

Aoife made the executive decision, if they were to work together on their projects, his search for a past, hers and his for a future, she should just move in with Tom. His condo had three bedrooms; she'd have her pick of the two not in use. Her needs were as Spartan as his own. She required only a closet for her clothes, a dresser for the non-hangables, a place to set up her computers, and, most importantly, her own bathroom. It was not that she had an overabundance of makeup and accoutrements, she had no need for those, it was simply a privacy issue. Everyone needs a modicum of privacy.

She'd been using her laptop while they searched for any clues as to where Tom's people had migrated from but if she were to do the serious business that her partnership with Tom would bring, she needed the big externals and her desktops.

Once again Tom found himself duly impressed with the mind of Aoife. She had no concerns for propriety or decorum, all that mattered was function and requirements. It took them a full day to set her up in the former dining room and run lines for power and some USB cables. Bluetooth could handle the inconsequential, less secure communications. She was meticulous, focusing on each detail to assure no one, no entity, could hack into her system. Nothing would go through Bluetooth that could compromise security.

Tom realized he had thought himself too smart to ever be hacked yet she had accomplished it without working up a sweat. He thought himself too clever by half and yet had left himself wide open to hacking in the most simplistic way, she'd just had to hack into his Wi-Fi. He laughed at his own naivete and arrogance, though that had brought him Aoife. Her presence completed his life. She was a friend and partner with a mind that left him astounded; and that's all it would ever be. But that was enough.

They worked side by side searching every available website that might have any information as to where his people came from. All the while he was teaching her the ins and outs of the programs he had created and she was discovering new applications for them all. It was several weeks in when Aoife sat up, startled, and exclaimed something akin to joy.

"What is it?" He asked trying to peek over her shoulder. "Found something of interest, I'm guessing?" He grinned.

"If it's true, I may have found the golden key to your family history," she sat back in her chair and rubbed her eyes to assure her tired eyes weren't seeing what they wanted to see, rather than what was actually there.

Tom pulled the padded wooden dining room chair up close to her so he could see what she was looking at. There was a newspaper story from a small Michigan town not far from the border with Ohio of a black woman and her son, Mary McHenry and Tom, taking up residence in a small farmhouse just on the outskirts of the town of Samaria. What made it noteworthy to the publisher of the small-town paper was she had paid cash for the farm, a total of one hundred and seventy-seven dollars. She claimed to have saved the money from a benefactor in their former residence in Amherstburg, Canada. 'She plans to farm the land with her son and hopes the fine people of the new town of Samaria will welcome them and allow them to live in peace.'

"And what has that got to do with me?" Tom found the article interesting historically but didn't see the connection.

"For one, I don't think your people were brought over on a slave ship, as we can find nothing about your ancestors in any web database. Not any site involving African Americans brought over or coming over later has even a hint of your line; not hide nor hair of any link to you. Now here is this woman come from Canada and settling into an area close to where your grandparents said their parents and grandparents came from. Right?" She looked to him for confirmation.

"Yes, I think I remember my granddaddy mentioning something about Michigan though I can't be certain it was this exact area." Tom did not want to get his hopes up. He had been searching through every line of code he could find for that tiny needle in a haystack the size of Earth.

"Well, I think we should try to find if this is them. Now we have someone, possibly," she cautioned, "to make the link. It's a reach, I grant you, but it's a reach I think we should follow."

"Agreed." It was the only thing they had found with any possible connection.

He had no names to go on. Just his grandfather and grandmother, he from the Webbs, she from the Jones line. She would almost be impossible to follow, there were more Joneses than grains of sand on the beaches.

Aoife thought they should follow the Webb line and see if that got them anywhere. After several false starts and dead ends, she found a line that she was fairly certain led them to Mary and Tom in Samaria, Michigan. She had come across Tom's great grandfather's birth notice in Temperance, Michigan. It was noted as the first black child born in Temperance since it changed its name in 1884. He had been born there quite by accident as there were no black citizens in Temperance at the time. Apparently, his mother was returning from a short trip to Lambertville back to her home in Samaria and the baby wouldn't wait. She gave birth in the carriage by the side of the road and was forced to spend the night with some good Christian folks at the town's edge.

The Mother's name on the birth record was Betsy Webb, father unknown. Now they had a connection to Samaria and his surname but they were missing a very important piece, the connection of Betsy to Mary. Time to get out the entrenching tools and dig a little deeper, though Tom thought he saw a light blinking at the end of this road.

Betsy, as far as any recordkeeping they could unearth, had never been married. Possibly because of the birth of her bastard child which would also clarify why Tom's great grandfather had never known any of this history to pass down. His mother might have told him of a father who never existed and an untimely death and he'd blocked out information not necessary for him. Still, they had to find the connector to Mary. They focused on Samaria and every newspaper, church announcement, mention of a celebration or death they could find from the time, the late 1800s, when young Tom must have gotten married or had children.

The stone wall was a hundred feet thick and impregnable. Newspapers from the time were almost completely destroyed by fires, need, and time. The fact they had come across the article about Mary and her son was pure serendipity. The great grandson of the publisher had tried to save some of his ancestors works but had only been minimally successful. The fact he not only had the newsprint but also had microfilmed and put it up on the World Wide Web was miraculous. But it would appear the miracles had run their course.

Aoife spoke quietly in the silent dining room, "I'm afraid," she began.

Before she could utter another syllable Tom chimed in, "The evidence, thin as it might be, points to the data available. It's pretty damn certain Betsy has got to be the child of Tom, right? The coincidences are too strong for her not to be. I mean, there are not a plethora of black folks living in Samaria, Michigan at this time. They might be the only ones." He sat back in the comfortable overstuffed chair that was his place of contentment.

"The evidence is strong," she conceded, "though not absolute. I think we should venture to this town and dig around a bit. We've been lucky thus far, all we need is a little bit more."

"The question remains, where to dig? It appears to be a rural area with small to nothing towns. It might take weeks to find any information," Tom felt the creeping of melancholy stirring in his soul combining with hope slipping out the other side.

"We start here!" Aoife stated jabbing here finger at something on her screen.

Tom looked over her shoulder to see a site for the Monroe County Historical Society. For such a rural area the building looked like it housed everything that had ever happened in the county and surrounding towns for the past few centuries.

"Can we just text them or email them our questions?" Tom was not averse to travel he just hadn't done much in his life and wasn't confident he could navigate through states, routes, back roads, and people he had never met or thought he would have need of. Would they have to fly to this Michigan? Did they speak the same language? He didn't want to appear a rube though he had to admit in some areas of life he was.

He knew his way around Chicago, could hail a cab, take the 'L', or a bus, if great need arose. He'd been to the wilds of Milwaukee several times with Chester when he had business up that way and had actually traveled all the way to Des Moines, a frontier town as far as Tom could fathom, for a meeting one time. He had begged the corporate hack in question to allow for a zoom meeting but apparently these frontiersmen wanted to have their meetings face to face.

Michigan was on the other side of the Great Lake which bore the same name. Would they have to take a boat? How many days would that take? Maybe he could take a train, he liked traveling by train, though the schedules could be fickle and volatile. Still, he could relax in the comfort of a train. He feared this trip would involve automobiles. It's not that he didn't know how to drive, it was just a few outings through the great metropolis of Chicago had cured any interest he had of ever getting behind the wheel of a car again.

Other drivers terrified him. Every single one appeared angry and aggressive. He felt they all knew he was a novice and thought him grist for the mechanical mill. They drove so close to the back end of his car he thought they might be attempting to hitch a ride in his trunk. They slammed on their brakes at eighty miles per hour for no discernable reason. And, they changed lanes, as quickly and blithely as they changed their minds. The thought of having to go through the city brought shivers of horror to his well-ordered mind.

Aoife watched with dispassionate curiosity, like a scientist observing a subject, as his mind worked through whatever horrors he was feeling. It piqued her interest in what it might be that could arouse such passion and fear in this man.

"Something wrong?" She queried ever so lightly.

"Just curious how we plan to get to this faraway borough," he was surprised his voice didn't crack. He sounded inquisitive not terrified.

"Well, we could drive there, it's not all that far," she suggested to his absolute dread. Unprepared for his visceral reaction, she tossed him a bone. "Or we could take the train into Detroit or Toledo and rent a car from there. It's pretty wide-open country, not a lot of traffic." She had deduced from his reaction he was not keen on driving or traveling through the congestion humanity presented.

"I think that would suit. Trains are a very civilized way to travel. One can relax, enjoy the scenery without a care in the world. Yes, I think that would do nicely," his words rushing like a salmon running up the last half mile to her spawning grounds, as he breathed a sigh of relief.

Their conversation was interrupted by the insistent buzzing of the front doorbell. They hadn't ordered take out or any deliveries so Tom was reticent about answering. Though it would seem the person with the finger on the button was not to be ignored.

Tom opened the door to a man in suit coat, white shirt, no tie, and wrinkled slacks. "Thomas Webb?"

No hello, is Tom home? My name is...nothing. Just a demanding tone to assure the person he sought was the person standing in the portal.

He reached behind him—and Tom jerked in memory of the cop with the gun—and pulled out an official looking envelope handing it to Tom.

"You have been subpoenaed to appear before Judge Henry Walsburg two weeks hence in the case of Sergeant Fredrick Pulaski's accidental discharge of his firearm. You must appear in person and I would suggest you bring an attorney." And with that he was gone.

"But he shot me!" Tom spoke to thin air.

A New Life, Again

1865-Early

There was little or no love lost between Thomas, Mary or her parents and the town of Kingston. They were happy to be leaving and the general feeling among the well-to-do was they were happy to have them removed from their town. They would not consider themselves responsible for, nor needful of caring, about the death of a black woman years past. It was a nonissue. They had no idea what happened to the bastard child or his new mammy and would not lose any sleep if they had suffered the same fate. There were several who proposed the concept of refusing to buy either house, that of the father or his daughter's husband, but the fellow from Ireland who had come to purchase the ships also decided to buy both houses for himself and his son, who would share in the running of the business. They even agreed to take Thomas and his family west to the confluence of Ontario and The Niagara. They could offload at Olcott and travel south overland to the general dominion of Buffalo; not in the city but near enough to enjoy all it had to offer.

Thomas had done some research of where they wished to settle in the new world. He wanted to remain close to the lakes and close to a center of civilization where the children could benefit from all the culture a new country could provide, though, not so close he would expose the children to others morbid dislike of those different from themselves. Thomas had spent a large part of his youth and early manhood traveling the world and intermingling with other cultures and people. He felt that once you got by color or religion most all were interchangeable. Everyone in the world wanted to raise their families, feed their children, enjoy an evening quietly contemplating the stars and blackness of space, and only sought a modicum of wherewithal. Greed, he had discovered, was an addiction that could not be satisfied.

He found a town, on a large island, that had existed for only a decade or so. The island had been inhabited by the Attawandaron tribe for centuries before being wiped out by the Seneca then becoming part of the British Empire in the middle of the last century before becoming part of the great state of New York in 1815. Though the Island would not be truly settled until several decades later, after a feeble attempt to turn it into a Jewish Homeland. It finally settled into its current iteration as Grand Island, from the French le Grand Ile, in 1852. It was now a bustling burg of several hundred people with plenty of land and room for a growing family. And, best of all, it was just across the Niagara from Tonawanda and Buffalo.

Thomas McDermott II was born on Grand Island in the State of New York and the burgeoning country of the United States, the first American born scion of the McDermott family. Both the McDermott's and the Haggerty's were living in a rude, raw, upscale log cabin. It had a large open area that served as living area, dining area, and sleeping area separated by blankets and promise while they built new homes on the island.

Days became weeks became months as time passed pleasantly between two men on a mission. Thomas and Mary's father, Earl, grew close as they worked side by side constructing first the McDermott home and finally the much smaller Haggerty home several hundred yards to the north. Thomas had friended several members of the Webb family who had resurrected portions the Whitehaven sawmill for their own uses. They were more than happy to have Thomas' coin to shape boards for his new homes. Months became seasons as they put the finishing touches on the two homes. As his own home neared completion, he had decided to construct a smaller, cozier log home on the back of his property as a place for he and Earl to have a sip and share cigars, a habit Mary and her mother found to be less than desirable. The McDermott's and Haggerty's were now well and truly established in the new world that Thomas had dreamt about since he was a child.

Two more boys would follow once the new homes were completed. Jack and Earl were born two years apart and were the apple of big sister, now five years their senior, Katherine's eyes and spoiled accordingly. All enjoyed the privilege of education—a school had been constructed on the property, a teacher imported from Albany and all island children invited. The children were exposed to fine cultural events. Reading, writing, and 'rithmatic were compulsory. In addition to an appreciation of art and other cultures, each child took up an instrument—Katherine learned piano, Thomas Jr. took up the piano and violin, Jack leaned towards cello and Earl, baby Earl, took up woodwinds, clarinet, flute, bassoon and, to his mother's suffering ears, percussion. They lived a refined life with evenings spent playing music, cards, croquet, and the new game catching on throughout the states, baseball; they could field, with the addition of a few friends, a decent team. All in all, it was a pleasant lifestyle.

Through it all Mary, continued to send along subsidy to the mulatto child and his 'mother' via ships, through trusted captains and sailors, formerly in the employ of her husband, who continued to ply the waters of the Great Lakes. The major difference now was she need only find a ship on the Erie side of the great Niagara Falls to take her packages to the boy in Amherstburg across the river from the growing city of Detroit. Until the day came when her package was returned with an almost illegible note stating she need not send further help as Mary McHenry and her 'son' Tom had resettled in America. Mary burned the letter. Thomas must never discover what she had been up to for the past decade. Only she would ever know the child's name, Thomas, for him, and Mary for the 'mother', the McHenry's after her former owner. Mary had to laugh at the woman taking her name and giving the child Thomas'. Some might have been incensed at the audacity, but Mary found it endearing and quite an honor.

A Court With Little honor, Your Honor

Present Day

The court case was set for three weeks from the date of the subpoena, not two. The server was near illiterate or didn't much care for accuracy. Tom and Aoife would've preferred either sooner or much later, as they were both anxious to go see what they could find in rural Michigan. They didn't want to rush the search, a search they had put much time and energy into, wishing to allow plenty of time to delve as deeply as they might need. They had no idea exactly where their search would take them but they both knew neither would be satisfied until they had learned all they could. The mission was to uncover some truth. The journey into the past would have to wait.

The court was everything Tom's apprehension had prepared him for. Just seeing the cop again brought back psychological terror and an intense panic attack. He would've preferred to let dead dogs lie and forgive, though not forget, ever! Tom wanted nothing more than to move on with his life. Unbeknownst to Tom and Aoife the sergeant had been put on administrative leave with the excellent possibility of losing his job, his pension, his future. Tom wanted him to pay, though he did not want the price to be cancellation from his life.

When Tom was finally called to the stand to testify, the witness stand was directly across from the man who almost cut his life extremely short. He tried to ignore the cop, yet he found he couldn't. The man stared hard at him as if daring him to say what he knew Tom must say. Maybe if he had appeared remorseful to Tom, a man who was midlife and had made an awful mistake or resembled a chastened soul seeking some mercy, Tom might have been willing to grant such. He was challenging Tom, his eyes taunting, provoking, and mocking. Tom told the truth of what had occurred on the night in question. It was short, succinct and to the point. Until the defense took their turn.

As Tom sat in the witness stand, he noticed that not only was the defendant glaring at him, but several uniformed officers also sat front and center just behind Sgt. Pulaski, never taking their eyes off him. If they meant to intimidate him, it was working.

Like a searchlight on a ship seeking safe harbor in a storm his eyes sought shelter. Flitting about the courtroom, avoiding the death rays coming from the eyes of the representatives of the law they found safe harbor. Aoife sat calmly in the second row just off the center aisle. Her expression was one of serenity, as if she were completely unaware of what was taking place. Totally unconcerned with the grilling Tom was about to undergo.

The attorney began his questioning gentle enough asking Tom to repeat his name, if he remembered the date of the incident and why he was wandering through this particular neighborhood. Tom realized immediately this was going to take an ugly turn.

Yes, he remembered the date, the time, and the conditions of the evening and the why; he was going to the Sushi shop, he was hungry. He was not 'wandering' through his own damn neighborhood but walking through it, as was his want and right. He enjoyed walking, didn't like driving, and the sushi shop was only a few blocks away.

"But it was raining, was it not?" Smiled the interrogator.

"Not when I set out from MY condominium," Tom felt his anger being stoked in the belly of the beast. He didn't like the tone of voice being sent his way. They were trying to make it sound like he didn't belong in his own neighborhood. He was just some random black guy—though he was more tan—

casing the rich white folk's homes. Tom was not conversant with racism especially as an accusation to prove a crime. His blood was coming to a boil. He took a deep breath to prepare himself for the line of questioning about to happen. It would do him no favor to lose his temper with these fine white folk in 'their' court of law. He pushed the anger down, cooled it with a soft intake of air conditioning. Bring it on!

"How long have you 'lived'", yes the attorney used finger quotes to indicate Tom's intrusion into somewhere he was not in the class of belonging, as if Tom was some kind of interloper or squatter, "at your condominium." His grin was malicious.

Shit! Hadn't these people done any research or investigation into him during the past months? All they had to do was Google him or check with the condo association to find this shit out. OK, play it cool.

"Ten years," cooed Tom coolly.

"I see," said the man who should have known, "So, you set out in a rainstorm to get some food, is that right?" It was an inane line of questioning but they were trying to show he was the one who was responsible for the shooting.

"No, I set out when it was lovely evening to get something to eat, after acquiring said food, some sushi and sashimi, the rain began a few blocks from my home." Again, emphasizing that he belonged where he was.

"Is there a reason you were walking with your hoodie in place?" This guy was trying make a forty something year old, overweight, light skinned—tan really—black man into a gangsta! Tom had to take a breath to stop himself from exploding in laughter.

"Yes, and I'll say it slowly so you will understand. It was beginning to rain, slightly, not pounding, not a storm, slightly, and I pulled up my hood to keep my head and sushi dry!" he probably emphasized that more than was necessary but this was idiotic. He glanced at Aoife to see what her reaction was and saw her hide her silent laugh behind a lovely hand. OK.

Now the lawyer had him right where he wanted him. "So, you were trying to keep your sushi dry?" He chuckled, "Isn't sushi fish?"

"Oh, for the love of God!" Tom thought he said that in his head but from the look the judge tossed his way he had been unsuccessful. "Sorry, your honor, but really..." he pleaded. The judge nodded. Well, there was one person in this clown show that might be on his side. "Yes, as foolish as that might sound, I was trying to keep my sushi dry as that seems to be the way I like it. I was walking along, minding my own business, eating sushi in the rain and didn't realize that was a capital offense." He took a long, cleansing, calming breath.

"Did the officer, Sergeant Pulaski," he emphasized the man's title, "request you to stop where you were?"

"He pulled up with his lights flashing, jumped out and demanded I stop, which I did, before I requested he speak to me, as a citizen of this city, in a more respectful manner."

"And what was his response?" Was this idiot trying to get this cop thrown off the force?

"He began to lose his shit," again Tom turned to apologize to the judge for his language. The judge waved the apology back into Tom's mouth. "He told me to drop what was in my hand," Tom regained his composure. "It was my dinner. He could see it was a takeout container. I wasn't going to throw good sushi—and it is very good sushi at our corner place—on the ground. I was hungry!"

"Did he request you to set down what was in your hand?" The realization dawned in Tom's mind! This cop had told this lawyer a completely fabricated story and this guy either had no idea what he was asking or he was as slimy as the cops.

"No! He was acting crazed like he had caught the most wanted man in the country and, to be honest, he seemed frightened to find a black man in my neighborhood." Again, making the point he belonged where he was, not the cop. "When I tried to show him, it was nothing but sushi and sashimi, he shot me! Who shoots a man over sushi and sashimi?"

"Is it possible he might have thought you had a weapon? A handgun? That he felt threatened by your motion?" Ah, the truth was coming to the fore.

"Not unless they make guns that look very similar to takeout from Yoo See Un's." Tom had had enough of this. He had shit to do and history to uncover. Instead, he sat in this ludicrous farce. Tom looked up into the glaring faces of the Sergeant and his cronies behind him, he may have erred, possibly, but he no longer cared. He glared back. Fuck these guys!

A light went off in Tom's muddled brain. "I have a question, if you don't mind, your honor." He looked to the judge for approval. A nod. "Aren't all these guys supposed to have body cameras on them at all times?" The corners of the judicial mouth twitched in understanding. A nod. "Why don't we go to the film and see what we see, so I can get back to my life!"

"Objection, your honor, the witness is out of order and has no right to demand anything of this court!" The lawyer reverted to his core being.

"Objection overruled," the clap of gavel on desktop absolute. "Tell me counselor, is this your first case of this sort? You don't seem to have prepared as well as one might for defense of such an action. Would you like a few minutes to confer with your client? You know, to straighten out any misconceptions or misinterpretations of what your client might have mistakenly overlooked in his deposition." Tom understood the judge was attempting to be fair and give the officer his day in court, though it didn't seem to matter, as the Sergeant sat steely eyed and silent, refusing to break eye contact with Tom. And Tom was not about to give in to the man who shot him for the crime of being black and in the wrong neighborhood with the wrong food.

It was peculiar, Tom thought, that he had never had just cause to think about his ethnicity before this incident but the more it came to the fore, the more pissed he became. He took another in the series of deep breaths to calm himself and slow his racing heartbeat, it was not a resounding success.

Sergeant Pulaski fidgeted in his chair; it was the first sign he might be coming to terms with a different outcome of this criminal case than he had imagined. The conclusion crowding into his racist, diminutive brain was, he was not going to intimidate his way out of this. He either thought that the victim would not show up or thought that by bringing his 'backup' it would intimidate the victim into not testifying or testifying he might have been at fault, rather than be put on the police shit list. It was going to be number three. The guy was standing up for himself and Pulaski was fucked.

"I believe in this city we have law that all body camera footage must be kept until no longer pertinent and also every police officer must engage the body camera when leaving his or her cruiser, am I correct counselor?" The lawyer nodded in ascent. "Good we'll take a fifteen-minute brake while someone runs over to the police department and retrieves the footage from the night in question." The bang of the gavel like the tolling of the bell of doom.

Aoife was waiting for Tom as he pushed his way through the half dozen off duty cops waiting for him at the door. He glared, they glared, he walked through the middle of them. He'd had enough of this obvious attempt to pressure him to recant his testimony. Nothing had been said, nothing needed to be said, it was implied and he didn't care for the implication.

"You are doing well, Tom," she nodded the compliment with a smile for reassurance. "though I believe once this has been settled, we should probably get outta Dodge," she grinned at the appropriation of the adage and how well it fit the situation.

"I could not agree with you more!" He was tired, aggravated, and done with this charade. "It just chafes that they think they can just paint me as some ghetto dweller out on the prowl when I had every right to be walking in my own damn neighborhood. I don't have to answer to anyone for anything I do! I have accomplished what I have on my own in spite of, not with the aid of, in spite of every roadblock put in my way." He was proud of what he had done with his own wit, intelligence and perseverance, and these assholes were trying to take that away. Well, not today.

"This digitization of the evening will prove all to everyone, yes?" She was unsure how all this legalese worked never having the imperative.

"We can but hope." Tom tried to be positive but he no longer was a believer in the legal system in his own country.

"What if they do not have the footage?" Aoife seemed surprised he hadn't thought of that possibility.

"I think they are screwed either way. He can't act like I attacked him when I was armed with only sushi and sashimi. And he has already testified I was at least ten feet away when he shot me." Tom shook his head. "You know I had a lawyer call me and ask if I wanted to sue the police department and the city over this. I told him no, I just wanted it to be over and done with. I may be rethinking my decision." She looked shocked. "Oh, not for the money," he reassured, "but so they might think twice before shooting another human being because they don't like the 'look' of him." He left it there as they were called back into the courtroom.

Of course, the intimidation squad awaited his attempt to return. Tom closed his eyes and just concentrated on passing through the blue wall to get some justice. Some odd sensation began in his gut and raced to his head. It was as if he wanted his anger to physically push them out of his way.

When he opened his eyes, he was surprised to find himself safely ensconced inside the courtroom. No one had impeded his entrance. As a matter of fact, the vanguard had moved aside to provide him with a corridor to walk down. The surprised expressions on their faces providing the proof they had not meant to move aside.

Aoife, at his side, grinned. "Don't know what you did there but your vibe changed and they felt it. Impressive!"

What the hell had just happened. New doors, new journeys, new discoveries. Tom was uncomfortable with all of it. He had been happy in his hermitage. He enjoyed his computers, his thoughts, being left alone by all but a miniscule percentage of the human race. Now, he seemed to have been thrust headfirst into life and he didn't care for it one bit. Though there was this stunning woman standing next to him and he thought, 'there are some definite benefits to this new world'.

Something was niggling at the back of his head, something so wrong with this whole picture. It was not supposed to be like this in America. He was a well-respected man about town doing his own thing so conservatively, so as not to draw attention to himself. It had been that way his entire life. Now he found himself the center of attention and not in a good way. You don't want to be the center of attention when the po-po are involved. It was then the harsh memory came back like a hot kiss at the end of a wet fist.

He was getting ready to go out with Chester, his only friend, for a night of being ignored by the more popular kids and being mocked by the privileged; privileged by way of their physical stature. His folks cornered him in the living room where he could not escape. They were about to inculcate reality into his brilliant head. They were hesitant and stammered for a moment with their message.

"You be very careful out there," began his hard-working, blue-collar dad, his mother standing next to him dry washing her hands in worry.

"I will," began the cocky rejoinder before his father held up a hand to forestall any further interruption. It was then he saw the deep fear in both their eyes. What the heck were they so afraid of? He and Chester would probably find some place out of the way to talk about books, games, and some new computer on the horizon. They were nerds, what kind of trouble could nerds get into? A bad chess match?

"I'm serious. I know with that big brain of yours you think no one can touch you, but you're wrong. They can hurt you bad." His father took a deep beath to steady himself and collect his thoughts. Tom waited. He was going to warn him about bullies and kids being horribly mean. The taunting, hitting, pounding on those who could ill defend themselves. In other words, what Tom and Chester had dealt with forever. But he kept his mouth shut to allow the man he respected most in the world to have his say.

"You think I am talking about the other kids in school, don't you? Well, I'm not. I'm talking about the police. They can make your life a living hell and more. They control everything when are you out just trying to have fun." Another breath.

"But you always told me the police were my friend. That I could rely on them if the other kids got too mean. To go to the police," Tom felt the pain of the lie deep in his heart.

"In many cases that's the truth but you are going to be out there, just the two of you, driving while black (DWB) and they are going to be gunning for you, looking for a reason to pull you two knuckleheads over just for fun. There are a lot of cops who just don't like black boys, especially if they are driving around enjoying themselves. You gotta remember that. They might have helped you when you was little, but you ain't little no more and they are looking for you." His father glanced over to where his mom looked about to break into tears. What the hell was going on? Why were they so afraid?

"You remember that skinny kid up the block? The one with the snaggle toothed grin? He was a couple years older than you but always friendly. Took you for ice cream couple times." Tom nodded. "He was out with some of his friends awhile back and the police stopped them. That kid was being friendly, having fun with the cop. Or so he thought. The cop wasn't having none of it. He pulled that boy out of the car window and beat him bloody with his night stick. Boy is still alive but he's in a home. Can't walk or feed himself. Never gonna be the same again. Cop told the judge the kid came at him and he had no other choice but to put him down. Put him down! His exact words. Like that kid was some kind of rabid dog or something!" His father's voice had reached a crescendo before he slumped a bit, his energy spent. "Look, all we are begging of you is to be careful. If the police pull you over, don't talk, don't sass, just do whatever they tell you and come home whole to your mother and me. You all we got and we love you." They both hugged him tight between them, gasping for breath beneath the tears. Damn! They were terrified for him. He began thinking maybe him and Chester should just stay home.

They went out and did their best to avoid any trouble. No police. No jocks. No nobody but the two of them. Oh, they still jacked around and had some fun, but they were always looking over their shoulders. That is what he felt in his gut right now as he made his way back to the witness stand. These people had instilled such a fear, worry, terror in his parents and now they were attempting the same in the court of justice. He assumed that meant that, yeah, there was justice, but only for just white folk. Well, not today.

He took his seat and stared out at the boys in blue seated behind the assailant. That's what they called people like that, didn't they? The cops watched him, though with a wary eye. Something had taken place as he walked through the door, but he could not for the life of him figure out what. They were now wary of him, as if he had physically assaulted them, though he hadn't raised a finger, just moved past them. He had wanted to push them out of his way—his father's warning stuck like a signpost in the back of his mind the only thing holding him back. Well, that and the promise of a severe beating, but he sure had wanted to!

His attention was pulled to the television being wheeled into the courtroom. Tom couldn't hide his amused grin as he took in the scene. In a courtroom in the richest country in the world where technology was worshipped, they had wheeled in, on a metal cart straight out of 1970s Junior High School, a television from the same period. He had to wonder if it was even a colored television or black and white. He coughed a laugh into his cupped hands.

The piece de resistance was the VHS player hooked into the back of the TV. All he could think was, 'we need to upgrade our justice system', before breaking out in a cackle of laughter at his own observation. This, of course, earned him a scowl from the judge before he, too, realized how sad the whole scene was.

Tom did not watch the video. He had lived it and felt no compunction to see himself assaulted by this officer of the 'law'. He had no want to see himself shot and squirming on the ground. He observed the cops in the courtroom instead.

Several of them watched the screen intensely hoping to note Tom make any kind of threatening move toward their fellow officer. Two of the men who serve all men kept their eyes on Tom. Tom's eyes locked with the biggest one and he refused to break the contact. Several minutes passed until the cop looked away and Tom realized a very important fact. The dynamic had changed between he and the officers. The power they assumed over him had diminished. As if they realized he was in the right and their pal was wrong. The video showed a man reasonably questioning why he had been stopped and why he was being treated with such disrespect. He was not angry, he was not yelling or cursing, he was in control at the scene and was in control now. And that frightened them.

Apparently, these men were not used to ordinary people, especially ordinary black people, being in control when the police were involved. They relied on fear and intimidation as the well of their power. Tom displayed neither fear nor intimidation, only intelligence and a sense of humor.

He heard the judge chuckle when Tom had asked if the sergeant was going to shoot a man over sushi. Though the laugh was cut short when the sound of the officer's gun went off. Silence smothered any further reactions.

Someone coughed. Aoife? He looked her way and saw the shock on her face seeing him actually shot. It is one thing to know and quite another to see it happen. There were tears in her eyes. She knew he was right here, sitting in the same courtroom as her, yet she had seen him shot and go down. He wanted to comfort her but he was still on the witness stand.

"Any further questions, counselor?" The judge stared hard at the lawyer and his client.

"No, your honor." He sat back in his seat and glared at the sergeant.

"Any further exhibits anyone want to enter?" Silence.

"I want to thank Mr. Webb for his cooperation in this inquiry. I know this has been extremely hard for you to relive especially when it seems the object of dragging you before the court was to attempt to make you out to be some sort of criminal. I apologize for the inconvenience and for the insult. I assume you would like to get back to living your life without further digressions. Please go in peace and our sincerest contrition. Court adjourned." The gavel made its presence known one last time. "Oh, and counselor, you might want to inform your client that all the evidence and testimony will be forwarded to his superiors for consideration and discipline. He should consider himself lucky that Mr. Webb has shown no interest in pursuing this further and he should consider himself blessed if he only loses his job!"

Aoife wrapped her arms around his large frame as Tom exited the courtroom and hugged him tight. "Just seeing that, seeing you, the blood, even knowing you are alright, it just, well, it just went straight to my heart." She hugged him once more before shaking off the terror.

"Let's get something to eat," he smiled, "and then let's get the hell outta Dodge." He found he really liked that expression, especially today.

Finding A New Purpose

1873

Thomas was becoming antsy with the lack of doing. He had been constantly engaged in something or other since he first hid in the bowels of the 'Avenging Mother'. Now, he sat and carved wooden objects out of fallen branches; a skill he had picked up while sailing between the myriad islands of the South Pacific. When you don't see land for months at a time or the boredom of becalmed begins to eat at your sanity the need to keep the mind and hands occupied is consuming. You find something, anything, to do or go stir crazy.

He had led an active life and now found his mind wandering back to his journeys. The wanderlust he thought buried was being excavated. When they had first moved to the island, he had been occupied with building his home and a new home for Mary's parents. Then more kids had come along and he had kept busy being a father to four precocious and very energetic children. He had loved every minute of it. Now they were older and no longer needed his guidance—in fact, ignored or were exasperated that he still wished to run their lives. He who had carved sheep, pigs, horses, and dogs for them when they were children; had carried them on his back and taught them to swim in the mighty Niagara River. They didn't need him any longer. It seemed as though no one did. Mary was busy with her women's groups and attempting to get men to see the wisdom of allowing their truly better halves to vote.

Mary's dad had passed a couple years earlier and her mother had moved in with them. Thomas loved the woman but the house was closing in on him. He required a distraction. He missed his ships and crew, missed being among the men as they fought off storms, pirates, and nasty currents where there should not have been any. He thought fondly of *Katherine's Waves*. She had been an excellent ship and he loved her. The thought of her at the bottom of that damn lake, where no one would ever stare in awe at her beauty, tore at his soul.

And there it was. He had found his purpose no matter how temporary. He would recreate the *'Waves'* in fine detail with his hands and jackknife. It would take months, time he had. He could remember every line, every curve of her hull, every board of her deck and each spar, yardarm, rigging and sail. He would create a miniaturized Katherine so the world would know her magnificence.

He would carve each board of the hull, each plank of the deck, every stanchion, spar, and arm with his own hands. He would carve the figurehead, not as it had been, but in the likeness of his Mary. He could use pieces of sailcloth for the actual sails and hemp for the rigging. Yes, he was excited by the project. It would take a year, maybe more, but it would be a work of art. Something to last in perpetuity of his time on the Great Lakes. And it would keep him out his wife's hair and away from the scheming. He might even entice one or two of the boys to lend a hand. Yes, a project for the family to bring them tighter together in common cause.

As if in answer to his quest, a massive thunderstorm blew in from the eastern coast dumping an inordinate amount of rain, hurricane force winds, brilliant flashes of lighting and crashing thunder. They remained warm and protected in the sturdy home Thomas had built. A fire crackling in the hearth and the children performing lovely chamber pieces including a Beethoven Violin Sonata, a Shubert String Quartet and Brahms Piano Quintet in which everyone played. It kept the storm at bay and lifted the spirits of all in the main room.

In the morning Thomas assessed the damage to his property and found an ancient White Oak, sixty foot tall if it was an inch, had been felled by the storm. Though it broke his heart to see this former playland of his children gone, it also gladdened him that here would be the plunder to create his chef d'oeuvre!

Though the ground muddy and puddled, and the tree immense, he strode to the tool shed to grab his ax and began to chop out the logs that would provide him with the raw material to begin carving each individual piece.

There was never a time when Thomas missed Mary's father by his side more than during the creation of his carving. He and the old man had become quite close over the years, sharing stories from the Emerald Isle. Now the old man had passed, you could almost see his specter waiting by the door. Thomas missed him as he would a brother. He had loved hearing Earl's stories from the homeland. No matter the reason why he'd runaway, he still missed the ancestral home he had abandoned at such a young age. He recalled with warmth his time as a child in Dublin, the love tugged at his heart. He would have been guaranteed a life of leisure in the church with a warm bed each night, safely tucked into the cloister, his only duty to God and the salvation of straying and lost souls.

He would've died from the boredom of it all. As much or more then he loved to hear stories from home, Mary's father had loved to hear his tales from around the world, his adventures on the high seas, pirates, and strange and wondrous native peoples. His father-in-law was the only person Thomas had ever felt close enough to express his loss of the island girl he had saved only to allow frigid hate and ignorance to kill her.

His thoughts were of the child she had borne as she lay dying. He hadn't thought of the boy in many years and found himself wondering how the child faired. Thomas had sent them to the town of Amherstburg in the west. He had done some investigating and asked many questions before sending the boy and his milk mother to the black town, where they might have a chance at a good life among their own. He felt it was the best he could do.

He hoped the woman would tell the boy about his mother and what a wonder she was. That she would recall and recant the stories Thomas had imparted to her. He'd wanted to assure she could pass on the glory that had borne him. Where she was from and who she had been. How she had survived on her island all alone by her wits and strength of will. She had been an extraordinary person. He found he missed her all these years later.

He set about the chore of chopping the logs into workable sizes that he could haul to the log outbuilding he had built for he and Earl, Mary's dad, to sleep in, share a whiskey, a cigar, and tall tales while they constructed the home the family now occupied. He'd cut the massive tree into five-foot sections and then drag them to where they could be trimmed down into even more workable sizes. The log hut would serve him well, as it had when he'd first built it on the path he had carved from the forest for the beginnings of a road to their home. It had served its purpose then, allowing him to bring wagon loads of lumber directly to the plot for the massive six-bedroom monstrosity he was constructing for his family. Mary's father had joined in the project as much as his body would allow, even back then.

It was a good time in all their lives. He and Earl would fell the trees, strip the branches, before taking them to the lumber mill where they would be split into planks to be used as the siding. At the end of the day, they would adjourn to the log hut they had out fitted with a small fireplace for warmth and cooking. A small table to eat and two cots of hewed branches and sail cloth to sleep. It brought the two close as brothers, with Mary, her mom and now the three children bringing food out to them once a week and providing them a family picnic. This hut would serve him once again and wrap him in the comfort of memory.

Thomas thought of those days not quite a decade in the past as he hooked up the harness to the work horse and begin dragging the five-foot section to the cabin. Yes, the cabin would be the perfect place for him to work without interruption. The boys would find him sooner or later and wonder what he was about. He would not allow them in to see what he worked on; it was a secret. Which would only pique their interest to the point of implosion. It would worm its way into their every waking thought. They would yearn to know what their father was keeping from them. Until he would finally allow them entrance and they would be taken in by the enormity of what he had set out to accomplish. He would have his helpers.

It was with this happy thought that he drove the horse to his workplace, the log carving another furrow in the soil, where he could begin to cut it into malleable planks for the hull. He grinned in the bright sunlight and noticed not a cloud in the sky. The storm had pushed back any inclement weather, he would have a week to chop, haul, and set up shop.

Once again, he reminisced about the bounty of life his impetuous decision had bestowed on him. He could accomplish this feat now due to his 'schooling' on the 'Avenging Mother of The Sea'. No one could spend any time on the great sailing ships without picking up skills in almost all the trades. From wood working, sewing and repair of sailcloth, hewing the proper size and shape tree on an almost deserted island with nothing but hand tools to replace a main or mizzen mast. You had to know the tools, learn the skills, be willing to work night and day to survive on a merchant ship. The sea taught you all you would need to know about life, about living, about death, and joy. It was going to be a good day.

A good day until he failed to notice his horse zig around a hole in the ground and his foot slipped down the still muddy bank where he twisted his foot between several large tree roots. He pulled and turned the leg, but the roots held fast. He tried moving himself around the gapping maw to where maybe he could slip the foot free but all he accomplished was further twisting the ankle and causing sharp, stabbing pain that shot like a bolt of lightning through his calf, up his thigh, exploding through his abdomen, and into his head. He was in trouble.

The sun, which just moments before had brought such joy into his being, now beat down on him as it reached its zenith. He knew this suffering. He had survived it many times out in the middle of the South Pacific with nary a whisper of a breeze and nothing to provide cover.

He laughed, a loud bitter, bestial cackle. Here he was on his own land, not a tossing, angry sea, but on almost dry land and due to his own inattention and daydreaming he may have affected his own demise.. There was no one within several miles of where he lay and no one would come looking for him, as he had let it be known he wished privacy. He had no food, nor water, nor shade. Hoisted by his own foolish desires and fate, he lay back, trying to find the one position where the pain was sufferable and rest before attempting escape one more time.

Closing his eyes, he thought to pray, then stopped. Would that not be a betrayal to all he had believed since escaping the seminary? Would his last act on this earth be one of hypocrisy? To die with a lie on your lips was the cruelest passage he could imagine.

She came to him. His Roisin, on the second day of his entrapment. He lay in the now drying mud, the heat sucking the life from him. He hadn't eaten and there was no water except the tiny puddles inhabiting the few depressions his body had made. He was already dehydrated by his work; he had no reserves. A man could live a long time without food, but water was a necessity. So, she came to take him to wherever her people believed your soul would settle after the body had been used and tossed aside. His heart flew to her, glad he was to see her. No matter it was in the afterlife.

She smiled at him and shook her head. "Now look what you have got yourself into, mister."

"Can you help?" He knew it was childish and selfish to ask but he thought of his wife, his children, they would need him.

Roisin's face reflected the sorrow and pain of the situation, as she shook her head with a helpless 'no'. She could do nothing; she was spirit and soon so would he be. She turned to walk away, closing her eyes with wishes and powerlessness. She would wait for him on the other side.

With a wistfulness she turned one more time to face him. "How is the boy?" Her love for the child shown through.

Thomas lay back in the mud, pain distorting his features. Though from physical pain or of the soul it was impossible to tell. He hadn't thought he would have to face this great sin while he still took breaths, but she was here, either in his mind or in spectral form and she would not be denied.

"I don't know. After you died, I found a milk mother to nourish his body but there was nothing I could do to change his future. The hate of the ignorant for those who are different is strong. It pains me to admit that humans need someone to look down on, to feel superior to, to think of as lesser than human so they can dominate and use them. I also believe there was communal guilt that their treatment of you had instigated your death which led them to abuse, rather than console. Guilt is a strange bedfellow, either an emotion to lift you to greater heights or one to turn your heart cold and hard. There is no telling with people. So, I sent he and his milk mother off to the west, to a negro town, where they might find some contentment among their own kind." If confession was supposed to be good for the soul, he had done it wrong. He only felt the weight of his decision and its aftermath. "I sent money so they would want for naught." Was his weak defense.

"You should have kept him with you." It wasn't an accusation only a statement of fact.

"I thought he should be with his own," he was near tears, drowning in remorse.

"You were his own. He was of your blood. You thought you dreamed on the ship. T'was not dream but desire on both our parts to come together. To create a life of us both, though we knew in our waking hours such a thing was blasphemous. Our unconscious minds knew better." She sighed, "He was your son." And she was gone.

Thomas wanted nothing more than to scream his denial to the gods who had abandoned him as he had abandoned them. He couldn't. He knew in his heart she told him truth. He had sent away his first born to a life of hardship and poverty, of never knowing his true father. He had denied truth. His soul was damned, if not by some nameless, faceless, uncaring deity then by his own hand. Let him die with his transgressions. He closed his eyes to accept his own judgement.

The sun was setting and shades of red colored the sky, highlighted by deep purples close to the horizon and on the underbellies of the clouds Yellows snuck through to accent the blues of the sky and the browns of the forest. It was a beautiful sight to die by.

He heard the sound of twigs breaking as steps made their way cautiously towards him. He had to decide whether to play dead, in case of a human, or to rise up and show himself alive and strong in case of wild animal. He waited.

"'Scuse me, suh." It was not a voice he recognized. He waited, holding his breath. "You dead?" It was a tentative verbal nudge followed by a quick poke with one of the fallen branches nearby. Time stood still, awaiting the letting out of a breath. Another poke. "Suh." More urgent this time. Fear and worry filled out the query.

Thomas managed to rise from the waist to gaze into the bright white eyes that rested in the dark brown face. His head swam with the effort. He swooned before righting himself like a ship in heavy waves. A hand took hold of his shoulder to steady the vessel, though the owner of said hand stood back as far as arm and shoulder would allow.

"Do, do I know you?" It was the first thing that made it to Thomas' tongue.

"Well, not by rights, I guess, but we have waved like passing ships from time to time," the smile genuine, the joy at finding this man alive evident in those eyes.

"You're the squatter, yes?" Thomas was so weak he barely pushed the question into birth. Thomas had always thought there was a squatter camping on the land he had purchased. He had seen sign of footprints in the dirt and smoke deep in the forest. He had even caught sight of him in the past and just waved, there was plenty of land and no reason not to share it. Besides, he had no way of knowing if the man be squatter or just a recluse, a hermit of the forest.

The black man took a step back unsure of where this might be headed. He had come to help whoever was laying on the ground, not be chained and taken to jail as a trespasser. He could see this man was trapped where he lay, he felt safe laying his truth on the hard packed ground.

"I guess, tho' I believe I was squattin' afore y'all done settled here. So, I guess it's a chicken and egg question, innit?" He chuckled hopeful of a cordial resolution.

Thomas admired the man's logic and honesty. "I seem to have fallen into a hole; do you think you might help dig me out of it? No strings attached, just a neighborly assist." Both men grinned, though one with more verve than the other. "I'd prefer not to lie here any longer."

It took well past dark to free Thomas' leg and foot with some extremely careful digging and precision ax work by the dark-skinned man that impressed Thomas to no end. He was convinced, several times, the fella was going to cut his foot off but he wielded the ax like a surgeon cutting just enough of the tree root to free Thomas. Thomas gingerly stood, with aid from his newfound friend, after a few moments to catch breath and rest. Amazingly, it appeared nothing was broken and just sprained, he leaned on the man's shoulder who then helped Thomas limp back to his cabin where they found a very hungry and irritable horse waiting on the wrong side of the fence around its paddock. The colored man grabbed the feedbag of oats hanging on one of the fence posts and filled a bucket with water while Thomas insisted on limping inside and cooking a meal for them both.

"Ain't your woman gonna wonder where you been this whole time?" James, Thomas finally got the man's name out of him, asked over a sip of after dinner Kentucky bourbon. Thomas had an acquaintance in town who made twice yearly trips to a cousin with a still.

"She knows when I am involved in a project I might not show up at the main house for days or even a week or two," Thomas' lips twitched wishing a smile to express how much he loved Mary and her understanding of his needs.

"What kinda thing you projecting?" James' interest had been piqued by mention.

Thomas considered the man and then remembered his expertise with the ax. "I'm creating a scaled down model of my ship, which sank with me aboard, several years back. She was one of the great loves of my life." He sighed as he took a sip enjoying the warmth of the whiskey as it slid slowly towards his innards.

"Must be a helluva story there, suh," grinned the 'old' black man.

Thomas couldn't tell how old. His skin was smooth, though his head was ringed by a pure white halo of hair. He was spry enough to be in his thirties, though his eyes had the depth of great age. Thomas guessed him somewhere between thirty and his final chapter. He would be a good man to know, to work with, to friend.

He couldn't tell if it was the whiskey—and how he wished it was good Irish whiskey, not this brewed in the forest under full moon when the conditions are just right, rot gut—or relief at having not died stupidly with his foot stuck in a hole but Thomas began to tell his story to this man. James sat quietly sipping his own cup as Thomas' story unfolded in the cozy log cottage lit only by the crackling fire.

James kept his commentary on Thomas' tales to himself, deciding interrupting the story would be rude. He exclaimed at the proper points of discoveries, fighting, survival, and the capsizing and inheriting of the ship south of South America. He ooed and ahhed at descriptions of lands he would never see, not even in dreams. Thomas' descriptions exciting the imagination with wonder and glory. And he felt the sorrow at Roisin's loss.

The old man was coming to respect this foolish, strapping, white man who almost caused his own end. He was enthralled with Thomas' adventures and exploits around a world James would never have imagined in his wildest dreams. He knew where in the south he had spent much of his life as a slave. He also knew this island in the middle of the mighty Niagara close to a grand waterfall he had never journeyed to see, though he had heard it in the dead of night when the wind came from the west.

He was impressed with what Thomas had accomplished thus far on his pet project, as he could see the lines of Katherine's Wave coming together in the carving and placement of hand hewed boards for the hull. He inspected the sailcloth and hemp strings and, though he had never set eyes on a ship quite like the one Thomas meant to recreate, he could see it in his mind's eye. It enticed and aroused the creative spirit in him. He'd thought that well beaten out of him on the plantation. He found it rebirthed and crying for release.

"Would you like some hep on this, suh?" He knew he shouldn't question a white man or ask favor but his want to couldn't be denied.

Thomas considered the man's skill with the hatchet and shovel, thinking if he was as gifted with other tools or had the want to learn, it would be nice to have someone to share this vision with. His boys' curiosity hadn't been stimulated. They were more inclined to hang out in the small town of Grand Island with the few pretty young girls who resided there.

"I would love to have an extra pair of hands, if you have the time." Thomas didn't wish to seem too eager as he didn't wish to be beholden to anyone. "Though please call me Thomas, sir is for powerful men. It is a word that can denote respect or disdain."

"I would mean nothing but respect," James shook his head never realizing words would have such different meanings, "I believe that unless we respect one and other, we cannot live with one another." He was silent for a few moments lost in a world as foreign to Thomas as Thomas' was to James'. "See, mister, I was a slave most my life, I know what disrespect is. When Mr. Lincoln freed the slaves, we was happy; though we came to wish he had freed the minds of the enslavers at the same time. They never could think of us as anything but animals. Less than they cows, sheep, pigs or, especially, they horses. They could never imagine in their wildest us being anywhere near equal with." He wiped a bead of sweat from his face, then another. Tears, Thomas thought, but kept his thoughts to himself. "The sad thing is they thought by treating us as less than we would be less than but it didn't. What we discovered was they was making themselves less than by not realizing we was all the same just colored different. We was human just like them, but they couldn't see through they hate. It made them small and frightened of us. If they come to think of us as equal, well then, what would that make them for what they done to us?" The fire crackled and spit in the silence. Shadows danced on the walls like ghosts come to listen to the telling, keeping silent not wishing to stay the man's tongue.

Thomas wanted to say something, anything but he also didn't want to interrupt the man. Yes, the man. He leaned over and poured a healthy dollop of whiskey in James' cup before pouring himself a dram or two. He had never considered what slavery had done to the soul of the enslaver. He guessed he had never thought much about slavery, about humans owning other humans, at all. Although his people had been kept down below their English overlords on their own island, they could leave. As many did during the potato famine in the years while he was at sea.

"I guess Mr. Lincoln thought he could change people's minds by making it a law but you can't change people by lawin' them into it, you got to start when they young and learn them by living it. Childrens ain't born hating, they taught that, if you can teach them to hate you can teach them to be brothers and sisters." Thomas was captivated with how James' mind worked. How simple, yet so erudite. He was enlightened by life, not by study. He was kith and kin to Thomas in that aspect. Actually, in all aspects but color, he realized.

"I think I am going to enjoy your company and would greatly appreciate your skill," Thomas shook James' hand.

"Just stuff I picked up on the plantation. If you want to live and have a chance your woman and children won't be sold, you got to make yourself useful." James tipped his cup in toast, "Though sometime ain't none of that matters." A great melancholy settled over him. Thomas wanted to ask, but he thought they had dug a deep enough well today. They had time to learn of each other.

The friendship was sealed with a toast and a healthy sup of whiskey. James explained he had put in his spring crops. He could do a little weeding and work around his cabin in the morning then come to work with Thomas. When they had a day or so to relax, he would do some fishing on the Niagara and check and set his traps on the far side of the island for more substantive sustenance.

The two would meet at the log shanty, delegate what work would be accomplished and then set to carving, chopping, and planing. They worked in silence most of the time, concentrating on the job at hand. When working with chisels, knives, axes, and homemade gougers it was best to keep the mind on the doing. It was good work. Hard work. Sculpting wood while sculpting bodies. Thomas had allowed himself to soften in the middle, his arms had lost their tone while he had gained weight sitting and enjoying the good life. He missed the hard life on ships, climbing the main to sit all alone throughout the night in the crow's nest; hauling nets, taking in sail standing forty or fifty feet above the decks, the wind and ocean spray, the call of gulls as you came into port and the screech of the albatross far out to sea. This physical exercise felt good for the body and soul.

James would sometimes talk about his previous life, though Thomas thought it pained him. He had never met his father; he had been sold off before James could walk. When he was a child of maybe ten—he never knew how old he was as they didn't care to write down when he'd been born, property don't need to know such things— there had been some kind of rumpus late one night in the slave quarters. Two fellas been sippin' the corn mash and got into it. Somehow his mother had been implicated. They had sold her downriver the very next Saturday.

James had been a slave down Georgia way with his brother and sister, all that was left of the family. They learned to keep their heads down, do what they was told, and try to stay together as long as humanly possible. Humanly never come into it as first his brother, six years his senior, was sold during a bad year and massa needed money. The master of the plantation reckoning he could just breed up more boys with the slave women. They could either breed with their own or he and his could help whiten up the black race with some mulattos. One way or another the girls would have to replace lost inventory, of their own will or raped, the white man cared not.

The pure evil of the slavers shocked Thomas. He had seen slavers crossing the wide oceans but had never given a second thought as to the cargo. Several of the crew on the 'Avenging Mother' had served on slave ships. They would not talk about their time except to say it was the most inhumane time in their lives. They wouldn't say what but they alluded to acts that would stain their souls well into eternity.

"The main problem was, and still is," James began one early afternoon when the weather had turned too warm to be inside and a cooling breeze was riding the Niagara from Canada, "Mr. Lincoln freed the peoples but never told them how to be free. It was a pretty confusin' time. Nobody knew what they was s'pposed to do. Some of the slaves wanted retribution for their treatment. They wanted the power to go after them what had been so cruel, but they had no weapons, no wherewithal to obtain that power. And to be honest I was just as glad they never did. I didn't want to see my people turned into folks what had done all this evil because that would mean we was just as evil." He wiped sweat from his brow with an old rag he kept in the back pocket of his overalls.

"You can't just set free what ain't never know'd freedom. They don't know how to act without being told. We been told what to do every second of our lives since we was born. Now we supposed to figure out the hardest thing ever, being ourselves. We didn't know what we was, we don't know what we ain't. All we know is white folk seems to hate us even more than they did when they owned us. At least when they owned us, we knew where we stood. We was nothin'. Now we nothin' with a little bit o something and the white folks want that little bit back. Got ugly, I got out." His attention found its way back to the mizzen mast he was sanding and preparing to connect the yards with the twisted hemp strings.

Crickets chirped in the deep forest while ducks splashed and swam in the river, which burbled playfully free as the wind, as if unaware of the fate awaiting it several miles upstream. You would think the river could hear the sound of the Falls, this far upriver the water was joyfully oblivious.

Never taking his eyes off the spar, James continued his story, "Thought about heading down river to try and find my mother but that was just asking for trouble. White man catch you alone wandering near his property, he might have a mind to see what you look like swinging in a tree. Or maybe his friends join in and drag you for a while behind they carriages or horses."

He took a quick glance over to where Thomas was meticulously carving the figurehead. His face was lined with concentration as his hand, steady as the island they stood upon, found lines in the wood to accent what he had in his mind. The face was stunning, innocent yet steadfast, the kind of face you wanted to wake up to forever. The hair framed this beauty in long flowing curls. They had the look of the ocean, James thought, though he had never seen the ocean. There was love in those eyes, James thought they might blink in the brilliant sun and ask for some shade. Lips pouty but not in a petulant way more as if in thought. Yes, that was one fine looking woman and she would add magnificence and allure to this ship.

"How'd you find your way to this island?" Thomas had listened to James' tales with intense interest. His respect for the man had grown exponentially with each new story. He was a man who had survived the worst that mankind could offer. He had worn their indifference like a suit of armor to keep their hate from his heart. His mind was a thing of wonder and beauty. How was it possible to think such thoughts when you had endured the beatings, the loss of family, the rapes of sister and mother, and every woman he knew, the violence, and still James did not want his own pound of flesh, just to live.

"I was making my way to Canada. Word on the railroad had been if you can get to Canada, you find freedom, a good life." He chuckled as he spoke at the innocence and gullibility of his plan. He was a little taken aback by the sound of Thomas laughing; or was that the sound of him gasping for tear filled breaths?

James took in Thomas without staring at him, give the man some privacy. Thomas wiped his eyes unsure himself whether he had laughed at James misconception of what he would find or wept at his memory of Roisin. Yeah, they had come to Canada thinking the same only to have found a sorrow that filled life.

"Yeah, I guess you know what I found," said James recalling Thomas' mention of his girl. "Wasn't so friendly, so I come back across the river and settled here. Didn't know nobody owned this land and when I seen you and t'other fella clearing and building never crossed my mind you might've bought my squat right out from under me. I was gladdened when you two would just wave hello and leave me be!" His white teeth gleamed in the afternoon warmth.

"I want you to know you are welcome to live on this land for as long as you or your family wish. Anybody says boo to you, you just mention my name and have them come talk to me. We'll straighten them out."

"I 'ppreciate that, I really do. I know it ain't my land, as it were, but it means a lot to have a home where I am welcome," he wiped a drop of rain that fell from a clear blue sky and landed gently on his cheek. "though I don't think I be makin' a family any time soon." To which their loud laughter set the birds to wing with joy.

Every Journey Begins With a Dollop of Trepidation

Present Day

"May I ask you something?" Tom eased the question across the room where Aoife was packing her few things along with her laptop and external drive. It would all fit in one small suitcase, she traveled light. Tom could learn much from this person, including how to travel. He had never been one for the road or flying to exotic ports of call. He had been happily ensconced in his cubby on the north side. Now he was preparing to venture out into the world of man with little or no knowledge of how to interact, relate to the normal person. He was, once again, grateful to have an interpreter and guide.

It was about this time that Tom realized he couldn't find his suitcase, bringing on the realization that was because he didn't own a suitcase. One did not need suitcases when the furthest one traveled was to the nearest dining establishment. How to tell Aoife?

She turned to see how he was coming along and saw the expression on his face. "What is it?"

"Well, you see, I don't get a round much, and haven't traveled very far, and, uh, well, you see. . ." he rumbled, stumbled, and bumbled.

"You don't own a suitcase, do you?" It was midpoint of accusation and pity.

"There was never any need, you see, I, uh, just . . ." it spit, backfired, almost turned over and then died.

"

"Grab your jacket and hat, we're going shopping." Tom sensed words entering his mouth but she shushed him before they could attempt an escape.

They hailed a cab at the front portal to the condominiums and Aoife told the man what they were in search of. Cabbies, the good ones, know where everything bought, sold, rented, drank, eaten, debauched, worshipped, and bailed could be found in the city. This was a good one. He knew of a luggage store with very deep discounted prices but excellent quality. They had him wait out front while Tom and Aoife went to choose a nice small suitcase for Tom. The Cabbie could keep the meter running so as not to lose a dime while they shopped.

Black, nondescript, large enough for several days of clean underwear, socks, a change of shoes and several comfortable shirts and two pair of slacks. His laptop would fit perfectly in the padded zipper pocket on the front and it had wheels that would take it in any direction. Tom was elated!

Back at the condo Tom carefully folded and placed his belongings in his new bag. Everything would hold everything else so nothing would wrinkle needlessly. It had straps to assure a tight fit. It was wonderful. As they exited the condo once more the same cabbie came around the corner to pick them up. He had heard them talking in the back about their upcoming trip and need of a ride to Union Station. They had paid him and tipped him well, he thought he should be there when they needed him.

They chatted about what eastern Michigan might be like, whether it would be wild and overgrown like a forest or tamed and civilized like Chicago. The cabbie chimed in that he was, in fact, from eastern Michigan and he could assure that the people there were as civilized as anywhere on the continent. He was from the southwest outskirts of Detroit and though Detroit itself could have a bit of rough trade the exurbs would be downright rural. Just like Chicago only smaller and less loved.

They asked if he had heard of a town called Samaria, to which he admitted ignorance. Though he perked up when they mentioned it was close to Temperance. He was from down near Luna Pier which was directly east of Temperance and much more fun. It sat on the banks of the western shore of Lake Erie; a summer town, though it had seen better days.

He stopped midsentence as he was reminiscing and glared into the rearview mirror. "You folks on the run from something? Robbed a liquor store? Murdered the Mayor? Parking tickets?" Though his tone attempted joviality his expression suggested something a tad more sinister.

"No, why do you ask?" It was Tom who sensed it first. He wanted to turn his head to look at what had the cabbie's attention but fought the urge.

"Nothing, just that, this cop has been on my ass almost since we left your home." Now he turned his head to glare at the two cops in the panda directly behind them.

Tom turned and did not like what he saw. He recognized both men from the courtroom, friends of Sgt. Pulaski. This did not bode well. And he was done with all this faux intimidation. "Pull over." He instructed the cabbie, "This will only take a minute."

The cabbie pulled the vehicle over to the curb where Tom made a slow show of getting out. It really was the only show he could make as his size and the proximity of the curb made exiting the cab awkward.

He straightened himself and stood ready for whatever these two thought to bring. He could feel the indignation churning in his bowels, either he was going to shit himself or he was going to make a stand. Considering he only had the other two pair of slacks in his new suitcase his body told him he had best choose well. He would make a stand.

"Hello gentlemen," he smiled graciously, no hint of threat about him except in his eyes, "something I can do for you?" He glanced over to see Aoife with her phone held steady in the window and recording the episode.

The two cops gave each other a wary shrug and shake of the noggin. "We see you are leaving town," said the squat one with the beady eyes.

"Is there some law you might have found or made up to impede my exit?" Tom found himself clinging to his control. What had he done but get some sushi and sashimi to have earned constant surveillance?

"No, actually we wanted to apologize for the scene at the courtroom." Now it was the taller of the two who spoke, his hand on his protruding belly in a convivial way. "We were standing with a fellow officer as our brotherhood demands. To be honest we don't much care for Pulaski. He's been a dick since he came on the force and worse since they made him a sergeant." He coughed his enmity into a meaty fist. "What you did in court, standing up to him and us, made us question blind loyalty. We did a little digging and found you are not the first innocent man he shot or browbeat to make himself feel like a big man. Though we think you might like to know, you will be the last he does that to in uniform. He has been taken off paid administrative leave and put on permanent dismissal." He offered his hand and Tom took it weakly before adding pressure. This was not what he expected, though it was far superior to the scene that had played out in Tom's head.

Back in the cab the tension melted like butter on a hot skillet. "That was interesting." Proclaimed relief as the body followed suit and relaxed noticeably.

The cabbie chuckled into the rearview mirror, "I seen a lot of things but I ain't never seen a cop fess up to a colored man!" The cabbie several shades darker than Tom found himself in a world he had never considered possible.

Union Station was a riot of humanity. Evidently every person in Chicago had decided to go elsewhere today. He was corrected as he bought their tickets and mentioned the cluster of humans in the station. The ticket agent explained that it was slow, as it was Thursday and just another workday. However, had it been one of the many three-day weekends the crowd would be three times the size. Enjoy the quiet, he yelled over the noise of the station.

The train was clean by human standards, though those standards can leave much to be desired. Tom had bought them first class tickets so as to avoid the hoi palloi as much as possible. It was not that Tom didn't like people, per se, he just didn't like them in large numbers or where something might spook the masses and they riot or stampede. Tom was of the opinion many human beings would've benefitted greatly from another year or two in kindergarten. Most could not color on the same page let alone within the lines. People were messy things best kept at home.

It was not that Tom was fastidious in his own personal care and feeding. If he was involved in new codes or programing, he could let his dishes pile up in the sink and there'd be an empty takeout container left on the kitchen counter, and the vacuum would know a solitude that would terrify humans. But, sooner rather than later, it would pick at his psyche until he would close the laptop, focus his attention on the 'mess' in the kitchen, cleanse his guilt and assuage his very slight OCD while taking the lonely vac for a turn around the abode. Most humans, at least from his limited observations were content to live, work, and sleep in their own feculence. They left a trail of refuse wherever they had been, including in the first-class compartment of this train.

The train was still in the station when he found the conductor in charge and begged for a garbage bag and a pair of rubber gloves. He had the misconception that if he asked, the person in charge would say, 'worry not, I shall endeavor to find someone to come cleanse the area!' She had not, she had simply found the items he had requested and brought them to him. He donned the gloves and carefully straightened the compartment while Aoife donned an amused expression, sat back in her seat, and watched him.

"I don't suppose you'd care to lend a hand?" he ventured.

"Oh no," her facial features morphed into seriousness, "I would not presume to interfere with the work of an artist." She opened her laptop and began tapping away.

Tom wanted to say something but choose the better part of valor and closed his lips against what would surely have been a loss. He completed the final touches on his cleansing and sat back in the seat as the train left the station and began winding its way through the railyards of Chicago.

As they headed east through Hammond and Gary, Tom found the rocking of the train somewhat disconcerting. He had believed, from previous excursions up through Wisconsin for business, the ride would be smoother, less rattling and swaying. Aoife explained that this is what happens when passenger and freight trains shared tracks. The freight trains, being much heavier and not as well maintained, rode on tracks where the 'passengers' cared little for their comfort. As such, the rail companies felt little or no need to do necessary repairs until absolutely necessary. The tracks were made for freight not humans.

The train at long last settled into a comforting rhythm. Tom opened his laptop to do some research on the area they intended to search. One of the great benefits to rail travel, he had discovered in years past, was the ability to be constantly connected to the world wide web. It was comfort enough for the nonce. His eye constantly wandered to the wide-open plains of Northern Indiana and Southern Michigan. He had been of the opinion that the great plains ended well before where the midwestern metropolis of Chicago, and surrounding greater Chicagoland suburbs and exurbs, grew. It would seem the land held its flat, open territory for quite a distance past that assumption.

They should be into Toledo around 11:30 pm with a car waiting for them at the station. That is, if the train was on time. Aoife also explained to Tom that since they shared the tracks with freight trains, and since freight lines owned the tracks, that if a freight train was approaching or catching them from behind, they would have to pull over and allow the trains to pass.

Tom was astounded! "You mean to tell me that in this day and age of computer operated everything where all things can be scheduled down to the nano second, they can't get the trains on a schedule that would alleviate such inconveniences?" He gazed out the window at the oncoming darkness, shocked such would be allowed to exist in a technological civilization. "It should be simple arithmetic to pull together all the trains, the times required to get from point A to point Q and plot a course for each and every one of them. They do it every day for tens of thousands of airlines!" He was truly appalled.

"That's true," she agreed wholeheartedly, "but they care about airlines and the millions who fly, not about passenger trains and the thousands who enjoy them. It's all in the numbers." She bent her head to better read her screen.

Tom stared out the window into the oncoming dusk and his mind wandered. What would they find? Would there be any tangible facts to tie him to this woman and boy. They had come from Canada, was he Canadian? And was Canadian even an ethnicity? So many questions, so many trails to follow, would any of them pan out?

He was tired. Tired of not knowing. Tired of his run in with the police and subsequent court hearings and threats. Tired of not feeling quite up to one hundred percent, though he definitely was running at eighty-five to eighty-seven percent of his pre-shooting self. He found himself acting even more timid than his usual self since the shooting, though Aoife was helping him overcome some of that timidity. And what of her? He wanted to search the web for any information there might be on her. She was too good to be true, stunning, brilliant mind, a joy to be near and way, way, way beyond his pay grade. He should get his laptop and do some digging on the mother and boy, and Aoife.

The sharp intake of breath brought him out of his revery. The shocked expression on the stunning woman across the seat from him pinned him to his own. What had he done? Had he accidently passed something he shouldn't have in the presence of a lady? He hadn't felt anything untoward happen within his physique. What was she staring at?

His laptop rested comfortably on his lap, nothing weird about that. It was where he always set it while working. But he hadn't been working, he'd been daydreaming and if he recollected correctly, the machine had been resting comfortably on the seat next to him when he took his brief mental holiday. He must have reached over and grabbed it without thinking.

He smiled a reassuring smile towards her and she shook it off like a pitcher not liking what the catcher called. What the?

"How did you do that?" It wasn't actually fear that filled the spaces between syllables it was more wonder and awe.

"Do what?" He may be slow on the uptake but uptake he would have.

"The computer was sitting on the seat and it," she searched her gifted mind for what she wished to express and settled on, "levitated off the seat and floated over to set itself on your lap. Like a dog being called to its master."

"I'm certain you imagined that. It's been a long day, the train has been taxing with its swaying and jerking, You are tired, that's all." He made it sound so reasonable.

"I am not now, nor have I ever been, prone to flights of fancy or wild imagination. I am a rational, well-educated, and sane individual and I know what I witnessed. Had I been quicker of thought or action I would have grabbed my phone and videoed the happening."

Tom wanted to quell her angst but he knew from their time together what she said was truth, therefore he had to believe that she saw what she saw.

"Do it again!" She spoke it like a young child that had just been amazed and astounded by the greatest magic trick ever.

"I don't think that feasible, as I have no idea how I did it in the first place. I didn't do anything except think I should grab my computer and do a little work while we traveled." His tone was hesitant and unsteady. If what she said had happened, had happened. Then how? Why? And could he actually replicate it?

After several frustrating and foolish attempts, he gave up. There was nothing he could imagine he wanted more right now than to pull a miracle out of his hat. Wrong hat.

Once it became obvious that Tom either couldn't or wouldn't repeat the trick of the floating laptop, Aoife returned her attention back to her own workstation bobbing in her lap. Maybe he was right, maybe she had imagined the floating machine due to the stress of the past few days and the bobbing and weaving of train travel. Or maybe there was more to this man and his history than either knew or thought feasible. Is it possible he has hidden powers of which not even he is aware? She thought back to the courtroom when the fifteen minutes had closed and all were being ushered back in. The cops were waiting, threatening in their stance, as she and Tom made to enter. They meant to block the couples' way, to create a wall of menace to give warning. 'Don't say another word against our comrade!' was implied or else. Though as Tom approached and made to walk through the doorway they moved back, as if pushed by an unseen force.

He hadn't done anything; hadn't raised a hand, made a gesture, or given them a dirty look. They simply parted, allowing a corridor to open for Tom and her to walk through, slightly surprised or flabbergasted by their involuntary action. One had even gazed down at his chest expecting to find a hand or arm pushing him back only to find shirt and badge.

Tom had appeared nonplussed. Either he hadn't taken notice or was too distracted by the affairs of the law. Could it be possible he had some latent magical or sorcerous power? Or was she imagining a story out of a fantasy novel read as an impressionable young girl. She shook her head to dispel the notion. There was no such thing in the rational world as 'magic,' though it would explain his genius with code and his brilliance at obfuscation. Maybe, just maybe, he had some hidden powers which allowed him preternatural skills that no one else possessed and that was why no one, no matter their acumen, could break his encryption.

She required a soft bed, quiet, and eight solid hours. She hoped the car would be waiting for them at the train station so they could go from passenger car to luxury car to hotel. She had made all the arraignments, now let's see if the other end had complied.

They pulled into the station only an hour late, though an hour more rail wearied, to find the gleaming sports car waiting in the parking spot her luxury car was presumed to occupy. A quick call to the rental company, an ensuing argument about what was ordered and what the prepubescent dolt on the other end thought she would prefer before a short half hour wait for the delivery of something more suitable and comfortable. Tom was not a sports car sized man and she was not a sports car ride woman. Something to smooth out the bumps of the railroads of America, not feel each and every one on her roads.

It was with mild trepidation that she entered the upscale hotel—when one is engaged in a folly which will result in a merger of intellect and information worth hundreds of millions, if not billions of dollars, one did not skimp on the accoutrements.

Yes, she had a reservation. Yes, it was under her name. And yes, it was for two suites with king sized beds and quiet. She held her breath.

"Hmmm, the reservation said you would be in by nine p.m., long day on the road?" She couldn't tell if the young man behind the counter was preparing her for disappointment or just making conversation, either way she wanted him to dance on the keyboard and give them room keys. "Ah, paid in advance. We have your rooms ready. If there is anything else. . .?" He handed them both their keys.

Aoife led Tom to the elevator in silence.

No Island Defines a Man

Late Fall 1873

"You meant what you said last night, didn't you?" They were sawing what was left of the tree trunk into movable pieces. They'd start on the larger branches tomorrow.

"About what, suh?" James thought about all they had conversed about the night before, there was much water in that hole. "Sorry," he said to Thomas expression, "it's going to be hard to break that habit. When a word been beat, whooped, and branded into your soul, it don't come loose overnight."

"About slavers not thinking of you and yours as human." Thomas could not wrap his head around the concept. Oh, there'd been a crewman or two he hadn't thought much of, but that was because of the way they avoided work, or tried to worm their way up the ladder by stomping on those below. Some people just were scum, lowlifes, schemers, and reprobates, though he never thought of them as less than human, just humans he wanted nothing to do with.

"Oh yeah, but it weren't their fault, necessarily. It was drilled into their heads just as surely as it was drilled and beat into our own. They done had generations of hate to build on. I once saw a white boy treating a slave like he was something other than property. Theys talking and laughing for just a minute, he didn't know no better, just a little man, and his daddy come out an whooped that boy from one end of the yard to the other. Then had the slave whipped for allowing such a thing. What was the slave supposed to do, the boy talked to him first, he just answered like he supposed to.

Damn near killed the man. Nothing nobody could do, slave was property, slaver could do what he want with him.

"Now if'n that white slave owner had allowed that boy to treat that slave like a person what would that mean to every other white person what owned slaves. They would have to look in the mirror every day and see someone who owned, beat, and worked to death, not an animal or some horrible thing what couldn't survive without the benevolence of the owner, but another human being. Maybe they got a soul just like the white man, maybe they got thoughts and wants and desires and could be trained just like white children to be more than property. Well, that would be just too much for that white person to bear. He'd have to admit he was a despicable, evil thing that his own God would despise. So, they turn them stories in their book to make it seem that they God wants them to treat us like they do. They God wants them to rule over us and beat the love of that God into us, though they know we going to they hell just by being black." He spit into the hole he'd been standing in while cutting the trunk. "They never stop to realize we was already livin' in they hell. They the ones what condemned us to it." He was silent as death for several heartbeats.

"You want to know what hell is? Watch your woman bein' raped by a half dozen of them or your daughter. Watch them beat your son almost to death while you stand impotent. Watch them sell your family for whiskey or land and know they prize the whiskey and land more than your own. Yeah, we know what they hell is." He picked up an ax and began pruning small branches off the larger ones needing something to concentrate on besides that past. "Our only hope was that one day, even after they dead, they would find out what they hell is."

A quiet wrapped the forest like a mother comforting her child, even the birds, the animals, the trees, and wind took soft shallow breaths as if respecting James' story and life. Thomas had no words to express his sorrow at the life forced on James and so many millions, yes millions, of others over the centuries. The brilliant sunshine, dancing in and out of tree limbs and shadows, afraid to show its full face, not wishing them to think it mocked.

"I'm sorry." It was such an inadequate declaration of sympathy Thomas almost wished he had held it in his mouth until the sour taste went away.

"You got nothin' to be sorry about," James smiled, "you never owned no one did you?" He waited for Thomas to shake his head, "not even that girl you traipsed around with?"

That brought a laugh from deep inside Thomas' soul and brought to the surface like a breeching whale some very hard, very sad, yet very wonderful memories hidden for decades. He hadn't thought of her often enough after marrying Mary and the birth of Katherine. It still set him aback that he had told the story to James. Guilt filled his belly, the least he could do was take time to remember. He guessed he had pushed her out of his mind in respect to Mary. That if he thought of her, it would be like he was being untrue to his wife. But it wasn't. It was taking the time to hold someone, a friend, a student, a kind soul, close to his heart, that was fine, wasn't it?

He laughed in release and shook his head, "No one owned Roisin." He said wiping a tear. "She was her own person whether here or on her island. Even her tribe could not pretend they owned even a piece of her. She was as independent and strong willed a person as I have ever known and deserved far better than the suffering and death she endured." Now, Thomas gazed into the clear blue sky as if seeking her spirit. If anyone could come back from the other side it would have been her. And he rekindled the memory of her coming to him as he lay in the mud, dying. There was a magic, a charm about the woman that he'd heard called Voodoo, though he thought that too dark of an explanation of her essence. She was pure. Created and raised by the jungle and reflecting the mystique of that holy place. He missed her.

"I guess I feel guilty about how things turned out." Thomas locked eyes with the old, black man so he would know the truth of his heart. "She probably would have been better off staying on her island."

"Thought you told me you rescued her from the abuse on that island. That everyone thought she a witch and treated her as such. Not even her own people wanted no part, ain't that true?" James challenged Thomas' self-pity. "What would her life been if'n she stayed there?"

"I guess," Thomas was not about to give in to the offer of absolution.

"Would leaving her on that island have changed the outcome of her life? At least when she was with you, she had a friend, a friend who defended her and took care of her. She was well-fed and respected, yes?" Thomas nodded, "Then if you ask me, she was given a great gift, you! If'n she'd a stayed on that island she'd a had nobody but the jungle and lonely. She might not have lived long, but she lived longer and free from their fear and loathing. You can't gage another's life by your own. One man's suffering is another man's freedom. It seem to be in the view." He reached over and grabbed Thomas by the shoulder and gave him a shake. "We got work to do 'fore sundown."

Thomas nodded his gratitude for the words, for James' wisdom. It made him wonder what in all hell could make someone think that another person, especially this person, was lesser than them just because of the color of their skin.

It took most of the rest of the summer, but with James' help and a little assist from his boys, who had finally found their curiosity as to what father was up to, to finish the ship. Earl had proved a bit of a hardcase not wishing to work with a black man, and a former slave, at that. He had been hanging around a group of the more affluent—if you could use that word when describing a small hamlet on an island in the middle of a river—boys in the town of Grand Island. These were boys who had grown up with most of their needs taken care of by servants, maids, and very permissive parents. The parents spoiled the children and the children then spoiled anything they touched. They also had a very high opinion of themselves and their place in society. And that didn't include former slaves and darkies.

Thomas had considered commanding the boy to join in the family ship building brigade but Mary talked him out of it. You can't command someone to accept others, they had to find their own way. He may carry his grandfather's name but it would take a bit of living before he earned it. James had heartily concurred remembering how the white folks down home had reacted to being ordered to accept their former slaves as free men.

Thomas decided the better course of action would be for he, James, Jack, and Thomas Jr. to never mention the work in front of Earl. They could talk, play, wrestle, anything else boys were wont to do but never bring up the ship, even if he asked. Just tell him it was coming along. Thomas kept the workshop locked and only he had the key. If the boy wanted to know about the progress, he'd have to earn it.

He guessed it was the thought of his grandfather's displeasure if he'd lived long enough to witness Earl's disrespect of another human being, that brought Earl to the cabin one day. He had always been close to Mary's father. He, being the youngest and therefore the babe, became the apple of the elder man's life. The other boys and his granddaughter had aged out of wanting to ride on his bowed shoulders or listen to his stories from the Blessed Isle. Peer pressure can be compelling but the love of a grandparent, even one who had passed on, overrode all other considerations.

Now it truly was a family project, working hand in hand with their neighbor. Even Earl came to respect the old man's skill and wisdom. Yes, thought Thomas, he was becoming a good man. All the boys learned the art of carving, whittling, and woodworking. They were impressed their father knew as much as he did and had a deft hand with carving knives, chisels, and gouges. They were even more impressed with their neighbor's artistic bent when they saw how he had sanded and cleaned up all the imperfections on the figurehead. It was the spitting image of Thomas' wife, their mother. They wept with the beauty, the perfection, it was as though she was about to come alive and speak to them. James nodded his approval at his own handywork.

It was magnificent, or so said everyone who came to the unveiling at the McDermott residence. There weren't but a thousand or so warm bodies on the entirety of the island. Far less than that came out to view what Thomas and James had created. The broadsheet out of Tonawanda called the workmanship and skill to be of Master class. They even mentioned James' participation and that he was a respected neighbor of Thomas McDermott and family. In honor of his contribution and masterful workmanship he had been gifted the piece of land adjacent to the backwoods of the McDermott property.

He had a legal deed for the land paid in full. No one was more shocked, astounded, and grateful than James himself, he had not expected anything so generous. His own land. A piece of God's green earth that was his and his alone. He wept openly at the benevolence.

As the years walked by, picking up their pace, Thomas and James became closer, spending many evenings sipping the whiskey Thomas now had shipped to him from the new state of Kentucky. They would swap stories, laugh, and cry at each other's adventures. Thomas, amazed and astounded by James' journey from slavery and unimaginable cruelty in the south, to his contentment once settled on Grand Island. James was equally amazed and astounded by Thomas' journey from religious acolyte to stowaway to sailor riding the waves, literally, around the world. He was amazed learning of the different people he had met in thousands of ports and islands throughout a decade of travel, how he had become captain of the ship, *'Daughter of The Sea'*, after losing the despicable, though very able, captain when they rolled beneath the waves of the Drake passage. He could not imagine the horror, the terror that must have run through Thomas as he held on for dear life.

He loved the story of Roisin, and Thomas taking her from the superstitions of her island. Though when Thomas told him of the weird and eerie occurrences involving Roisin and the supernatural, he had to admit he might have been more than spooked himself. James could tell Thomas loved the woman though he never touched her in that way. Thomas was too good of a man to despoil someone he respected and loved.

Thomas never spoke of her visitation while he lay delirious waiting to die, nor what she told him. The child was his. He found it hard to contemplate the possible truth of that statement. She was dead, he was near death and having visions, maybe wishes, as his life played out on the blank parchment of his fevered mind. Had he sullied her in his dreams? Had he a deep-seated desire to mate with her? Had her spirit lied to him when she told him the child was his? It had the ring of truth when she had come to him, now he couldn't be so certain.

He thought James would lose respect for him if he told the man what Roisin had imparted to him. James was his friend, his only friend truth be told, and he feared what he would see in the man's eyes if he knew. He would keep his secrets deep in his soul until death weighed them and then God could determine the truth of the matter.

It was late one evening, the sun well put to bed and sleeping, when Jack came barging into the library where Thomas sat reading. He was overwrought, sweaty from running, and having difficulty finding his tongue.

"What is it, son?" Thomas tried to calm the young man but he would not be calmed.

"Some of Earl's old chums, the Edsen twins and one or two others. They have been drinking pretty hard. They started in on him about his negro. Earl's fury found fodder and exploded. He took great umbrage at their talk and language; a fight broke out and Earl took a beating. He's being cared for in town!" Jack took a breath to compose himself as Thomas leapt from his chair.

"I've got to go to him this minute and see if he lives!" Thomas found his own fury aroused. He wanted retribution but first he had to find the condition of his son.

"Thomas Jr. is with him. I came to get you because the whiskey and the fight ignited their hatred and they are on their way to James' cabin. We have to go and stop them or get him out of there!" Now Thomas found himself between the hammer and the anvil. He wanted to go to his son but he also had to save his only friend.

He grabbed a hatchet and a gouge as he ran past where he had been working earlier in the day with James. They had discovered they worked well together and wished to begin another, much larger creation. Now Thomas needed the tools to fend off evil.

He ran through the forest not caring whether his feet touched ground, rock or root, Jack hard on his heels. They had worn a path between the two homes over the past year and he ran down it with abandon. How long ago had this occurred? Did he have the time to get there before these entitled brats found James alone? His breath hard and ragged as he pushed himself to pick up his pace.

They saw the glow of the fire before they saw the flames. James' cabin was engulfed in an inferno. Where was James? His eyes searched the property seeking any sign of the old man. He saw several of the young toughs standing well away from the flames, laughing, and pointing, while taking long draughts from the jug being passed.

Thomas felt his rage ignite and erupt. All he saw was red, he felt nothing but righteous anger and launched himself at the circle of laughing, foul, fiends. He took out the first one with a fist to his temple, he knocked another senseless with the face of the hatchet. He would've killed the third had not Jack tackled him to the ground. He made to take a killing blow to whoever had stopped his fury until he saw his son laying on the ground next to him.

He rose from the ground and turned to where the cabin was collapsing in on itself. There was no sign of James anywhere. He called his name. Waited, called again louder. One of the boys lifted his head and grinned, " the nig's in there." He laughed pointing at the cabin before crumpling to the ground.

Thomas ran to see if he could see James in the rubble. There were only charred remains of a home. James was somewhere under the desecration. Thomas fell to his knees. He wanted nothing more than to rise and finish the job he had begun until he heard James' voice in his head begging him not to.

'Killing just leads to more killing and then, where does it stop?' He heard James' calm wisdom and knew he was being given a chance to be better. 'You gave me peace, land, respect. I am grateful. You gave me life, don't waste that gift.'

The silence was only broken by the sound of the crackling of dying flames and the moans off to his left.

Riddles in The Palm of The Hand
Present Day

Tom slept fitfully, it was not the bed or the unfamiliar surroundings—though that had been a concern as he was a man who rarely slept in any bed other than his own—but his mind ran in circles until he was certain he would fall asleep from exhaustion. He was unaware that Aoife was running right next to him on her own treadmill. Though Tom was running faster in place, digging deeper in an old hole, and going over and over the same ground he and Aoife had traversed previously, she was plotting a new course without a map.

On the night of the shooting things had transpired at a lightning pace. He, walking home with his dinner, sneaking bites behind his own back, enjoying the neanderthal experience of shoving food into one's maw by finger only. There is something so freeing about leaving civilized proprieties on the tree lawn and living on the edge. He was lost in the experience and thoughts of the new life he hoped lay just beyond the next corner when the flashing red and blue lights yanked him back to the reality of the now. Then the idiotic exchange with the cop. The anger, the fear, the hate in the man's eyes. Of he himself attempting to lower the temperature before someone got hurt, as he was well aware if someone was getting hurt the odds were he would be the one on the receiving end.

That was when everything slowed down and he could observe events in quarter time. He saw his arm hold out the sushi so the cop would realize he was no threat. He hadn't realized the threat was already well-placed in the cop's head.

The threat had been there for years just seeking release. The fish released it. He looked down the barrel of the pistol, mentally computed the end points, took in consideration vectors and distance formulas and his chances of avoiding the projectile from entering his chest at the exact point where his heart hid. He knew intellectually there was no possible way for the officer to miss his target. If only Tom could alter the trajectory, force the man's hand just to the left. He saw the shock on Sgt. Pulaski face as he pulled the trigger his hand moving an inch to his left, changing the course of the bullet. He felt it enter his body. He guided the bullet through his interior, missing all major organs and exiting out his back. How had that happened? Wishes only came true in fairy tales and drunken dreams. But it had. Had he somehow mentally forced the action just as he had, apparently, cause the laptop to levitate from the seat and softly land in his lap?

Here's where things got hinky. He had to consider that he might be a sorcerer or had some kind of magical powers. He laughed. A hard loud, belly laugh he was certain would wake up everyone on the floor if not in the entire hotel. How naïve could one genius be? He had already been gifted with an amazing mind that could figure out mathematics and coding faster and more thoroughly than anyone he'd ever met or known, wasn't that enough? Or was it possible that his 'gift' with technology was actually based in his 'gift' in the paranormal?

And that was why Tom Webb was awake most of the night. He floated between wanting to believe and the realization of how foolish that belief was. He would have to accept he wasn't brilliant and intellectually superior; he was simply magical. And here, he couldn't contain the laughter anymore; he thought he might wet the bed.

Tom was tired, cranky, and upset with himself for the loss of sleep. He considered himself to be a disciplined individual, in control of his mind and emotions, but his head spent the better part of the night wishing and pretending he was imbued with some kind of mystical powers like a character out of a Harry Potter novel. He wasn't. He was a rational, intelligent, balanced individual, not some preteen, pimply faced child wishing on a star. He had gotten to where he was by intellect, hard work, and deductive reasoning, not magic.

So, it was a cranky Tom that came down to meet Aoife for breakfast. He required coffee, eggs, a meat product, toast, and juice. Then, maybe, he could face the prospect of sitting in an automobile for several hours. He had never driven anywhere except in the confines of Greater Chicagoland and he found that experience miserable. The idea of spending several hours wrapped in the insanity of thousands of other vehicles filled with rage and screaming humans caused his body to shudder uncontrollably.

His hands shook as he pumped the dark roast into his paper cup, and filled his Styrofoam plate with hash browns, scrambled yellow, hockey puck sausages, and a thimble full of blueberry yogurt. These hotels would supply you a breakfast but they were not about to go overboard on folks they would, more than likely, never see again.

He sat across the table from his stunning companion who, by the look of her, had managed her time much more efficiently than he. Jealousy raised its ugly noggin before he slapped it back in place. His lack of sleep was not her fault!

Tom was pleasantly surprised when Aoife explained that it was but an hour tops to reach the historical society of Monroe County, not several hours. They would head there first, discover what they could from the volunteers, and then drive the twenty minutes to Samaria and see if they could locate where Mary and Tom's farm was. That would be the most difficult search as she was certain nothing of their presence would still exist, but it was worth the short drive.

The voyage up north was far more pleasant than Tom could have imagined. It would seem that driving—when not surrounded by the majority of the civilized world all hell bent on going to the exact same speck of earth with undo haste, anxiety, and rage—was far more pleasurable than he had ever experienced in the confines of Greater Chicagoland. Yes, there was traffic but one could observe emptiness between the properly spaced vehicles. No one looked to be aggressively seeking a victim, someone to be dashed to smithereens, along this stretch of highway.

They arrived safe and sound in the mighty metropolis of Monroe, Michigan, with nary a scratch and mentally relaxed. Housed in a 1911 Georgian Post Office, the museum looked to contain all the knowledge and history of greater Monroe County. It was brick and stone and had a sense of permanence. It should, it had survived well over a hundred years of harsh winters and blazing summers, intense storms filled with howling winds and driving rains, it was not a structure to be trifled with. Aoife was confident it would hold all the secrets they meant to unfold.

It had exhibits from the 18th and 19th centuries, Native American Woodland Cultures, French Canadian settlers, Victoriana, and the Civil War. It had everything one could wish to find except intimate information on people who had lived within the boundaries of Monroe county. It was all too general. It was history, sure enough, but not genealogy. They were downcast as they made their way to the information desk to inquire if there might be more information on the populace. Maybe in the basement or the attic?

The nice gentleman in the very strong bifocals and dressed, in what Aoife guessed was supposed to be the attire of the period, smiled at their query.

"This is a museum," he gently informed them, "I believe what you seek might be found at the Monroe County Historical Society. They are the keepers of family histories, the movement of the populace to and fro in the county. They are the repository and guardians of folk lore, myths, gossip, and scuttlebutt. They would be the ones who would have any information of the sort you seek."

They thanked the gent and then thanked him again for the directions and times when the Historical Society would be open. It was time for lunch. They asked if he would be kind enough to suggest a place for afternoon libations.

If they wanted someplace close, one that would not require more than a few blocks walking. He suggested the Public House. It was just across the river and had a comfortable atmosphere with good comfort food. It was just the remedy to revive their spirits.

Basking in the early summer sunshine, bellies happily filled, they perambulated the half dozen blocks or so back to where the Johnson-Phinney House sat behind the museum. They enjoyed idle chatter about nothing and each other's company. Tom shoved the emotions aborning in his heart back to where they had taken up residence in his late teens. It had become quite evident that he would lead a pleasant, if solitary, life; he had come to accept that fate. He had a brilliant mind and found most people to be quite obtuse after only moments. The concept of spending the rest of his days with someone who bored him, or worse, chatted about insipid and banal happenings endlessly, had filled him with dread. There was no need for progenerating, as he had no desire to pass on defective genes. Genes, it would appear, that were not as defective as had been advertised.

He treasured his time with Aoife, keeping all expectations well in check. Even her small talk and idle chatter was interesting in its detail and implication. He was almost disappointed to find himself standing at the entrance to a beautifully restored three-story Victorian home and indicated such to Aoife.

"Actually, it is in the Federal style and is one of the earliest examples of that style this far west." She did not lecture, only informed which she found quite liberating, not belittling. Around most of humanity she always felt as though she was instructing them of things they should know and came across as professorial or pompous. She did not have to concern herself when around Tom, he would accept the information as a gift and be thankful.

They were met as they entered by a slightly zoftig woman in a flowered pinafore worn over a pure white blouse. She had a pleasant, open face, not the pinched, annoyed look adopted by so many spinsters over the ages. She was a woman happily ensconced in her chosen profession and wished to help those seeking knowledge of her specialty.

"We do not give tours of this building, if that is what you are hoping for," she explained, not chastising, not wishing to offend, but wishing only to expedite.

"It isn't a tour but information we are hoping to find here," Aoife chided with a tinkle of laughter that immediately put the woman at ease. There is something about an Irish lilt, a tone that makes it almost impossible to take offense at anything said.

"Then you have come to the right place. How may I help." Her face lit with purpose, though she regarded Tom with a measure of apprehension. He was a large man, close to six foot and a half, he was, by all indications, a black man, though light skinned—tan she thought—but did not appear threatening in any way. She shrugged.

"We are chasing down my ancestors and believe one of them may have landed here back in the latter half of the 1800s," Tom offered as a way to defuse any concern the woman might have.

"Do you have a name or any particulars?" She asked as she made her way behind a large desk with an impressive desktop HP and settled in to begin the chore being laid before her.

"We believe," and here Aoife took over as she opened her own laptop across the desk and settled herself in work mode, "the mother's name was probably McHenry, Mary, and the boy was Tom. From all indications and scraps of information I can find I believe they may have emigrated from Canada." She looked up as her screen came on illuminating her face slightly to see the curious expression on the woman's face across the desk. "We think there might have been a grandchild or child with the surname of Webb, if that helps."

"Hmmm," said the curator thoughtfully. "This would have been in the 1860s or early 1870s?"

Aoife took a peek toward Tom whose gaze was bouncing between the two women. They both had the identical thought, paydirt! Aoife cautioned him with a slight crinkling of the eyes and a shushing expression before he could speak. She did not wish to spook their luck. She would take it from here.

"Yes. We believe, though without any facts or proof admittedly, that they sought a new life thinking they would find welcome now the war was over. We can't find any information beyond their, apparently short time here. Nothing before; whether they were servants brought to Canada and given freedom or whether they were escaped slaves hiding in the north until they thought themselves safe." Aoife sat back in the ladder-back chair with an air of despondency, "We are seeking two very small needles in an extremely large haystack."

"Needles do have a way of finding the bare foot, though, don't they?" The other woman laughed. "I have a tale to tell. It is not based on anything verifiable. There are not written histories about any of this; no newspaper articles that have survived. These are rural legends, stories passed down from generation to generation of a mother and son who sought refuge in a small town not far from here."

"Samaria." All three said simultaneously.

Frieda, as her name tag proclaimed, stared at the two of them as if they were mind readers. Astonished she composed herself before, "I'm guessing you did a little homework before venturing out to the wilds," her smile was genuine, she was pleased they had not come a begging with naught but hope.

"Yeah, as much as we could, though we are hoping to fill in the myriad gaps," Tom glanced at Aoife and his breath caught in his chest for just second before regaining his composure. He hoped she never noticed how he looked at her or the jig would be up and he would be gone. "Aoife can fill you in on what we've discovered and then we would love to hear the tale."

Aoife explained what they had found about Mary and Tom in a news article, found and kept by chance by a great grandson of a newspaper man of the time, coming here from parts unknown with enough money to pay cash for fifty acres of land with a home already standing. But they could discover no more. No way to find where they had come from, where they got the money, and if they lived here long or where they might have set out for. And most importantly, if they might be Tom's long lost antecedents.

"I believe I can help. if you have time for a bit of a trek down the roads of history." This was her calling, her raison d'etre, and it had finally come a-calling.

"That's why we have come," Tom intoned.

Frieda busied herself in a file cabinet behind the great desk, rummaging through several drawers and selecting papers and what appeared to be a few photographs. Would Tom be given the privilege of gazing into his past?

She returned with scraps in hand and settled herself like a cat easing onto a favorite pillow. "First let me tell you what I know and then what is conjectured, and finally what is rumor and legend," Tom was entranced. "From the gossip of the time passed down from generation to generation, as that is the only evidence we have. Newspapers did not last. They were either used as kindling in the evening or deteriorated due to exposure to weather, lack of caring—people really didn't see much use in preserving the local broadsheets, though luckily some in bigger cities kept them safe until they could be microfilmed for further generations. So, stories are told of those who came and went. Mary and the boy stood out for several reasons where most would have been lost in the annals of the passing of several generations and a century. First off, it was very peculiar at the time for a black woman and her boy," she chanced a quick peek at Tom to see if any offense might be in the offing. When reassured he only wanted facts and that was what she presented, she continued. "that they would have the wherewithal to pay cash for land. She might have had five or ten dollars if she was very lucky and had a generous owner," again a glance, Tom sat mute, "when they were freed. That was the assumption, that they had been slaves and been freed after the conclusion of the hostilities.

"Here they had come with coin enough to pay full price for fifty acres with house. That would have been a whopping hundred and seventy some dollars. A large sum at the time. Now where would a former slave come up with that kind of money?" She literally beamed with joy as she opened the first folder on her desk. "According to the bank records— thank the lord they kept excellent records and being banks they kept them forever—she claimed to be a free woman from Canada. A small black town across the river somewhat from Detroit, called Amherstburg. It still exists! Back then black folks were tolerated in the north as long as they didn't get above themselves. They lived in black towns, only associated with black people—unless they were working for white folks—and kept to themselves. Amherstburg was one of those 'black' towns. According to her testimony to the banker, she had a white former employer who had gifted her the money over time for excellent service." She took in their doubting expressions, "It was not totally unheard of that after a certain length of time, decades usually, when a slave or servant would begin to physically decline, the master would put them out to pasture with a little severance of appreciation, though not to this extent." She took a deep, cleansing breath before continuing.

"Yet according to legend, she never wavered on her story. She claimed to have letters avowing to this but refused to reveal them to anyone as she had promised to keep secret the identity of her benefactor. She required not a loan only the deed. She was polite, by all accounts, but insistent. That would remain her temperament throughout her time in Samaria.

"From what I understand, and again this is conjecture created from anecdotal evidence so it comes with an immense grain of salt, they lived quietly on their farm. Working their fifty acres and storing produce for the winter. She bought a dozen chickens, a couple pigs and a milk cow which was enough to sustain the two of them comfortably. They kept to themselves.

"Apparently coming from a black town," again her eyes found Tom who shrugged as if to say, 'the past is the past and cannot be changed or ignored.' He accepted that without shame, without offense, without blame. "they were used to not associating with white folks. Well, they hadn't been allowed to. But they were friendly when they would come into town and didn't seem to offend anyone's sensibilities." She purposely did not look towards Tom.

"They lived here almost a decade, seemingly set to end their days there. What changed it all for them was an act of kindness," here she hesitated as this was the crux of the story. "According to legend and this is really why we know anything at all about them—it is what stood out in the stories even more than their color, background or financial resources. And I will tell the tale as closely to the way I heard it from my grandmother who got the words from her grandmother so, again, keep the saltshaker to hand.

"The neighbor boy was chopping wood one brisk autumn morning, stacking the wood for the coming winter. I don't know if you are familiar with rural Michigan winters but they can be quite brutal. Anyway, the boy had been chopping and stacking for several hours in the cool air and his muscles began to cramp up. He wished to complete his chore so he could retire to the homestead and warm up without the need to return to the cold. He swung the axe and missed the log, cutting almost clear through his ankle. His screams brought his ma and pa running from the barn where they had been putting up hay for the winter. The mother fainted and the father tried to tie the foot to the leg, to no avail. Tom had, apparently, been chopping his own cord of wood a quarter mile away and heard the screams. He dropped his axe and ran to see what had befallen the neighbor.

"He came up on the scene with the neighbor boy passed out from lack of blood, the father weeping over his son, who was now unconscious, and the wife, revived from her faint, pleading with God to intervene. Without thinking or pausing or considering consequence he reached down and grabbed both foot and ankle—now remember, this is all hearsay as there we no actual witnesses to the act except a very distraught father and mother—he grabbed them and held them in place, closed his eyes and lifted his head to the skies as if in prayer. The father swore, under oath, that as he watched, the skin, the veins and arteries began to find their mate, like snakes or worms growing back together, the bones reattaching themselves, and within, oh, who knows how many minutes or hours went by, the boy was healed. Tom nodded to the farmer once and passed out from the exertion." The listeners and reciter all let out a breath they had held in far too long. Panting they took a sip from a water bottle that had appeared, as if by magic, from the lower drawer of Frieda's desk.

"Now, you would think the neighbor would be grateful. He would not mention the incident for fear others would think he had lost his mind or taken to drink and flights of fancy. He certainly didn't want to cast aspersions on Tom who had saved his son's life, but it was a miracle. It had to be.

And no matter how hard you try to keep a miracle under your hat, it is going to peek out sooner or later." Frieda dug into her folder once again and pulled out a yellowed, brittle, handwritten letter.

"This kind of describes the course of events from the discovery on. This is from a young woman who lived in the town of Samaria to an aunt back east in Buffalo. She begins, 'What a week we have had in our small, sleepy town. One boy almost died from an accidental slip of the axe and another saved him. Now the savior is on public trial. Not a law type trial, a trial by public judgement. It would seem one man's miracle is another's act of a demon. And when one boy is white and the other is black, well, the demon takes precedence.' She goes into great, and I must say, gory detail of the injury and the healing but it boils down to whether belief in God or fear of the devil rule your world, I guess. Some wanted Tom to remain a resident. It appeared to them he was a miracle worker, healing the sick and mending the lame like Jesus. But the true believers recoiled at the idea of a young black man being compared to their lord and savior. They were aghast and wanted him banished from the town, the state, from their sight." There were tears in Frieda's eyes seeking their freedom but she held them in check. This story might tear at her heart but she was a historian and had to complete the tale. That was her calling.

"Wait a minute, just a sec, are trying to tell me that this Tom, possibly my antecedent, had some kind of mystical power? Some kind of voodoo or supernatural ability to heal people?" Tom shook his head in denial, though he took a quick side glance at Aoife who was doing her best not to react to the implications of the story and her companion. "And the fact he could heal people caused a good portion of the town to rise up, proclaim him a witch or demon or spawn of the devil, and, so, banished he and his mother from their sacred grounds?" He wanted to laugh, he really did, the laugh wedged itself somewhere between the fifth and sixth ribs just below his sternum.

"As I explained earlier, these are tales that probably evolved some over time. Have you ever played telephone, maybe as a child or a party game?" Frieda grabbed hold of a thin lifeline to pull them back on board. Tom nodded; Aoife stared in ignorance of the subject.

"It's a game where you whisper a story to the person sitting next to you in a circle of friends. They then whisper to the person next to them and so on and so on, until it circles the group and the last person whispers it to the originator and they see how much the story has morphed since the first telling." Tom explained, "It's an interesting experiment that teaches children a valuable lesson in believing what you hear without crosschecking data."

"So, you can understand how this tale may have transformed over the decades, though almost all these tales are born of a germ of truth. Something did happen. Now, the actual occurrence may have mutated with a hundred tellings. It does not mean that the facts are not buried somewhere in the story. I have investigated many bizarre tales and they almost always can be traced to an incident, sometimes minor that got blown out of proportion and sometimes important enough to have been chronicled." Frieda shrugged not wishing to give the tale any more credence than it deserved but wanting to impart that something had happened, "All I can say for certain is that soon after there are no longer any stories or mentions of Mary or Tom as far as Samaria is concerned. They apparently moved away." Silence filled the room while consideration filled the minds.

Tom shot a questioning glance at Aoife. Were they done here? He felt frustrated and yet intrigued by what they had learned. Maybe somewhere deep in his psyche or his life force there lurked a magical power just waiting to be unleashed on all of mankind or to move his laptop three feet from where it sat.

"Any clue as to where they might have moved to? I'm guessing it was far enough to leave the rumors and accusations behind. They would have to go far enough away that the tale wouldn't follow them." Aoife spoke, though deep in rational thought.

"Rumors," Frieda said, "though one would think they shouldn't be that hard to find in this day and age. A black mother with a twentyish boy in tow showing up with money to live and sustain themselves would stand out anywhere in the country." She suddenly perked up, "Wait!" She dug through her folders seeking something and finding a yellowed piece of paper, "here it is!" She proclaimed triumphantly, "I knew there was some piece of information tugging at the back of my mind like a puppy in need of a scratch. It would seem that since the town, not everyone but enough, wished them to leave she forced them to buy her out. This is a letter of intent dripping with chagrin at the deal. It states that since the unwanted refused to leave and threatened the town with a curse if forced out, they demanded the town buy them out. I guess when people believe you are some kind of sorcerer or witch or whatever, you have a little leverage in negotiations. So, she forced the bigots to buy her out at handsome price, almost double what she paid and promised they would never hear from her or her son again." She grinned at both the piece of paper in her hands and Mary's gumption.

"A shrewd woman," Aoife nodded approvingly. "But where would she go?"

"They came from water, Amherstburg is where the Detroit River empties into Lake Erie. She came to Samaria, which isn't on the water but damn near it. I would look to west Michigan. Far enough away that no one would have heard of them or Tom's special qualities. They might have settled near Lake Michigan." She trailed off as a thought came to her. "How long are you going to be in the area?"

"As long as it takes to follow any leads we find, why?" Tom was on the hunt and would not be denied.

"I have a friend over in Holland. She knows west Michigan and everybody that could help. Let me talk to her and have her check with all the folks in historical societies over there and see if we might get lucky and get a bite." Frieda was all in. This was her passion and she had been handed a very meaty bone; she was not going loosen one tooth without a fight. She wanted answers as much, or maybe more, than these two.

Optimistic Plans Make Excellent Kindling

1874 Summer

When the flames had died down enough so he wouldn't kill himself by entering the shell of James' cabin, Thomas pushed inside to find the charred remains of his friend. He had held a slim hope but that hope had burned with the inferno. He bent down and as carefully as a mother picking up a hurt child, he lifted his friend in his arms and slowly, lovingly carried him out to where he could be laid on the soft green earth.

Thomas forced his eyes from the charred corpse of his friend and gazed at the well-kept, immaculate patch of property surrounding the cabin. He saw by the light of the glowing embers that James had not taken any more than absolutely necessary for him to live. A small half acre garden, rows perfectly straight with green a half foot tall running down each one, sat to the right of the cottage. An outhouse to the left with a modest outbuilding for storage near the back. It was perfect in its simplicity. No wasted space, everything just so, just like the man himself. He wanted to weep, though the fury still simmering in his belly would not allow such, not yet.

Jack was sprawled out on the ground where he lay after tackling his father. Thomas quick stepped over to check on his son. He had a knot growing on the side of his head, apparently, he had hit Thomas' elbow or rib cage with his temple, but other than that he appeared unscathed. Thomas sat down on the grass next to him and cradled him in his arms. He thought of the righteous fury that had raged through his body, causing him to almost land a killing blow on his own boy. Now, the tears came. His body wracked by sobs and impotent entreaties to the sky. It was the moment when any belief he may have harbored about a kind and just god perished. They had been incinerated in the white-hot blaze.

His emotions spent, his rage burned away, he only wanted home, though first he had to bury his friend. He would give him a good Christian burial, as he knew James was a firm believer and he would want Thomas to honor that belief. Thomas made his way to the small outbuilding and found a shovel.

As he patted the mound of dirt completing the duty to his only friend, he closed his eyes and prayed to a god he did not believe in. "James was as fine a man as I have ever known. He was a hard worker and a skilled craftsman. He never harmed another and never allowed malice to enter his heart. It don't matter what I believe or don't, he believed in you and so I ask that you take this good man into your loving arms and give him the reward he earned. Give him peace, give him love, give him his freedom without want."

He heard laughing sprout up behind him, he turned to see one of the other boys, one he had knocked cold rather than kill him, laying on the ground and coughing out laughter. "Don't you know them nigs can't get into heaven, old man? They ain't got no souls! They are just animals."

It was all Thomas could do to resist killing the real animal right there. Instead, he helped his middle boy rise from the ground, put his right arm behind Jack's back and under his armpit to help him walk back to their home. Before they entered the forest Thomas turned to take in the scene, he saw the other young man getting to his knees.

"If I catch you anywhere near me or mine, I will kill you on the spot. I would do it now but I have more important concerns. You mention that to your friends and your deadbeat family. If I have to, I'll kill every single one of you and not shed a tear." He turned and walked into the forest.

Mary met him as he entered the home still bracing Jack before gently laying him on the couch. Earl was resting in the overstuffed chair. His head bandaged, his arm in a sling, a deep purple-green and black bruise covering most of the right side of his face. Thomas hoped he had given as good as he had received.

Mary knelt in front of her second born to check him out for herself. Thomas had told her Jack had injured himself on his own father, attempting to stop him from killing the men who had killed James and burned his home. Mary took her eye off Jack only for a moment to take in her husband. Thomas looked exhausted of body, mind, and soul. He hung his head as he slouched in the matching chair to where Earl sat.

"Are you alright?" Thomas knew what Mary meant. She wanted to know if he had been physically injured during the melee. He nodded his head in answer to what she had asked, not what he knew. He was not 'alright', he was scarred to the core. He had lost his friend, almost killed several others while lost in a blind rage and had—and this was the act that would rest on his soul until the day he died—almost killed his own son. He had not felt that blinding, burning, mind numbing rage since the attack on Roisin in New York harbor. He hoped he would never feel it again. He had lost control of all his senses. He had become an animal bent on revenge. It would take years before he would forgive himself.

Mary wanted to go to him. To wrap him in her arms and shield him from the pain he was experiencing. She had many friends, people to whom she could turn at a time of crisis or share a meal, a glass of wine, and an evening, comfortable in their company. Thomas had James. He had never made friends easily. He was a man of the sea, of his ships, of solitude. She knew in her heart he must be suffering to the bone.

She had no idea how deep the pain had settled. How much more complex the suffering was in his mind and heart.

He was a man of peace, though he'd had to fight many times. He had fought with intellect and to protect his men and the ship. As far as she had ever known he had never fought out of pure animal instinct and rage. He had never been blind to another's suffering; until now.

He was scarred to the soul. It is never easy to look in the mirror and assess the person reflected. It was much harder to have to face the man in the mirror and realize he was not the person you thought he was. He was far more evil than he thought possible. In his mind he no longer recognized the boy who had hopped a ship in Dublin hoping to find a new life in America. Now after circumnavigating the globe so many times and sailing the Great Lakes for a decade, surviving a shipwreck or two he had found that new life, and it was ugly. He would have to change, to try to become the man the James, Mary, and the children thought he was.

They spent the rest of the night in silent contemplation, each lost in their own thoughts. Reassessing life and what was important to each. They would talk in the morning. Thomas knew he would not sleep tonight. It was well past midnight when they climbed the stairs to bed. He thought he might stay downstairs, maybe go for a long walk through the woods. Think. He changed his mind when he saw the worried weariness behind Mary's eyes. She needed him. Even if he lay staring at the ceiling all night long, he would be by her side, as she had been by his.

Morning brought a brilliant, golden hued sunrise, pink around the edges and deep greens on the horizon, it promised a beautiful day. A day of renewal, of moving forward and not looking back. Thomas had decided he would go back to James' cabin and clean out what he could save to keep in his own workshop as a constant reminder of the man. He also thought he might tear down the rest of the cabin before it fell down; and clear out debris to clear the land. This would now become the official family plot. Generations of McDermott's would be buried alongside James. He thought it a fitting tribute for a man who had lost all his own family. They would now be his family for all eternity.

The breakfast table was quiet, no one wishing to break into anyone else's thought's. Mary finally could take the silence no more. "What do you want to do?" a simple question that carried the weight of the future on each word.

Thomas considered his wife. He knew what she asked but chose a different path. He told what he planned for the day. What he planned for James' property, which actually had been Thomas'. He told her each minute detail of the how's and the why's.

"So, ye wish to stay?" She adopted the dialect of her youth. It was a serious question told playfully. She knew before she asked what his response would be. She had to be certain. He had been so downcast the night before, a state she had never in all their time together witnessed. The blow might have been too much. She should've trusted the strength of the man more. He was the strongest – physically, mentally, and spiritually – person she had ever known, but even the strongest can be broken if hit long enough and hard enough. He had not.

"Yes, where would we go?" He took her hand, "This is our home. We built it with our own hands, our sweat, our love. We have raised our children here. The only way we leave here is feet first and fighting all the way." His Irish was showing and she was never so proud. "Where would we go?" He asked again, searching her eyes for all answers cloaked and concealed.

"Where what we believe and live would be more accepted? We left Kingston because of hate; we can certainly leave here for the same. We could find some place of peace, without the memories of last night hanging over our heads." She spoke with no conviction, as she knew the answer before the words spilled from her lips.

"And where would that be, Mrs. McDermott?" He knew she only wanted him to voice what he was thinking, she wasn't really prodding him to leave. "The problem is, no matter where you might run to there are always people. I have been to barren coasts where people scratched out life one fish at a time. They worked together, they shared together, they starved together. Even in that shared existence there were always a few who thought they deserved more, were better than others. You can't escape humanity or the lack thereof. I spent time on islands that were paradise, with more plenty than any man or woman could ask ... fish jumping into their nets, fruit falling from the trees, sunshine, warmth, a veritable cornucopia of life. And still there were some who thought they should have more. They would demonize others who they thought less deserving and try to convince their friends and others that the lesser than were taking food from the mouths of the deserving. They had no need. Their bellies were full, they wanted for nothing yet they could not be satiated as long as they perceived others having what they thought rightfully theirs. Their share should always be larger, worth more, to show their significance, their standing. When is enough, enough? There are people who are not human, they think themselves superior, yet they only prove their inferiority by their actions. We are none of us superior, we are all the same. And the sooner we realize that the better off we will all be. James was of the finest cloth, just a different dye. I have met many throughout the world who were the same. We stay and live our lives for him, for them, for all of us. We will hold last night to our hearts and remember, every day. We will remember a good man and live accordingly." He kissed her hard as promise. She kissed him hard as acceptance.

It was then that the germ of an idea took root in Thomas' head. What better way to turn the tables on these hateful, violent, ignorant sonsabitches than to flood them with immigrants and former slaves. Thomas had no idea how much of their venom could be siphoned off with examples of how wrong they were but he was willing to put his money where his heart was.

Several days later he took the ferry across the Niagara to Tonawanda where he hoped to set his plan in motion. He spent several days surveying the lay of the land, how much of that land might be available, and what the cost would come to. After running his figures and seeing how limited his options were, he changed his plan and took a carriage into Buffalo proper to find desolate or unused properties. Especially properties no one wanted and he could buy cheap and develop.

If he could command enough contiguous land, creating neighborhoods, he would buy them up. He would then develop small homes in rows with room for commercial development, groceries, cordwainers and cobblers, dress shops, maybe a saloon, a small meeting hall, all the accoutrements of a neighborhood. He would then target freedmen, new immigrants from Ireland and Italy, Germans, and Poles. If he could give them something in common, he believed they would grasp that commonality and work together for the benefit of the community. He hoped they would see that they all shared the same disrespect from the established natives and would bond in their near poverty and workplaces.

If he could find enough land available in the center or close to most neighbors, he would set up a park with a gazebo for Sunday concerts. A way to enrich the cultures of all who would come. It was a grand scheme and had it not included human beings it probably would have been an amazing accomplishment. Instead, the people settled into their own neighborhoods and would not have anything to do with the people the next avenue over, because they were from somewhere back in Europe who had insulted their ancestors a hundred years previously. Hate is a strong and overpowering emotion; it even overpowers the instinct to survive and thrive.

Even the freemen, whom Thomas had envisioned becoming the bedrock of the town chose revenge over prospering. He had to admit James had warned him of the same, Thomas had prayed the ensuing decades might have ameliorated some of their hate. Born and raised under the whip and rape. It was a far greater chore to breed out centuries of hate than his optimism envisioned.

Despondent, Thomas remained on the island for the rest of his life without ever stepping foot on the mainland. His children and, then their children, though, would go on to create great things.

The Hardest Needles to Find Shine Brightest at High Noon

Present Day

A sliver of yellowish gold was the line of demarcation between earth and sky in the rearview mirror on Tom's side of the car as they headed west across the breadth of Michigan. Frieda's friend had discovered some interesting facts about a special township on Lake Michigan between South Haven and Benton Harbor. Frieda was tugging at the tether that held her at her job. She wanted nothing more than to hop in the car with these two and truck on over to western Michigan and investigate. She was nothing, if not dedicated, and her dedication to her mission in life was the determining factor. She would hold down the fort in Monroe and they would report every minute detail of what they found. She gave them her phone number, a fax number to send copies of whatever documentation they found, and a promise they would return so she could hear every juicy tidbit from their own lips.

They rode in silence while the sun made her presence known as humanity came to life on the highway. They cruised west on Interstate 94. The air was warming as they passed through Ann Arbor and Jackson. Tom was lost in a dream from the previous evening that had disturbed him enough to create the circles under his eyes.

After learning all they could from Frieda the previous day they had set out to see if they could find the location of the original farm outside Samaria. They had ridden the backroads and farm roads of Monroe county until Tom hollered for them to stop. He didn't know why, there was nothing to indicate there had ever been a homestead on this particular piece of land but Aoife obeyed and pulled over. She turned her gaze on him with a question struggling for freedom in her eyes. He shrugged and got out of the car.

Walking the land felt familiar though he had never stepped foot on this farm, never been in Michigan, nor had he ever been much of one for the rural. But he could feel something as he walked. There was a pull on him, a force leading him, where? There was no indication of any kind of building still standing or a foundation where one might have been. Yet, the land called to him. Dumb as he considered the idea, he felt quite certain that if he had or could find a divining rod, he would discover water. He didn't care, he was just as certain he would find something, a piece of furniture, a hand carved log from a wall or barn, a castoff chunk of metal that had survived time. Nothing.

He continued walking, searching, kicking dirt. He was so immersed in his search he didn't notice the elderly man come sauntering up with a bemused expression.

"Lose something?" He asked with a mischievous grin.

Tom almost bumped into the man. Startled he look up and got lost in deep introspective eyes. "Have you lived here long?" He didn't know how he knew the man owned the land but he was a farmer and this was a farm, so the math worked in his head.

"Most of my life." Which, from the look of him, could mean from the beginning of time. Tom didn't think he had ever gazed upon a more permanent human being. "Something I can help you with?"

"I am in search of my ancestors and I think they used to have a farm here," Tom was struggling to explain.

"Around Samaria?" Asked the ancient one.

"Yes. To be more precise I think it was right here. Is this your family farm?" The man nodded. Tom thought he should have piece of straw sticking out of his mouth but there was none available.

"Been in my family since the aughts," he scratched his head as if that would cause the exact date to rise to the surface.

"Well, we're guessing she would've had it probably in the 1880s before selling and moving her and her son west." Tom gave him the scant details he'd recently been gifted.

The old farmer stared at Tom, then looked over to Aoife to gage her expression, then back to Tom. "A colored woman?" the farmer asked without any hint of racism just habit. "Supposed to be witches or some such?"

Goosepimples raced down Tom's arm. He glanced at Aoife and saw the look of surprise tinged with joy. Had they found the right plot? And how had he even known to stop right here in the middle of a thousand acres of farm country. "Yes." It was a whispered prayer.

"Yeah, my old man bought the farm from the fella she sold to. Guess they wanted out after everything that went down. Lotta superstition and foolishness, you ask me, but they made the town buy them out and give it to the neighbor. Apparently, he had almost lost his son and the boy, though I guess he was a man by then, saved the kid's life. Woman wanted the man to know there weren't no hard feelings and wanted him to have the land. That was the deal, or so my pop was told and he told me. Woman was a might bit put out that after they lived here for some time, and then saved the boy's life, that folks turned on them like that, but folks can be funny when it comes to religion." He spit on the dirt. It was evident he thought the whole incident was much ado about naught but simple folks, simple minds.

Tom shook the man's hand vigorously in thanks for the information as it confirmed everything Frieda had told them. It wasn't just hearsay or myth, it was true. They had found the start of his line in America.

"I might have something you'd be interested in seeing if you got the time," the farmer hinted with a tilt of his head in the general direction of his own home.

They walked along sharing small talk. Aoife asking a few questions, as was her wont, while Tom took in the vast open fields. He was a city boy, born and bred, he almost felt agoraphobic out here in the middle of nothing. Crops were growing in every direction as far as the eye could see, how was it possible you did not get lost out here without any landmarks or signs, no buildings just miles of green crops?

They came to a bare spot in the middle of the beans and cucumbers, nothing grew here. Without a word the farmer started kicking the dirt, digging with the toe of his boot. Within seconds he kicked a buried squared log. He looked up at Tom. Tom fell to his knees and began digging with his hands. Soon, Aoife joined in. Within minutes they had uncovered most of the beam buried under years of soil.

"My guess, is that'd be the foundation of where your great, great grandma and your great grandpa made their homestead." Tom though he might cry.

Tom's dreams that night were filled with visitations from his far past. He met his antecedents though he had no idea what they might look like. The photos Frieda had were washed out and only showed ghosts. He dreamt of whom he thought they might be. Sometimes dreams could fill gaps, even if the filling was false. Tom ruminated on those dreams as he and Aoife passed Battle Creek. They would be to the hotel in South Haven within an hour and half. Let the discoveries continue.

After settling into the hotel, they decided it would be best to grab a late lunch/early dinner somewhere. Tom suggested they call Frieda's friend and see if she would like to join them. They could go over what it was they hoped to find and familiarize themselves with each other. Toni, a middle-aged white woman who kept herself in shape, though allowed her hair to choose the color it wished to be, mostly white, met them at a favorite restaurant of hers, Taste. It had small plates so you could sample a few things, a decent wine and cocktail list and was quiet enough they could hear themselves think. She'd chuckled at her joke, which both Tom and Aoife found charming.

She was a lovely woman who accepted age rather than fight it and was comfortable in the life she had chosen. She reminded them a bit of Frieda, who it turned out was less friend than acquaintance in the same line of historical societies. They shared a love of preserving the past and had talked at great length on the phone, though had never met face to face. Tom and Aoife assured her, she would find Frieda to be just as engaging in person as she was over the radio waves and encryption of their cells.

She was excited about their search and wanted to know everything they had discovered thus far and their hopes for what might lie ahead. The conversation was convivial over a bottle of Rombauer Chardonnay and blackened chicken, salmon, and Cuban shrimp small plates. She listened intently without interruption as Tom told her of his quest, with Aoife filling in where his excitement or disappointments left him speechless.

They made a good pair, Toni thought, grinning to herself, if they could ever realize that they'd make a good couple. She wanted to help them but she also had to be honest and upfront about their prospects. When they had completed their recitation, she sat back in her chair impressed with what they had accomplished. It wasn't easy digging in the past, so much of it had been lost to the ravages of time, weather, misuse, and abuse. It was time for honesty and facing of facts.

"I have to admit you have done more, and learned more, than 98% of those who set out. It isn't easy chasing down the line of our relations. Time eats facts and events as surely as a hungry wolf eats a small chick, but you have done well and should feel a sense of pride. Here are the major obstacles we face," she took a swig of the fine chardonnay and then a moment to organize her own thoughts. "Those of us who attempt to preserve history and sift through the myths, tales, and legends deal with a dearth of facts and data. The great difficulty in siphoning through bits and pieces of letters, newspapers and broadsheets, diaries, and spoken word passed down through the generations is, it only provides a skeleton of actual facts. I can't guarantee we will find much to appease you. You will need great luck and a bit of serendipity, which, from what you have said, you seem to have in spades.

"And here is the real kicker, though also, possible savior. When it comes to black, brown, red, and other minorities, much has been erased on purpose. Not lost through the degradations of time but through the degradations of humanity. Those who are the conquerors, those who control the narrative usually like to whitewash, and I mean that literally in these cases, what has been done." She hung her head in shame for those who either could not because they had passed on or would not because it would mean they would have to admit their guilt in a crime of weakness, to cover up the horrors their ancestors had committed.

"You are saying that the people who conquered this country wiped clean the lives of those they eliminated?" Tom was aghast that anyone would delete from memory the true past of any epoch in history.

"Not entirely." Toni quickly answered, "Just those who made a difference. They retained the parts where the people existed, but erased as much of their valor, their fight for equality, their successes as they could, though you can never erase all of that. Too much lives on in the memories of those who lived it, survived it, and passed it down as sacred to successive generations. Those who survived told the stories, engrained the names and deeds of their heroic ancestors into the minds of their children and their children's children with the promise they would remember every word, as if it were holy. Which it was." She smiled at the determination and intrepidness of those who kept their history alive. "Keep in mind how challenging that was. At the time most of these indigenous and black people could not read or write. It was illegal to teach black people how to write and read. Same for the indigenous folks, and they were having their language, myths, and tales bred out of them. They were whipped and beaten if they spoke their native tongues. So, they only did so in the quiet of the night. Whispered to each other to keep their cultures alive. And, thank the gods they did.

"Did you ever hear of the code talkers or Windtalkers?" Tom nodded in affirmation; Aoife appeared puzzled. Toni continued, "They were indigenous soldiers during WWII in the Pacific theater. They used the languages that white people had been trying to breed out of them to send military information over the radio. It was their own code. They were Navajo, Lakota, Cree, Choctaw, Cherokee, Tlingit, Mohawk, many tribes, and they developed a code using native languages to send tactical messages. Their code was never broken."

Aoife glanced at Tom whose code had also never been broken, did he. . .? She shook her head to push her thoughts back on the road they traveled at the moment.

"Yes," replied Tom, "But they are well known. There was a movie and everything. Their stories were not buried or discarded."

"Not yet, but they are erasing them from websites as we speak. Along with many others of Black, Brown, Red, and women. They wish to make it so the only deeds that are known and celebrated are those of white males." She sipped again gaging their reactions.

"Talk about insecure, narcissistic children," Aoife said almost under her breath.

"Well, leave us say that it is not a new concept. The point is it makes our job much more difficult than it should be.

White people didn't consider it of utmost importance to save and preserve the utterings, writings and communications between those who were not like them." She could see the disappointment wrangling with the anger both of them felt. Their search was being betrayed by hate; stupid, insecure hate.

"Here is where we might be lucky. We, Frieda and I, believe that your ancestor might have landed in Covert, Michigan. It was a rural community in Van Buren county, which is right south of where we sit and right on the beaches of Lake Michigan. It was a great oddity at the time as it was formed by a group of freed slaves and white folks who thought all people should learn to live together. Founded in 1856 it hit its stride around 1866 after the end of the war. They were people who believed in equality for all. At the time it was illegal for black children to share a school with white children, so the township never listed the ethnicity of their students. It was illegal for black folks to vote but not run for office. And so, they elected a 70-year-old black farmer who oversaw road projects. They went on to elect another twenty-nine black folks as trustees, sheriff, and Michigan's very first Justice of the Peace. If there is any place on this continent that will have preserved any mention of your antecedents, Colvert is the area we should scour." She clapped her hands in pleasure as she completed her dissertation.

She was a woman born to the career, just like Frieda, thought Tom.

Tom and Aoife spent the evening walking about the town of South Haven lost in conversation. They decided to rise early and mosey on down to the Covert Historical society which, according to Toni, was only fifteen or twenty minutes south of them. They wanted to get an early start, as the day promised to be warm with full sun all day. The beaches of the area called to Aoife. Tom would accompany her but his feet would stay dry. He was not one for the open water, a pool possibly if they had it to themselves but he was, and always would be, apprehensive about being seen in public without a shirt covering his girth. Aoife tried in vain to quell such fears, he would not hear of it.

Tom was excited to begin digging into the history of the area. He had no idea, nor did Aoife, that they had landed on such a treasure trove of history. Tom had never had much truck with history thinking the past was just that, past. One could learn about all the injustice and horrors of the past, learn the names of those who had lived and died fighting such, but it would change nothing. The past would always be what it was.

He had gravitated toward math and science, and especially computer sciences, as they were the future. He could work with 1s and 0s to change what would be. Plus, they spoke to him, challenged him, dared him to be bold and create something no one had ever created. He thought of the Code Talkers and what they had accomplished. It amazed him that they built on the courage and cunning of those who had kept alive the language and culture. And those who sought to extinguish the language and erase the people only to have those same people and language come back to save their asses eighty or so years later. It was humanity at its zenith.

He also considered how he, himself, had used some of that same ingenuity in creating his own code. The wheel spins and comes around even though those who spin it are unaware. Unbeknownst to all who wished to break his code, he had been able to obfuscate the code by hiding it in Feng and Tshiluba, little known and almost lost languages of Africa. He had studied the languages of where he thought his line ran from. No one would ever know he had studied such things, as he never mentioned them or used the language for anything except encryption.

As he and Aoife had ambled back to their hotel, he almost let it slip. The night was marvelous, the company was exquisite and the three glasses of wine had made their way to the locked door where he kept most of his secrets.

It was a quick trip to Covert with anticipation running at full intensity. When they arrived at the historical society/museum they found the doors locked and no one about. They had planned on getting an early start so there would be no sense of rush. There was no sense of rush as there was no sense of movement. Toni arrived just as they were getting back in the rental car to try and make do with the free time.

"Shit!" slipped out as she exited her car. "I forgot, they are only open two days a week, Tuesdays and Fridays and, even then, for a few hours each day. The conversation was so intriguing and delightful it must have slipped my brain. Let me see if I can call someone and beg them to allow us in to do a little searching. They might want to lend a hand if they're not busy." She pulled out her cell and began punching numbers.

After a quick series of calls and negative responses, though with suggestions as to who might be available, they found Ed. Ed was the caretaker/handyman/all-around-good-guy of the historical society, the township, and the surrounding area. He was retired and always seeking something to occupy his time. He'd be right over. He loved a good hunt.

The pickup that pulled into the gravel drive looked to be part and parcel of one of the museum's exhibits. Tom was not a car guy, but he knew from the style it had to be from well before he was born.

"1948 Ford," said the man as he stepped down from the cab. "runs like new 'cause I ain't never messed with her. I wash her, wax her, put gas in her and leave her alone. Like a good marriage, I don't tell her she needs fixing. If she wants something done, she'll do it herself." He grinned and held out his hand in greeting. His grip was strong without being overbearing, he wasn't trying to impress anybody but he couldn't help the strength in his hands, he worked with them all the time.

Tom liked the man. Here was a fellow who had nothing to prove and wasn't wasting any time trying. He was here to help people he'd never met and would probably never see again because that's what people do.

"We really appreciate you coming all the way down here when we can't even be certain we'll find anything we are seeking," Tom showed his gratitude with a slight slap on Ed's back. It was what Tom hoped was a common expression of thanks.

"Just live up the road, no bother at all," Ed reached out a hand to the pretty girl. Like all old men, he might not have much keenness for pretty women anymore, but he still appreciated the view. He unhooked his keyring from the belt loop on his jeans. There had to be at least thirty keys denoting the importance the man had in this community.

Ed noticed Tom staring at the plethora of keys and chuckled. "Ain't use but for maybe a half dozen. Guess I jess can't part with the rest. Like old friends, they remind me of doors I used to open." He sorted through the ring until he found the one he sought. How he could tell one from another Tom had no idea, it was like watching a magic trick, he concentrated on Ed's hands just to see if the illusion worked.

Inside there were about a dozen displays of yesteryear. Manikins dressed in early 20th century clothes, furniture from the late 1800s if Aoife was any judge, articles from papers and stories of logging. What drew their attention were the washed-out photos on the walls of groups of black and white children all standing in front of what had to be an old schoolhouse. Tom remembered what Toni had told them about the uniqueness of Covert.

How sad, thought Tom, that this would be odd. Why could these people on the banks of Lake Michigan, away from the rest of civilization, find a way to all get along, blacks and whites, there might have been some Mexicans and Indigenous folks in there as well, while the rest of humanity struggled so. If they could do this a century and a half ago, why in the hell did we have so much trouble getting along now? A question for the ages.

What he found of most interest was the multitude of articles on African American writers, politicians, abolitionists, philosophers, and inventors. He had no idea of the contributions of so many black folks. He had never been taught the names or the accomplishments of these people while skating through the entirety of his education. He found himself embarrassed that he had never paid attention in school when he assumed, now, this knowledge had been discussed. Black History month had circumnavigated his interest while the teen years beckoned. Nor had he ever had the inclination to investigate the contributions people of color had made to his country in the ensuing decades. This was as good a place and time to start as any.

He asked Ed if there were copies of these accomplishments he could take with him, or if they could be found online.

Ed grinned, "I'll make them available to you but, yes, they are also featured on websites like *Unique Coloring.* I'll write them down while you folks have a look around. If you have any questions, I'm not going anywhere."

Aoife, with the assistance of Toni, began wandering through and examining what there was on display in the main room, while Tom went in one of the side rooms. Most of what was displayed, obviously, was pretty general and, if people were mentioned, it was because they were the movers and shakers of the eras portrayed. They would need to see if there were any mentions hidden away in boxes or file cabinets, the heart and soul of historical societies.

In every historical society and museum in the world there are boxes of letters, newspapers—usually torn and tattered and unreadable but still kept—cards, work missives and orders, that are windows into the everyday lives of those who came before. Covert was no different. They had stored these relics where the humidity and changes in weather would bother them no more.

They all gathered in the main room where Ed was bringing the treasures to be sorted. They took great joy reading letters to lovers and loved ones while wondering why they didn't write more themselves. For Tom that was an easy answer, he had no one to write to. There were handwritten orders for lumber—Covert having been a lumber rich town with mills and jobs—and pieces of torn papers that tantalized in their partialness. They would read half or a third of a story only to have the rest gone or worn to the point in being illegible.

It was Ed who uttered the startled exclamation. "What did you say the names were that we are looking for?"

"We believe they went under Tom and Mary McHenry," Aoife said tentatively.

"Tom got married on August the 5th, though I can't make out the year." He handed the bit of newsprint to Tom's shaking hands.

True to form for Van Buren county at the time, only the names were mentioned, not color or ethnicity. The groom's name was Tom McHenry his wife was Tonia. Interesting, thought Tom, if that was taking place today, he would assume that Tonia was a white woman as it wasn't a common black woman's name. But this was more than a century in the past and he had to assume black folks back then had white people's names. His head was spinning.

Well, they had a starting point, they would dig deeper into this box and those close by assuming whoever had sorted them would probably try to keep them chronologically in order. Aoife found the birth announcement and squealed with delight.

"Here it is." She held up the scrap of paper no larger than her first three fingers. "Birth announcements!" She read them silently. There were several listed on what she could only assume to be a church bulletin.

"Well?" Tom's impatience was fraying at the edges.

"Sorry, I thought I was, nothing, nevermind. Tommy, me boy," and the Irish lilt was strong, "You must have done something very good in your life because on this scrap of paper they mention a girl was born to Tom and Tonia McHenry end of May 1873. Seems they didn't waste any time having a family. Her name was Betsy." She let out a whoop!

"I don't want to be the one to pour water on your fire but her name then would've been Betsy McHenry. And if memory serves, my great grandfather, according to what you found on the other side of the state, was born to a Betsy Webb." As he explained, the others noted his mood deflate. Hopes born, ignited, put out within a very short epoch.

"Women change their names when they marry." She shot back at him.

"Then why wouldn't the father's name had been noted on the birth certificate in Temperance?"

"They had a fight, they weren't together, he died, she killed him! How should I know?" Both of their tempers were running short. They had been chasing phantoms for weeks now and she was offering him a lifeline and he was being obstinate. This was the first time they had been short with each other and they both found it chafed. They were reasonable, rational, logical human beings. They needed to take a step back and breathe. "I think it is too much of a coincidence to be thrown aside. The daughter is Betsy, your great, great grandmother was Betsy." She took a deep breath. "Maybe she made up the name for the birth certificate."

"Or maybe she didn't!" Breathlessly spoke Toni. "Here is another mention. This family seems to have made an impression on the folks of Covert township." She held in her quivering hand the brittle, fragile scrap of a newspaper page which she then carefully, gently set on the small table they were using for sorting. It was an announcement of a name change for Tom McHenry, wife Tonia and daughter Betsy. For personal reasons, the patriarch had decided to formally change the surname of his family to Webb. No other details were visible or attached just the mention of the name change.

"If they made such an impression then why has it been so difficult to ascertain their movements from point A to point me?" Tom was confused.

"Well, like most people throughout history they made an impression on those close by them, though not to the greater, wider world. Many people affect neighbors, small communities, friends, and family though are lost to the wider world. What makes the local weekly doesn't cause a bleep two towns away. Be grateful, we were lucky to find anything on average folks at all. The vast majority, all but the upper millionth of a percentile, are not remembered past a generation or two." Toni barked a laugh to take any sting out of fact. "You are a very fortunate individual that your forebearer made a mark on this township."

"I guess, but why Webb?" Tom sought answers and was afforded naught but more questions.

"We'll probably never know. It says it was a personal decision. Something he probably discussed with his mother and wife but none others." Toni said, shrugging off the impossible.

"We found the needle buried in a mountain of hay," Aoife gestured at the boxes of flotsam and jetsam of a thousand lives lived over a couple centuries in a small, very unique corner of the world. "It has been a long journey, though, the end result has been some closure, would you not agree?"

"I guess. Though it almost fits together too completely, too easily. Too fortuitously. Like we were supposed to find these pieces of the puzzle without even knowing what it was we sought." Tom could not shake the feeling they were missing something. It should not have been this simple.

"What are you talking about?" Aoife allowed her frustration to find release, "We've been on this search for, what, a month or more? Using the best technology available, search engines that can find a certain molecule in the middle of an ocean. We have traveled here, discovered your ancestor had some kind of healing powers, probably the reason people remembered him, and followed his tracks. What was too easy about that?"

"You know, if he was some kind of healer and people thought so poorly of him, so frightened of what he had done or could do that they chased he and his mother out of their town, maybe that's why he changed his name. To give his children and their children a clean slate. It wouldn't be the first time someone had tried to outrun a past." Ed was thoughtful as he considered possibilities. "People are funny creatures," he continued, "they are superstitious, especially the uneducated. Rumors and lies ran fast in those days, even without the help of the internet, televisions, radios, and such. Word of mouth and exaggeration are dangerous weapons in the hands of the foolish." Ed might seem a bit of a backwoods simple man but his mind was a sharp as any Tom had met.

"The thing is, we now can be sure of your lineage. Your people, as far as we can tell, didn't come over on a slave ship. They were not bought and sold." She did all she could to remain upbeat and offer up any and all positives she could muster. Tom was a brilliant man who had accomplished much against great adversity, his insecurities and self-doubts had come along for the journey. The curious addendum to that was instead of finding his peculiarities to be weakness she found them endearing and humanized the man. He was a much better find than she had originally thought, most of the 'geniuses' she had encountered either were devoid of personality or were arrogant to the point of chafing, hard to suffer for more than an hour or two. She thought she was buying a brain, like she was purchasing a computer or something. How arrogant and cold-blooded of her. What she had found was a wonderful, caring, decent individual who happened to have one of the most original and magnificent minds she had ever come across. Some reevaluating was in order.

He settled his insecurities around him, fitting back into the skin of a rational, patient man who sought answers logically and methodically. "So, where do we go from here?"

"Back east, across the Detroit river and into Canada. Amherstburg here we come." Aoife, like Tom had not been an outgoing venturesome sort, but now that she had the wind in her sails and a project to bring to fruition, she was all in. They had a quandary and a possible route to solution; she would follow the path until they either solved it or ran out of data. First, they would celebrate their good fortune with Toni. They had invited Ed to please come along and enjoy a fine meal, but Jeopardy and Wheel were on and it was a tradition he and his wife had shared for more than half a century. Even though she had passed several years ago, he would not stand her up.

Peace and Tranquility are Ethereal

1885

Thomas had settled into a leisurely, mindless, pointless exercise of retirement from the human race. Disappointment in his fellow man had chased his vitality and slaked his fervor to better the condition of mankind. People would always let you down. It mattered not the color of the man, the religion, where he was born, nor to whom he could trace his parentage; rich or poor, righteous or wicked. If you expected them to stand before their god and proclaim they had lived the words handed down from the religious texts gifted them, you would find yourself frustrated by the reality. Oh, there were a few who could proclaim such, James came to mind, his father-in-law, his wife and, he hoped, his children, though they were the exception; not rule.

He still enjoyed working with his hands in the workspace he and James had created. Sometimes one or more of his sons would venture out, though his sour mood made the space feel cramped and they would leave. He would walk the forests alone, conversing with nature, arguing with the trees, and hunting game only to let them go free once he'd 'captured' them. He spent much time at the site of James cabin tending the garden and weeding the grave. It was a quiet, secluded, contemplative existence.

He grew his beard out, wore tattered work clothes and spoke in a soft tone and then only when it was someone he truly wished to communicate with; they were few and far between. He maintained his stature physically, broad at the shoulder, narrow at the waist, and strong of heart and mind. His favorite companion was his first born and only daughter,

Katherine Ann. She had grown into a lovely young woman, intelligent and gifted on the piano, a physical strength that was belied by her slight build, and a spirit that could not be tamed . She was Thomas in female form.

He was beside himself with joy when she announced that her beau, John, had asked for her hand and would be coming to ask her father's permission and formally propose within the next several days. Thomas had never met the young man but, if he had stolen her heart, he knew the young man would be of admirable stock.

What he hadn't been prepared for, and discovered upon introduction, was the man was a Saxon. An Englishman! No wonder Katherine had not brought the young man around previous to this occasion. Thomas would have thrown him, bodily, from his property. And would have done so now had he not just come from James' cabin. It was a place of peace and reflection. A place he could hear James' voice, as if he stood side by side, could hear the man's wisdom and sense.

Thomas shook John Webb's hand and welcomed him into the family. No one was more shocked than Mary, who, apparently, was taking the English connection far harder than her husband. She would save her words until they were alone, and she had plenty to share.

Thomas and Mary would settle their differences before the wedding took place. Mary found it inconceivable that Thomas, a staunch Irishman—though he had stowed away as a boy to see the world, his heart and soul remained steadfast in his love of the Emerald Isle—would so willingly and swiftly accept an Englishman into their family. She had come from Ireland years after Thomas had sailed. She had lived the Great Famine. lost an uncle to the Young Irelanders Rebellion and a brother to the Irish Republican Brotherhood Rebellion. Though her mother, father and she had lived in Canada for several years, her brother had remained to fight. His loss remained as fresh as the day they had read the words written in a letter of condolence. To say she was not fond of the English was the understatement of the century.

Thomas had used every tool of reconciliation at his disposal though he found the words of James and his forgiveness—though not forgetting the pain and suffering of generations—of his former 'masters' was the most compelling. Mary had loved James and his explicit kindness and generosity of spirt almost as much as Thomas. If he could be gracious and magnanimous, how could she not follow, especially for her own daughter's happiness.

She could not deny the love she saw in her daughter when John was around her. If he left her side, she would wait for him to return and he would be greeted with eyes that smiled, a nose that crinkled with love, and a coquettish smile that tugged at the corners of her mouth, as if she were overjoyed at his return yet unwilling to give the entire game away.

The wedding was an island wide celebration with most of the islanders invited. The family and kin of the men who had killed James were the exception. Thomas could only forgive so much and he would never forgive them. Nor would he forgive the officials of Tonawanda and the Island over which they had jurisdiction, for not bringing those same men to justice. While it was a grudge he would take to the grave, he would not allow that hatred to infect his daughter's day of joy.

The family came together to play for the dancers with many of the islanders joining in with their own instruments. They had brought over several of Thomas' former tenants from the mainland to cook the grand meal and bake glorious four-tiered cakes. Though some of the islanders might have been taken aback at the sight of a dozen or more black folks on the island, once again, they kept their concerns to themselves. Thomas had made his societal designs well-known. They were here to help, not be indentured or considered 'help', but invited guests with their gift being their culinary skills.

The celebration lasted well into the night, the music becoming more boisterous as the wine flowed and the food continued to pour from the kitchen. Thomas opened a couple of jugs of his Kentucky whiskey in honor of Mary's father, Earl, and James. It was a festive occasion filled with love, welcoming spirit for all even the Englishman and his friends and family over from the mainland. They sang and danced until the last man standing emitted contented snores from the chair he had fallen asleep in. Thomas would have a crick in his neck for days due to the awkward position.

He smiled through the pain recalling all the compliments he had received the night before on his woodworking and paintings hung around the home. People oohed and ahhhed at his skill with brush and tool. He was proud of his work though thought it amateurish, he reveled in the praise and vowed to spend more time with brush, canvas, and easel.

Thomas demanded his home be a place of acceptance, not hate, where all were welcome as long as they came in peace. He had taken up painting just for something to do with his hands when he was not working with wood. He loved to create beauty where none had previously existed. A branch found in the wood would be transformed into an object of beauty through his hands. A bird or woodland creature that one thought might spring into action they were so lifelike. Painting his favorite sites around Grand Island and Tonawanda relieved much of the stress and animosity he carried. He, at least on the surface, appeared content with his lot in life.

He had lived a full life before ever setting foot on the island. He had sailed the seven seas and ported in some of the greatest cities in the world. Beautiful metropolises filled with the great works of man. Cathedrals whose spires seemed to touch the sky. Block after block of human habitation crowded into such relatively small areas with buildings five and six stories high filled with people living on top of people on top of people. They may have been the greatest cities in the world but they stunk of the great populations with few methods to rid themselves of their effluvium and dregs, whether garbage or human. While they may have been magnificent on the surface; he could sense the reek and decay beneath.

He loved the islands and primitive lands they would travel to collect oddities and gewgaws not available to the nominally civilized. Handmade silks and fabrics from the West Indies. Pelts, precious minerals, and gold from Africa. Sandalwood, Copra, and pearl shell from the Pacific Islands. Everywhere they would port they would find the people willing to trade what they thought plenty and insignificant to the sailors who would trade the same. If you had plenty of somethings and a dearth of others, especially those that came from faraway places, well, one man's treasure. . .

He began a series of paintings that told those stories. Watercolors depicting islands and jungles, oils of the brown and black people who inhabited those places and their way of life. He used dark foreboding greys and smudges of black with perfectly straight lines to show the cities, though if you looked closely, you could see and feel the dilapidation behind the pristine walls. Tenement houses filled with the poor and broken, disease crouching in the shadows, children wailing in puddles of waste.

It was during this period that he painted a portrait of a beautiful young dark-skinned woman of late teens or early twenties standing on a beach as if waiting for someone or something to come rescue her. The sadness in her posture, slouched and bent, was superseded by the hope that shone through her perfect white eyes. There was an aura surrounding her, as if imbued with the light of God or some sort of magic. In the corner of the painting, just visible under a large elephant ear demarking the border of jungle and sand was a babe, laying, wrapped in leaves.

Mary took a sharp inhale of breath when she saw the work. First, because the work was so magnificent. The woman looked about to step out of the canvas. And second, because she knew without ever having seen her, this was Roisin. She was lovely in a primitive, natural, pure way. Her husband must have loved this woman in his own way, knowing he never could actually be with her. A shock of jealousy ran up her spine before she could staunch it. The woman was dead these many years, that her husband carried her in his heart was a tribute to both of these people.

She could not be resentful, not after all he had given her; four children, a beautiful home, a life and love she hadn't dared dream of, and a freedom most women of the time never knew. He had pushed her to learn and grow as a person. He loved to debate her on the issues of the day. She was his rock, as surely as he was hers. He treated her as an equal not as a possession, as most men treated their wives. No, she would not demean their years and love with petty jealousy. She would admire and love him for his heart.

The family continued to grow with the boys, Thomas and Jack, marrying within a several years after Katherine. Both found nice Irish girls to satisfy their mother. Children soon followed and the McDermott homestead was quickly filled with the cries of laughter of children at play and babies' cries of hunger and joy. Katherine led the pack with eight children in all before she and John called it quits; Tom, Dick, John, Kate, George, Ed, Annie, and Ruth. Thomas followed with a small brood of his own with two girls and a boy, Jack brought up the rear with just his two girls. They filled the house with love and laughter. Thomas and Mary could not have been happier in their twilight years.

Earl never married and lived a life of solitude and loneliness having never forgiven his friends, nor himself as an abettor in the death of James. Thomas had spent several years trying to get his son past the past, though the pain was embedded too deeply. He had loved James, as all the

McDermott's had. He was his friend and no amount of his father explaining that he had done all he could — almost losing his own life trying to stop the action before it got that far—would assuage the guilt. He would die alone and drunk in the depths of Buffalo's ghettos. Samaritans had found him and recognized him from attempts in the past to save his life. They brought the body back to Grand Island where he was buried in a plot next to James.

Several weeks later Thomas made the trek out to the cabin to lay fresh flowers on the graves and found them defaced with feces and he could only assume urine as well. The crosses had been kicked over and broken.

Thomas had made every attempt to get by the anger and hatred that threatened to consume him over the ensuing years, however the fuse had been lit. The next morning the family barn of the Edsen twins was burned to the ground with two of their prize bulls inside. Message sent. If they wished to reply they could, but Thomas would not recommend that action. He was now well past midlife and cared not a whit if he made it any further. He had lived, they would know his wrath.

A few days later he heard through the island grapevine that the other two men who had been involved in the original sin had fled the island for western parts of Canada. Fine, less rats to chase off his ship.

Mary never asked, and he never brought it up. When they came into town people gave them both wide berth and respect. By now Katherine and John had moved their passel into Tonawanda and only rumor made its way to them. Thomas Jr. and Jack may not have had their father's size but they did have his name, respect was afforded out of fear of retribution.

The family preferred peace, all hoped the incident with the barn would put the final nail in the hate filled coffin. None ever mentioned the conflict nor the end result. All considered it well and truly finished. They'd spend time wrapped in quiet discourse, music and dance at home, foregoing the barrooms which were springing up on the island for summertime distractions of mainlanders.

The Edsen patriarch, Robert, had become a regular inhabitant in those same barrooms and had been drinking, carrying on and causing mischief most of an afternoon. He would leer at the gentle ladies as they passed by and shout obscenities at the men who would stand by their women. It would seem the apples had fallen at the foot of the diseased tree where they had rotted. Now, the root was rotting as well. He was full of rum brought from the Caribbean Islands probably in barrels made from staves from the White Oaks the island was famous for.

Thomas and Mary happened to be passing by in their surrey when Robert exploded out the door of the public house he had holed up in. He staggered for several steps before steadying himself and attempting an upright position. He saw the couple and he staggered towards the side where Mary sat.

Thomas was in no mood for the drunken fool of a man, especially when he was making a swaying, teetering motion towards his wife. He had thought his interactions with the family over and done with. Robert had other ideas. He grabbed the surrey as if to stop it. It dragged him several blocks through the muddy street before Thomas pulled up.

"Is there something I can do for you, Robert?" He demanded.

"You killed my cows and burnded down my barn, you sonofabish!" he slurred in response.

"Apt payment on a debt well overdue." Snapped Thomas.

"And what might that be, for your nig?" Now he found his balance and spread his feet apart to steady the ship on these rocky waves.

"I would mind my tongue, if you wish to see the end of this day," Thomas' tone was chilling. Calm, soft, threatening to the core.

Robert was not in any condition to note the danger. He had fueled his anger with rum and now it had found purchase in the form of Thomas McDermott. He would not be dissuaded by sense or threat. He took a roundhouse swing in the direction of Thomas' head, which was easily sidestepped.

"I give you one more warning, Edsen, back down or pay the consequences." Though his own anger raged, Thomas understood the man was drunk. He had given up on life when his boys deserted him for greener pastures on the mainland. He had nothing left, nothing to live for except this. Let him die where he swayed.

He charge Thomas, head down, arms out, intending to wrap Thomas in a bear hug and wrestle him to the ground. Thomas had fought men on a raging sea with a ship bucking and trembling beneath him. He easily grabbed the big man by the shoulders and threw him, unceremoniously to the muddied ground.

"Go home, Edsen. You're making a fool of yourself and I have no desire for more blood on my soul." He turned to go back to the surrey and his wife.

Robert had come up from the ground, swayed, steadied, and tackled Thomas from behind before he took three steps. They both went down in the mud of the road. People had begun to gather round when the shouting first took place, now dozens stood by to watch the fight.

Thomas was a big man, a strong man, but Robert was also a large man. Not in muscle or breadth but width and fat. He weighed almost three hundred pounds, though he only stood five and half feet. And, with the alcohol flowing through his body and his brain, he had neither the sense nor the ability to lift himself off Thomas.

The stench of the man was near enough to put Thomas out for the count. He must not have bathed in months and it, combined with the rum, was sweating out every pore on his body. Thomas had to get out from under him before he passed out. He took a dep breath, braced his feet, and hove to for all he was worth. The large drunk disentangled and rolled into the street. Thomas stood, brushing mud from his clothes while keeping an eye on Robert. If he came at him again, Thomas would end this.

He came. His face twisted in rage. Rage at Thomas, rage at life, rage at his own impotence. He closed on Thomas and just as he was about to tackle Thomas, once again, Thomas came with a rounding punch to Robert's temple. He crumpled in a heap on the dirt street.

"If you ever bother me or mine again, any of them, I will kill you. Let that be the final word between us." He turned and took in all those gathered. "You have heard my vow. If this man comes near any person of my family, it is considered a threat on their lives and I will respond accordingly." He climbed back into the buggy and turned the horse's head towards home. They rode in silence. Though Mary did not appear annoyed.

Getting To Know You,
Getting To Know...

Present Day

Tom jerked awake. Gasping for air, his body soaked in sweat, he had a sense of disconnection with the world. He had no idea where he was. He gazed around the room. It was not his room; this was not his bed. He had been a small babe in his dream. His mother held him to her breast so he could suckle, but there was something desperately wrong with this scene of motherly love.

She was dying. His birth had killed her, though that wasn't exactly true. She had been quite ill for some time. How he knew that he couldn't fathom, he was newly born. He'd entered the world cold, hungry, frightened and seconds away from being orphaned.

As his pulse slowed and his heart stopped pounding in his breast, he could feel his chest heaving with sorrow. Tears streamed down his face soaking his pillow. Where was he? Who was he?

He had never been prone to nightmares. Over the last several months he felt he was living in two completely different realities. One he was familiar with and one he could not comprehend. Taking slow, deep, cleansing breaths the room came into focus.

He was in a hotel in South Haven, Michigan, where he and Aoife had traveled to learn more of his ancestors. They had made a solid connection between a family from Canada and him. Now, Aoife wanted to see if they could trace where that trail would lead.

Tom was tired. They had been tracing leads and genealogy for weeks, months, and he was no longer certain he wanted to know. It was all shrouded in fog and uncertainty. He guessed this was how it was for almost all those with African roots in North America. Hell, probably throughout the hemisphere. They floated, untethered to a world where they had no roots. Yanked from a reality they had known for thousands of years and dragged across an ocean in the belly of a monster to a world they could not recognize and would never truly be a part of.

And yet, that was not his story. At least, it did not appear to be. He was rudderless in a sea of misperceptions. He had no way to trace his beginning to Africa or anywhere. Canada could not be the origination story, his people had to come from somewhere else. But where?

Sub-Saharan people were the darkest people on the planet, weren't they? Though where had the Aboriginal, the Torres Straight Peoples, come from? They had taken root in Australia but they had to have arrived from another place. They didn't evolve on the continent of Australia. He had no idea and had never had any reason to wonder. Until now. Maybe he was from the Caribbean, weren't there black people there? In Cuba or the hundreds of other Islands? Where had they come from. Were they indigenous or had they been brought as slaves just as surely as most of the dark people in America? Too many questions and his mind was fogged.

Tom was not used to having a mush mind. He had always been clear headed, logical, his thoughts precise and sharp. He was an intelligent, rational being not some superstitious backwoods jungle dweller. Dreams were just dreams, fantasies of the mind, not something to be feared, some kind of portent of the future or a glimpse into the past. Just cartoons to entertain while the conscious took some time out from the day to day. Same reason people go mindless in front of the tube.

Of course, Tom had never felt the need or desire to go mindless at any time. He enjoyed exercising his prefrontal cortex. Solving for quotient was play time to him. If he wanted to entertain himself, he would find impossible equations, unsolvable theorems, and work on them to occupy the mind and hold boredom at bay.

Now he found himself entangled in a riddle he was quite certain had no resolution. He wanted to go wake up Aoife, bang on her door, and explain that he no longer craved the knowledge they had pursued.

What would she think of him then? Would she come to the realization he was weak? That he would fold the moment life made him work? She would back out of their deal, which, to be honest, he had almost chased from his mind.

He had become so embroiled in their quest he'd forgotten she was here so she could prove to him she was on the up and up when it came to acquiring his secrets. He had allowed himself to fall into teen angst and believe she liked him for him. Or maybe he was more like the timid, little man who convinces himself the stripper really likes him. She was a good and decent individual; he would gladly sell her the secrets behind his magic. And then, she would be gone. There was no use in kidding himself there would be any other outcome.

Stop! His logical mind yelled, as loud as one could, inside the head of an insecure man reliving his teenage timidity. He got up and went into the bathroom to get a glass of water.

He had to get some sleep if they were going to be back on the road in the morning. Canada called and Thomas Webb by any name, would answer.

He was quiet at breakfast, sipping coffee and enjoying a bowl of Raisin Bran. Aoife sat across the table trying to assess his mood. She knew this had to be wearing on a man who barely left his neighborhood for years at a time. He was set in his ways and his ways were what made him who he was. She knew that peeking outside of one's comfort zone, though frightening, could also be enlightening. One just had to be open to the possibility. They would press on until he cried uncle or great, great, great grandfather.

"If we take it slow and easy, don't push, I still think we can be into Canada and heading down to Amherstburg by mid-afternoon," she broke the silence.

"What do you think we'll find there?" His tone was far more upbeat than when the words had formed in his head.

"People, answers, questions, blank stares, and a kernel of hope," she made a show of getting up, taking her dishes to the bus tub, and motioning for him to do the same. It was time for wheels to turn and rubber to hit the road.

They rode in silence, Tom staring out the passenger window at the flat open land passing by, broken only intermittently by a few small towns and the larger Kalamazoo, Battle Creek, and Ann Arbor. Aoife wanted to ask what preoccupied his mind, to get him to talk about whatever was obviously bothering him, yet knew she should wait. He would open that can when he was ready.

As they passed into the outer exurbs of Detroit he sighed. "I'm just curious, why are you spending so much time assisting me? Shouldn't you be running your business or preparing to take over mine?" He was not accusing her of disregarding her responsibilities, it was more a general curiosity of her end game.

"Well, I thought since we were going to kind of be partners in the one venture why not get to know one and other by engaging in another. Especially one that has nothing to do with the first," she gently avoided the actual question.

"You don't consider this a colossal waste of time?" He was going to push until he got the answers he had ruminated on throughout the night and morning.

"Yes, I do. Though I also consider it a necessary waste of time." Dribs and drabs, she would make him open up and work for the answers he sought.

"What is that supposed to mean?" A speck of frustration landed on his words.

"Let me tell you a story. It's a bit involved and might take a few, but I think it will help you with whatever it is you're feeling. We'll start here and finish over lunch, probably on the other side of the bridge." She checked her mirrors and slid over into the right lane setting the cruise at a speed that would allow all to pass and keep the rest off her bumper. "We have the time."

"Speaking of time," he bought a few moments before she could begin her narrative, "shouldn't we run down to Monroe and report into Frieda? She must be at wits end wondering what we have discovered. It seems almost heartless to keep her dangling like this." He settled back in his seat assuming he had bought a little more time before entering a foreign country.

"Done and done." She smiled, "I called her this morning to report in and sent along copies of what we had so far. We shall report in again when we have more to report!" She appeared quite pleased with her evasion of his attempt to detour there progress to Canada.

"Now, as I was saying, do you remember a young genius out of South Africa around the turn of the millennium. Back when everyone was certain civilization would end due to the turning of the year. No one had thought about the double aughts and whether the computers would compensate or if they would think it was 1900?" She waited while he nodded his head, turning his gaze to listen.

"A young girl, late teens, out of South Africa, without much fanfare had reassured the world that all would be fine. The computers would roll over the date. All they had to do was set dates to four digits instead of two. It was such a simple concept the experts laughed at her, but she was right. She had recognized a simple solution to what everyone thought was a monumental problem." Again, she waited until the smile crept across his features as he remembered how silly it all seemed now. Though admittedly he'd had some of the same concerns, he immediately recognized the brilliance of the solution when he'd heard it back then.

"She went on to found her own multinational concern that rivaled Bill Gates. She created unique solutions to computer created conundrums. Or I should say, programmer, engineer, and developer created conundrums. That was the key. Every new program, every new code, created new riddles that required new solutions. She was the solution. Made millions and was the subject of every enquiring mind on the planet. How could such a young girl accomplish so much before the age of thirty? Who was she dating? What did she eat? Did she sleep on satin sheets in the nude? You'd be surprised at how invasive curiosity can be." Tremors of revulsion shot through her body as she took a sip from the water bottle nestled in the holder on the console.

"She hadn't considered what wealth and fame would bring. She became a bit of a recluse. She thought if she could just accumulate enough money, enough wealth, she could keep the world at bay. However, the interesting fact about wealth is that the less you have the more you crave it, and the more you have, the more you crave it. It becomes the means to an end that does not exist. It is its own self-fulfilling prophesy. Sooner or later, it will destroy everything you once valued." The sound of the road, tires slapping the road joints, the wind whipping by the windows, other vehicles passing or being passed filled the interior.

Tom was about to interject a thought when the obvious slapped him upside the head. "You're her!" he blurted out. It was staring him right in the face.

She nodded once, "Yes, it was me. And, if you recall, I disappeared from the planet for a decade and a half. I bought a nice property in Ireland, nothing ostentatious, it wasn't a castle or mansion, just a nice three bed, three bath out in County Clare, outside of Ennis. It was lovely. I could bike to the shore or into town. No one knew who I was or suspected that one of the richest women in the world would be holed up in a comfy cottage on the far end of town. They left me alone. If I allowed, I would enjoy some companionship. The Irish are wonderful people, they sense what you need and they provide just enough. You want to chat over a pint or two, they're pleased as pie to share them with you; especially if yer buying." And the brogue came on strong, she laughed at the brogue and the memory. "If you wished solitude, they respected such and would only pop in to see if ya might be needin' something."

"Oh, I still enjoyed messing with programmers and coding, but I kept my identity secret. It was while messing with your corporate raiders that I came across you. I'd heard rumor and seen a few articles. You kept a pretty low profile for a man who has accomplished so much," admiration washed over him as he could feel her approval. "In you I saw a kindred spirit. After much frustration and a multitude of attempts to break through your mystifications, I realized I'd met my match. I also recognized the road you were heading down. I admired you. I found myself wanting to share your journey. If I am honest with myself, I have to admit I wanted someone to share mine as well. It's lonely being the smartest kid in class." She chanced a glance his way and was rewarded with his acceptance of this admission.

"So, you just wanted to come along for the ride 'cause I'm such an interesting fellow?" He laughed.

"I wanted to come along to say there is more to life than work and money," she sounded tired.

"So, It's not about the money?" He chortled, "Every time someone says that it is either because they don't have any or they don't want you to have any. It's always about the money." He now accused.

"It doesn't have to be. It shouldn't be. It should be about the creative, the doing, helping others with what you've done."

"So, you don't have the money you were offering and now the truth comes out!" Tom had been through enough ringers and just wanted the truth one time.

"You can have every cent I've got, which is substantial, I don't give a fuck about money anymore and haven't for a long time. The truth is I am tired of having no one to share my life. Everybody wants a piece of you when you have money. I wanted to find someone who just wanted time." She slumped down in the seat as she drove. This was not going well at all.

"So, a woman that looks like you, with baskets of cash, is just looking for a guy that looks like me?" the laughter that exploded from his mouth was abrasive to her.

"Yes. I don't care what you look like, though I find you attractive. You have a mind that intrigues, a way of thinking that excites, and if you don't like the way you look then change it. Don't judge my reaction or wants by your own standards." The sigh that escaped her lips carried the disappointment of almost half century of living. "I had hoped you would've known me better."

"We've only known each other for two or three months," his reply sheepish and embarrassed.

"Three months and four days, unless you count the face time, then it's three months and eleven days," she shot back.

How would she have known exactly how many days they had known each other. Tom was a genius when it came to numbers and cyphering, but he had no clue, which only made it worse. Geez, moron, think you could be a bigger asshole? The hush that fell on the interior of the vehicle was smothering.

"Three bathrooms, huh?" He tried.

"Yep, never a wait," she forgave.

"Look, I'm sorry to doubt you but when you look like I do, act like I do, and think like I do, pretty women don't exactly throw themselves at your feet, let alone stunning women who are brilliant," he said almost under his breath. She heard.

She chose to let the addendum lie. "Understand that I understand. Just because we might have great intellect doesn't mean we don't suffer from the same self-image insecurities as a low IQ person; we may just dwell on it in a more in depth, analytical manner." She spoke to the windshield, forcing herself not to lock eyes with him. Keep it reasoned and grounded. "Imagine being a somewhat attractive, intellectually superior female who has been quite successful. Every single person assumes you have hundreds of suitors climbing over each other to woo you." Why she chose 'woo' instead of a more contemporary designation she would never comprehend. She sounded like an 18th century school marm. "The Catch-22 is that no one will talk to you or ask you for a cuppa or dance because they fear retribution from your very large, sculpted physique, man friend, husband, or lover. Which, as it turns out, is a figment of both imaginations. So, the pretty girl sits alone with her imaginary beau and buys herself a drink to assuage the melancholy."

"I guess I never considered," he began.

"No one does," the pained and lonely teen inside her head completed. "I'm sorry, I guess we are both allowing our assumptions, angst, and youth to stand in the way of a more mature relationship." She turned her head so he would know she meant what she was about to say from the heart. "Look, I don't know if this relationship will ever grow beyond a professional partnership but I believe in setting my cards on the table. I really do like you. I find brilliance sexy. I find insecurity attractive. I find the possibility of two middle-aged, intellectually powerful people forging a path, a journey, together exciting. So, let's enjoy each other's company. Let's seek the truth we set out to find. Let's allow life to go where it will and have some fun along the way. That's all I'm saying."

"And the money?" He couldn't help himself.

A profound, deadly silence threatened to explode in the car. What actually exploded was her laughter. She laughed until tears flowed down both cheeks and she had to pull over on the shoulder. His roaring laughter only egged her on and the two sat on the shoulder of interstate 94 laughing like two idiots playing thumbs and tying every single time.

Once the tears had dried and the laughter begat chuckles, which begat giggles and dying embers of titters, they both took deep breaths between ragged barks of residual guffaws.

"Yer an asshole, Mr. Webb!" And their bodies shook with gaiety for another five minutes.

The Wheel Turns

1885-Early 1900's

Thomas finished washing up before dinner. He'd needed a bath after his roll in the mud with the pig but it had been worth it. He hadn't beaten the man into the ground as he deserved, he'd only beaten him, and that should suffice. He thought Mary might be upset by the free-for-all, instead she was composed, almost gay, as if proud of him. He would never understand her and that was a prize worth fighting for.

Dinner called and from the scents emanating from the kitchen, cook had outdone herself once again. Where the woman had learned to prepare such delectable fare, he had never bothered to ask. She had shown up on their doorstep fifteen years ago, while James still took breath and life held as much promise and joy as any man could ask. There was this diminutive black woman of indeterminate years come seeking employ. She had heard they had a full house of growing children and knew from experience that an extra pair of hands was always welcome. She had a welcoming smile, bliss deep in her eyes, and a jovial laugh that could cure any man-jack of his sorrows.

She had been a welcome addition to the family. She offered to work for room and board though Thomas and Mary would hear nothing of the sort. If she was to be employed then she would be reimbursed. The children took to her immediately calling her Aunty Jo, short for Josephine. She claimed she was named after a queen or an empress. She didn't know and they didn't care, in this house she was royalty and afforded the respect that came with the title.

She didn't cook until she had been with them for almost a year, but when she did Thomas was almost angry; she had held back her greatest redeeming quality. He forgave her as they ate. From that day on all her other duties were curtailed. The children could help with all the chores, cleaning, chopping wood, mending their own clothes, laundry, and grooming the horses. Aunty Jo was the official cook at the McDermott home.

With that memory to warm him, he answered the insistent knock on the front door with a smile. The smile evaporated at the sight of the town sheriff. Thomas knew immediately the purpose of the visit.

"Hello Sheriff Thompson, what can I help you with?" He forced the smile back in place.

"I guess you know why I'm here. Got a complaint, gotta check it out." Sheriff Josiah Thompson was a good man and had no desire to interrupt what smelled like a feast about to happen.

Thomas had no need to make the sheriff spell out what the complaint was. The man was doing his duty, there was no need to make him work harder to do it. "It was quite simple. I came into town, he snarled and yapped. I smacked him a good 'un on the nose, told him he was a bad dog, and came home." Thomas hid his grin behind a hand wash of his face.

"And the knot on the side of Mr. Edsen's head?" Asked the good lawman.

"Must've fell against the wheel of my rig when he slipped in the mud." Thomas dared the man to challenge his account.

Silence. "Care to stay to dinner? Almost on the table and it's a good half hour back to town."

"You know I am going to have to check your account against Edsen's," Josiah said around the mouthful of fresh baked bread. He had no desire to ruin a good meal with business but his job was his job.

Thomas understood and respected the man for not shirking his duty. "You do what you think necessary, Josiah, but there were easily thirty witnesses that saw Edsen attack me when my back was turned."

"Yeah, I talked to several, they also say you threatened the man before you left. Any truth to that?" He set the rest of the piece of bread down. He wouldn't take the man's food, if he wasn't going to take the man's word.

"No, there isn't." Thomas said while eye to eye with the law. "I threatened no one, I did promise the retribution of god if he ever bothers any of mine again. And you should understand one thing here, I am a man of my word."

"Chicken is delicious, Aunty," Sheriff Josaih said to the woman sitting to his right. Everyone called her Aunty and everyone knew she ate and lived as part of the family. It was a changing world, thought Josiah, he hoped it would be for the best.

When Aunty smiled that beatific smile and patted his hand in thanks, he knew it would be.

They never heard from Edsen again. Thomas had to assume either he was shamed into silence or the sheriff had warned him to stay away, if he wished to stay alive. Either way, their lives were the better for it.

Thomas concentrated on his carvings and paintings. His children and grandchildren would come often to spend weekends during school and summers when school was on break. Unlike most of the children in the area they did not have a farm or family trade to take up when not studying.

Days and weeks were spent cavorting in the woods, swimming, and boating on the Niagara. Evenings were spent reading, carving, painting, and in parlor concerts. Some grandchildren excelled at music and one or two were more interested in the visual arts. All took pride in what they accomplished and the competition between siblings only intensified the desire to create. Sports entered into the activities as a way to occupy more than a dozen high energy grandchildren. Left to their own devices they would have annoyed each other to the point of injury. It is one thing to play a trick on each other but that escalates and blood is usually the result.

The coming new century promised great things for those in the upper classes while the working classes saw only more of the same. Thomas had always treated those he employed for disparate tasks with respect and a proper wage. He believed a man should never be treated as "less than" just because of his place of birth. Given the opportunity and support any man could rise to the position Thomas had.

He had begun life as the son of a merchant. He ran away from the priesthood and found himself spending most of his youth swabbing decks, fighting off pirates and merchant seamen bent on taking what his ship held, and trying not to end up at the wrong end of a spear while roaming jungles. He knew what it was to have nothing. He knew hunger and pain. He had survived where others had perished.

He wondered, many times, if he was not doing his children and grandchildren a disservice by allowing them a life of leisure; a life devoid of trial and failure. He loved them too much to force the issue. Let them fight the woods, get bloodied in their own battles, compete with each other for the prize of being the best at whatever they tried or feel the pain of failure when beaten. They would live. A guarantee he had never had.

He grew close to his son-in-law, Englishman though he may be. He was a good, solid, hard-working man who took nothing for granted. He did not expect a free ride from Thomas, though neither did he return the gifts sent their way. And he was a more than a passable violinist, something that helped endear him to Mary. She could fault his Saxon roots, while loving his musical skill.

In the midst of this peace and prosperity, the new century had hardly caught its breath when Thomas took ill. What had promised to be a century of new ideas, modernization—Henry Ford had built a mammoth factory over in Detroit and employed hundreds to build his new automobiles—soon turned ugly. And then war. Mankind had learned nothing.

Mary thought that might have been the cause of Thomas' illness. He believed that man was evolving into a more intelligent species. One who could solve his disputes peacefully. One that could find ways to end poverty, hunger, destitution for all. His heart broke on news of the war.

He stormed around the house cursing those who could not find ways to make peace but hungered for death. He spent days alone in his work cabin painting and carving all hours of the day and night. It was as if he thought he could wipe out all of the ugliness in the world if he could create enough beauty. That was until they got the news that his youngest grandson, Ed, who had joined the Coast Guard when the war began, had contracted meningitis. He was coming home to die.

All anyone in the family concerned themselves with was providing comfort for Ed and not allowing George, his closest brother, as he was nearest in age, to find out. He was serving in the balloon corps overseas and they felt it would destroy him. Someone from home, who thought he was doing a kindness, told George he had heard Ed had passed away. Though premature by months the news broke George's heart. George took it hard and began drinking the pain away. He almost lost his commission until others in the unit, from home, got hold of him and helped him straighten himself out.

It all carved Thomas' heart from his body. He had stayed in the cabin working himself into exhaustion until one night he fell. Passed out from fatigue. He knocked over one of the oil lamps in the cabin igniting all his work. Jack had seen the flames and run out to save his father but all his paintings, his beautiful carvings his life's work went up in smoke and flame.

He laid abed for weeks. His condition worsening as he refused to eat. His will to live had burned with all his creations. At eighty-nine years old he didn't have the want, nor the will, to live anymore. He passed peacefully, surrounded by almost all of the family. George was still overseas and Dick and John, who had formed a popular band, were out west performing. They did catch a train from Cleveland back home in time for the funeral.

As was Thomas' wish he was buried on the left side of James, closest to his heart, with his son Earl resting on the right. They used to say that on full moon nights on the Niagara you could see Thomas aboard his love, *Katherine's Wave*, sailing towards the open water out at sea. He is standing at the wheel on the bridge, midships, with a grin that lights up the night. And behind him, if you concentrated and knew exactly where to look, you could see a young woman, black as the night, standing at the rail behind him. Mary hoped it was true.

Still Searching, eh?

Present Day

The tension had evaporated like a puddle in the desert. Tom and Aoife rode through Detroit in companionable small talk and trying not to predict the future. They had found information at historical societies. That would be where they would begin in Canada. Tom Googled while Aoife drove. All his anxieties about spending time in an automobile had evaporated as well. The driving experience was night and day when compared to driving anywhere in Chicago. Annoying habits remained, aggressive behavior, driving so close to their rear Tom was quite certain they were attempting to hitch a ride. Yet, it wasn't out of anger or petulance, more out of habit. They saw nothing wrong with their driving it was how they were taught. People still used the one finger wave and glared as they passed, but it wasn't threatening like in the city.

Until they entered Detroit proper. There were a few times Tom was quite sure they were either going to end up in the Detroit River or a hospital. Too many people occupying too few lanes. As humanity spread out, he noticed they became less aggressive. Compact multitudes in a cramped area and tempers rose, killer instinct kicked in, and it became every man, woman, and child for themselves. He swore an infant in a car seat flipped him off as they passed. He prayed Canadians would live up to their reputation as kind, polite, nice folks.

Reputations are funny things. One man's kind and generous is another man's last nerve. Put any people on queue for any length of time and tempers flare, patience wears thin, and Canadians come to resemble Americans. The Ambassador Bridge was backed up a good half mile. They came to an abrupt halt halfway across. Tom glanced over at Aoife with a question burning its way out of his head through his eyes.

"No," she murmured, "this is the only bridge to Canada unless you want to wait until the Gordie Howe is completed."

"How long?" He didn't grin but he could have.

"Some time this year," she sighed taking in the absurdly long line of vehicles attempting entry to their northern neighbor.

"Might get a chance to use it." Tom snickered.

"Just might," her mood lightened.

It was but a mere forty minutes later they found themselves face to friendly face with a Canadian border guard.

"Reason for entry." Succinct and to the point, friendly though gazing at the long line of cars behind them.

"Knowledge." Tom blurted out without thinking. Well, he thought it amusing. He stood alone on the deck of that sinking ship.

The border guard ripped his glare from Tom and settled comfortable on the nice, stunning woman behind the wheel. "Care to try door number two?" He asked pleasantly.

"We are here in an attempt to trace my friend's," and here she turned her gaze on Tom, smiled beatifically, though her eye warned him to keep his lips sealed, "roots." She completed the thought and silently awaited further inquiries.

She did not have a long wait. "Anywhere in particular you plan on excavating?"

"We believe our best first step is in Amherstburg." Don't say more than is absolutely necessary. Name, rank, and serial number.

"Stay on 3 about two kilometers to the 401-W. Go half a click and you'll find 20 south. Take it all the way down to Amherstburg." He initiated a turn back to the booth before changing direction, "How long you plan on staying in our fair land?"

"I would guess several days to a week, depending on what we can discover, thank you." She pressed the power window switch and they were off. "You can't be flippant with authority figures," she scolded, "I would have thought you'd learned that lesson. Especially when traveling between countries."

Tom took the scolding like the man he was; quietly and petulantly. It reminded him of the warning his parents had imparted. He took the rebuke with their love.

"Ain't traveled between countries before." He defended weakly.

"Instead of sulking," Aoife pushed the brogue though not too hard, "Why doncha, find us rooms for the night?"

Without a word Tom pulled out his Android and begin tapping the screen. "I found a lovely hotel that is but a kilometer from the Freedom museum and close to restaurants. Looks perfect if a bit on the pricey side." He knew he had the money, and she had more, but a lifetime of frugality did not dissipate within a few weeks' time.

"I think we can afford some luxury. See if they have two rooms for the night, maybe two nights." She reconsidered. They might get lucky, as they had in Michigan, though the chances were slim. Slimmer when you considered the ancestors had resided here in the middle of a century almost two centuries previous when this would have been considered the frontier. What were the chances this town would keep records from that far in the past? Only time, and fate, would tell.

Checked in and very happy with their rooms, it was time to grab some grub.

"Would you like something a little more upscale or down home?" Tom asked as they met in the lobby.

Aoife didn't much care. She was hungry and tired from the drive across Michigan, the wait on the bridge, and getting through customs. She didn't know why, but she hadn't considered customs. Canada was a neighbor separated by a river, lake, or nothing at all, depending on where in the United States you started from. It wasn't really a 'foreign' country, more like cousins.

Cousins argue, she thought, and they didn't want you trashing their house when you came to visit. She understood. There were people in her adopted country she wouldn't want to be judged by and wished they would stay in their quaint towns and their pubs. She smirked to herself thinking of some of the people she knew in the US as well. It was probably a good thing they had guards at the entrance to The Great White North.

"Something simple and quiet, I would think," She answered his query.

"The Pepper Cat looks a bit nicer and quiet. The Salty Dog has the feel of a local sandwich shop. I could go for either, though if you want a glass of wine, I suggest the former." Tom perused the menus popping up on his phone.

"I think wine."

They sat in the half empty restaurant wondering if they might have made the wrong choice. It was dinner time and they thought they might have had a bit of a wait, but they were seated right away. Undeterred, they each ordered a glass of wine and both went with the Aveleda Vino Verde, a light white to begin the evening.

Small talk came forced; both knew why. It had been the clearing of the air on the drive over. Well, clearing might be a stretch. Tom could not get his mind wrapped around the concept she might find him attractive by any stretch of the imagination. He knew he wouldn't send women running from him screaming in horror; but look at her. He swished his wine like he was a connoisseur or a sommelier hoping it would open up a little or buy him some time, either would have been fine. What he truly desired was for it to open up the conversation from earlier. He wondered if Vino Verde had that much body.

Aoife watched him, wondering what was running though his mind. She sipped and almost spit out the wine. How stupid could a brilliant woman be? Here she was with a man whose insecurity with the opposite gender made her seem like she was a red-light harlot. The reputation had come back to haunt her. She remembered intimately what had been written about the ravishing, young billionaire and the multitudes of men chasing her; hoping to bed her and capture her heart. The press can be so cruel. He must assume she had bedded hundreds of men when she was a wild, young, headstrong child. Time to nip this or there would never be peace with him and her.

"You wonder, don't you." She dipped a toe into frigid waters.

"I'm sorry, what?" Tom had been lost in his inferiority complex and hadn't heard exactly what she said.

"You are staring into a glass of white wine, well, Vino Verde, to be precise, and wondering if I meant what I said in the car." Her voice soft and easy, she didn't want to scare him away.

"And that would be?" Not that he was being obstinate but if there was clarity being offered, he wished to know what was being clarified.

"Look I know a great deal was written about me during my youth and rise to power," she air quoted the word, "but very little truth would be found in those exposés."

"You don't have to explain anything to me. I mean, I'm not some new-born rube just fallen off the arugula wagon." He cleared his throat which seemed to have filled with self-doubt, bravado, and fear. "I've been, I've been around a few blocks in my time." It had reverberated with such boldness bordering on bravado in his head, he couldn't think why it had come out like a sad whisper.

Aoife studied him like an equation that they said couldn't be solved. And then solved for X, and X marked the spot. If she was wrong, she was going to have to live with it, but in for a penny. . .

"You're a virgin." It came out as hushed exclamation. It was not a denunciation more an exclamation of finding a unicorn amongst a vast herd of wild stallions.

Tom wanted to deny it. Wanted to claim a thousand conquests. Wanted to throw her down on the table and put the lie to her statement. He sat mum, glass halfway to his lips. He began to tremble, God, not even Chester had ever guessed such a thing and the truth of it almost crushed him.

She waited, not willing to press the point. She knew the truth. Now, what would he say. It mattered not she had her own truth and if she was going to lay bare his, then hers must be a gift.

"So. Am. I." It was a profound pronouncement. They stared at each other; she assessing his reaction, he assessing the truth.

Could it actually be she was telling the truth? No, she was attempting to mollify any ill-will she may have brought with her original statement. No way this highly accomplished, extremely wealthy, People magazine socialite was what she claimed. God, he couldn't even get himself to think the word. How much of a prude was he?

"How is that possible?" Was what dribbled out past his lips landing on his chin and trickling onto chest. "You are stunning, intelligent, strong-willed, had men flocking around you like ducks to breadcrumbs. You were seen in the company of the most handsome, perfect playboys of your day. You couldn't turn on the news without your exploits being broadcast throughout the world." After she had made him aware of who she was, all of the tawdry dribs and drabs of the salacious came to the fore. Plus, he had Googled. "Why would you say such a thing?" Why was she placating him? Did she honestly believe that his 'condition' was something to feel shame for? Maybe it had just never been a priority for him. Maybe he had just never gotten laid.

She interrupted his ruminations, "I know the reputation. I also know it wasn't earned. You ask how it is possible, considering my youth and press. Well, yes, I was pursued by the most eligible men on the planet but they never got what they wanted." She steadied her shaking hands and trembling limbs. Having never been this open and honest with any human being, maybe even not with herself, she found she had reverted to the terrified, vulnerable child being tested and prodded, pushed and scolded for not living up to all the expectations that came with intelligence. Being denigrated for not following the path her parents had laid out for their beautiful, brilliant child.

So, she lied to them. Told them what they wanted to hear. Morphed herself into the computer they saw as the end result of their fucking. They'd made her, she should now give them what they craved. Money and power provided by her intellect. She performed and they benefitted. She didn't care. She only wanted them to leave her be. They could have what she earned and live the lives they wanted, if only they would afford her the same.

They pushed her off on every eligible man they could find. Every handsome, empty husk that wanted to lay on top of her. All so they could breed her like a champion mare. She'd rebelled. The funny thing to her was they were so surprised when she had.

"You're saying the press, all of it, was fabricated?" His disbelief was palpable though he really did try to keep it in check.

"Not all. I did go to the parties, to glamorous playgrounds throughout the world. Usually accompanied by some sloth barely able to construct a sentence." She took several cleansing breaths. Reliving her youth, adolescence and twenties pushed her towards the nervous breakdown of her early thirties. She had to keep it where it belonged, in the past. Tom deserved to hear her truth from her, not salacious reports from magazines to boost sales to those who thought they wanted her life. "Do you have any idea what it is like to be with someone who only wants one thing from you?"

It was interesting, he thought, that he did, as he recalled the one or two opportunities he'd had to lose his own virginity. That thought could wait in the queue.

"And I'm not even stating the obvious," she continued. "Yes, they wanted to bed me because I was beautiful and sexy, but their ultimate goal was to take over where my parents might have left off. To take control of my gift, as they called it. They wanted the power and influence that came with what I had accomplished. They wanted to control me, like a dog at the end of a very short leash. They thought they could domesticate me!" Her voice rode the anger of past endeavors at manipulation. Her fury found purchase and began to ignite before she regained control and tamped it down. Tom had nothing to do with past indiscretions.

"How can you get intimate with someone you have no respect for or interest in. Mental midgets. You can't have any kind of intercourse as the frustration level makes any intimacy, physical or mental, impossible." She ran out of steam, "I just let people believe what they wished and ignored the leers. I had my little breakdown, as my 'friends' called it, removed myself form the glaring eyes of the overly inquiring, found a pleasant little village where no one knew or cared who I might have been, and took my time finding out who I was." She chanced a glimpse to see how her confession fared.

Tom sat dreadfully quiet and absolutely still. He picked up his wine glass and drained the contents. He stared at the table, glanced around the, still, half-filled restaurant, out the front window at the darkening sky, everywhere but at her.

"I know you will find this hard to believe," he began softly, "but I had, I guess, a kind of similar experience, though not to the degree you suffered." Now his eyes found hers and held them gently. "There was one instance in particular of a woman I had met through my business connections. She was physically very attractive, well-spoken, mid-level intelligence, a nice person and honest to a fault." He chuckled. "She told me she did not find me attractive in any way but she would be willing to have sex with me because she desired my DNA. I explained that intelligence was a throw of the cosmic dice and bearing the child of someone with exceptional intelligence guaranteed nothing. She told me she was willing to chance it, if there was even the smallest odds she would bear a child of exceptional skills." Tom shook his head at the memory. There was a slight twinge of pain though, moreso, a feeling of the absurdity of the incident. "I know it's not the same but I kind of get it. Any attraction there may have been superficially died on the spot. I guess it would have been nice to have done the deed, but my conscience and dignity would not allow it to occur." He shrugged his own folly.

If Aoife believed she couldn't have thought more of the man than she had previously, she had been wrong. A man with scruples. Yes, a unicorn indeed and in action.

"We are two peas buried deep in a singular pod." The arrival of the waiter forestalled any further discussion of the matter.

Aoife ordered the Lobster Raviolis and Tom got Yellowfin Tuna, a small; truly a small order, please, he begged the waiter. He had made the commitment to drop some weight and inches while they were driving over and today was as a good a day to start as any. The conversation faltered while they ate before he kickstarted it with laying out the plan for the next day's activities. Best to avoid the open wounds for now. They would find the historical society, though he felt their best course of action was to invade the Freedom Museum. They bantered back and forth the pros and cons of both before settling on his initial plan.

An after-dinner cocktail to settle the dinner, he a Stormy Night and she a light Pomegranate Gimlet, before they walked back to their hotel a few block away. Tom was pleasantly surprised when halfway back she slipped her cool, soft hand into his. It was as natural an act as he could remember. He almost commented before choosing silence and mood over breaking of same.

It was a pleasant evening and a more than pleasant walk. They climbed the stairs to their luxurious lodgings. Tom's heart was beating at 127 beats per and he was quite certain he was sweating. It was not from the exertion. They came to a rest at her room. He turned to say goodnight and maybe, just maybe… she stopped the action with a hand gently placed on his chest.

"I think we should concentrate on the task at hand before we do anything we might regret," he said before she could. The better part of valor and all that.

She nodded. Was that the dim glow of regret burning deep in her eyes? They both had known loneliness and isolation for a lifetime, it would only be natural for them to jump at the first true offering of companionship. It would have to wait. They had forestalled intimacy thus far, it could wait. Things could change and then a continuation of the partnership would be destroyed. Hang on to what you had until a change in course was the optimum course of action. He kissed her hands, one at a time, before turning to go to his own room.

"Tom?" She turned away from her door, he turned to look at her. "Goodnight. Thank you for everything. See you in the morning."

Entering the room, he leaned against his closed door as if to hold against an assailant. She mimicked his action and closed her eyes against the same only meters away.

It was two sleep starved human beings that met in the lobby the next morning. Neither had found rest in their beds, as the previous evening roamed the inner sanctums, pulling band aids off old wounds and worries did not lend itself to rest. The beauty of the human psyche is it never completely heals. All those doubts and perceived trespasses were as patient as stopped clocks waiting for someone to install new batteries or give a quick wind.

They walked down the street to a diner three blocks away. The hotel was perfectly situated for food and history. They would get in some much-needed steps for people not used to spending their days in cars.

The breakfast was solid Canadian fare, eggs, Canadian bacon, toast, coffee, fresh squeezed orange juice, unless their taste buds were sorely mistaken, and potatoes. A filling meal to begin the search. They exchanged ideas and hopes as they ate, keeping their distance from subjects best left sleeping. They would keep, they had for decades. The focus was on the hunt.

Sated and juiced, they set off to find the historical society. The lovely woman at the front counter of the diner informed that the historical society was actually the Amherstburg Freedom Museum. That would simplify the search. They had asked the cashier for directions, always best to check before the walk begins rather than when it had gone awry. She informed them it might also be worth their while to check out the Park House Museum which was even closer to where they stood. If it didn't have what they sought, the distance would be negligible backtracking to the Freedom Museum. A nice lady.

The Park House was a chock-a-block of knick-knacks and information of the period they wanted to search. It was mostly mid 1800s clothing, China, glassware, furniture, and documents on the people who resided and made an impression on history. They spent several hours combing through documents, letters, bills of lading and sales receipts with the help a young man who volunteered at the Park several days a week. He enjoyed sifting through history for fun though he loved panning for specific information. Once he was informed of the names and time frame, he was a Lagotto Romagnolo sniffing for truffles.

He knew the approximate location of the boxes that might contain any correspondences from that era. He was the one that found the bill of sale for a shack on the river sold to a Mary McHenry for $50 in 1867. That was the extent of any paper trail they could uncover in four hours of meticulous page by page sorting.

It was a needle, what they hoped to find was a trail. They found a post with a yellowed sign nailed to it saying, 'she was here but she moved.' They knew that. They knew where her future lay, the question was, where was the starting point and why.

"Best bet is probably the Freedom Museum," Jacob, the volunteer bemoaned. He had become so invested in Tom's search; the letdown felt personal.

"Don't feel badly," Tom spoke to the tone of Jacob's voice that flooded the room with despondency. "We have proven another step along the journey of my family. Maybe we'll find the jumping off point."

Aoife gave the kid a hug of thanks as they left the Park House. Outside she turned to Tom, "Maybe we should see if he'd like to tag along to Freedom House, you know, as our local sherpa."

"Why not, if they can do without him for a few hours. Let's ask."

Jacob was overwhelmed they would ask him. He'd wanted to suggest it but didn't want to be pushy and interject himself into their quest. Here were two intelligent, pleasant folks with a holy crusade. It made him feel as though he was part of something noble, a great cause. He begged off work, explaining to his supervisor, the only other person in the Park House, the quest, the journey and how he could help. She smiled with pride at his exuberance and told him not to be late to dinner.

Neither Tom nor Aoife had noticed the similarities of features until that moment.

Jacob fairly skipped down the street leading the way and talking the whole time about his love of the city and its history. He explained how Amherstburg was considered a 'negro town' back in the 1800s. It was a place that African and Caribbean folks could come to escape a modicum of racism.

Both Tom and Aoife were slightly taken aback that there was such ill will between people in Canada back then. They, like most, they supposed, thought it was concentrated in the USA. Jacob explained that though there wasn't necessarily slavery in Canada, there was still a great feeling of supremacy among the other immigrants. The Scots, Irish, English, French all chimed in to help keep black people 'in their place'. It may not have been as awful as it was down in the states, it still would not have been a pleasant experience. Jacob was a chocolate brown man whose ancestry could be traced back to the Caribbean and, more than likely, to the Motherland herself. He explained that all the brown and black people could trace their heritage to west Africa.

He loved discussing history without a hint of bitterness or hostility towards those who had practiced racist attitudes in that past or those who continued. He considered it a flaw in the genetic make-up or upbringing. He believed, and the numbers bore him out if you'd care to see, that these imperfections could be bred out or that evolution and knowledge would smother it with data, interaction, and understanding. He was a paragon of innocent hope. Tom envied him, though he had been the same, up until the shooting. Maybe he should try and put that hate behind him.

They arrived at the Freedom Museum and were greeted by a middle-aged black man in suit and tie. He stood easily as tall as Tom, though rail thin and exuding a welcome that swaddled them in warmth and love. He greeted Jacob in a familial way, though there were no physical attributes that would align them. Tom put it down to teacher/student affection.

Jacob explained Tom's situation and what he and his 'friend'—and here both men slightly bowed in respect to Aoife—were searching for. Walter, the custodian of knowledge for the museum, listened intently.

"Not sure I can be of much help." He scratched his head in thought. "Trying to discover where people came from is a quandary. Most just showed up, either walking or on an old plow horse. Some, admittedly, had wagons with some belongings, but they were the few. This town was a last resort for many. They had no place else to go. Well, no place that they could hope. And hope is essential for a man's soul.

"I am sometimes so amazed that our people, and I include all people of color, survived to tell the story. And that has become as ingrained in us as our DNA. It's as if our ancestors survived just to keep the stories alive. It's why I'm here and my Jake," apparently his pet name for this favored student, "is at the Park. I stand in awe of our forebearers, especially those who, for generations, endured the horrors of slavery. I cannot imagine the strength, the courage, and the magnificence of those who watched their parents and grandparents beaten, worked to death, raped, sold, and taken away, knowing their children would suffer the same fate, yet continued on. It boggles the mind." He turned to take them into the museum. "You must forgive me; I get a bit riled when I'm allowed to pontificate on the subject. I am prone to expound when I have a captive audience. I am inspired when someone shows up—and they are few and far between—to find their personal history." He apologized but only just so. "Let's retire to the back rooms and see if we can uncover your personal trail of tears and joy, if I may borrow from our cousins in the first nations."

They entered a room filled with bookshelves, filing cabinets, boxes, and exhibits that were either waiting for their day in the light or enjoying their retirement. Tom was overwhelmed by the enormity of the task at hand. If they had to go through every one of these old, ragged, time worn books on the shelves, through each file cabinet, the boxes, the loose papers, someone would find their dried bones a century from now still bent over the past.

Walter walked over to a desk, pulled a blue plastic sheet off a recent model desk top computer. He turned and grinned, "You didn't think I was going to make you go mining through all this, did you?"

Tom could only laugh while Aoife let out a breath she had taken when they entered the room. Jacob pressed the power button and waited while the screen lit up and the computer came online.

"What was the name of the person you think might be your ancestor?" Walter took his place, sitting at the wizard's portal. "We spent a couple years entering everything you see here by hand. Talk about a daunting task, though we knew in the end it would pay off in spades, and it has. If I had to search through every single thing in this room every time I needed to find a name, a place, an incident, I would be certifiable by now." He barked a congenial laugh.

Computer up and running he typed in the name. The search was on.

"I think it is admirable and remarkable that you have all this at your command." Aoife's tone was that of wonder, as if she was witnessing a miracle right in front of her.

"When the rest of the society, and this has been the truth throughout history, wants your civilization to disappear, to erase your very existence, you do everything in your power to save each scrap, each story and tale, myth, every memory in case you are the last of your kind. You become the repository of your people. It becomes your ultimate responsibility to keep your kinsfolk, your ancestors, forefathers and mothers alive. If the stories die, if the tales, accomplishments, and exploits disappear, wiped from this earth, then you never existed and that is the worst possible outcome for any people." Walter looked away from the screen to face her. "Imagine if we had never heard of the exploits of the Greek sailors, of Zeus, Jason, Athena, of Thor, Poseidon. Think if we had lost all that. Think of Plato, Aristotle, Socrates, of the Pharaohs of Egypt. If all these people had been erased from our history how sad and pathetic our lives would be.

"When our people," and here he included Tom, Jacob, and himself with an apologetic nod to Aoife, "founded towns like Amherstburg, it was decided they would be the keepers of as much of our history as we could possibly save. Our ancestors learned to read, write, collate, sort, and file. We painstakingly preserved every scrap we could hide from those who would destroy. Yes, those who came before us were heroes and gods in their own right." He clapped his hands as he gazed at the screen.

"We have a couple hits on her name." He said tentatively, "Now we have to hope it is the right Mary McHenry." He began moving the mouse and clicking. "It is not exactly a unique name," he said to Aoife's puzzled expression, "African descendants when either granted their freedom or ran for it, had a tendency to retain the names given them by their former owners. They had no cultural ties to the motherland, no mother tongue that would translate their heart's desire for connection to their ancestral home. They did not have the means at their disposal to name themselves, no reference point, so they kept what they had been given. And many were given the same names over generations. Or, they adopted the names of white folks they admired or had treated them with some kindness. If there was a woman by the name of Mary McHenry who had treated her slaves well, with kindness, fed them, took care of them—as much as society would allow—maybe gifted them with small tokens of appreciation, then several may have taken her name as tribute to a good white person." He shrugged his impotence over history. What was, was. What had been, was carved in the historical stone and wishing wasn't going to make steak out of hamburger.

"Boy named Tom?" he glanced up at present day Tom, who nodded in the affirmative. "Let's do some digging." He gestured to the few chairs scattered around the room. The others pulled them up behind where Walter sat and made themselves comfortable.

"She bought a shack," he began before being interrupted by Jacob.

"Yeah, we found the bill of sale at the Park," Jacob mentioned before seeing the fleeting of irritation cross Walter's features. "Sorry."

"No, you were right to stop me from giving you information you possessed." Walter patted the young man's arm assuring him he'd done the right thing. "There is another, a letter from someone back east. A Mary. Might be where our Mary took her name, that would be a find. Yes, Yes, Yes, it is a letter sent with a stipend to help care for the boy she was mothering, interesting vernacular, though there is no mention of the connection betwixt the two women. Curiouser and curiouser." He went silent in thought.

Time moves at its own pace. To Walter, in his ruminations, it may have stopped to allow him to consider. To Tom it dragged its feet like a recalcitrant dog. He waited, impatiently, for the man to come to whatever conclusion his thoughts would lead. He could take the suspense no longer.

"Well?" pled the man begging a favor.

"Oh, excuse me, I oft times lose myself when faced with a dilemma that requires thorough examination. I hop on the treadmill of thought." He took a brief peek at the screen to assure what he was considering. "I think it is obvious from this missive that the boy is not the genetic get of this woman. She is not his mother. Well, not his birth mother, though she appears to have been handed the role and fulfills the role admirably. With a financial assist from this woman back east."

Tom caught the reference this time around. "That's the second time you have referenced a woman 'back east'. Is there a return address stating the town you refer to? Or some other indicator that tells you she is from somewhere back east?" His frustration grew with the vagueness and his weariness. He hadn't slept well and they had been studying minutia for several hours. He was tired and just wanted some thread to hang his hat on.

"To be honest, it's just something we say because everybody, at one time or another, came from back east. So, it is an assumption as well as a saying. More than likely our Mary came from somewhere back east as there was little out west in those days. East she may have come from Toronto, Quebec, Montreal, or one of the smaller lake towns. Places like Kingston on the far east end of Lake Ontario were growing and thriving towns attempting to grow into cities. It was an exciting time in Canada as well as the USA. We shall attempt to narrow down the back east as we delve into her history or any other correspondences." He leaned back in his wooden chair in order to stretch out dormant muscles. It took several minutes to force blood into sleeping appendages before he leaned back towards the monitor, scanning the results for the most promising.

With nothing for them to do, the remaining three began to browse through boxes and shelves, careful not to displace anything that might be important. They soon realized everything in this room might be important to someone, so slowed their prying fingers to show respect for others lives.

It was in one of the large books containing newsprint that Aoife gasped, then let out an audible 'hmmm' before returning to whatever had caught her eye. Tom sensing a change in the vibe in the room and being well acquainted with her intelligence and eye for detail made his way over to where he could peer over her shoulder.

There was a side bar article about a young African boy with a special talent for healing. It bordered on the mystical. He had cured a woman of severe abdominal pains and an elderly man of stiffness of the joints. Some were claiming miracles while others raised their voices in doubt. And, as was the case in the later part of the 19th century, 'witch' was thrown about by the superstitious.

"Looks like your great grandfather was practicing without a license again." She grinned over her shoulder. "It got him in some trouble over in Michigan once they had resettled there. Seems he couldn't keep his 'gift' a secret, to his own detriment."

"When you have a gift like healing, I suppose it would be incredibly difficult to contain it. And even if he could, if he was a man of morals and empathy, it would go against his integrity, his code, as it were, to not help someone suffering. He would not be able to sleep at night nor look himself in the mirror if he did not alleviate the pain." Walter spoke with reverence and admiration of this man-child heretofore unknown to him. It would have made this person's life much easier, he supposed, to keep his gift to himself.

Family

1919

Mary loved having the house filled with her children and grandchildren. Sound and love permeated every empty nook and cranny with yelling, exclamations of joy, and laughter. The aroma of cooking pies, bread, hams, chicken, and fish gathered like old friends gossiping in the corners of each room, following you everywhere you walked in or near the house. The Grandkids that used to run rampant through the house, out through the yards and gardens before scampering like wild Indians through the forests, pretending to be the former inhabitants of the island, had grown into young adults. Mary missed reminding and scolding them over and over that the former inhabitants, the Seneca, were silent as they hunted and strode through those same forests. Noise scared the wild game away, they had to be quiet if they wished to eat. Well, it was quiet as a church now.

The home slipped back to house when family was absent. Just her and Auntie Jo sitting quietly reading, darning, or doing needlepoint. The tick of the clock echoing through what had been a space filled with love and the sound of her husband hammering, sawing, chipping, and whistling out back or on some project in the house. He was always so happy when he had a project that required his hands.

Sadness and loneliness permeated the entirety of the structure. It was early evening when Mary sat staring at the river flowing by out past where the land rolled down to meet it. She sighed.

"Do you need something, Miss McDermott?" Auntie Jo always referred to Mary as Miss. Old habits die hard or not at all.

"Yes, but nothing you can bring," a wan smile and eyes once again found the river.

They sat in silence until Mary put her stitching down on the ottoman with some force. "You know what, Auntie Jo? You can do something; you can start packing what we need for an extended stay on the mainland. We are going house shopping. I am tired of sitting here wishing he would come back, he is not, and this house is a mausoleum without his presence." She tore her gaze from the constant flow of the Niagara and locked eyes with the dark woman across the room. "We are not going to sit here, entertaining the ghosts of lost loved ones. I miss my son. I miss James' sweet, calming voice as he talked Thomas around from some real or imagined slight, and I miss my husband. But you know what I miss most?" She waited a half breath for the other woman to respond knowing she would hold her tongue as she had been trained to do long ago, "I miss living. Leave us go across the river, find suitable lodgings for two old women that is within walking distance of a passel of extremely loud grandchildren and soon to be great grandchildren. I wish to enjoy what time we have left on this earth!"

It was time to rejoin the human race and her family full time. Yes, she was involved in their lives when they would make the trek over. The grandkids would catch her up on what was happening in their lives in this exciting 20th century, but it wasn't the same as sharing that life to a more intimate, day to day, degree. The grandkids were becoming adults and she wanted to see them come into their own.

Ruthie had told her about some young man that was pursuing her and she thought she might like him. Mary thought Ruthie too young and inexperienced for such, though she couldn't say so to a girl she hardly knew. The news had been several weeks old then and was far more remote now. It was time to get involved.

Dick and John had put together a band, a real band, of a half dozen fine musicians and were making a go at Vaudeville. She'd never heard them or the new kind of music, jazz, they told her about. Grandson Tom had become a well-known painter with pieces appearing in many of the new magazines and receiving requests for portrait work from the well-to-do in New York City. They had "adopted" one of the town boys who became a dear friend and, apparently, the suitor Ruthie was so enamored with. Ruthie gave the distinct impression she was getting serious about this Ike Alliger fella, kin to those they had traded with when building the house here on the island, and Mary wanted to check out his bona fides. It was one thing to be hanging around with the boys, quite another to be wooing her baby girl. Time to live, to be a part of the human race.

George was still recovering from his bout of drinking and depression after Ed had died; he needed her. She would help nurse him back to health. She had abdicated her role as the perceived head of the family, it was time to reclaim the title. She would live closer to the action and be involved. If any of the grandchildren, or her children, needed advice, financial help, or just a place to get away from whatever was crushing them, she would provide. Well, she and Auntie Jo would.

They took the morning ferry between Grand Island and Tonawanda. The three remaining children, Katherine, Jack, and Thomas II had all moved to Tonawanda years ago with their broods in tow, as it provided more opportunities, culturally, economically, and socially, than the Island. There were plays to see, orchestras to hear, discussions on the new century and what prospects the new mechanizations would provide. It was an exciting time, especially now that the war had ended.

The kids knew there was family money they could live on for the rest of their lives, but Thomas had imbued each with a yearning to make it on their own. He had been proud of what they accomplished, as was she, and all the grandchildren found enormous satisfaction in the pride of their parents and grandparents. Tonawanda would bring Mary closer to all still making their homes in the towns surrounding Buffalo.

Buffalo was now a thriving metropolis with regular train service connecting it and all the major cities of the new world, which suited the Webb boys and their band as they traveled the vaudeville circuit. They could hop a steamer and be in Cleveland in just four to six hours. Depending on what problems the mechanical transport would encounter. Chicago was a mere twelve hours or so away, again depending on the will of the locomotive divinities. Hell, they could be in New York City in time for dinner and their shows. Yes, it was a magical, wonderous time, and Mary wanted to experience all she could before she rejoined her one true love.

With the help of her brood, they found a lovely home on Broad St. a block from Clinton Park and an easy walk to the river and town. The children could stop by day and night to talk, have supper, share a lemonade out on the porch and talk. They would bring by their instruments and play almost until midnight. She feared the neighbors would complain of the noise, and they might have, had not the houses been laid out with some distance between and the quality of the players. Dick and John had developed into extremely talented young men and would stop by when their tours brought them near. And though the others may not have had professional aspirations, they all could hold their own. They had always been competitive with each other, from toddler on, and now that they had graduated to late teens and early twenties, the competition took on a decided edge.

Each wished to prove their worth, their creative bona fides, their mastery of what their father had set before them. Learn, learn all you can in every subject. If one line of endeavor proved too difficult or uninteresting, they'd find some discipline to yank off the scab until the blood of desire flowed. Learn the hard stuff, not just what came easy. Learn an instrument you loathed so you would know how it should sound and where it should fit in a score. It was the knowing, the conquering of ignorance in any discipline, Music, Algebra, English, Science, Art, Painting, Sculpting, Pottery. Knowledge was king, all other pursuits were avoidance. It would be through the study, the practice of art that they would find the great answers to man's most arduous questions.

They would use their art, their music, their wealth of knowledge to help lift all mankind, not just the rich and privileged, but the poor huddling in their ghettoes who also sought some way, any medium to express themselves, their pain and suffering, their wants, desires, and dreams. For, as their grandfather had explained over and over with the great example of James, one did not require great education and years of study to want more from life.

Mary gazed out the window of her new home and wished Thomas could observe how his lessons had manifested in their scions. She could hear him pontificate on what he believed to be the great truths in life. "You had to have your eyes open and digging tools at hand if you wanted to excel at any endeavor, to understand life from as many aspects as was humanly possible. Know yourself, do not fear looking deep into who and what you were. Seek forgiveness and learn to forgive. Do not expect to be handed what you had not earned. Show you were worth more than would be 'granted' by those who ran industry and government. If you desired a more lofty position in life, you had to work for it. And you should give to those with less rather than horde what was not needed.

"How arrogant," he used to rant, "that the privileged few thought the hoi palloi too lowly to appreciate remarkable beauty. James was a former slave. He'd had to fight every level of bigotry to learn his letters and numbers. A grown man with less knowledge and education than a small white child. By all rights he should've given up and stayed with what little he knew of farming, carving his needs from forest debris, relying on rudimentary skills passed down from generation to generation without any improvement that would lead to beatings and hangings."

Yet, James had risen above the expectations of his white masters. He would constantly remind his children. "They believed the negro ignorant, incapable of appreciating the finer things in life. Knowledge was wasted on such. Attempting to make them more than what God had created was futile. They were lazy. There was no need to instill a sense of ingenuity, hard work, creativity, and inventiveness. The white man wasn't superior to the negro, it was more as if he feared him. Feared a black man with knowledge, with words to inspire his brothers and sisters, feared that a negro with intelligence would show the world he was human and lay bare the guilt of how slave holders had treated another human being. The colored had to be kept in their place, perceived, treated, and dominated as stupid, simple animals. An educated negro would use that knowledge to show his people they didn't have to be subservient but could stand side by side if given half a chance."

"Fear is a great motivator," James had mentioned over and over, "not just to hold others down, to rule them and beat them into subservience but also to raise them up. A person who is terrified to remain in his station in life, or more importantly, to have his children and their children remain stagnant, illiterate without the tools to improve their lives, will fight with his or her last breath to climb from where others would force them down. When one realizes there is only way out of abject poverty due to bigotry and hate, and that lies in anger, education, skills, and refusal to obey. When one has nowhere to go but claw the way up or die, that person will claw and fight with every breath."

Mary remembered James had used that fear as motivation to leave the south and seek freedom.

"The great quandary," James had chortled, "was how to overcome the paralyzing fear of retribution with the fear of remaining in an unsustainable situation." He laughed hard at his own creation of a puzzle based on the better angels of man. The fire raged in the oversized fireplace Thomas had built in the parlor. The cold winds of a harsh winter blew down from the artic on this February night. Thomas had insisted James come stay at the house until the winter storm passed. He'd opened a bottle of his 'special' whiskey from the Kentucky frontier to warm their bones and help the conversation. The evening fresh as yesterday in Mary's recollections. She working her needlepoint while the two men shared philosophy, belief, and history. Now she heard James as if he sat next to her.

"You see," James added as he supped from his cup of bourbon, "How that anger takes hold depends on each individual. For some it becomes violence, the least desirable result. Violence can only lead to more violence worsening until death is the only solution. But anger focused can be a tool to delicately slice away that which stands in the way of progress. One can use their anger to learn, to educate themselves, to force growth and that growth becomes power.

Thomas had pontificated often to his children the wisdom of the former slave. He had drilled into their heads what James had drilled into his.

"People can be dominated only so long before they realize, out of necessity, they have the power to rise. The great divergence is dependent on course of action. Violence begets hatred, it does not snuff it out. Those who hated your people previously will not suddenly see the errors of their ways in the mirror of hate and violence. They will plot and scheme vengeance for the perceived injustice you have wrought. And retaliation for death and violence rained down upon them will make itself known ten-fold, on and on ad infinitum. The hate and retribution never ends until the last person standing. A lonely and empty victory. It may have taken centuries for the negro to break the yoke of slavery but break it, with the help of the northern army, they had."

"Anger affirmatively and peacefully put into action can have positive results. It will not be immediate and will need to be reinforced constructively through cooperation and collaboration, there will be setbacks and resistance. However, if you begin to educate the children, reward the adults, and prove beyond any doubt the benefits of these actions the majority will see the light. When you remove the antagonists, those who use their perceived power—money, possessions, ancestral authority, or physical prowess—and expose their weaknesses they lose their influence to pit one group against another." Thomas would laugh at his own naivete when he would ramble on, he had witnessed what those beliefs had wrought when he'd attempted to put them into practice. And yet, he held those beliefs close to his heart.

Unfortunately, a part of human nature has always been to lord over 'others.' Any group might succeed for a while, if they can convince those with little they are treated unfairly and that others, who are different in color or religion, are taking what little they have, he reminded himself. He still hoped if you could make the impoverished see that they had no more, no less, than those deemed different, it becomes far more difficult to arouse passions. Individual success is celebrated rather than envied when all are given the same opportunities to succeed and success is defined by spiritual or emotional contentment rather than material. He hoped he had instilled in his children and grandchildren those basic tenants.

Mary could hear Thomas' voice as if he stood next to her, his arm around her waist, his touch gentle and reassuring, his voice soft yet steel. She found her joy in the presence of, now, three generations born of her body and raised in her loving embrace, nurtured by the strength of Thomas' conviction to lifting all boats and embracing of all mankind. He had lived as an example to his children and they infused each ensuing generation with the same.

Lost in her thoughts of the goodness and righteousness of her dead husband, Mary hadn't noticed the decided change in the weather. The wind had begun to kick up and storm clouds scudded across a formerly clear, blue sky. Something big was approaching from the east. The rain pounded against the windows of the new house. The windows rattled in their frames, threatening to explode into the interior. None of the occupants of the McDermott house had ever experienced a hurricane except the former master and he rested beneath six feet of dirt on Grand Island. This was but a remnant of a great storm that had made landfall four hundred miles to the east. The fact that it packed this much power after traveling across the entire state of New

York made all glad they hadn't had to feel her fury when it was at its full strength.

Mary hunkered down in the root cellar with Auntie and the girls Ruth, Kate, and Annie. Never had she wished her husband by her side more than she did now, impossible though it may be, she would have given anything for his solid strength and presence. If wishes were horses, ran the mantra through her mind as she held her granddaughters close.

The massive nor-easter howled its wrath for more than an hour as they quaked and prayed. Thomas might not have been a religious man, after his experiences in the seminary, but his wife had made certain his daughters would be. His sons followed his footpath until Ed had passed from typhoid and George had been converted. She thought if the boys were down here, they might change their tune.

Dick and John were working their way out through the wilds of the American west toward Portland and California, Tom was safely residing down in Florida with his artist friends and wouldn't be heading north for another three weeks. George had made an attempt to come to the aid of his sisters and mother when the storm first reared its ugly head, but the storm had come full and angry. He had not come and she prayed he'd been smart enough to turn around and go home to his own wife.

Mary wanted to cower in the corner and wail, begging the storm to cease. She might have except Thomas would have expected her to do exactly what she was, holding her progeny close and filling them with her strength.

The howling and hard pounding on the windows, roof, and walls, finally diminished after the interminable assault. One could almost hear one's own thoughts in between the occasional buffeting of dying wind. She lifted the root cellar door to see what damage had taken place and if the house remained intact. A hard insistent pounding on the kitchen door froze her where she stood half out of the cellar.

Was the storm regaining strength? Had only the eye passed over and now they would be assaulted by the rest of the monster?

No, the banging was too constant and insistent. Someone was banging on their door and would not be denied. She pulled back the locks and flung open the door to find a soaked and disheveled Ike panting on her porch.

Here was this rail thin, early twenties, man/drenched rat, clinging to the porch rail as gusts of wind buffeted his meager frame. Hair all akimbo, being tossed and flung in every direction and looking for all the world like a survivor of shipwreck having made it to dry land. Mary grabbed him by the arm and pulled him into safe harbor.

"What were you thinking coming all the way over here in this hurricane?" She covered his shivering body with dry towels handed her by her youngest daughter.

Ruth had heard the commotion and knew in her heart who had come banging on their door. She and Ike had made common cause in secret, she had not divulged the news to her mother. They had spent hours together, huddled on the front porch swing planning their lives together. They had discussed running off and eloping in Canada, though Ike had vehemently opposed that idea. He did not wish to begin their lives together in the ill graces of her mother. They would find the right time to sit down with Mary and he would ask for her hand in marriage.

"I've, c-c-c-come t-t-t-to," he pushed the words past chattering teeth.

"Dear god, Ike, come over by the fire and warm up before you shake yourself into pieces," Mary steadied him as they made their way to a seat in front of the fireplace where she had a roaring blaze heating the front of the house.

Ruth brought over a steaming cup of tea and held it to his lips. He sipped the hot liquid gingerly, blowing on it to cool the surface before Auntie shoved a snifter of brandy in its place. The shivering abated, he steadied himself physically and summoned his courage. This was not how he had envisioned asking for Ruth's hand, but the storm had taught him there is no time like the present.

"I've come to ask you for Ruth's hand in marriage," he hung his head in shame as his voice cracked like a prepubescent child.

Mary could not help herself, she laughed. The whole scenario was ridiculous, yet it pulled at her heart with memory of Thomas asking her father for her hand. Thomas was a successful shipper and owner, he could have run off with the woman he had come to love and no one could have stood in his way, yet he knew in his own heart how important it was to ask, to show respect, to her father and family.

"I'm sorry," She calmed his shocked expression, "you stirred an old, particularly fond memory." She patted his hand as she offered a hug of apology. "You know you could have waited until the rain had ceased." Her smile showed she did not blame or fault his impetuousness.

"I had not planned on coming today. The storm, the ferocity of it spoke to me. It told me we are not guaranteed tomorrow or next hour and, if I wished to make my case, time was of the essence." The love in his eyes sought and found Ruth's own.

"Of course, you may. If you two love each other, honor each other and pledge yourselves enough to challenge the very gods, how can I refuse?" She hugged him tight before turning to hug her daughter. As Ruth found her way into his arms the other girls came, giggling and loaded with food and drink, into the parlor. They would celebrate surviving the storm and a new future.

The wedding was a small event as society affairs go. Almost all of Katherine's eight children were there with partners and broods in tow. Of course, Ed was not there, and George came solo as he did most every occasion. He would never fully recover from his brother's death though there was nothing he could have done to prevent it; he still carried the belief that if he'd been there, he could have. His wife stayed ever the outsider, though Mary and Katherine had done all in their power to change her perception.

The day was warm and bright, the wedding gay and filled with laughter, as all weddings should be. Many of the upper crust of Tonawanda and Buffalo attended. Though there were also many of the middle and lower classes there as well. Auntie Jo was there with some of her extended family, her two sisters and her brother and their children, which caused a not inconsiderable stir among the upper crusts. She had offered to cook and cater the affair but Katherine would not hear of it. She would be an honored guest as part of the family. She had helped raise Katherine, as well as most of the grandchildren.

Some of the workers who had aided in the maintenance of the Grand Island property and the home in Tonawanda had also been invited. One great lesson Mary had learned from her Captain was to appreciate and respect those who worked with their hands and minds. The financial status of a man usually had very little to do with the moral and ethical status of same. Money did not mean decency nor kindness. Too many with money thought that was proof enough of their worth, Thomas had found that to be a fallacy.

Mary and Katherine had demanded all the boys come to the wedding. Tom had taken up temporary residence after arriving from New York City the week before. Dick and John had arrived in time by the skin of their teeth.

The music was to be provided by the local chamber orchestra though Ruth's brothers and sisters had another notion. What had begun as a staid, respectful, religious ceremony soon devolved into a raucous, celebration of family, gaiety, jazz, and revelry. Those who were taken aback by the boisterous nature of the celebration either exited soon after the ambiance resolved or made merry with the celebrants. Wine flowed like the mighty Niagara; Auntie Jo grabbed several of her entourage to whip up more vittles in the kitchen with Mary by their side. Katherine and John, though he was considering a run for Mayor, joined in the revelry, and danced until almost midnight.

He had feared the Irish in his children would raise its drunken head. He had to admit the evening was far merrier and jovial than any Englishman should experience. He found himself with a cousin of a cousin from Canada, whom he had never had the pleasure, discussing and comparing English authors to the Irish. Shakespeare was a fine writer, quoth the Irishman but he didn't have the heart, soul and depth, nor especially the cutting wit, of an Oscar Wilde. The argument lasted until the final glass was empty and almost came to blows at one argumentative point, though calmer and wiser heads prevailed. They shook hands and left on convivial terms promising another rowing in the near future.

The happy couple honeymooned up at the Falls for several days before spending two weeks in New York dining and dancing with Tom. When they returned to the wilds of western New York they found that Katherine, John, and Mary had purchased them a lovely home on Elmwood Park. They settled in to begin their new lives.

Discoveries Without Solutions

Present Day

Following an afternoon learning the history of Amherstburg and the accomplishments of former and current residents Tom and Aoife required sustenance and rest. They had discussed their next best course with both Jacob and Walter, if they were to follow the trail to the end. Tom now had rekindled the need to know the where and when his roots took hold on the North American continent.

Walter was of the opinion they would be best served by searching some of the oldest and well-established towns and cities lining the lakes, especially Lake Ontario. As Mary and Tom had sought to always live near water and, especially, by the Great Lakes, he surmised they had an affinity born of conversant knowledge of same. People tended to want familiar surroundings, comfort, especially when settling in the unknown. Mountain people sought hills and mountains, shore people sought the rhythmic crack of waves, lake people sought rivers and lakes. It soothed and eased the transition from one locale to another. He suggested they follow the shorelines of the lakes to the end of Ontario.

Though Walter felt their most advantageous towns to search would be along Lake Ontario they decided to make a vacation of the search and check out the small towns and villages scattered along the northern shores of Lake Erie. It would only take a few days from what they could ascertain and neither had traveled Canada to any extent. They would concentrate on towns and harbors that had existed in the mid to late 1800s.

They discovered there had not been many and none really afforded them much in the way of history or information. Though Port Dover had an interesting tale of a shipwrecked captain and one crew member finding their way there after their ship had been sunk in a great storm in the mid-1800s miles west of the town. They had been thought lost to the waves. The story was interesting though not pertinent to their search. Still, Tom was here to learn and so begged the story.

After more than a week of floundering on the great Lake Erie, their makeshift raft washed up on the northern shore. They were found quite by accident, so the story went, near death by a French-Canadian trapper and his wife. The couple took them in and nursed them back to health over several weeks. Whereupon they forged their way through forest and muskeg until they arrived half-starved, looking more like wild red men than civilized white. They stumbled from the forest, clothing ragged, beards weeks old, and crazy eyes, as described in the scant historical records. No one could prove the veracity of the tale, but a good story lives where truth might lie beneath the surface.

Through correspondence with friends, family and business associates in Hamilton, Toronto, and Kingston it was discovered the one man was possibly a well-known laker thought dead. A celebration was held on the off chance it was this said missing Captain and the, presumably, happy news sent on ahead. The Captain and his Lieutenant, Merritt by name would be returned to the loving arms that waited. It was quite the tale and a point of pride for the town.

Tom and Aoife enjoyed an evening and night's stay before heading towards Hamilton and Lake Ontario. They found the expectancy, the thrill of travel soon dulled into drudgery. It's fun, if it's for a day or two, with discoveries each step of the way. When you are seeking needles and the haystacks are barren it wears on the psyche.

The small towns and villages that dot every lake throughout the world morph into one. There are the exceptions. The lake destination points with small amusement parks, and lanes lined with bars and restaurants, live music, and marinas, those are the exceptions. Most are places that fishermen hang out with other fishermen and are content to keep the city-folk away. They have no need to update their fishing shacks and single room cottages. Fishermen sleep there, eat outside, and wash up wherever water might be found, but only so as not to offend their fellow fishermen. The aroma of fish, centuries of filleted bass, perch, walleye, discarded entrails and scales, permeate the air. To the fisherman these are the smells of freedom. They catch, they gut, clean entrails and rinse, then toss the fresh catch on an open fire all while quaffing a few cold beers. It is heaven. Why bathe or shower when you are returning to the lake early the next morning?

Tom and Aoife realized they would find nothing of note in any of these outliers and concluded they should stick to the towns of fair size and history. Port Dover had demonstrated they should concentrate on well-established burghs. They would make much better time and with less offense to the olfactory nerves.

Tom had dreams of the captain and his lieutenant from Port Dover. He knew they could mean nothing to their search, yet he found the closer they came to Hamilton and then, on through to Toronto the dreams intensified. Almost as if calling to him across the decades. But the captain had been a white man, by all accounts, and he had, according to legend, only spoken of returning to his wife and child. All white. Though some accounts spoke of him as an Irishman who had sailed the world before setting in along the shores of Lake Ontario. No one could recall which town, just a town or maybe a village. Toronto seemed their prime candidate.

Toronto is a marvelous city. It is chock-a-block with immigrants, Asians, Chinese and Black. It is a thriving, bustling, youthful metropolis on the banks of Lake Ontario. It has a lively lakefront, an energetic downtown filled with music spaces and world class food. They have embraced cultures from around the world with joy and acceptance, rather than focusing on a singular culture and forcing their will on any newcomers, as many further east chose.

They found a lovely hotel near the lakeshore. Tom didn't know why but he wanted to be near the water. Maybe his genes were calling out to him over the generations. He now believed with a great degree of certainty that Tom Webb was his great, great ancestor. He also was coming to the conclusion that he had inherited some kind of gene that manifested in an ability to physically control events surrounding him. He hadn't discussed this with Aoife since she had witnessed his 'magic trick' on the train. Yet events, coincidences—how often they happened to run into people who could facilitate their search—had the impression of far more than happenstance. He was a man of logic and sound judgement, give him the data and he could parse out any conundrum, but this was different.

Or was it? He had the data. Both he and Aoife had observed curious and weird events—he more than she—had he, himself, created these events? The police moving out of his way as he entered the courtroom, the way the cops arm jerked as he pull the trigger, the computer floating to him as if on command, and the plethora of people they had encountered finding little eggs of knowledge buried for almost two centuries, wasn't that data? And, if he was to accept what they had independently observed, was it that farfetched to think it might be real? They had discovered his ancestor possessed some kind of healing power that got he and his mother exiled from several towns, why wouldn't it be possible that whatever he possessed could be handed down through the generations?

Of course, that brought up the possibility that others in the family had had the same affliction. Mayhap his father or grandfather had this genetic quirk. It is possible it showed itself early in their development, someone, an auntie or uncle, parent or grandparent noticed and affectively quashed the ability before others could observe. It would be considered a defect, something evil, diabolical, something to be hidden and never shown the light of day. His predecessors were religious folk, he could imagine their reaction to one of their own having the capability to affect their surroundings. It would terrify them!

He and Aoife should discuss this interesting subject in far more depth than they had. He trusted her intellect, her opinion, and her reason, he would broach the subject over dinner.

Playing into the kismet of the adventure Tom found a place to dine right on the harbor front, Miku. It was upscale, a quiet atmosphere where they could talk, and they served sushi, nigiri and sashimi. He thought it humorous considering how his last sushi dinner had gone. Aoife did not miss the intent.

Her grin as the taxi pulled up in front of the restaurant told him he had scored on the location and choice of menu. Her beauty continued to fascinate him, yet their closeness, their friendship softened the effect. He knew she was lovely, she knew she was lovely, though not as lovely as he might see, yet it no longer defined their relationship. They were bright, perceptive, scholarly, yes, he thought, that was the word, scholarly people. They could see beyond the surface to the depths of each other. The grand drawback was he found it only enhanced her beauty. Ah well, such is the heart of the hopelessly shy.

They were seated at a window table overlooking the harbor. The night was clear, an early cool evening, with full moon completing the scene. The waiter was mindful of the current between these two. He asked if they would like to see the wine list. Tom declined stating they would each have a glass of Chardonnay to begin the evening.

Tom sat back in his seat and gazed momentarily out the window. A marina and an amusement park lit the waterfront, a park off their left framed the harbor perfectly. It was enchanting and fit the evening. He sighed, brought himself around to the subject at hand.

"Do you remember what happened on the train?" He broached the subject from the side.

"There was much that took place on the train trip over to Toledo," she teased. Aoife knew where he was headed with this thought. She admitted to herself she thought he had brought her to this romantic spot for a completely different conversation. She settled back and waited for him to be more specific and for the wine to make an appearance.

"The thing with the laptop," he whispered not wishing to be overheard by the tables close to hand.

"Ah, magic," she nodded knowingly. "I thought we had agreed that was fanciful, a product of tired minds and overactive imaginations." She was prodding him, goading him into admitting it may have been real and he had performed the 'trick' they both had witnessed.

"I don't know what it was, but I've had plenty of time to reassess and reevaluate several occurrences, as well as consider the facts we know about my ancestor. Supposedly, he performed feats that would be considered miracles in his day. Well, miracles, or witchcraft, which seems to be the route taken by the majority of his contemporaries."

The wine and water made their appearance. The waiter asking if they were ready to order. Tom relayed they were not in any hurry. The waiter bowing his acceptance with a side glance indicating he had overheard, at least, some of their conversation. Curiosity can kill the tip, thought Tom, though he brushed off his paranoia.

"What I am saying," he leaned in so as to protect what he was saying, "is, there was something that happened in the courtroom, there was some pressure or force that made the gun jerk in that cop's hand, and there is some weird energy that continues to point us to the exact person we need to talk to pushing us in a certain direction." He sat back and quested answers from the empty harbor. None were forthcoming.

Aoife considered his consternation and realized she had, intermittently, traveled these same roads. Though her thoughts had remained at the back of her mind where she could sift through data and myths surrounding such happenings. His conversation had brought them to the fore.

"I must admit I have had the same thoughts niggling and pawing at my reason since the train trip. Though I hadn't experienced that same dynamism you obviously have. I know I witnessed the cadre of officers, with the intent of cowering you, back off when we stepped back into the courtroom. I had tried every way from here to eternity to rectify how a trained police officer with years of experience could miss your heart from a few feet away. Still, logically there is no empirical evidence anywhere in history or science that can account for these phenomena. Still, to assume, no matter how preposterous, that you possess some kind of inherent gift, if you will, that allows you to affect events. . . I just don't know." She shrugged her impotence to discover an explanation.

"So, the question is, if I have possessed this power my entire life why did it not reveal itself well before now?" His irritation at not solving this query made itself known.

"There is the possibility it has made itself known through your singular ability to create unique code that allows you to stupefy the most proficient programmers in the world. You have a way of seeing, discovering paths no one else has ever considered." She grabbed the frayed thread of thought and followed it to its logical conclusion. "Though, it appears when you have needed it most, when it was matter of survival on some level, it awoke the latent physical capacity." Tom closed his eyes appearing to be contemplating her reasoning. "It fits the data we have. Great need becomes the mother of exposure."

Tom sat back, thinking, wondering, and trying to recall if this 'gift', this ability, had shown itself at other junctures of his life. Maybe when being threatened by the ignorant who were thin skinned and insecure in their own abilities and so had to pound him down to their self-images. He never understood why some felt the need to belittle those who just happened to possess above average intelligence or aptitude rather than breaching the primordial slime themselves. Most of the geeks and nerds he had associated with over the years would have happily assisted others who struggled with assimilating information. He had offered those he knew to be struggling to mentor and take the time until they understood all assignments. They had rejected his entreaties.

It had taken decades until he realized they were threatened and thought he was mocking their disability rather than offering help. It saddened him they never comprehended he only wished to lift them, not push them down. They thought because they reacted in such a way, that any and all would react likewise. His contemporaries could not see past their own automatic responses. He didn't remember a time when he had sought to physically dominate anyone, though there had been times when his anger almost got the best of him. In his mind he could imagine fighting back, using his size to overcome their physical capabilities. Yet, he never had. Or had he?

There was the time he had come under the scrutiny of the local street bully, the tough kid at school, the one all the other boys would follow and do his bidding just to remain in his good graces. Tom had managed to stay out of his notice for the first six years of grade school. That changed as they entered middle school and the stakes in academia grew more profound. As the kid began to fall behind in learning and his grades lowered, he became meaner and more aggressive. That's when Tom's accomplishments began to stand out.

The kid caught Tom in an alleyway one evening with no way out. His followers began hooting and howling like chimps safely situated in trees and far from the focus of the affronted. Tom frantically tried to find any avenue of escape. There was none. He prepared himself for the beating he knew was forthcoming.

He wished with all his heart something would forestall this bully, he'd trip or stagger if only for a second, long enough for Tom to make a run for it. The kid was agile, an athlete. There was nothing to stop him. Tom waited. His heart pounding in his chest, the back of his shirt soaked with fear. Just as the bully was about to land his first blow something did happen. Like a reprieve from the governor to a man on death row, the kid slipped on a pipe no one had noticed. He stepped, it rolled and he went backwards onto his ass.

Tom slipped past him and made his escape down the crowded street he never should have left. Over the years the scene had played out in his mind. He'd glanced at the pipe laying inert next to an empty trash bin. He remembered thinking if he could only reach it, free it from its prison between trash bin and curb, he might stand a chance. But he was not a fighter and it was wedged where it would not come loose. And then it did. As if of its own volition, it broke free and rolled right where his antagonist would step on it. Good fortune had found a way to smile on him, or had it? Could it have been this hidden genetic defect came to him without his conscious mind knowing?

His long dead relative had healed people, though it would seem he was well aware of this power and had used it to heal rather than as a weapon.

He became aware of the complete silence that had enveloped the table. Aoife sat patient, studying him as if attempting to read his thoughts, though not wishing to intrude. Her wine glass empty, a smirk playing around her lips.

"A hundred and thirty million for your thoughts," she chirped.

The waiter, standing close by, took a quick, deep intake of breath. Someone could not contain their curiosity.

Tom wished there was a way to make their conversation silent. There were things he wanted to discuss with Aoife and he didn't want prying ears leaning in. This guy might be waiting for them to order but he was being served an earful while he waited. Tom wished he could put a cone of silence around them and then snickered at the reference. He hadn't thought of Get Smart since he was a kid.

"Interesting number you pulled from the ether," he commented to her.

"Just seemed to pop into my head."

The number struck Tom as peculiar as it was the number he had played around with when considering what it would take for him to sell his secrets and retire. It was not that he required that much money, he had no personal need, it was what he could accomplish with the funds. To finance research into Syckle cell and support those who suffered. He could set up scholarships for the impoverished and disadvantaged. He could leave his mark on this world.

"I was only considering all you have proposed while tying up some loose ends in my life. I believe we should investigate the possibility of what we believe impossible and see if it might bring aid in our search." He downed the last gulp of wine before signaling to the exceedingly curious waiter—who scratched and dug at his ear as if trying to dislodge something—they were ready to order.

Spinning Wheels Kick-up Mud and Snow
1920's Forward to The Present

Though Ruth was well aware that her new husband's name was more a nickname than his Christian name, she preferred it. Ike was how she had been introduced to him by her brothers. Ike was who she had fallen in love with. Ike was someone fun and relaxed, and though her parents preferred his given name, she found Ike to be less formal. Ike's given name was Frank, named nominally after his father, Franklin, though not a Junior or third, whose father was also a Franklin. It was a family name though none could tell the story of why. He went by Ike to differentiate from his forefathers. The wedding ceremony featured Frank, but she had married Ike.

His father was a well-known and respected member of the Tonawanda community. He had served as Mayor of Tonawanda and set the land speed record between Buffalo and Rochester in his roadster. He came from a family that was well-to-do but not arrogant. They worked hard and lived well. Between the largess of both families, Ike and Ruth would never have to worry about having enough wealth to put bread on the table and a roof over their heads.

The newlyweds lived the lives of the privileged with a maid, a cook, and men to help around the home when needed. They never came off as self-important or superior, they knew where their privilege had come from and were thankful for their antecedents. Their wealth had been earned, though not by them. They were grateful for all they had and gave to those less fortunate. In other words, they kept the values of their forebearers.

They never considered it might be inappropriate to have live-in hired help to do most of the dirty work, it was de rigueur. Many of those they associated with had the same. Those of the elite and wealthy thought nothing of the arrangement. In fact, they considered it beneficial to those they hired. They provided work, paid them well, considering what most earned at the time, and they were permitted to live in far grander surroundings than they might have expected considering their birth, and far superior to those they had shared their upbringing with, most of whom lived in squalor.

Ike dabbled in hobbies rather than a career. He had never found any vocation that called to him nor held his interest for any duration. He enjoyed working with his hands though his attempts at carpentry, masonry, or electrical (a new skill when he was a young man) would never fool a professional. He tinkered with automotive mechanics attempting to follow in his father's footsteps, but to no avail. He just did not have the aptitude. Still, the workers and craftsmen he employed encouraged him and took joy in his attempts. He was born into a life of leisure and it would appear he would live his days as same.

Ruth bore two children a girl, Carol, in 1924, and a son, Frank, in 1927. Like his father he was not a Junior nor even the fourth, though he was also sometimes known as Ike. They were raised as Ruth had been, immersed in music, art, and literature. Carol took to all scholarly pursuits soaking up every lesson like a dry desert drinks in fresh rain. Ike preferred running with his friends to running to classes, libraries, and recitals. Carol took up tennis as was expected of her place in society, while Frank played hooky. They were as different as night and day.

Given every opportunity position could afford they were destined for disparate lives. As Carol completed high school she was expected to go on to college where she would major in education. When the second war to end all wars came along, she had to put her degree on hold. She joined the WAVEs and served in Washington as a cartographer for the Navy, which, in later life, would strike the family as quite humorous as she could hardly read a road map. Apparently, water was far less complicated than the highway system in the United States to decipher. Frank would also join the Navy though the war had ended by the time of his enlistment. After the war Carol became a teacher, one of the few professions open to women at the time; Frank joined the police force once his military service was completed.

They were an interesting Mutt and Jeff from a wealthy family, with both choosing to serve their community, just in different ways. Frank joined the Tonawanda force while Carol went to teach in a small town in upstate New York where she met a handsome, broke, school bus driver and married him. Carol and Robert eloped. They had been married for several months before informing her parents. A rebellious streak born more than a hundred years previously ran strong in her and would nestle in the McDermott DNA of her children. Her parents were not thrilled to find their daughter married to a farmer/bus driver/neer-do-well who came back from his time in the war with a noticeable wild side.

The young man had survived the depredations of war, poverty, and itinerant listlessness. He had returned from war with no plan except to drink heavily, wander where his feet took him—Florida to work banana boats, along the east coast as a day worker and manual laborer, truck driver, a skill picked up out of necessity, and field hand—and see what life would send his way. It sent him back home to upstate NY broke and in need of employ, hence the job as bus driver.

This young woman from privilege and wealth, who had never learned to cook or take care of a household—she'd never had the need—now found herself married to man who worked the soil, picked up odd jobs to help pay the bills and was the first born of his family in America. Mutt and Jeff reincarnated.

They picked cherries and apples during their summer break from education and transportation, which became her first encounter with blisters and exhaustion. He lost fifteen pounds while she learned to cook dinner, not burn it to a crisp or place raw meat on the table. She wept while he choked down what she had prepared with a smile of gratitude. It was love and learning, growing and adjusting. Hard times either broke you or brought you so close together nothing could split you apart. They did not break.

While Carol and Robert survived on love, working the fields, teaching, and learning the skills of homemaker and couple, Frank took to the police force like he was born to it. He enjoyed enforcing the law, keeping old friends on the straight and narrow, and roughing up those who just wouldn't listen. He never crossed any lines and he knew where they were. He was a straight arrow who wouldn't bend the rules. A good cop. He found his own love several years into his career and produced two children who would bear the family name: a boy, the first born and a girl several years later.

Robert and Carol produced four children, one girl and three boys and a hankering for travel. Early on they moved from the rustic, rural lands Robert had grown up in, to Tonawanda where Carol could be closer to her family. Robert found many odd jobs but never fit in until he got hired on as a dock worker for a trucking company. Unbeknownst to him Carol had gone to the manager, after they had turned Robert down for employ, and explained he was the strongest and most capable man they would find. It was the truth. It would also be years before she would confess to the crime of helping him. Nonetheless, he had found his calling. Robert worked hard in the trucking business, he learned everything they would teach him, from dispatch to bills of lading, to paperwork that would bury a lesser man. He wanted to know it all. He already knew how to lead men, due to his time in the military when he'd been made a sergeant out of necessity, knew how to drive a truck, learned during his wandering years, and how to keep a schedule. They showed their appreciation by moving him up the corporate ladder. With each promotion came a move to a new city, new house, new friends, new adjustments.

Moving every few years can wear on a family. Though the brothers and sister found ways to fit with each new society, making friends with similar interests, social webs, scholastic pursuits there is always one who doesn't fit in. Enter the third child, a boy, and rebel to the core. Always being the new kid in class, attempting to make friends with people who stared at you like you had two heads because of your thoughts and expression thereof. Making some kind of effort to fit in can lead to a wonderful expansion of experiences, or trouble. Some kids just gravitate toward the 'friends' who were more rebellious, rule breakers, and trouble with a capital T. This third child, the second oldest boy, Jacob, fit that mold perfectly. He had tried to fit in wherever the family landed though there were too many angles for any hole no matter the force used to push.

He found with each move the degree of difficulty fitting in with his own kith and kin to be increasingly challenging as well. Both parents and siblings wondering why he couldn't get along with what they considered to be normal people, people who held similar interests as their own.

Of course, each had their own likes and dislikes, none of which overlapped. It was easy to find people of like mind when your interests were confined or limited to what society expected. However, when one lived outside the expectations, it was not so simple to find like minds. Especially when it came to music. Jacob could not be contained by any niche in life, politics, literature, artistic interests, or music. He loved music. All music. He found it especially bewildering that people could only enjoy one particular genre of music. He had been exposed to every kind of music throughout his life. Mom was a classical and jazz fan, dad loved hillbilly country, his sister, the eldest of the clan, turned him onto rock and roll, the Beatles and, later, Hendrix, Stones, Cream, and the new psychodelia. He took to it all like a fish to pot. He experimented with mind expanding drugs and became involved in the counterculture of the crazed 60s.

He began to play music and hang with the hippies early on and never looked back. He rebelled against anything thrown his way. Like Brando in the 1950s movie The Wild One, when asked what are you rebelling against, he would say, 'What have you got?' Marching against the war, against racism, for equal rights, for women, gays, Lesbians, trans, black people, brown people, anyone who was being denied the promise, the rights, the benefits of living under the auspices of The Constitution. Rebellious parents raise rebellious children. Though sometimes the children will leave the parental revolutionary in the dust. His mother could only shake her head in frustration.

However, throughout his revolution and rebellion he still held close to the family values. Treat everyone the same, only observe actions of people, words mean nothing without action to support them, learn everything you can, read every book offered or suggested, and, most important of all, understand what anybody does in the privacy of their homes was no one else's business. Love who you love, don't fuck anybody over, do unto others, and work for peace. Know where you came from and don't ever think you have all the answers, just more questions.

Following in the footsteps of great uncles, those who played the Vaudeville circuit, he took to the road as a traveling musician. Though he had promised his mother, after an afternoon of stories from one of these great uncles of their life on the Vaudeville road, that he would never consider such a lifestyle. Apples and groves are going to produce more apples, sometimes they shine like the original stock, sometimes they are a bit more bruised as they bounce on the rock-solid ground. Rebels are going to rebel.

He performed wherever and whenever anyone would allow. Benefits to raise money and awareness for the hungry, the disadvantaged, the homeless, those who slipped between the cracks. They would throw together fundraisers for folks who needed medical help, assistance from disasters of any stripe, flood, fire, hurricane, tornado, you name it, they had a concert. Money for himself was not important, it was for the benefit of those less fortunate. He could couch surf, sleep in his 'classic' car, eat for next to nothing, and survive on songs, comradery, and idealism.

He met and married a woman whom he thought shared those ideals and values. In nine years they produced two daughters, also gifted with the McDermott DNA for insubordination and rebellion, several albums, poverty and hunger, and an exceptional seductiveness towards both the latter. He soon found out money fluctuates in value depending on the hand holding it. Still, he stood for those less fortunate and the oppressed.

"Who is less fortunate than we are?" Asked his wife one day. "You hardly make a living playing your music and when you do you give it to someone else."

"I give it to those who need it more than we do," replied the idealist. "we have food to eat, a roof over our heads, and each other." He soon found that ideals can't feed a family nor hold a marriage together. She moved onto greener pastures and fuller bellies. He moved onto the next town and the next possible gig until he found an empty stomach and sleeping in your car proved nothing to anyone. You had to survive if you were going to stand for anything. It is hard to stand for your fellow man when he has to hold you up because you haven't eaten in days.

He was bruised but not bowed. When his music career came to a slow, ponderous halt he threw down his guitar for jokes and stories and kept traveling. The beauty of the entertainment industry is it attracts every sort of oddball and outcast there is roaming the planet. Gay, straight, lesbian, bi, trans, black, white, women, men, Asian, Indigenous, the druggies and the drunks, the egos, narcissists and the decent, 'lend a hand, everybody can succeed together' folks. And second chances. If you fail at playing music, try singing, or dancing, or production, or acting, or stand on a stage and tell jokes, carry equipment, and build stages, there is always another avenue to cruise down and, if all else fails, write a book about all your trials and failures in life. He shared the stage and life with an ever-growing cadre of folks. Nothing makes you more open to different people than travel, especially when you are sharing the bathroom.

"Don't ever let someone tell you, you can't succeed just because you've failed. You just haven't found your niche yet!" He would drill that into the teeny heads of his children. They had no idea what a niche was but they deduced it had to have something to do with not listening to those in authority as that was the single greatest attribute their father possessed.

Though he spent most of his time on the road he, evidently, still had enormous influence on his daughters. They took the baton of contempt for any and all authority and ran their own obstacle course with greater precision and speed. He seemed the turtle compared to their hare. His one blessing was the children maintained the family virtues and values as they forged their own paths. Always give back, don't judge, make the world a better place by your having lived in it.

They would not walk easy paths. Each road would be filled with potholes and craters that could swallow a life. The surrounding forests and deserts would be populated by misogynists, users, takers, and disgusting humans who used their positions to force themselves on you. If there are humans, there will always be a few rotten apples. If you wished to work in their world you had to play by their rules. The girls would fight and refuse, they would hold their morals high and not let any man, any power broker, try to force them into salacious situations. They had earned their positions by hard work and study, by outproducing, working later, and learning more than any of their competitors. They had proved themselves to be equal by being so much more. Unfair? Yes, but necessary in a society that prized anatomy more than brains and skill.

Apparently, thickheadedness was one constant in the McDermott gene pool. Though Jacob and his children may not have known it at the time, they were following a family tradition of stubbornness.

Jacob raised a 'Katherine' of his own. He named her Peaseblossom from his favorite Shakespeare play. Though she had been taken from him at an early age and had the age-old truth that her father was a useless drifter who would never amount to much of anything drilled into her head, she believed differently. She was as stubborn and filled with idealistic notions as her father and she believed in him contrary to all outward appearances. Her sister was no better, the more you told her no, the more time you spent explaining why she couldn't do something, the more she proved you wrong. It might involve her living hand to mouth for an extended length of time but she would stick it out just to prove to you she could accomplish what she had set her mind to. It mattered not whether the subject was vocation, love, or lifestyle.

There was much head banging and some incredibly loud discussions between father and daughters. The love for each other ultimately won out, even when he incredibly found another woman who was willing to share her life with a broke down, worn out, musician with two daughters. The woman was just as stubborn as they were and she was thoroughly convinced she could fix all that was wrong with these three. She'd just need time.

When the children came to live with them as preteens, she began to doubt her conviction. Preteen and teenage girls can try a man's and woman's souls. After several years she had 'fixed' nothing, adjustments were made but adjustments 'fix' nothing, they just smooth the edges and allow love to work its magic. And work its magic it had, though it had taken the better part of a decade or more, they all came to realize they were family. Dented cans and bruised apples, but a family none the less and they might not have much but they had each other.

Daisy, the younger of the two daughters, now grown and still curious about everything, was the one who engaged in digging into the family history. She craved to know where they, this misfit collection of humans that comprised her family, had come from. How her forefathers and foremothers had lived. Where they had lived and what they had done. She knew she might find horse thieves and pickpockets, or drunks and neer-do-wells, as a matter of fact it was more than likely her family tree would be inhabited by the dregs of humanity, but she was adamant in seeking where she had inherited her own willfulness. She was the one who noticed the genetic defect of pigheadedness in the family. At first, she assigned it to her father's father's side of the family. Pigheaded dirt farmers, immigrants only a couple generations removed from their origins in Holland, who bought and lost a few farms. They took odd jobs and worked other, more successful, farms to finally keep the last one they had. Farmers are extremely stubborn people. They stand in a field full of unrealized hope and believe the crops will be better next year, sometimes next year never comes. Where would find a more eccentric group?

Upon deeper excavation she discovered the people on her father's maternal side might hold the key. That was where she found the octagonal pegs attempting to force the rest of the world into reshaping for their eccentricities. Painters, musicians, photographers, people who lived off the resources earned by those forefathers fortunate or blessed enough to accumulate wealth through guile, luck of the draw, hard work, sacrifice, or, possibly, piracy. Oh, they also worked hard to achieve in their chosen fields but it takes some of the fear, the trepidation, out of flying by the seat of your pants when the seat is cushioned by the largess of previous generations.

She had learned some of the family lore at her great grandmother's knobby knees. The woman had been known to embellish on ancient family stories though she had also lived a very long time over at least two centuries. Still, Daisy was one for truth not conjecture or fairy tales. She wanted to know who her people were and from where they had sprouted and blossomed.

She began searching through old records from, what she believed, was where the family had originated; Tonawanda, New York. No one from the family had resided there for decades. The last was her beloved great-grandmother who had returned from Florida—a place she dearly hated—to spend her last few years in her beloved Tonawanda. A place where her father had been born. When she passed most of the history of that side of the family was lost to time, erased, or burned in fires. Daisy was not one to let dead ends stand in her way. She hadn't professionally and she wouldn't in her new hobby.

She followed the line all the way back to the first mentions of the McDermott family on Grand Island. The question was, where did they come from? They couldn't have just materialized on the island, they had to have immigrated from somewhere else. She dug through her great-grandmother and great-grandfather's ancestry, quite pleased to have found a Great-great grandfather on the great-grandfather's side who was on the wild side. She had assumed all the wackiness came from his side of the family. Instead, she found a politician and speed demon who set land speed records while running with a fast crowd from Buffalo. Though it seemed the really wild ones were on her great-grandmother's side. This surprised her as the elderly lady she had known for only a brief period of time, seemed rather staid and proper. It was a pleasant surprise to find she had such a whimsical family.

Her great-grandmother had been a Webb by her great-great-grandmother's marriage to an Englishman, one could only guess against her own mother's wishes. The mother was of solid Irish stock, the hard Irish who didn't much care for the other side of the Irish Sea. It was all very confusing to a daughter of America, though she loved that her great-great-grandmother was a rebel. A family tradition was a-borning.

Soon sister Peaseblossom became involved in the search. The two had been talking for several years about Daisy's quest and Peaseblossom caught the bug once she heard what Daisy had uncovered. They had butted heads for years, sisters will revert to rivalry when allowed by absent fathers, overwhelmed stepmothers, and feelings of abandonment. This quest seemed like a way to bring peace between the sisters, if only a temporary one.

They found they enjoyed digging in the past together, possibly because it didn't afford them reason to argue. It was a common pursuit with a shared interest in the outcome. After forty years of knocking heads, they may have found common ground.

It was deep in the night when they came across a site that claimed they could find their roots. It would cost them a subscription of a few hundred dollars but there comes a time when it truly isn't about the money. They'd split the cost and hope it wasn't wasted. That was the chance you took with the Web, you paid your money, you took your chances. Both had wasted hundreds of dollars buying something that had the look of quality only to find it was cheap crap from China that would cost more to send back than it had cost to learn the lesson. They paid the subscription and began digging anew.

It was easy to find their parents, and their grandparents but that was where the branches began to grow. Everyone thinks they and their family are unique in a word of commonalities. Unless you are a Smith, Brown, Williams, or Jones, you believe your surname can only have a few turn-offs on the genetic highway. With their father's father that was mostly true. They could trace his lineage back several generations to a small town in Holland. Simple.

However, on the matriarchal side things got a bit more complicated. They followed the lineage that Daisy had found for the patriarchal side of their grandmother. The Alligers were pretty straightforward when it came to when and where they had come. Daisy had followed that line without much assistance to their great-great-great grandfather born in 1868, though it got murky after that. There were many more Alligers, cousins, second and third and beyond, as well as people with the name who bore no familial connection. It was time to focus on the Webbs.

The Webbs joined with the McDermotts where Daisy had found earlier, with their great-great grandmother, Katherine. Peaseblossom was as pleased as Daisy had been to find that obstinacy, the backbone in the family didn't appear to be choice but, rather, in the gene pool.

Once becoming aware of the great search for the origin story of the family, their aunt on papa's side rummaged through old boxes of communications with her grandmother, their great grandmother, and came across some old handwritten histories of the family.

She had written what she knew, and what she believed she knew, in an attempt to save what she could of the family story. Some was quite illegible from age, though there were still pages and pages of familial anecdotes and accounts to piece through. Was every story true? They would never know. All the participants in these stories were long dead and gone, but there were enough tidbits to try and piece together the trail from their origins in Dublin, Ireland.

There had been a rebellious young man in the 1840s who had gone against his father and his mother's wishes for his future. They wanted him to be a priest, which, as the sisters were to discover, was fairly common in mid-nineteen century Ireland. The first-born boy was expected to take Holy orders. He, the patriarch of the American side, had other ideas and hopped a ship he thought bound for the New World. Not much was known about his adventures until he finally made landfall in Canada a decade or so later.

They had their starting point. They also found that he had emigrated to the United States and lived most of his later years on Grand Island, New York. They were aware that their grandparents had close ties to the island, so, they would begin their physical search there. What they hoped to find was the initial family plot. They dug in and discovered what they could online.

It was time to travel to Grand Island and see what they could uncover in ancient records and the dirt of their family's plot, though first they had to find its location.

Both decided it was worth taking a leave of absence, accrued vacation time from their jobs would not necessarily provide the time required to chase down the root of the family tree. Peaseblossom's husband was not keen on the idea. They had bills to pay and appointments to keep. They could ill afford to put their lives on hold while she took off on a wild goose chase. She explained this was her family and her quest. They had chased down as many leads as they could on the internet, now, they had to go, to see, to feel, to find the where and whys of how they came to be. Wasn't he curious about his own ancestors? Wasn't he the least bit intrigued about his history?

No, he proclaimed, the past was the past and it had nothing to do with the present. If she left on this stupid quest, she would find him gone when he came back. She didn't think she would miss him.

She and Daisy would meet in Cleveland—home to their father most of his life—drop off Daisy's gas guzzler and take Peaseblossom's hybrid and drive to Grand Island. There was a Holiday Inn Express on the north end of the island that should be convenient to both the towns of Grandyle, Tonawanda, and, if and when they decided to head over, to Canada. They had never gone to where their father and his mother were born and raised but had addresses and points of interest recommended by his memories. They would find the house where he had been brought into the world and raised in, and some of his favorite haunts, assuming they remained standing and his memory hadn't taken leave. Sixty years can change a town.

They would begin their search at the Grand Island Historical Society and hope for the best. Most historical societies managed to collect old newspapers, letters, and books, as well as having some knowledge of historical figures—which their great, great, great grandfather certainly was, according to his granddaughter's musings. Most of these societies were rife with myths, tales, and rumors of what happened to whom and when. Sometimes you just had to be lucky.

Checking into the hotel they thought they may have mistakenly booked something further away from where they wished, though the nice front desk clerk assured them there were no other hotels closer of the quality than they would find at the Holiday Inn. When faced with either/or and or was nothing, you took the either. The rooms were clean, comfortable and there was complimentary breakfast each day. The price was right, they were tired of driving and anxious to begin the search.

The historical society is housed in a home built in 1877 called River Lea. It has been restored several times and was once supposed to be torn down for an eighteen-hole golf course but saved by the historical society in the early 1960s. It was museum and container of all things Grand Island. It had boxes of letters, books, and maps but nothing that mentioned their ancestor. It was as if the history of the family—prior to the son of a former Mayor of Tonawanda and his wife moving back in the mid-1950s—had not existed. They came across newspaper clippings of the Alliger side of the family. They, apparently, were the respectable group, but not the side the two sought information on.

They needed information from a hundred years previous and on the Webb/McDermott side. The folks who volunteered were helpful but only so. They had other duties besides helping a couple young women find where their great antecedent might have lived. Even though the sisters assured the keepers of antiquity that the young women believed there was history involved that should and would interest all who loved the island.

One would have thought even busy antiquarians would find time to dig through or try to find information for those seeking knowledge. One man's family is another's history. It would seem those members of the family had shown up at the wrong time of the past, and the young women the wrong time of present history to be of concern to the limited staff at the historical society.

"Is there another museum or historical group we might consult either on the island or Tonawanda?" Asked a disheartened Daisy.

"None, though, on second thought, you might want to check in Tonawanda at their historical society or the Tonawanda-Kenmore Society," suggested the pleasant woman who had helped them with what little she could.

As they planned on remaining in the area for another day or two, depending on what they might uncover and where it might lead, they left their hotel and personal phone numbers with the volunteer. The volunteer nonchalantly laid the numbers on her desk where she could toss them into the waste can later on.

Despondent, though not defeated, they thought they would head over to Tonawanda and scope out where the other societies might be. They would take the opportunity to grab a bite at the local hot dog stand their father had suggested, though first they would go in search of the family home.

It was a tiny house with an attached garage that had been added long after the family moved to Ohio. They spent an hour or so attempting to find some of the special spots their father remembered. Sadly, most were empty lots after more than sixty years. Thankfully, they did find the hot dog spot, Old Man River's, and the sad discovery they had changed the hot dogs from what he loved. This trip was turning into farce with little potential for success. They would not be deterred. Tomorrow was a new day and there was digging to be done.

Toronto on a Whim

Present Day

As Tom and Aoife walked along the harbor front, they spoke in whispers as if hiding their words beneath the lapping waters. They had things to discuss and Tom wanted privacy to talk freely. The lapping of the lake against the manmade shore became the slow rhythm of their steps. The cool, clear night air seemed to bring his thoughts into focus. He knew he wanted to say things to Aoife, but what? To say he loved her? He hardly knew her. Yet, he felt as close to her as he had any human being on the planet. She understood him on such a visceral level, a level no one had ever attempted before. That was it. He saw her as a future, his future. He wanted to ask her if she might, possibly, even consider the same thought, and then shame, reality, knowing the answer before the question could even form in his brain, shut down his voice.

How could he think about the future, any future, until he had his answers of his past? What could he offer her? An empty husk parading as a man. A man had to know who he was, his origins, before he could be complete. No man was an island, wasn't that the quote? An island has no connection to the rest of the world. It sits alone, without touching another piece of land. Without the ability to reach out through an archipelago and know another stands close, a much larger continent where it was born, where its history lay. Not an orphan, alone.

He was an island. Oh, he could see where a few other Islands had been, but they were gone now. Swallowed up by the sea; the same sea that was lapping at his feet, the feet that could no longer touch the bottom of that sea. He floated without anchor. He had to find his past before he could think of having a future. Where in Africa had his people been born, evolved? Where in this new land had they put down new roots? Roots that, maybe, were not deep, maybe had shriveled before they could grow strong yet had kept alive long enough to allow his tertiary root to break through and breathe in clean, clear air and bask in the bright sunlight of freedom. Whatever strength he had was earned by generations who survived, those who had stayed alive long enough to procreate until along came the genius. His debt could never be paid, though he would make the attempt.

What was the use of wondering what lay ahead when he couldn't see where he had been? So, they walked, now wrapped in the gentle murmur of waves. He kept his thoughts, his grand plans to himself. He did not speak to her of what he hoped would be his legacy, those thousands of underserved poor with no hope for a future.

Tom and Aoife would go to the historical societies and museums and dig until they found his roots. Then maybe, just maybe, he could gently push them beneath the warm, fertile soil of hope and promise and they would take hold and grow strong and deep and then these children without a future would become his legacy. Mayhap she would join him in fostering a generation of children who, without the wealth and mentoring of two well-educated, intelligent, decent 'step' parents might fall between the cracks.

"I thought we should try some experiments." He spoke softly, thoughtfully, so as not to disturb the night.

"And what kind of experiments did you have in mind?" Her tone was playful, almost, coquettish.

"To find if your theories hold water." He halted his progress and turned to look directly at her. "If I do have some sort of 'inherent power' or ability, it would be helpful to know. Then, maybe, we could figure out how to best apply it. A long shot at fantasy but a shot none the less." All his doubts, worries, and half-baked plans, slid into the harbor. He now had a course of action, granted a flimsy one, but any course was better than running blind. He was now fully prepared to take the first step.

Aoife locked eyes with him. She read his temperament, his thoughts, and where this was directed. His logic had kicked in and he had found his path, that was evident. The question was, how should they proceed? She had been the one to propose the conjecture, she hadn't considered whether she was prepared to see it through.

"Let's go back to the hotel and begin with a few physical experiments, as per the train and the laptop." Decision made she was fully engaged in the idea. Time would not be wasted wondering if they should put it in gear. Yes, let's play magician's assistant and see where it led.

After more than an hour of frustration and continuous laughter after each attempt, Tom struggled to continue. He hadn't a clue as to how to summon this hidden faculty, his 'magic.' It remained hidden. How does one summon something that you don't believe exists? No amount of hocus pocus, or reorganized thought could produce the results they both thought they had witnessed on the train. They admitted defeat, coming to the conclusion that each instance either they, or Tom, could recollect had to have been an aberration of the mind. Memory could be such a fickle thing.

It had been proven, Aoife admitted at long last, over the past decades, that eyewitness testimony more often than not was hazy at best. People remembered what they subconsciously wished to remember. The mind was always willing to give you the results you most desired.

Tom shot a glance at Aoife wishing to argue they were not the normal man and woman on the street. They were logical humans trained in the disciplines of science and observation. Yet, he had to nod in agreement. If you wanted it bad enough, the mind would find a scenario to make desire real. Maybe they had been tired after the rush to the train station, the run-in with the officers, and the ride over. Maybe the laptop had bounced into this lap. Maybe the cop had only misfired, his hand shook, every single instance could be logically explained. Maybe they were chasing parked cars and barking at an empty tree.

They sat in silence next to each other staring out the window into the dark night. Neither felt the effort wasted just without the desired results. The evening had been more than pleasant, a dinner of excellent sushi and sashimi, the walk had settled their full bellies, the conversation and experimentation had been stimulating. They would just have to chalk all the hopes up to just that, hopes.

It was getting late and they had much digging to do in the morning. Tom turned his head to bid Aoife a goodnight when he became aware of the soft purr of her snoring. He considered her position on the sofa for several seconds. He could leave without moving her. He could, though she would wake with a terrible crick in her neck and a tremendously worse attitude. He could attempt to reconfigure how she lay and see if he couldn't alleviate the pressure points. Or he could pretend he was a knight come upon a gentle lady and gently carry her over to the bed.

Tom had never seriously attempted to pick up a woman, either physically or sexually, though he knew that either required a remarkably delicate sensitive approach. One wrong move and there would be hell to pay. He considered all delicate points and where not to make contact. Time stood still.

It was now or never. One arm under her knees and one, slowly eased under her back he lifted with his legs, not his back, and was shocked at how light this human being was. It was as if he held a thought or a wish in his arms. All he had to do was turn, not trip over his own two feet, walk the several steps, and lay her on top of the bedcovers.

But hadn't there been an article that caught his eye on how bedcovers in hotel rooms were one of the most germ and microbe infested places on earth? No matter how he adjusted his grip there was no way to pull back the covers while he held her form. Unless. He tipped her upper torso down enough he could grab the coverlet and gently ease it back, lay her down on the clean sheets, and remove her shoes.

Whew. It had gone much smoother than he could have imagined. She never opened an eye, there had been no change in her deep breaths, he had successfully put her to bed. He tip-toed to the door, and turned off the lights as he opened it, slipping into the hallway. As the door whooshed shut, he heard a soft, pleasant, 'good night' from her room. He had done his best.

At breakfast the next morning Tom sat quietly soaking in the ritual of the waking of humanity. Dozens of denizens of the small caves people occupied while traveling began to filter down in various stages of dawning. It was simplicity itself to pick out those come for business and those who traveled to view. The men and women in their fresh pressed shirts, slacks with creases you cut cheese with, perfectly shined shoes and grabbing newspapers as they entered were obviously getting a jump on the business day. Others were disheveled, hair akimbo, eyes flying at half-staff and wishing they had remained safely encased with a head resting on a soft pillow. Some wore slippers of fur or feathers, others were barefoot, too tired for footwear and hoping for a reprieve to their warm, firm beds. They were in t-shirts, shorts, pajamas, and blue jeans, caring not a whit who might observe them in this state of disarray.

Tom sat comfortably in a polo shirt, slacks, and comfortable shoes for walking. He was ready for the day. Aoife would make an appearance soon, or so he hoped. He was ready to begin their search in the first large metropolis they had encountered since Detroit, which they had bypassed.

Tom was quite content to sit, sipping his coffee, gazing out on the sun filled harbor glistening a short dozen or so yards from the hotel lobby, and waiting on Aoife. He hoped she had slept well. He had placed her in as comfortable a position as he could, considering she was completely dressed and the covers were wrapped around her.

Bleary eyed but dressed for the day she made her appearance. She smiled as he set a cup of coffee down in front of her and quietly asked if she would care for some eggs, or cereal, or toast, or whatever might suit her mood today. She smiled her thanks but grimaced as she turned her head.

"Stiff neck today?" He inquired. "I tried. . ." he began

"Yes, thank you for putting me to bed. You are a kind, decent gentle man." She sipped her coffee as she rose from her chair to grab a glass of juice from the machine behind her. She silently shushed him and motioned for him to stay seated when he made to rise to get what she might require.

"You knew?" It surprised him that she might have been aware.

"I was awake, though barely. I appreciate your kindness." Again, that smile.

"Why didn't you stop me? I thought you slept. I would not have. . ." He stumbled as his apology stuck in his throat.

"Because it was nice. It was comforting to have someone I trusted tuck me in for the night. I can't tell you the last time that happened." Now her face lit with the joy of a pleasure not experienced since childhood, if ever. "It was the safest I think I have ever felt in my life." She kissed his cheek as she made her way back to her chair.

Tom wasn't sure how to take that. Was he so ungainly and unattractive she thought he would never try something while she slept!

"Crick?" he hazarded.

"Slept funny, I guess, though I shouldn't have considering," she refused to look at him.

Interesting, he thought, he hadn't tried anything. They hadn't done anything. Well, if there was one absolute truth in this world it was that Thomas R. Webb had no idea how the female mind operated.

"Sorry," he began before she shushed him again.

"It's not your fault. You were kind, gentle, a real mensch. I just tossed and turned once you were gone." She shrugged off her concerns. "I did have a thought in the middle of the night, around about the fourth flip."

He waited.

"We tried everything we could think of and half of what we had memorized from Harry Potter, nothing worked." She waited for his accession. "Maybe, just maybe, this 'gift' of yours, whatever it is or isn't, real or imagined, or, I don't know, what the fuck."

Tom started where he sat. He didn't believe he had ever heard her swear.

"Anyway," she mumbled to his startled expression, "I think it's possible we're trying too hard. Maybe you can't control it as a tool, per se. What if it is a latent ability that only comes to the fore when you need it. I mean, you can't use it but it can assist you when it decides you require an assist."

Tom stared at her as the wheels ground through the rust and began to turn in his head again. What was she saying? They had tried every single thing they could imagine, every trick ever seen in a movie or TV show. They wore themselves out trying to prove the impossible. Now, she was throwing them both a lifeline to the unimaginable.

"You're saying," He began.

"I'm saying we re-examine every possible incident where this supposed power came into play." She smirked at the obvious. "Let's start when you were a boy," she prodded, "when was the first incident that you can even tangentially connect to what we previously believed was possible."

Tom began with the story of the bully, moved onto the cop who shot him, then the cops in the courtroom and before he could begin to talk about the train, other instances began to coalesce in his mind. Things he had always considered coincidences, although now examined in this new light he had to wonder. Add to that the fact that each time he got stuck on solving some issue, some glitch, all he had to do was lay back, relax, close his eyes and the solution would present itself in all its glory. He thought that was just the way it worked. Move the equation out of your conscious and allow the subconscious to take over. He mentioned this anomaly to her as he summed up his entire sorcerous existence.

Aoife's gaze threatened to slice him in half. He was talking about a certain kind of genius that she had never experienced. For her to solve some interesting equation or glitch she had to painstakingly work her way, step by step, through until she could find the solution. He just fucking dreamt it up? She wanted to strangle him, though she knew he had never considered how those solutions came or how easily.

Deep, calming breaths. He wasn't cheating. He hadn't found a shortcut, it was gifted to him without his knowledge. "It is all in your subconscious. If you push yourself to make things happen, they never will, or so my thinking goes." She sat back while he cleaned up their dishes.

Tom could see how frustrated and aghast Aoife was that he, apparently, had been able to solve complex issues not because he was brilliant but because he had a little magic. He shook the thought from his head, though it hadn't left, only hidden itself in the recesses waiting for him to acknowledge its existence. Yeah, it would piss him off as well.

"Look, I'm sorry, I didn't know, I thought it was just how my mind worked, not that I was cheating or taking the easy path." He had no idea what he could say that would relieve the palpable tension that had instantly arisen between them.

She closed her eyes. He had voiced the exact words and phrases that had run haphazard through her own mind only seconds before. She inhaled deeply before shaking off the insanity of this. "It's not like it's your fault." She began. "You didn't know, it's not cheating if you don't know you're being abetted." She soothed his bruised ego. "I mean, it doesn't make any difference what form your brilliance takes it is still brilliance. All you did was recognize the solution when it was presented. Now let's see if it can point us in the direction to answers to our myriad questions." She required motion to engage her own reasoning and evaluations. Walking, she found over a lifetime, was a great stimulus for the mind.

They walked their way in silence to the Black History Museum thinking that would be their best bet of a starting point. Each was lost in their own thoughts, some pinpointed on the task at hand and some wandering the might be's, could-a-beens and what-ifs of life. For Tom, he had to consider whether he was who he thought was or was he an imposter riding the coattails of chance. Though wasn't chance what created great sports stars or musical genius or any kind of other genius. It was a genetic gift, no more, no less, others might possess such though used it for a myriad of purposes. Weren't there evil geniuses and those who excelled at athletics or business acumen? Was it just a roll of the dice that gave any person that extra boost? Neither mind accomplished much except mental timekeeping against the sound of leather on pavement.

They could have saved themselves some steps. It was soon apparent that whatever impression Tom's forebearer might have made on the people of Michigan, if they had wandered through Toronto or the surrounding area, they had done so quietly.

They had not given into despair when faced with solid, brick walls previously, they would not do so now. Instead, they would find the Toronto Historical society and see what secrets it might hold. The first secret they discovered was that there are approximately a half-dozen historical societies in Toronto. Official, unofficial, East, West, North, Beach, you name it they got it.

After a full day of pounding solid, and extremely hard, pavement they were beaten. They both agreed a glass of wine and a nosh would help soothe the savagely worn-out souls.

"How can there be so many possibilities and such a barren desert of results?" Tom was despondent at their lack of results and the dearth of assistance from his latent and missing gift. Nothing from no one had led them nowhere with not a clue as to where they might go next.

"Remember, Walter said we might do better in some of the smaller towns and villages as young Tom and Mary might have stood out more in less populated areas." She sipped as they watched the populace stroll by on their way home. It was an outdoor café with the sun continuing to bless those taking the time to notice with warmth.

"I think we should spend one more night before heading out," Tom's attention was not on her but something far in the distance, though whether it was an actual point of reference or someplace only he could see Aoife couldn't discern. "I got a feeling," he said, turning towards her, "I know it's not much and probably won't amount to anything but a waste of some time, but what else to we have to do? Maybe we could take in a museum or ride some rides." He chuckled. There was an amusement park they could see from the windows of their rooms.

"Roller coaster fan, are you?" Aoife grinned.

"Not really but they looked to have some tamer amusements that might help pass the time and clear the mind. I sometimes think we are so intent on finding the needle that we keep walking by the haystack with a flag waving and shooting rainbows to get our attention." He shrugged off his discontent, "maybe we just need a day off. There really is no hurry, no deadline. Neither of us has to be back to our lives any time soon, unless you have someone or something waiting for your return." Now his full attention was on her, had he missed something? In all her recollections and stories had he missed a mention of a lover, a 'friend'? Had he unconsciously made another person disappear from his thoughts?

Sisters, Sisters, There Were Never Such Devoted Sisters

Present Day

The phone rang. It was early in the morning though both Peaseblossom and Daisy had been up for a short while. Still the sound startled them both.

"Who the hell is calling at this time of morning?" Daisy glared at the clock sitting on the nightstand. It wasn't all that early, almost eight.

"When's checkout?" Peaseblossom peeked from around the corner of the bathroom door where she had been applying a new coat of make-up for the day. She'd decided to get ready for the day in her sister's bathroom so they could talk while readying themselves. She didn't really care about her appearance, neither of them did, it was more a ritual and a sparse one at that.

"Not for another couple hours. Shit!" the phone continued its insistence. "I'll get it."

"Hello?"

It was a male voice on the other end. "Is this the room of the two women who came to the historical society on Grand Island yesterday?"

"Yeah," answered Daisy cautiously.

"Look, I know you won't remember me but, my name is Billie, I was one of the volunteers you kinda met." He rushed his intro.

Daisy glanced over at the bathroom as she cupped her hand over the mouthpiece of the receiver. She called out Peaseblossom's name insistently, quietly. Then with more force and volume to her sister who either didn't hear her or was being her sister.

"It's the guy from the historical society on the island," she half whispered and half shouted.

Peaseblossom came over to listen while the guy nattered on.

"I'm really sorry no one seemed interested in helping you yesterday but there is some kind of attitude when it comes to your family. Not everyone, but certainly a faction of this island has a shit attitude. Goes back a century or more from what I can figure." He rattled on, "the thing is there are old plat maps in the back rooms here."

"What the hell is a plat map?" Peaseblossom said out loud. Daisy shook her head, not a clue.

"It's a surveyor's map that shows property lines so you know where yours is and the neighbors and such." Came the voice on the other end of the line. "Anyway, when you left, I went in the back room pretending to be searching for something else but dug up the plat maps from when your ancestor lived here." He wanted them to know he had put himself in the line of fire.

"And?" Asked Peaseblossom to the incredibly pregnant pause on the other end of the line.

"I made copies with specific points of reference so you can find your family's property." His voice almost cracked with his pride in finding what they sought. He couldn't help himself, they were pretty, though far too old for him, probably his mom's age. He still sought praise.

"That's fantastic! When can we come and pick that up?" Daisy was straight to the point.

"That's the thing, I'm at the historical society and won't be off until well after lunch. Can you meet me at Old Man River's around four?"

They knew the place. It had been on their list of to-dos and they had-dones. It was kitschy though the hot dogs had not lived up to their billing. They'd switched from what their father remembered. But hell yeah, they would meet him. Now all they had to do was fill the next eight hours. They could continue their search online and pray.

He was pacing inside the ramshackle establishment when they showed up at the appointed hour. He was nervous and kept shooting glances out each window like he was some kind of spy about to be exposed and taken down. It made both of them giggle.

He pulled the papers from inside his jacket and handed them to Daisy. She glanced at them and saw property markings with pencil marks showing where new buildings, homes, and roads had been added since the mid-1800s. She nodded to Peaseblossom that she believed they could find where the old property lay.

She leaned in to hug Billie for his heroics, which she thought was the right way to thank a young man, when he stopped her. "I also took the liberty of using my access to our database to see what I could find about your great, great, great grandparents." He let that hang in the air for several moments while they allowed the information to soak in.

"Here's what I found." He handed Peaseblossom a piece of paper.

She glanced at it.

"I tells you your great, great, great grandmother came from Ireland, I believe Thomas did as well, though they did not meet until both were living in Kingston, Ontario. I'm guessing that would be the origin point of that side of your father's family in North America." The words spilled from his lips like the falls of Niagara. "I hope this all helps." He said as he made for the door.

"Wait! Is there some way we can thank you? This is all wonderful!" Peaseblossom's hand dove into her purse reaching for whatever cash she might have. Daisy just stood and gaped at the man who had brought them so much yet seemed to be trying make a quick escape. Shit! He could at least let them buy him a hot dog and a milkshake.

Billie shook his head as he snuck out the door and made for his car, which he'd parked several blocks away. Daisy and Peaseblossom just stood staring at each other and the papers in their hands.

"I think we get a good night's sleep and then go find the family plot tomorrow and then we'll decide where we want to go from there." Peaseblossom made for the door with Daisy hot on her heels.

"I think we should find a bar and get a drink and a sandwich." Responded the younger, quicker on the suggestion.

They stopped at the Town Tavern smack dab in the middle of the island. It was homey, comfortable and had cold beer and good food. It was early in the evening, still warm, and the sounds of the island wrapped them in nature, almost as if they were camping. That is if the campsite had cold beer, a jukebox, fried pickles, and Beef on Weck. They talked excitedly about the next day. They would get up early, head to the east side of the island, East River Road, according to the maps Billie had provided and follow it around until they found the first landmark. He had it plainly noted on the map; all they had to do was hope it was still there.

From there they would take a one lane service road along Spicer Creek. Not far, maybe a quarter mile and they would find what was left, they prayed, of the original family home. Billie had explained that it was a substantial home two stories high with several outbuildings. It had five bedrooms, a den, a parlor, large kitchen, and servant's quarters, which were said to have been as nice as most people's homes. The servants had been hired help, not acquired help, if you knew the difference. Thomas had been antislavery in his time and thought anyone who worked for him should be accorded respect, a decent place to live, and welcome anywhere in the house as a guest. Where he unearthed all of this information while no one else even pretended to care, well, they hoped someday to ask.

They were both pleased to hear their great ancestor was a good and decent man. Billie couldn't guarantee that any of the buildings were still standing. Over time people wanted smaller family homes that were far cheaper and easier to maintain. The days of the grand homes had passed. No grand pianos with talented hands stroking the keys lovingly could be heard for miles around They had been replaced by cheap radios and yelling. Such is life.

Supposedly, there was a path from the house to where a log cabin had been constructed, though for what reason no one seemed to know or care. None of the inhabitants throughout the years had bothered to go searching for what might be hidden deep in the forest. And then, as the forests disappeared to make room for more housing, as time passed, people forgot. Most of the people, Billie corrected, but the elders passed down the stories and tales from the far past. He was enamored with the tales his great grandfather would relate when Billie was not much more than a toddler.

The two women felt as though they were about to embark on a treasure hunt out of pirate novels. Well, they were in search of treasure just not the monetary kind.

Dawn broke, though they remained abed. One too many glasses of the cold local brew had put both of them out for the night. Now groggy, the sunlight stabbing eyes with knives of pure white light, Daisy called over to Peaseblossom to see if she was alive.

The drive to East River Road was silent as both attempted to find their equilibrium. There was the great tree marked on the map. They almost passed the single lane access road, as it was not officially marked. They bounced down the lane until their teeth chattered and their heads remembered the ache they thought cured.

The pulled over to the side of the lane and got out to walk and dig. Billie was certain the foundation would have survived the decades. It would most likely be stone and masonry. All they had to do was trip over it.

Peaseblossom let out a howl of pain as she discovered the first of the large stones used for the foundation and cold cellar. The house may be memory but Billie had been right, the stones remained. As they dug with small garden tools they had purchased at the local Ace Hardware, they were as certain as they could be that this was what they sought, though the forest had taken back all of that which surrounded the former home. Left to its own devices, nature will reclaim what man thought everlasting. Mankind would never, as a species, understand how much a of a blip they were on the face of the Earth. What may have been a beautiful, solid home was now rotted and mulch for the forest. To say they were disappointed was the understatement of the decade.

They walked in slow circles around the stones hoping to find any other relic of those who had lived here, but all they stumbled on was decaying logs, thick underbrush, and a firepit kids had used for warmth while they drank beer and smoked cigarettes, as evidenced by the bottles and cans and empty cigarette packages. It was time to head out, there would be no great awakening here.

As they turned to head back to their car Peaseblossom came to halt. She stared into the woods. First looking this way, then looking back the other. She had seen something, though she could not be certain what that something might be.

"What is it?" Asked her sister brushing off some of the dead leaves and dirt from her pants.

"I think that's a path," Peaseblossom whispered and pointed at what might be a trail or might be trees that just grew that way.

"It's nothing." Daisy was tired and despondent. "If it's anything, it's a deer trail or an optical illusion." Her voice took on a mystical tone before the laugh burst forth.

"Well, I'm going to see where it goes." Peaseblossom turned and began walking in the direction she'd pointed.

"I'm telling you there is nothing there!" Daisy had spent time wandering in the forests around the Carolinas, Tennessee, West Virginia, and elsewhere. She was conversant in forest signs.

"You got something better to do?" Came a voice from the forest.

"No!" came the dour reply.

They followed the path a good quarter mile before it came to an abrupt end.

"Well, shit!" Proclaimed the elder of the two adventurers. "I really thought this was going to lead some place."

"It did! Into the forest where we hopefully can find our way out." Daisy began to turn back to where they had come from when she stopped. "There's something odd about this clearing."

"What? Too small? Not enough mud and shit on the floor? What?" Peaseblossom was ready to find a cold beer and another Beef on Weck.

"No, it's just, I don't know, unnatural." Daisy began walking around the clearing. "the forest should have taken it over, like it did back where the house stood. But there was no old growth, no new growth. Oh, there's shrubs and such but no trees. It's like they refuse to grow here." She stood, rubbing her chin attempting to resolve this oddity.

"You're just trying to spook me out." The tone let Daisy know, though that had not been her objective, her sister was definitely spooked.

It felt wrong, or so right it was wrong. She didn't know.

Peaseblossom kicked a rock to pry it from the ground, you never knew when you might need a weapon.

"Jesus, this thing is huge!" she proclaimed as she dug deeper and opened up the hole she had begun. "and it ain't natural."

"What do you mean?"

"It's been shaped," she said pointing at where she'd been digging.

The curved top was becoming apparent. The sides, though not perfect were straight lines. It had the look of a, the shape of, shit! It was a Tombstone!

"I'll go get the trowels and the mats out of the car! We've got some digging to do." Daisy began the long walk back to where they'd parked the car.

"I'm going to keep looking around. If there's one grave there might be more. Hell, there might be an entire graveyard out here. Or any other wild thing of the forest. " She shivered as she took in the forest closing in around her. Anything or anyone could be hiding in those trees. It was dense old forest, overgrown with bushes, prickers, saplings and mighty trees of some sort. She wasn't an arborist; she was a programmer.

As Daisy made her way back to the gravel lane, she was brought up short by the sound of rustling in the dried leaves and trees. Someone was approaching her from the lane. She'd been lost in her thoughts about who was buried in the middle of a clearing in the middle of a forest and hadn't been paying attention to the path or her surroundings. She'd spent enough time in the woods to have a feel for where she was headed but she'd also spent enough time in the woods to know there were large predators hunting and prowling about. Whatever was heading her way was large and coming in fast.

She took in her surroundings seeking a sturdy tree with low hanging branches she might grab hold of to climb out of the way of whatever was crashing through the woods. She had just found her route to salvation when the attacker made his appearance.

"Billie!" she screamed much too loudly. "What the fuck are you doing crashing around the forest?"

"I took the day off thinking I might help you two." He looked embarrassed that he had, obviously, frightened her. "Sorry I scared you. I just thought I could be some help."

He was carrying a shovel over one shoulder and a pickax in his other hand, hence the noisy approach.

"I knew the house probably wasn't standing and you might want to dig in the former cold cellar, but when you weren't there, I got worried. So, I figured I could follow your trail into the woods. You guys don't exactly move through the woods unnoticed." He said gesturing at the clear trail of broken twigs, stomped on weeds, and large scruffs on the path.

Well, she thought they hadn't been attempting to hide from anyone. She was glad to see Billie with his far sturdier digging tools than what she was going to retrieve. And it would be nice to have an extra pair of hands to help with the excavation. Yes, he would be a welcome addition to the archeological dig.

She turned back in the direction of where she had just come from, grabbed the shovel from him, insisting if he was going to be helping them. then she could help carry what he'd brought, and began marching back to where she'd left her sister.

Peaseblossom was kicking and scaping dirt from another headstone when they returned to the clearing. She turned at the sound them tromping into the glen.

"Billie!" she didn't scream, her tone one of happy welcome.

Daisy thought, well, of course, she'd been expecting someone. Daisy hadn't!

Peaseblossom showed them the other site she had discovered with Billie chiming in that there might be more, as this looked to be a family plot. Back in the ancient times, he explained, people didn't use graveyards but chose to bury their family members on the family land. There could be dozens of their antecedents buried here or it might only contain these two. Only one way to find out, and he dug the blade of his shovel into where they'd found the first headstone.

As they struggled the heavy stone into a laying position, the dirt caked and packed on the surface, Daisy removed her light jacket and began scrubbing.

"You're going to ruin that jacket," Peaseblossom admonished.

"Don't give a shit. I ain't walking all the way back to get a rag or something when I'm wearing one." And continued her work.

Billie pulled out a large water bottle he'd strapped to his waist and poured the water on the mud and dirt, loosening it until the face could be seen. He pulled out his jack knife and began carefully scraping the imbedded dirt from where the name had been carved into the surface.

James.

That didn't ring any bells. James who? They guessed they would never know. Time to excavate the other headstone.

This one came out harder as it was larger. It was almost twice the size of the first headstone though no more ornamented. There was name, dates, born and died, and a quote.

Thomas McDermott
Born June 24, 1829—Died July 2, 1919
A friend beyond the end and a mate for eternity
Loving husband and best mate to Mary

There it was. The marker of the birth of their family in America.

Yet, that didn't tell the tale of James. Who was he? Obviously, someone close to Thomas, but friend? Child? Brother? They feared the answered was lost to time.

"Should we maybe do some probing and see if there are any more buried her?" Billie spoke in undertones respecting where they were and in whose presence.

They decided, why not? There was plenty of daylight and they had no other plans; they could eat late. The Town Tavern would be open. Billie took the pickax he'd brought and began methodically swinging it in a concentric circle, poking and prodding. The tip of the pick burrowing several inches deep into the forest floor, searching for anything that might be another stone.

If each headstone was placed at the actual head of each grave then Thomas' had been to the left of James. They assumed that since Thomas was the head of the family anyone of his kin would be buried around him. Either to his right or farther to his left past James. It was as good a plan as any they could think. Billie found nothing to Thomas' right, it was time to go on the other side of James and try their luck.

About three feet out he hit pay dirt. The pick actually sang as it made contact with another headstone. Peaseblossom grabbed the shovel and began digging while Billie turned the pickaxe over to make better use of the adze. Soon they had the face of the stone cleared and Daisy went to work with her now ruined, jacket.

Earl McDermott

Born 1871—Died 1897

That was it. No other information, though they could deduce from the dates and names it would be Thomas' son. They spent another hour digging and clearing debris searching but finding nothing. Just these three graves. A father, a son, and a mystery. It would be all they would find.

At dinner the sisters, along with Billie, who they rewarded for his prodigious assistance with a fine dinner of Banana Pepper dip, Buffalo Chicken Mac and Cheese, and a Beef on Weck to take home, couldn't help but wonder about the mystery grave. About what had happened to the property. Why had the family allowed it to go to rot? Certainly, someone in the family would've wanted the house and property if for no other reason, than to keep it in the family.

Billie kept his own council, munching on the free meal, though he'd earned it, listening to the two sisters. It made him smile, hearing them working out the who, what, and why of the situation together. He thought they must be very close. He nodded at the right statements and shrugged at the unanswered questions but offered no opinion.

As desert arrived Peaseblossom had to know. "Don't you have any opinion about any of this?" Her sister nodding emphatically.

"It is impossible to form an opinion without facts." He stated concisely. "I would need to spend hours, days, weeks digging in every site for data, stories, rumors, hearsay, scandals, search newspapers, if any remain. It would be intense and time consuming, but I think we could find some word. Your Great-great ancestor appears to have been someone that made an impact on this island and its community. Both positive and negative. Certainly, there is some article, some letters, some dirt about him and/or the family, somewhere." He took a deep breath and slowly let it out.

"OK, how much?" It was Daisy who spoke up. Let's get to the nitty gritty, her attitude screamed.

"Oh, I couldn't charge you. I wasn't asking, I'm sorry if I sounded like, oh, nevermind. I would be willing to take this on for the experience. This is my passion, my calling. I love genealogy and this would be the quest of a lifetime. Well, for around here. I'm offering my services; with the caveat it will take some time. It might be weeks or months before I turn up anything, but I sure would like to try." He beamed, head nodding, almost pleading with them to allow him to be part of their quest.

They laughed hard. The tension of the question shattered by his puppy dog enthusiasm. Of course, they would allow it and they would cover any and all costs and give him complete credit for all his work.

"You'd put that in writing?" He asked.

"Sure, why?" Now it was Peaseblossom's turn to be wary.

"This is what I am attending college for. If you make this official, I can use the experience for credit, maybe even apply it to my Masters." You couldn't fault the kid for being motivated.

After a cup of coffee or two for Peaseblossom, who was driving, and a beer for both Daisy and Billie they concluded the girls would go to Kingston where Thomas and Mary had begun. Billie would stay and concentrate on any and all knowledge of their time on the island. He told them they could take the Peace Bridge over to Canada or continue on across the island from their hotel and cross at the Falls or any of a few other crossings. Then they could follow along Lake Ontario to the east end and Kingston.

As much as both would have liked to see Toronto and the northern edge of the lake, they decided taking interstate 90 across New York would suit them better. Especially since the current administration had gone to war with Canada, though the rest of the country was refusing to join in the battle. Besides, they could stop off in Oswego and visit their cousin.

It would be a delightful distraction to the search and they could fill her in on all they had accomplished thus far.

Driving Lessons and Learning Lessons

Present Day

The rain had begun about ten miles, or sixteen kilometers, east of Toronto and gave no indication of ceasing anytime soon. The pounding, driving downpour was accentuated by brilliant flashes of lightning and booming concussions of thunder. Tom had never had much time behind the wheel and he was not relishing it now. White knuckles clung to a sweat slick steering wheel. Aoife had her phone in her hand and searched through the torrential rain for a place to pull off, maybe find a place to grab a bite, and allow him to decompress.

They had discussed the routing and settled on taking 401 out of Toronto and then pick up Route 2 for what they hoped would be the more scenic route. They had plenty of time and Kingston wasn't going anywhere. They might even stop along the way, get a hotel on the water, and find some place nice to eat. It would be a relaxing trip allowing them to decompress from all the travel thus far.

It had turned into a death march fighting wind, rain, sleet, hail, and fear. Christ on a saltine, it was the end of July, the temperatures were supposed to be rising into the comfort zone not assailing them with ice pellets and near blackout conditions. Aoife considered talking to Tom to alleviate a level or two of terror. She knew he wasn't used to driving anywhere, let alone through a frozen, gully washing hell, then thought better of the idea when she saw the terror on his face.

If only they could find. . . and there it was, like a divine, pure light shining through the darkness, guiding them to safety and surrounded by walkable dining options. The Best Western Hotel and Conference Centre.

Tom pulled the car under the awning at the front door, now all they had to do was pray they had rooms available. One. They had one room. Apparently, a storm of this size and fury had chased most everyone off the road. Especially since it showed no signs of letting up any time soon. At least the room had two queen beds. They should survive the night. After all they had become close friends over the past couple weeks, hadn't they?

"We'll take the room," Aoife declared. She didn't care if they had to share a room, share a bed, or sleep on a couch, as long as they were inside, out of the weather, and dry. "Any chance this will clear up by dinner?" she asked the front desk clerk.

He stared at her, not hard but as if he wished to say something he probably shouldn't. He had given them the side eye when they walked in together, not that he was openly hostile, just that he wanted to register his displeasure.

Whether that displeasure was brought about by them being Americans, who were not well-thought of since the elections and their poor choice, or because they were an interracial couple. She knew they weren't a couple, couple, but he certainly didn't. It had to be the American thing. After all, it was 2025 fer Christ's sake, not 1865. And weren't the Canadians supposed to be more accepting, kinder, gentler, less hateful than their neighbors to the south? Whatever, she just wanted to change clothes, stretch out on a firm mattress and relax for a couple hours before dinner.

Tom was giving the man the one eye, up and down, assessment. "Is there a problem?" Tom was going to grab the bull by the horns and wrestle it to the ground. He had never been one for calling out racist behavior though that had evolved since certain occurrences in his life. And he was not going to allow any man, woman, or child to insult Aoife by word, attitude, or implication.

His nerves were on fire from the drive, he was tired, his head ached, and he wanted a room, now! Along with two aspirin, a cool wash rag, and maybe a cold glass of white wine.

"No sir," the clerk's training kicked in. No matter what his personal beliefs, the hotel chain that handed him his check each week for filling rooms. "Just thinking."

"About what?" Came out more brusque than Tom had intended.

"About the closest and best place to send you for dinner, eh? Let me check the weather and see if there is going to be break for you to run over." His sardonic grin claimed victory.

"Don't tell me, your wife owns this hotel?" Tom was tired, his nerves were frayed from the drive, and he was in no mood for snarky front desk clerks.

"No, my husband has a jewelry store in Toronto." If Tom thought this guy had attitude before he had not seen beyond the depth of the first layer of skin. The fury embedded in this man's DNA had wormed its way deep into his soul. He was pissed at the world and most of the known universe.

It also explained his vexation when they entered. It wasn't that they were a black man and a white woman, it was that they were a man and a woman. He'd heard of this reverse bigotry but had never observed it. Gays and lesbians, who from Tom's experience were quite amiable around heteros, could sometimes allow years of derogatory remarks and outright sexual bigotry to color their interactions. This guy just didn't like heterosexual couples. Maybe interracial couples most of all as they seemed to be getting a complete pass on most bigotry these days. Tom shoved his irritation down where it could stew in the boiling kettle of his intestines.

Sometimes you had to take a moment to stand in another's shoes to understand the pain and suffering endured through life and take that into account. You didn't have to like how the horrors they lived came back to slap you, you just had to take a breath and forgive. Tom was in a forgiving mood, and hungry.

He took the offered keys, picked up both their bags—he was, after all, a gentleman—and headed in the general direction the clerk had pointed to the room. They would rest up, clean up, then fill up. Tom required an hour or two of stationary rest.

He was not a man born to the wheel, more a man born to living close enough to everything essential so he could easily walk to and fro without the need for bi or quad wheeled locomotion. He certainly had never had to brave driving through a hurricane of biblical proportions. Though Aoife tried to reassure him it had been a mere thunderstorm, though of an intensity above the norm, he closed his ears and eyes to her rationalizations.

She chose the bed closest to the bathroom, as was her prerogative. He chose to keep his thoughts to himself, as was the prerogative of an intelligent man. She purred when she slept. He did not know nor care whether it was considered snoring or just a lovely gift from the gods, either way it was a pleasant sound that resonated through his dreams.

He awoke while she still slept, tiptoeing into the shared bathroom so as not to awaken the sleeping princess. The shower was soft enough to not create a cacophony and arouse her. Cleansed, clothed, and combed he exited the bathroom to find her lying awake on her bed watching a news program on the CBC. Unlike most American news programs, it was well-balanced, reasoned, and impassive, just the news, no pontificating or editorializing. Refreshing.

The Symposium Café was a five-minute walk, which both would relish, as a stretch of the legs was always welcome after several hours in a car and a quick bed rest. She washed up, brushed up, and changed into comfortable walking clothes. The rain had let up considerably and the hotel clerk, now resigned to their presence, let them borrow one of the umbrellas reserved for just such an occasion.

It was not a fancy joint, more blue collar and family friendly, but they had wine and enough choices to fill weary travelers. Aoife got the Tuscan Tomato Bean Soup and Mediterranean Salad while Tom settled for the Blackened Halibut Gnocchis. They both sipped two glasses of passable chardonnay while Tom conspicuously checked his phone over and over for the weather report. Clear and cool for the next few days; perfect!

They would get to Kingston in the morning, drop off their bags at the hotel, and begin the search for history.

What Tom hadn't counted on was Aoife getting into bed with him in the middle of the night. He didn't say anything, she got out of her bed and slid into his arms. It was the most pleasant sensation he had ever experienced. He wanted to shout to the heavens with glee but kept his joy bottled up, though the cap showed signs of failing.

"I just wanted to know how it felt being held. It's nice. Don't take this wrong, but I feel safe and comforted. Thank you," And she closed her eyes.

He didn't know if he should be mildly insulted that she wasn't concerned about his possible behavior or take pride in that trust. Pride won out as he closed his eyes. She was absolutely correct; it was comforting and safe. He would sleep the sleep of the righteous.

The next morning no words were spoken of their night's arrangements. There was no tension nor remorse, just a pleasant beginning to the new day. Tom woke rested and filled with an emotion he had never experienced; contentment. Aoife woke rested and completely secure in her actions. They packed their bags, went down to the lobby for coffee and eggs, then checked out.

Tom couldn't help himself; it was the same clerk from the previous day. "Hate burns and smolders until it consumes everything good about your life," he filled each word with compassion and understanding.

The clerk immediately picked up on the meaning. His eyes filled with fury as his tongue prepared to spit his life's pain. "You have no idea what it's like to be looked down on, almost as if an animal, despised because of who you are. People are quite cruel and not by accident, they mean it." He was about to continue when he realized to whom he spoke. Their eyes locked as understanding and shared contempt for those who hated out of rote rather than loved out of understanding. He sealed the contempt boiling in his soul with a stopple of realization of kindred spirits.

"You'll find they lose their power when you forgive and move on," Tom shook the man's hand as the right side of his mouth raised itself in a half grin. It had taken him a while to learn and understand the same lesson. A good teacher shares knowledge.

The drive to Kingston was pleasant. The sun was bright, the scenery pleasant, the company perfect. They shared what they wished to discover in Kingston, what they had uncovered thus far, and where all this might lead.

"What if I find that I have relatives scattered throughout the land? And what if they are all Caucasian and wish nothing to do with a black man intruding on their family name?" It was a worry that had niggled at the back of his mind ever since the inception of the quest. Not every white person was eager to learn there were actual black sheep in the flock. It was one thing to have a reprobate or drunkard or even a horse thief dangling off the family tree like rotten fruit, but to find an African invading the orchard was quite another. They may despise him for inserting himself in their history, for having the impudence to believe his purported ties to their lily-white ancestors. Prove it! They would bawl to the heavens and cry an ocean. Proof, we demand proof beyond the shadow of the shadow!!!

Whatever happened would happen, Aoife reassured. If they found that he was related to a white man, then so be it. He would not be the first black man to find he had some white roots in his hair. Right now, their main concern should be finding all they could discover and letting truth will out. He was light skinned. She believed that showed the probability of white ancestors. Worry would not change the outcome, only facts and data.

Sisters, Redux

Present Day

After more than two hours of pounding rain, whipping, swirling winds, and hail pounding so hard on the top of their car they could not speak to each other (which was a positive happenstance as it quelled the bickering that had begun with the onset of the torrential downpour). So far, they had done well avoiding the sniping and sticking jabs that had defined their relationship for decades. It had reared its ugly head with the tension brought on by the end of the world they drove through.

Peaseblossom spoke calmly, at first, of her concerns for their safety amid the onslaught that Daisy considered an inconvenience. Peaseblossom noted the number of vehicles exiting the turnpike seeking safe haven in the myriad hotels and motels lining the turnoffs. Daisy considered those who left the field of play to be sissies and good riddance to them. They were all driving like frightened old women anyway.

As the intensity of the storm increased, so too did the heat of the discussion of 'pull over or drive through'. Daisy was quite certain they would soon be out of the gale, though her definition of soon proved to be as malleable as the weather. Peaseblossom was convinced they would exit the storm, only to find they had been eliminated from the human race with her only hope the sight of angels and a golden gate. Daisy attempted to assuage Peaseblossom's growing angst by relating that Buffalo walked into storms knowing they would come out sooner than walking away or standing still, she was following her spirit animal. And considering they had only hours ago left the city of Buffalo, she considered it a sign they were on the right path.

Peaseblossom thought her sister had lost her mind and was demanding they pull over, find a hotel, and get out of this fucking typhoon! The rain lessened, the wipers slowed from their frantic attempt at clearing the Atlantic from their windshield, and tempers were put on simmer.

"What is the cut-off for Oswego?" Daisy asked her navigator with a noticeable smirk on her lips and an evil glint of victory in her eyes.

Peaseblossom muttered, "Take exit 40 to route 34 north to route 104 into Oswego." She ignored her sister's silent taunting.

They spent two days in the pleasant company and restorative waters of their cousin Jenn's company. They loved her husband and her son. Rediscovering their equilibrium, they reinstituted the peace accord. They would survive this trip if it killed them.

They discussed with Jenn and John, the husband, all they had discovered thus far. Jenn was thoroughly impressed with the quantity of information. They had been able to walk the family back almost two hundred years to the beginnings of their line in North America. The McDermott's had instilled in Great-Grandma's maternal side a love of learning, art, music, literature, rebellion, and weird.

They all were far more aware of their grandfather's side, as they had come to the new land just over a hundred years past and settled not far from where Jenn and John now resided in upstate NY. They were good, solid, hard-working, nose-to-the- grindstone Dutchmen. They accomplished much in their chosen fields, though their chosen fields were not exciting or glamorous. They were bankers and insurance agents, trucking people and farmers. The girls did not wish to knock any of those "normal" professions. Grandma's side had all the oddities one family could hold. Grandpa's were the meat and potatoes. Grandma's were the Baked Alaska, Bananas Foster, and Baclava. Grandpa's family was shots and beers. Grandma's were champagne, Mai Tai's and Mojitos with Bumbu rum.

Jenn wanted to hear everything they had discovered. Drinks were poured, stories were told, and promises made there would be a full accounting once the expedition had been completed.

Peaseblossom and Daisy explained their next stop would be Kingston up around the east end of Lake Ontario, not more than an hour or so from where they sat. They had determined that was where Thomas McDermott had settled and began his life in North America after circumnavigating the globe for more than a decade. They hoped to unearth the truth of that conjecture, stories of his travels, and his time on the Great Lakes.

They left on the morning tide, with not near enough sleep and slight headaches. So it was that two hung over young women presented themselves at the border an hour later. They had considered crossing at Wolf Island but couldn't seem to locate where it was in their condition, which prompted the extra driving to the Thousand Island crossing, almost thirty miles to their east. They justified the slight error by remembering they were in no hurry.

The friendly attitude of the border service officer lasted approximately one minute and thirty-four seconds. It may have been the flippant attitude of the two women in the car. It may have been the words 'investigation' that Daisy thought made their visit official, or it may have been the long line of vehicles attempting entry into his country, it mattered not.

He instructed them to pull over to the left where another officer would be happy to accommodate them.

Neither Peaseblossom nor Daisy had much familiarity with border crossings. Most interactions with officials of foreign countries had come from flying into friendly countries while, obviously, on vacation. Mayhap they shouldn't have used the word investigation. It would seem they would require some work on their terminology; that was for another day.

The nice officer asked them to wait inside while he searched their vehicle. They watched as he pulled out both their bags and rifled through each searching for weapons or drugs or hidden secrets—they had no idea what—before he took to the trunk of the car, which of course was filled with flotsam and jetsam that all American cars are equipped with. He then turned his attention back to the interior checking under the seats, behind the back seat, the glovebox, under the dash, and finally, under the chassis of the car.

"What the hell is he looking for?" Daisy asked the universe.

"How the hell should I know," answered the only speck of the universe actually listening.

He entered the waiting area obviously frustrated at not finding they were either terrorists, drug dealers, or transporting illegal aliens into the country.

"Purpose of visit." He asked without further explanation of the search.

"As I explained to the man in the booth, we are here to investigate our origin on this continent." Daisy thought she sounded scholarly, like a student or something. Peaseblossom glared at her, as if she could stare a clue into her sister's head that that had been the word that had brought them into this hovel in the first place.

"I see," which was a lie, "and how long do you intend on remaining in our country."

"A few days, tops," Daisy still had not caught onto the seriousness of the situation. "Is there a problem?" She saw the bull and came to the conclusion the correct strategy was to grab both horns and wrestle it to the ground.

"It would seem that many of your countrymen," he pointed out the window at the long line of vehicles stretching into the distance, "have come to the conclusion over the past few months, they would like to move upstairs." He sighed. "We now are coming to the realization of how our brothers on the southern border of your, formerly, great nation feel. We are being invaded by disgruntled Americans running from your country's poor decision." Frustration covered the anger, while exasperation added just the right tint to color the man's features.

"Oh, we are not looking to relocate," offered Peaseblossom, "Just a little digging in the family history which we have been led to believe lies in the bowels of Kingston."

"Well, from your licenses you seem to have taken the long way around to enter Canada." He mentioned the obvious.

"That is easily explained," noted the elder sister. "We began our search back in Ohio, where most of our side of the family live, traveled to Buffalo and Grand Island, where we were told our family, on our father's mother's side, settled, and could've crossed over to Canada there," she noted to his nodding head, "but thought it would be a nice side trip to visit our cousin in Oswego before coming here." It had been a succinct telling, though not succinct enough for the tired Border officer.

He handed them back their IDs and personal affects as he opened the door so they could exit his life. Daisy was smiling and humming as they exited the border area and began their western voyage. They should be in Kingston within forty-five minutes or so, find the hotel, check in, and begin their hunt.

Peaseblossom had found them a nice hotel, The Delta Waterfront. It was reasonably priced, right on the lake front, and convenient to some of the museums and historical societies they planned on visiting. One of the first they had deduced would be the Great Lakes Museum a mere few blocks from the hotel. It appeared to be a good place to start their search as it was about all things sailing and lakes. Sounded like a place that would have info on their Great-great-great- grandfather.

"You seem quite pleased with yourself." Peaseblossom threw across front seat of the car.

"I thought it was fun. Those guys were so serious. Did they really think we had some kind of contraband?" She laughed, her eyes dancing a jig to music only she could hear.

"You don't fuck around when crossing international borders!" Chastised her elder.

"It's not really an international border," the younger shot back complete with air quotes.

"It is!" emphasized the passenger, "and keep your hands on the wheel." She glared at her sister which was a wasted gesture as the younger child was too pleased with herself to note it. "If you get me killed or thrown in jail or the hospital, I swear I am going to find a way to kick your skinny ass!" Someone's dander was doing its own jig and the feets were pounding hard on the headache which had made a redux entrance after exiting the stage in the last act.

"Oh, cool your jets. Nobody got whacked, nobody got hurt, we're on our way to Kingston where there is sure to be a treasure trove of information on the fam!" The chipperer of the two dug into an inside pocket in the waistband of her jeans and pulled out two gummies.

"ARE YOU INSANE!!!!" Peaseblossom was beside herself and both of them were pissed. "You brought drugs across the border?"

"They're not drugs, they are gummies." Daisy calmly popped one in her mouth.

"They put you in prison for possession of a half of one of those!" Peaseblossom had visions of a barred door slamming shut on her future. Who, the hell, would hire a druggie felon?

"Want one?" Her sister held out a gummy in her right hand tempting the conviction of the righteous.

Unlike the biblical Christ, sometimes the righteous cannot resist temptation. So, with happy hearts and happy heads the two sisters found common ground and the hotel. A happenstance, a miracle, that under the hat of some others might have meant sainthood, here it just meant a nice shower and a nap.

A quick nap and they both were ready to explore, though the grumbling in their bellies demanded action before ambulatory roaming. Diane's fit the bill for consumption. It was seafood and bar-b-que with a Mexican flair in a Canadian town. What could possibly go wrong. Loaded Gumbo skillet and Lobster Rolls, that should sit well with empty stomachs or maybe the gummies hadn't completely worn off.

The food delicious, the weather just north of cool, the skies clear and the moon almost as full as their bellies. The walking would be much appreciated. There was much to discover on the waterfront, including several of the museums and societies they wished to delve into that were strategically placed within blocks of the hotel. They should find all they wished for and more. Tomorrow would be an early start so this evening should be an early end. They would walk off the meal while locating the nearest sites they wished to check out.

Back in the room they both found it hard to sleep. Anticipation of what lay before them was running a marathon through both heads.

Never were two sisters so much alike, yet so different. Both were adept travelers though Peaseblossom tended to be the more cautious of the two, always wanting to plan ahead and suss out problems and pitfalls before venturing forth. Daisy, maybe due to her life constantly on the edge and health issues, was one to boldly go where no one had gone before and see if she could extricate herself from whatever dastardly danger she had fallen into. Together they butted heads about the right and wrong of both concepts.

Next, morning, The Great Lakes Museum was first up and was actually the Keewatin, a former passenger lake liner, and several permanent buildings. They wandered through all and enjoyed the distraction, though they had come in search of buried information on their great ancestor. He was, after all, a known ship owner and sailor on the lakes. Or so they had been led to believe. They sauntered over to the information desk and the lords and ladies of data.

"We are trying to find any information about our fourth great grandfather and grandmother whom we believe lived in Kingston around the mid-1800s." It was decided Peaseblossom should be the spokesperson here as Daisy did not suffer people well. "He owned several ships from what our great grandmother wrote. We thought he might be mentioned somewhere in here, but everything seems to be more general information on the lakes and the town. Could you point us in the general direction of where we might start digging in a more personal direction?" She used her sweetest tone on the young man behind the counter.

"Wait!" His confusion evident in the squint of his eyes and the scrunch of his nose. "You had four great grandfathers and grandmothers?"

"No, why would you think...where would you get the idea...How?" Peaseblossom was now the one confused.

"You said you were seeking information on your fourth great grandfather." He didn't blink, didn't change his expression, gave no indication he might be leading her on.

"Yes, our great-great-great-great-grandfather," she kept the frustration out of her tone by the miracle of years of customer service. Calling people idiots might have worked for her father, though intermittently at best, but she preferred a different approach.

"Ah, I see," he said as he bent his head to gaze at his computer screen. She couldn't see his face clearly so had no idea if he was smirking, still confused, or had no idea he'd said anything funny or peculiar. "Name?"

"Daisy." She was not going to be left out of this.

"His name was Daisy?" If this young man was leading them on, he was brilliant in his execution.

"Oh, his name, you meant," if innocence was chocolate syrup it would have fallen from her perfectly naïve expression and have flowed across the desk before dripping down his computer screen and puddling on the floor. "Thomas McDermott." And the world stopped.

"I'm sorry, can you spell that, please?" eyes never leaving the screen though she could see the tightness around his eyes and his shoulders straighten.

"Is there some problem?" asked Peaseblossom, trying to force his eyes back up towards her own.

"I can't seem to find any information for that name. I thought I may have misspelled it." He may have been brilliant at playing the fool, but lying did not come natural. "Mayhap you should consult the Blue Book of American Shipping rather than Canadian!" As he turned and walked away.

A Search For The Lost is Found

Present Day

Kingston is a town renowned for their multitude of museums. Ensconced within the city limits are the Museum of Health Care, The Miller Museum of Geology, MacLachlan Woodworking Museum, Royal Military College of Canada, Canada's Penitentiary Museum, The Original Hockey Hall of Fame, Bellevue House National Historical Site, Pumphouse, Murney Tower Museum and a host of others. Tom and Aoife required information from a few, though they had yet to come to terms as to which few.

They began their search at the Murney Tower, as it was operated by the Kingston Historical Society. That was where they had had their finest successes thus far. Historical societies were filled with nerds and geeks who loved nothing more than pilfering through dead people's memories, letters, scandals, tales, and disputes of the past. There is no greater joy for some than examining the lives of those past who can no longer take offense at the intrusion. Leafing through an anonymous dead letter of the most personal nature brings them a titillation seldom experienced. Words of love, passion, sorrow, stories told only to those most trusted, knowing no other eyes will ever lay upon the words gives a freedom of expression. The most titillating of all is the opening, 'Please burn this once you have read this letter. If it should fall into the wrong hands, it would be the end of my family, my good name, my fortune.' Yet here you stand with those words and that confession in your trembling hands.

The trespass on confession, the spyglass trained on the heart of a person more than a century dead allows inner sanctum on the most sacred feelings.

Tom and Aoife stopped by the information desk to ask the questions they prayed would direct them to where the answers lay buried. They asked the right questions, the same questions they had asked at every place previously, they were quite certain, though the blank expression on the face of information made them question their questions.

"Maybe they prefer French?" Aoife suggested to Tom in a stage whisper.

"I think we are still in Ontario," replied Tom in same. "It isn't until we cross over into Quebec that language should come into play. At least that is what Mr. Steves cautions."

"Let me try," She lay her hand softly on his arm to stay any further discussion.

"Nous recherchons toute information sur les anciens résidents, en particulier les résidents noirs." Her French, parfait. The expression unchanged.

"OK, maybe we are asking this wrong. I am seeking information on a possible antecedent of mine we believe lived in Kingston in the mid-1800s. Is there somewhere we could begin that search?" Tom used his most patient and obsequious tone. Nada.

"Are we bothering you?" Aoife's last nail was slipping from her patience.

"Well," began the automaton behind the desk. "Not really though I don't think we can be of assistance." Ah, the royal 'We' used to express a much larger presence than was evident to the naked eye.

"Might WE ask why that is?" Tom had come to know the tone now emanating from the vocal cords of his closest friend.

"We don't really have any information on the blacks who lived here as no one kept any notes or accounts." She stated the obvious.

"Why not...Why wouldn't...you've got to be joking." Tom stammered and stuttered his confusion. How could you express such sentiment without any empathy or emotion? "You are telling us that no one kept any histories or stories or accounts of people of color anywhere in any of the pages of any books of Kingston history?"

"I didn't say I agreed with the practice just stating the fact. There is little or no information on the African ancestors of that era. You might try Stones History," She shrugged her impotence at the situation, but she couldn't make information appear out of thin air.

"Maybe you could direct us to any information on a white man," and Aoife emphasized the words so as not to be misunderstood, "by the name of Thomas McDermott." She nodded towards Tom remembering something they had picked up along their travels.

Now the mien of disinterest was replaced by one of vexation. "I would have no information on that person. Thank you for visiting the Murney Tower." With that she turned and walked away.

Tom stared at Aoife; Aoife glowered at the empty space once occupied by a far emptier space. "I thought Canadians were supposed to be kind and gregarious." She took his arm to turn him about and head for the exit.

"Most of us are quite accommodating," said a male voice behind them.

"Excuse me?" Aoife was the first to recover.

"You will have to forgive my associate, the name you tossed her way is one that elicits varying degrees of emotional response in this area." He glanced to the left, then to the right conspiratorially to assure they were alone and would not be overheard speaking of things best left unsaid. "If you seriously would like to know more about the person you inquired about, meet me later this evening. Where are you staying?"

"We are down by the waterfront," Tom coolly answered in a hushed tone. He would have said more but he noted in spy movies they never were succinct in information given. And even though he wasn't certain why secrecy was paramount in this instance, better safe than in prison.

"There is a local kitschy place a few blocks from the waterfront. They have local brews and comfort food if that serves. I'll meet you there say sevenish?" Again, his eyes ping ponged about the room in search of meddlesome ears.

"That would serve our purposes." Replied Aoife just as conspiratorially, evidently used to the cloak and dagger world of subterfuge and corporate secrets.

"What's the name of this pub?" Tom was unused to conspiracy and didn't know not to ask the names of clandestine rendezvouses.

"Kingston Brewing," replied the still unnamed operative, tossing a withering glance Tom's way so as to indicate his umbrage at having to speak the name aloud.

"Sevenish it is!" Tom smiled having missed all undertone and nuance of the conversation.

Never Say Die! Maybe Quit or Run or 'Oh, Shit!' but Never Die

Present Day

Our intrepid archeological/genealogical sisters spent the day traipsing from museum to museum to historical society. From Murney Tower—where unbeknownst to them a roadblock had been set up no more than an hour before—to Fort Henry, the Penitentiary Museum to Bellevue House, they even stopped by the Pump House, the Original Hockey Hall of Fame and the Frontenac County School museum to no avail. They were worn out, disgruntled, frustrated, and hungry.

Daisy suggested a gummy, Peaseblossom thought she could use a beer. Trudging their way back in the general direction of the Delta Hotel they passed cafes with aromas wafting aimlessly to their olfactory senses but no alcohol, and places that promised every alcohol they would wish but only bar foods. They were about to call it quits and head back to Diane's when they came across the Kingston Brewery.

Peaseblossom was not a snob of homebrews but the aromas teased and the beer offerings included a few regular Canadian standbys. It would do. The food was a step or two above bar food. Hunger and thirst have a way of transforming average into superb.

The music was loud but not so as to drown out the spoken word, though the after-work crowd was louder, impairing quiet conversation. They were about to about-face when they spied a table in a corner by the outdoor patio. It appeared an island of relative quiet in between the patio and the bar. It would do. They took one of the empty booths next to a trio apparently having sought the same ambiance.

The waitress was convivial, a welcoming smile, glasses of water, and an offer of pre-dining drinks. Peaseblossom ordered a Blue, to the disapproving snigger of the formerly upbeat waitress. Daisy piled on with a glass of Tawse Reisling. Double snigger with a side of scorn. Though she left on an optimistic, 'let me know if you'd like an app!'.

The two couldn't see what the problem was with their order, both had stuck with Canadian offerings, not asking for American beers or wines. They thought they had been quite continental. After perusing the menu briefly, they decided to share a few appetizers, as all the food selections were quite heavy and calories add up whether at home or abroad.

Peaseblossom's eye could not resist the allure of the open laptop at the table with the trio. She was a geek to her heart and soul; she could not refrain from evespeeking at the screen. Though the trio spoke in hushed whispers, the screen screamed for her attention.

While Peaseblossom tried to focus on the screen, which was at an angle that made it hard to read what the trio were studying, there were enough hints to pique. She couldn't hear what the three were discussing but she could see by their expressions the discussion was intense and involved, she could only guess. At least two of the people at the table appeared allied while the third presented information; information he was not supposed to be sharing if she was any judge of body language and spy movies.

Her younger sister was oblivious to the happenings literally three feet away and was prattling on about what she was missing at home, at work, what they were doing at work, their new garden in the backyard, which her boyfriend was going to have to put in by himself, as she was a thousand miles to the north of him. She should probably think about ending this as they had what they had and should be satisfied by all they had discovered. The dog was acting up because her momma had been gone for weeks now and her baby was not used to that. She should, honestly, think about putting an end date on this venture and where was her glass of wine. She was ready to order some apps, they could split the spinach dip or the nachos but she felt it would be too much for one person, maybe a salad to balance all the salt and fat in either. She knew she should have brought her own food from home, this eating out was going to play havoc with her digestion and blood numbers.

"Hush!" Came the muted command from across the table.

It was then that the junior sister noted the presence of the people at the other table. Could it be that her sister was eavesdropping on stranger's conversations? How rude, she was about to chastise the busybody when her sister glared at her putting finger to lips and indicated silence.

Well, that was ruder than listening in on another's private conversation. Peaseblossom pointed at the open laptop on the table and mimed she was attempting to read what was on the screen. Shit! Her sister was eavesreading something on someone's personal computer? She had crossed a very distinct line. What if those people caught her? What if they demanded satisfaction? Did they still duel in this country? Daisy was about give her sister a lesson in manners when her eye caught what Peaseblossom was obviously attempting to read; Daisy having the better angle to see.

"Holy shit!" she exclaimed much louder than had been the intent.

Silence claimed the territory between the tables as the three ceased their conversation and glared at the two staring at the information on the laptop. The laptop closed of its own accord. No one reached over or slammed the cover, it just closed. If it had been silent previously it was as if the sound had been muted all over the world or, in this case, the bar.

"Do you mind?" glowered the younger man as he gingerly turned the computer away from their prying eyes. His fingertips barely touching the surface like he feared it would burn his hands. The damn thing was possessed!

"Do you?" Replied an affronted Daisy. "Why are you showing these people whatever you have on our great-great-great-great grandfather?" She had seen Thomas McDermott's name prominently displayed on the screen a moment before it closed.

If there had been absolute still between the two tables, throughout the bar and most of the region, now it was as if the universe had gone dumb. Words were impossible. Questions by the millions poured from every corner of, at the very least, two minds across the great divide that separated the two tables. The declaration was of such magnitude it stunned all who believed themselves to be the only humans on the planet that would be concerned with the life and times of a certain Thomas McDermott. Yet, kismet did a slip jig combined with a hornpipe across the table executing the landing flawlessly. Fate was about to announce something momentous to the world in general, and these five in particular. It would appear they were part and parcel of a much larger cadre. All they could do was sit and stare across the abyss where coincidence winked a conspiratorial eye.

"Your what?" asked the shocked black man—more tan, to be honest—sitting next to the lovely dark-haired woman.

The tables exploded into five conversations, all concurrently, attempting to scale the heights of each other, creating a cacophony of babble the bible would've approved. No one was listening, everyone was talking, questioning, declaring, attempting dominance, and none succeeding.

"Stop!" Brought the bruhaha to an abrupt cessation. "Who had the wine and who had the Blue?" the waitstaff of the world instinctively knows what is important and how to bring almost any hubbub to a halt.

"I had the beer, she had the wine, and whatever these three want is on us. Just set them here." proclaimed Peaseblossom as she pointed to the table with the three, while moving her purse over to the same. She pulled out a chair and took a seat.

Daisy scowled as she grabbed her bag and a spare chair from a nearby table, without asking, and sat at the corner of the table. All five exchanged glances before the three seemed to come to a silent agreement, shrugged their indifference, and welcomed the two women.

"It would seem we all have a common interest in Thomas," Aoife said, extending her hand in greeting to the new arrivals. "Aoife."

"What?" Daisy questioned before shaking it off. "EE-fa?"

"It's Irish," Tom answered extending his own hand, "Tom Webb. And I can't wait to tell Frieda and Toni about this turn of fate." He glanced at the stunning woman seated next to him and communicated an entire Encyclopedia Britannica in that furtive glance.

Daisy took his hand weakly as she stared into his eyes, then shook it heartily. She laughed. Looking over at her sister's shocked expression, which she was certain matched her own.

"What?" Tom caught the interaction between the two. "It's the family name."

"And a common name at that," added Aoife. "Many from England bore the name."

"And handed it off to their slaves or servants." Tom didn't understand why his surname would evoke such a response from these two, it had never done so before.

"It is also part of our heritage," explained Peaseblossom. "Our grandmother was a Webb. Her mother married John Webb in the late 1800s." The plot thickened.

"Hmm, an Irish girl, I'm assuming from the McDermott stock, marrying an Englishman? Must have been quite a dustup in the family." Aoife laughed.

Tom grinned at his friend, "Almost like an interracial or interdenominational marriage." He knew the history of the 'troubles' between the two island nations, at least the brief synopsis Aoife had explained during their hours in the car.

The sister's introduced themselves to grins of amusement. "Parents were hippies, one would believe," Tom laughed. "Daisy and Peaseblossom? Yeah, hippies." He grinned ear to ear though not in a condescending way, more approving.

"It's from Shakespeare," muttered Peaseblossom remembering a tortured childhood and teen angst. Children can be very cruel especially when they don't understand etymology.

"Knew it sounded familiar," Tom laughed, "Mid-Summer's Night's Dream, yes?"

Peaseblossom nodded self-consciously.

"If you hate it, why didn't you change it?" Now he was curious.

"Because I didn't hate the name, I hated the need to explain, to break it down for people who could only stare uncomprehending why anyone would choose such a whackadoodle name, especially from some dusty old book. All because they had never read any book, certainly not Shakespeare. I loved the play; how could I not love the name?" She thought it was the first time she had ever explained to people who might understand the explanation with explaining further.

"How long have you two been together?" Asked Peaseblossom, intrigued by the interaction between the two and wishing to change the subject. She was who she was and that's all she could be. A change of name would not change her life. The name made her unique and there was always a price for unique. "And who are Frieda and Toni?"

"Frieda and Toni were very instrumental in our scavenger hunt for my past. Oh, I guess our mutual past. Oh, and we're not 'together', together," Tom stated without looking at Aoife seemingly taken aback by the question. Why would anyone think they were together? "We're just associates, working together, friends, ah, we've only known each other a short time." Now his eyes found Aoife, her eyes held her own mirth, though there was more there, much more. She kept her opinions locked behind those beautiful eyes.

There was much being said, Peaseblossom thought, and a ton and half not being stated. There was more than a morsel of regret in the way the man had stated the fact. She also found it curious how quickly each of them had accepted or adjusted to the possibility they all might be related. It was evident in how personal the questions became and how instantly they fell into a familial line of fire.

"Ahem," interrupted the young man with the laptop. "If all the chitchat is completed, let us get back to the chore at hand."

"Please," Daisy was more than curious what these three had been in the middle of when she and Peaseblossom had interfered. And she cared not a whit about the two and their relationship.

"First off, let me get this straight, if my simple math skills are correct, Thomas McDermott was your fourth great grandfather, yes?" He spoke to the two sisters.

"Yes, on my father's, mother's, mother's side. He left Dublin in the mid-1840s. At least, that is our understanding.

We have determined he showed up in Kingston after a dubious career as a sailor circumnavigating the world. According to the story he came here to settle down after some run-ins with pirates and authorities. Though he came here and bought six lake freighters, so we're not exactly certain whether he was pirate or merchant seaman or both." Peaseblossom told the succinct tale to Daisy's nodding agreement.

"And you two believe this Thomas McDermott had something to do with your lineage as well, yes?" He turned his attention to Tom and Aoife.

"We have no proof he was directly involved in my line. It's just his name kept coming up in the stories about the first person we could trace with any connection to my familial history, whose roots also have their toes firmly planted in Kingston. Or so we have been led to believe." Tom tried his best to sound confident though came up short of the finish line.

"We believe," Aoife put her hand possessively on Tom's arm, "there are far too many coincidences for them to be just that. The evidence, though circumstantial and unconfirmed, points in that direction. Though what the connection might be we can't determine without further data."

Peaseblossom watched the interplay between the two with mounting interest. They might not think of themselves as a couple but their subconscious certainly did. She grinned inwardly at what was obvious to an outsider though hidden from the participants.

"I don't mean this to sound like it is obviously going to sound, but you're black, right?" Daisy was always the sister to get right to the point. No sidelining or diversions of who's dating whom, or what it all might mean. She was white, her sister was white, shit, the whole frigging family was white as ghosts. How could a black sheep sneak in the flock and nobody, but nobody, took note?

"Last I checked that was true." Tom prepared himself for what he feared would come when white folk found a black man might have snuck into the same root cellar.

The laughter bursting forth from the diminutive younger sister caught everyone off guard. Peaseblossom, more accustomed to her sister's antics and outbursts sat patiently awaiting the cessation and, what had better be, a damn good explanation. Tom sat stewing in offense, while the woman, Aoife, laid a calming hand on his shoulder, as if holding him in place, though he showed no signs of leaping across the table and strangling her sister. Which, to be honest, Peaseblossom was also considering.

Daisy found her equilibrium at last. She took several final deep breaths to staunch the embarrassment of her outburst. "I'm so very sorry, I apologize, I just had a visual of some of the relations, tangential as some might be, learning this fact and it amused me," she downplayed the explosion. "I know there are not many but there are a few on the far-right side of the wrong side of history. This is just the best thing ever!" She calmed herself, giggling, while containing any further eruptions.

A deathly still settled over the formerly effervescent woman. Daisy sat for several very long, drawn out, moments, quiet, as if the weight of the world had settled on her shoulders and it was crushing her. The others waited for whatever had changed the course of her levity to one of deep deliberation. Some thought had dug itself into her conscious and it was not a pleasant one. She took a cleansing, considering breath before espousing what she felt had to be brought to the fore. "If you are part of this family, there is only one way that could happen if I remember my history right. White folks didn't marry black folks, it was illegal. Even for them to even be consensual lovers would have created an uproar and time in prison. So, what we are left with is the possibility that our ancestor took advantage of," she really didn't want to say raped, though that was the word she locked tight behind her tongue, "your ancestor." She sat back, stunned by the realization she faced. Her ancestor had, more than likely, brutally attacked this man's ancestor. She knew the past was the past but no one wanted to find out their ancestor had been a monster. Yet, that didn't jibe with what Billie had told them back in Buffalo.

Tom and Aoife sighed, their fears coming to fruition. Peaseblossom sat wrapped in shamed silence, while Daisy considered the depth of the implication.

"Well, then I have a story to tell." The young man interrupted as he glanced at the screen of the laptop before the telling began. "According to legend, scuttlebutt, and gossip passed from generation to generation, scant though it may be, it would seem Thomas McDermott arrived in Kingston accompanied by a young black woman in mid-1850s. According to what little I can find in letters and snippets in the broadsheet of the time, he claimed her as a student he was mentoring originally from some island in the Caribbean. The gossip at the time seems to indicate general consensus was there was more between the two than they let on." He took a sip of his craft brew. "You were correct about that, it would and did cause enough of an uproar in Kingston that people wrote others about the relationship and it led to a great chasm between Thomas and Kingston. Hence, the attitude you all have been stymied by.

"It would appear the young lady did not fare well in the norther climes, the winter was cold, colder than the norm, especially for someone who had never known such temperatures. She took ill. Our fair city was not far beyond a small town at the time, though expanding and flourishing due to its proximity with the lake, and its former position as the capital of the Province of Canada, it retained small town attitudes racially. It was fairly common at the time throughout the world that racism was acceptable and slavery a given. Though from a letter I uncovered in our storage boxes only last year, written by Mary, Thomas' wife, meant to post though instead lay dormant in a box discovered in the demolition of their home, one would guess, Thomas did not share in that mindset. One could surmise from the way she spoke of the woman and her husband. He treated the young lady as an equal, something that did not go over well with the rest of the constituency. He was something of an outcast, as was the woman. They were offered no medical assistance nor comfort of any sort. It's amazing what one can discover if willing to dig past the surface layers of history. People have always been far more willing to confess their private thoughts and attitudes with ink, quill and paper." He looked up from the screen at Tom. "I believe she was your fourth great grandmother." He paused. "She died in childbirth." He wished there was another way to convey the fact, some way to gentle the words, there was none.

Tom's breath caught in his throat. Aoife leaned in to offer comfort and support. Yes, it might have been his relative from over a hundred and fifty years previous but to hear her story told in such a cold, dispassionate manner. The birth, her death, he felt it to his soul. A tear found its freedom on his right cheek.

"Shall I continue?"

"Please." All four responded as one. The storyteller noticed Tom's were not the only tears seeking freedom.

"The child lived." And a breath the universe had held for almost two centuries found release. "It would have been easy for Thomas to give the child away to another black family in the city, he chose not to. He kept the child and hired, bought or found a milk mother to feed and care for the child."

"One would have to assume she took to the child she fed, cared for, and mothered as her own. Thomas took to the lakes whether out of necessity or, as a romantic might believe, to forget the death of someone he loved. Take your pick." He scrolled through what Peaseblossom saw were microfilmed pieces of ancient papers, pieces of letters, and broadsheets. Before the screen went black. "what the...?" The young man seemed verklempt. He began pressing the on/off button, unplugging, counting to thirty, then plugging back in, pressing the on/off button on and off. Nothing. All his work was gone. Had he saved it? Or was it banished to the ether sphere? He sat dejected, not knowing what to do. All his work. All his digging and finding snippets and minutia, gone! What to do?

His eyes found each of the others, there were no words to describe the remorse he felt. He would own this failure. He could attempt to piece back together what he had discovered but it had now become one more unsubstantiated tale without data. Daisy thought he was going to cry.

Tom cleared his throat to attract the young man's attention. He refused to make eye contact with the man he had let down. Tom again cleared his throat and held out his hand, silently asking for the laptop. No response, he was lost in the betrayal of modern technology. It dawned on him he should have made hard copies as backup, he hadn't.

Tom, again, gestured with his open hand for the desolate youngster to hand over the laptop. Nothing. The young man appeared frozen by failure. His mind might be telling him to hand over the laptop but his arms would not respond. Tom gestured one more time, more emphatically, until the laptop moved of its own volition almost jumping into Tom's hand. A whoosh of 'WOW' followed immediately by near silence filled the space surrounding the table. The miracle had, at long last, been replicated. Aoife clapped her hands and squeaked with the joy of a small child.

Aoife leaned toward Peaseblossom, whose expression was one of great wonder and whispered, "He has a way with computers that borders on the mystical." She grinned, her eyes dancing, and clapped her hands once again. Her face glowing like a child who has been saying she saw something, something wonderous, and no one believing her. She knew she hadn't imagined what she had seen with her own eyes.

Tom ignored all the hubbub and began typing on the dead machine. His strokes were rhythmic, pulsing, as if performing cardiopulmonary resuscitation. Like a vascular surgeon weaving a limb back together, the machine began to come back to life.

Daisy waited, holding her amazement thinking if this thing actually revived, Tom would stand and shout to the skies, "It's alive, alive! Do you see? It's Alive!" Just like in the movies.

Peaseblossom could not take her eyes from the wizardry happening right before her eyes. "He's a geek!" she half whispered in awe.

"Oh, he is that and so much more," laughed Aoife, "He is the greatest computer genius living." The pride and love, yes, love, that filled her words may not have been obvious to her, but Peaseblossom heard them as if shouted from a mountaintop.

The screen filled with nibbles and bytes until they became megabytes and gigabytes of information flowing once again across the monitor. The dam had burst and information raged down a steep valley.

It dawned on her that these scraps were the bones, teeth, the skin, and last meals of history. Like an archeological dig she watched as Tom's fingers danced, pirouetted, a pas de deux as he retrieved minute bits and pieces and placed them in such a way as to form a skeleton. From the skeleton he could formulate the skin from past experiences and studies and formulate what the body would resemble. It was art on the fly. The familiarity he exhibited with finding each piece made it clear he was intimately conversant with digs like this.

"They lived as a family, though separated by station and color." Tom took up the narration where the kid left off. "She, apparently, lived in a glorified shack out back while he lived in the manor house. Though neither milk mother, nor child, wanted for anything. It was another thorn in the eyes of the sophisticated residents of the growing town. If you want the rest of the country to treat you as something more than an outback, rural, hicktown, you have to exhibit the same glaring feeling of superiority to others, especially those on the lesser rungs of humanity by virtue of color, origin, or religion. To consider one of them your equal might raise them in your own eyes yet to those of the superior race it lowers you into the primordial muck with the darker folks." Tom knew these to be his own thoughts and conclusions yet felt confident in his summation. He thought he might spit on the floor though he restrained himself. He gazed at the four others seated with him and knew mass generalizations served no purpose. And then he mentally rebuked himself for another faux pas in good manners.

"Tell me, uh, er, what is your name?" Tom realized none of them had been properly introduced to the person who had done all the grunt work on their expedition.

"Randy," he nodded the implied apology for not asking sooner.

"Randy how is it you have been able to uncover so much information when no one else even seemed interested in trying?" Tom pointed at the plethora of tidbits scrolling across the screen, his curiosity reignited. Though some of that spark had been originally spurred on by the discovery that doctors had kept their knowledge of his lack of a condition from him out of institutional racism.

"Thomas was not a beloved figure in this area. When his colored girl died, sorry, just reiterating what was thought back then," Tom nodded his acceptance, "due to a refusal of any and all to come to her aid, even knowing her condition or maybe because of it, Thomas turned his rage upon everyone in this town. Everyone except Mary Haggerty and her family who had only arrived months earlier from Ireland and years after the original sin. He swore he would never forgive the town, the people or their children's, children's, children and cursed them all. Though he remained in Kingston until he sold his ships and left for America. Some here believe, those of deep superstitions and religion, at least, that his curse put a stain on the town that has never been completely scrubbed clean. I am not a great believer in superstition, more inclined toward facts, data, you know, science. As I mentioned, if you are willing to dig, search for bits and pieces of history and are patient, and love puzzles, or in this case past sins and shame of an entire town, which I glory in," he grinned, "you find the fun of unearthing important details of folks' quest for their past."

"So, you're saying," Aoife made the effort to drag the train back upright on the tracks, "It is quite possible that Tom is the great, four times, grandson of this Thomas McDermott?"

"Anything throughout history is possible." Randy nodded.

Peaseblossom and Daisy had remained silent allowing the play to follow its path but now they wanted answers as much as the others.

"If what you're saying is possible, and it sounds like it might be more than possible, how do we prove any of this?" Peaseblossom raised the question that tugged at both their tongues. "Personally, I would like some kind of definitive answers, I think we all would. If Tom is our 'cousin', then I want a proper family reunion!" Daisy vigorously nodded her affirmation, though whether she was excited by the prospect of another relative or that the discovery would cause distress to some in the family not even she was certain.

Silence. Silence and meticulous review rolled and rumbled through the two most brilliant minds at the table.

"DNA!" shouted Daisy stating the most glaring solution.

Of course! Tom's and Aoife's eyes locked in embarrassed silence. Why hadn't they thought of that? The solution to his quest had hovered just out of sight of two of the most intelligent people on the planet. Why hadn't they grasped it and remained in the comfort and familiarity of Chicago? Tom could've Goggled and found a hundred people, companies and charlatans who would've happily, joyously taken his money and told him grand tales of his family. They would have been of African potentates and kings, grand palaces with hundreds of well-formed and physically stunning wives and lovers. They would have gazed into their crystal balls of want and told him any stories he wished to hear.

Instead, he and Aoife had traipsed around the countryside, meeting the hoi-palloi of the working historians, sleeping in unfamiliar beds, discovering frustration and dead ends in life they had not discovered previously. They had sought truth. It was the only way. They had to uncover the past with their own two hands and heads. They had to put in the time, the want, the great desire to know. And by digging with their own hands, they had discovered part of his lost family who, to his great almost bursting heart, were not shamed, horrified, or phased by his appearance but seemed genuinely ecstatic to have found him.

They had been so confident in their amazing abilities they failed to see what was right in front of their eyes. They had fallen prey to the same ill-considered and thought deprived strategies known throughout history; attempting to make the simple difficult. They were fools and had traveled a foolish path.

Or had they? If the DNA confirmed their suspicions, would it not have been inescapable for the son of a son of a sailor not to hoist the cloth, catch the wind, and follow the current wherever it may lead? Was he not of the blood of a man who as a boy could not refuse the call of the sea, to travel the unmarked path of the waves to ports of call exotic and unimagined? Just as he and Aoife had done by visiting such ports as Amherstburg and Kingston, Ontario, Samaria and Covert, Michigan, and the other small towns they dropped by, all in the name of adventure? He was a product of his heritage, if this proved true. And then what?

Randy's discoveries had given them every detail they could ask. He had singularly done what all others could not accomplish by force of his will, his desire to uncover what others skimmed over. He was just as much a man of his passions as Tom. Randy was a historian, archeologist, and would become one of the leading experts in the discipline of genealogy. Though he would lose his job at the historical society in Kingston once it was discovered that he had used their websites and rifled through the files, boxes of historical debris, and time not his own to assist foreigners. He cared not a whit or a hundred whits what the overlords of the historical societies of the world thought, he was a man driven by a love for knowledge. If that cost him his job as a volunteer then he would strike out on his own. He was a man of principles.

Much like Billie, thought Daisy, at the exact some moment the Tom thought the same about young Jacob. Maybe these three boys should meet! Though the thought was about different boys and Tom was considering another option.

And Daisy's phone dinged. A text from Billie. He had made some discoveries of his own he wished to share and reminded her of their promise to put in writing all he had done. His professor had confirmed he could, indeed, use this experience as credit for his PHD. She would back him completely. Good news all the way around. She showed the text to Peaseblossom who nodded the unspoken question of whether these two, she did not know about the third, genealogists and historians should meet. They would set it up. It was the least they could do in thanks.

Daisy explained to the rest who the text was from, where they had met and their promise to him to use their genealogical search for credit for his PHD. Randy's eyes lit up with the dawning of possibility.

"Could you use the same recommendation in your studies?" asked Aoife, the only one observant enough to note the light in the young man's eyes.

"I would never ask," he replied sheepishly, "but if the opportunity arose..."

"I think we know another who might benefit from an endorsement if we could all act as advocate," Tom grinned while a new idea was a-borning. They might have their first three student waifs. He was quite certain he could sell Aoife on the idea and from their brief interaction with the sisters probably them as well.

Peaseblossom watched as each considered where life had brought them. These were good people and if those two ever took a moment to slow down, look at each other in honest and open assessment of each other, they would realize how perfect a fit, a completion of each other, they would be. Then again, it was none of her concern.

She and Daisy had journeyed to learn of their past, to know who they were, the birth of this side of the family in the Americas. They knew intimately their father's patriarchal beginnings but his maternal origins had been obscured in the fog of time. They believed they had uncovered a wonderful truth, though it was possible not everyone in the family would be pleased to hear all the details. Too bad. Knowledge is knowledge, it is not meant to be pleasant or unpleasant, it just is. Just like life.

Daisy knew what her sister was thinking, they were far more closely aligned psychically, in their hearts, than either would ever admit, and that was ok. It was what rubbed them the wrong way around each other, they were too much alike, and yet it was the tie that bound them forever. Yeah, she had embarked on this quest alone but she was so very happy that she'd been allowed to share those discoveries with her sister. Two peas, one pod, a lot of chafing.

"I know we have only met but I have a favor to ask," began Tom.

"We don't have a lot of money," answered Daisy honestly, "but if we can help in any way we would do all we could."

Tom and Aoife donned the largest smiles their faces could hold before breaking into loud, uproarious laughter. "No, no, no," Tom shushed her, "money is not the issue, but I hoped if you were going to write your friend in Grand Island a letter of recommendation, if you might write three?"

"Three?" Peaseblossom gasped. "Can they all be the same with different names? I mean, I don't mind," she said to the affronted expression Randy now wore, "It's just, once I get back I have to try to save a marriage," though in her head she had to question whether she truly wanted to save it or throw it a rock to let it sink faster. "Sorry, I was, thinking, I, uh, shit, never mind, but, of course we would each write a litter for our friend as well as yours." She apologetically stumbled her way back into good graces.

"So, cuz, when do you want to meet the rest of the reprobates? We should plan a reunion so you can meet all!" Daisy was always in for a party and this one promised to be a doozy.

Tom side eyed Aoife. Damn! Was this all coming to an end? Was his time with Aoife really coming to a close? He certainly didn't want it to. Did she? He could ask, but would that be too forward, too aggressive? He had never been aggressive around women; he had been terrified. They would go back to Chicago, complete the merger of his secrets with her money and then never see each other again. Shit! What would life be like back in Chicago? Did he even want to return? When the future materialized in front of his confused eyes, was he still standing alone? There was Chester; Aoife was no Chester, nope she was better in a lot of ways. And now he had family, family he had never had the audacity to dream about, and they appeared to like him. Yes, Aoife would be the icing on top of an extremely delicious cake. Still, he was just this dumpy, mid-forties, lost soul and she was a stunning, brilliant. . .

Peaseblossom saw the silent interplay happening, the insecurity coming to the fore, the hopes being crushed, the knowledge that whatever he might have thought possible crashing against the cliffs of reality. "We would love it if you brought your friend," she nodded towards Aoife extending the reunion invitation to both. "as a matter of fact, it would be open to all your family, who are now our family, as we are one big happy family until one of us pisses off the rest!" Now she hugged her sister as if to say, 'just kidding' while not.

"All we've got to do is pick a spot that everyone can afford and we'll bring the party," Daisy ignored the dig.

"Have you ever been to Ireland?" Aoife asked as she took Tom's arm in her own indicating more than he had hoped.

"Three bathrooms?"

"No waiting!"

Addendum

They all agreed the reunion and introductions would take place in Ireland, the place of half the family's origins. It would involve all the cousins and extended members from the Webb/Alliger/McDermott side. Tom and Aoife would set up housing for the whole family in Ennis. Aoife guaranteeing they could find enough rooms for all the members attending. It took several months to arrange the get-together and for the clan to save up the funds necessary but all were hell-bent on making it happen. As they all wanted to extend the vacation/gathering to include a few days in Dublin for research.

Peaseblossom's marriage did come to a close, more of a mercy killing. She found that life could be so much fulfilling and gratifying when not being smothered. She began to blossom in a new relationship with an old flame that should never have been extinguished. Daisy and her beau continued down the path they had enjoyed since finding each other. He even agreed to come along on the excursion to the Emerald Isle. Neither had any idea of the wealth of Tom or Aoife nor did they care, family was family. They'd love them even though they were filthy rich.

The rest of the family was gobsmacked by the discoveries made, the knowledge of the beginnings of the family in North America and also wanted to do some digging into what they might find in Ireland. There was the hope for discovery of a pirate, a horse thief, or someone who was shot while sneaking out a married woman's window.

Tom and Aoife were still feeling out a relationship they had been denied for most of their lives. It had its moments, its ups and downs, and the usual adjustments involved in creating a new life out of two separate planets orbiting the same need. What they couldn't get enough of was the promise of a future.

And to that end they brought into their circle their first three 'adopted children', Randy, Jacob, and Billie, who they were financially assisting through University and PHD's. They had begun the legal process of setting up a philanthropic nonprofit to send children from impoverished and disadvantaged neighborhoods to college or trade schools. They joined with several other billionaires setting up programs to feed those in war torn areas or victims of natural and unnatural disasters. They would provide vaccines and health care to those who had none. They could not appease all the world's needs, though they could make their mark.

Author's Note

Money does not salve all the pain and suffering of a world, only compassion, empathy, hard work, acceptance, and love can hope to overcome centuries of hate and misery.

Mr. Zonneville (aka Charlie Wiener) Has spent his life as a professional singer/songwriter/ musician and Comedian traveling throughout the United States, well, 49 of them, Canada, Ireland and the Netherlands. He is married to the love of his life, Nancy, and has two beautiful and accomplished adult daughters, Katie and Adrienne. Completing the family are his two very spoiled, very loved dogs, Greta and Harper. He lives in Shangri-la.

www.ingramcontent.com/pod-product-compliance
Lightning Source LLC
Chambersburg PA
CBHW070156310726
48976CB00001B/113